THE ETCHED CITY

I despise and execrate pride and the indecent delights of that extinguishing irony which disjoints the precision of our thought.

Lautréamont, 'Poésies'

THE ETCHED CITY

A NOVEL BY
K. J. BISHOP

PRIME BOOKS

Grateful acknowledgements to Trent Jamieson, Geoff Maloney, Garry Nurrish, Kris Hemensley, Antonia Franchey, Cherry Weiner, and Ron Morris.

THE ETCHED CITY

Prime Books, Inc.
P.O. Box 36503, Canton, Ohio 44735
www.primebooks.net

ISBN: 1-894815-22-X

First Edition February 2003

For Stuart

PART ONE

ONE

THERE WERE NO milestones in the Copper Country. Often a traveller could only measure the progress of a journey by the time it took to get from each spoiled or broken thing to the next: a half-day's walk from a dry well to the muzzle of a cannon poking out of a sand-slope, two hours to reach the skeletons of a man and a mule. The land was losing its battle with time. Ancient and exhausted, it visited decrepitude on everything within its bounds, as though out of spleen.

In the south of the country, arid scrubby plains alternated with stretches of desert. One road crossed this region, connecting the infrequent hamlets and oases, following the line of a derelict stone wall built long ago by a warlord. Along it, at distant intervals, were the remains of watchtowers and small forts. The greater part of the wall and its fortifications lay in complete ruin, but occasional sections stood intact enough to provide shelter.

One evening, late in the Husk Month, as the sun was getting on towards the horizon and the bite was at last starting to go out of its rays, the road brought the physician Raule to a tower with three intact walls. Raule's dark features lifted out of the scowl they had settled into during the stifling, monotonous afternoon. She had traded tales with the Harutaim nomads whose way took them along the road, or rather beside it, for they held man-made paths in low esteem. They never camped near the wall, and cautioned Raule not to do so either. They believed the ruins were haunted by evil spirits, the ancient and acrimonious undead. But Raule preferred the stone places to the empty land outside.

Inside the tower she found the ashes of someone else's campfire, a bottle, an empty meat can, and a wad of blood-soiled bandages. She alighted from her camel and left it to graze on some thorny plants that had taken root in the gravel around the stonework. After kicking the rubbish into a corner, she pitched her small tent against a wall, and built a fire on the remains of the litterer's. She ate, chewing down some strips of dried goat meat she had bought from the Harutaim. With more relish, she speared some dates on the point of an old knife, and cooked them until they were hot and soft to eat. When she had eaten them all she stayed sitting in front of the fire, wrapped in a blanket and her thoughts, tired but unable to sleep, as night came on.

The temperature dropped sharply after the sun set, and a fierce wind blew up and went hooting back and forth across the sky. As Raule listened to it she thought it might be easy to imagine djinns and ghouls out in the darkness, or to fancy that you heard the camel-bells of a phantom caravan passing along the road.

When she slept at last she had dreams about the dead, but these days she always did.

The wall ended at the town of Proof Rock. The sun was a late afternoon bonfire, the earth overcooked and flyblown. Raule slouched in her saddle. Sweat glued her shirt and breeches to her skin, and her feet were baking inside her boots. She looked around without excitement.

Like most settlements in the Copper Country, Proof Rock was seemingly assembled from the detritus of other, defunct habitations. The only visible souls were a few old men and women, dozing on porches and balconies, as still as pegs of wood. Closed doors and shuttered windows completed the picture of an empty nest.

At the edge of the town there was an inn built of motley scrap metal. It had a brick porch, shaded by a tarpaulin and a mangy palm tree. A blanket slung over a wire served as the door, while sacking covered the windows, concealing the interior. Four camels were tethered to a rail in front of the porch. Raule appraised them. They were fit-looking mounts, handsomely caparisoned, but conspicuously lacking bells.

Raule dismounted, tied her camel to the palm tree, and went up to the doorway. She carried the medicine satchel that advertised her peaceable trade, while keeping her right hand near the scattergun she had made by sawing a shotgun short of most of its barrel.

She pushed the blanket back. Inside there was gloom, a sawdust floor and buzzing flies. The air was searing, almost unbreathably hot. The temperature outdoors felt pleasant in comparison. The only customers were four men sitting at cards around a table crowded with bottles, glasses and piles of banknotes. All four were clad in sombre-coloured outfits, decked out with weapons and ammunition bandoliers, and wore wide-brimmed hats that hid their features in shadow. Spectres of trouble. They all turned and looked at Raule.

One of them, a slim man, was fully muffled in a black domino, with a dustveil over his lower face. Raule smiled inwardly at such a caricature of a ne'er-do-well. Then a sword hanging at his left hip, with its point resting behind him on the floor, caught her eye. The long, slightly curved scabbard was familiar to her.

The man tugged the brim of his hat down, as though he was wary of her eyes. But then his fingers, clad in black gloves, drummed on the table in apparently idle fashion, and Raule read their movement:

Nice to see you. Wait till later.

The other three gave her looks that plainly said "later" as well, but with different intent. She was unconcerned about that; later they'd be dead drunk.

Excepting the ghosts in her dreams, Raule hadn't seen a face she knew, either friend or foe, for more than half a year. Though she thought about leaving then and there, life had been too lonely lately, and so she chose to stay. Wanting a drink, and water to wash with if any was to be had, she walked to the bar. No one was there. Her nose picked up a raw smell.

Looking over the counter, she saw the body of an elderly man who was no doubt the innkeeper. Something sharp and heavy had broken his skull open like an egg. The blood around him was still wet. A shelf behind the bar held a few bottles, but Raule decided to forgo alcoholic refreshment for the time being. There was a gap between two sheets of tin in the back wall, with another room visible beyond. Without looking at the men again, Raule moved towards the gap.

"Woman, stop."

It wasn't the voice of her acquaintance at the table. It was of iron and clinker. Raule halted.

"How would you say that man died?" the voice drawled.

"I would say," Raule answered, not facing around, "that he fell and hit his head."

There was ugly laughter, briefly. Then the shuffle and snap of cards signalled the resumption of play.

Just teasing.

Raule went through the opening, and found herself in a bedroom-cum-storeroom. The shelves held a few sacks of beans and some hoary sausages. On the floor lay a strongbox, broken open and empty. An unlikely leadlight door of yellow and green glass roundels led out to an open yard. Raule squinted in the sudden light. In a corner of the yard there was a pump with a bucket beside it. She tried the pump, which yielded brown water. She cupped some in her hands and splashed it on her head and neck. A muddy residue stayed in the lines on her palms. She wasn't going to try drinking it, but in case the camel was thirsty she filled the bucket and walked back around the side of the building. The camel drank a couple of mouthfuls, then gave the bucket a disdainful kick, spilling the water, which the dry ground rapidly swallowed.

Raule drank from one of the several canteens she carried, then settled under the palm tree and let her eyes close. However, she kept her ears open.

The sun inched down the sky. Shadows lengthened. An emaciated, three-legged hound limped across the road. Brass-coloured ants that were half as long as Raule's thumb came crawling out of a hole in front of her feet. She kept count of them.

Nine hundred and thirteen ants later, gunfire erupted indoors.

Even though Raule had been half expecting it, the sudden ear-splitting noise gave her a jolt. She jumped off the porch and lay flat. She heard what sounded like several pistols being rapidly emptied, and men bellowing like bulls.

Then all went quiet again.

Raule crept to the doorway. Squatting, she lifted the bottom edge of the blanket a little and peered into the room. Dark figures lay prone on the floor amid overturned chairs and broken glass. Only the veiled man was standing, wreathed in gunsmoke, lit by a cat's cradle of thin sunbeams threading through new bullet holes in the walls and roof. He reloaded the pair of long-barrelled revolvers he had in hand and holstered them. Then from the curved scabbard he drew a yataghan, and swung it down three times, severing each fallen man's head. That had always been his preferred way of making sure of a kill. Raule thought it was something of a comforting habit, too, like some people's habits of straightening crooked-hanging pictures, or always wearing a certain item of clothing.

She got to her feet. As she went to move the blanket, the wire fell down. The man started, and brought the sword up. Seeing only Raule there, he lowered it again.

Raule stepped inside and took a few paces into the smoke, stopping several feet short of the man and the mire of sawdust and blood he stood in. She glanced down at the bodies. "Who was cheating?"

"Who do you think?" The voice from behind the dustveil was pleasant, with the slightly breathy timbre of a northern accent.

"It seems you've still got your sweet touch, Gwynn."

"You use it or lose it," he said with a slight shrug. He wiped the sword on the nearest corpse's sleeve, and sheathed it. He removed his hat, then the domino and veil, disclosing foreign features: a white, finely tapered face, graced by an expression of urbane serenity. His eyes were waterish green, as though they held brine. His long black hair was tied back in a queue. "It's good to see you, Raule," he said. Locating an unbroken bottle and glass on the table, he poured himself a drink. "One for yourself?"

"Maybe later."

When he had quenched his thirst, he stepped over the bodies and held out his hand, smiling. With that smile the strange peace in his looks dissolved, and a baneful quiddity showed itself.

Raule had a moment of hesitation. There were other people she would have preferred to meet. But Gwynn had once been a comrade, and in some ways one of her better friends. She didn't have so many of those left that she could afford to be choosy. She took his grip.

"I had thought you must be decorating a gallows by now," she said. Their old foe, General Anforth and his Army of Heroes, liked leaving enemies alive no more than Gwynn did.

Gwynn cocked an eyebrow. "I? A jig was never my favourite dance, you know."

Raule heard less bravado than self-mockery in his words. Having become famous, or at least infamous, Gwynn had always professed amusement at the disparity between the grandeur that myth demanded of a famous man's life and death, and the bathos and indignities that actual circumstances tended to force upon both.

"Is Anforth still after you? I can't imagine he's given up," said Raule.

"Oh, he never will. The old bulldog pursues me as ardently as ever. He's made me worth a fortune. If only one could buy shares in oneself, I could be a rich man. You must have been keeping well to the back-blocks if you haven't seen my face on a reward notice lately."

"I'm afraid I've dropped out of the social circuit."

The unpleasant smile crossed Gwynn's face again. "I've heard all the parties are deserted this year. Even people of quality only want to hobnob with the lynch mob of an evening. I take it you're doctoring in this territory?"

"Around and about. There's enough work."

"Of the paying kind?"

"No, not really."

In fact, Raule was close to destitution. Few of the people she treated had the means to pay for her services with anything more than a night's shelter and a frugal meal. When they did manage to scrape up a little money, she couldn't always bring herself to take it. Not wanting to dwell on the subject of her poverty, she asked Gwynn whether he had news of anyone else.

"I saw Casvar at Flat Mountain," he answered. "He was rotting in a cave, with gangrene in a broken leg. He asked me to do the decent thing, and I obliged him. In Quanut I saw a grave with Red Harni's name on the marker. Have you seen anyone?"

"Evoiry, a few months back. He was selling firewood at a souk. He looked all right."

Gwynn nodded. His left hand fingered the hilt of his sword. Raule's eyes went to it. Gwynn had brought it with him from the north. It was of Maghian manufacture and its true name was Heron's Wing Scythes Over A Mountain Lake, but Gwynn had given it another name in his native Anvallic: Gol'achab, meaning Not My Funeral.

Raule noticed that the gemstones which had decorated the hilt were no longer there. Gwynn saw her looking. "Some time ago I traded all that rock-candy for a few necessities," he volunteered. "She might have lost her beauty, but she still works, and she saves me bullets from time to time."

Raule glanced in the direction of the late innkeeper. "Was that one?"

"No." Gwynn stepped back and nudged one of the bodies with the toe of his boot. "This fellow took exception to something the man said, and was somewhat over-enthusiastic in his response." Looking down at the corpse, he shook his head. "Poor bastard. His nerves were wound up like piano wires. I never saw him look happy. Life must have been a burden to him."

"They all must have been pretty high-strung, to get in a four way firefight over cards," Raule commented.

"I dare say."

"What are your plans, then?"

Gwynn walked past her. "Sleep. I want to leave at nightfall." He disappeared outside, and shortly returned with a sack. He took off his gloves and rolled up his shirtsleeves, and began stripping the corpses and gathering up what money had escaped drowning in the blood on the floor. Raule left him to it and went out into the comparatively fresh air. She squatted on her heels under the palm tree, surveying the street, where the oldtimers slumbered on. *I know how they feel,* she thought.

In a while, Gwynn came up from the back yard, gloves tucked in his belt, shaking water off his hands.

Raule crossed her arms behind her head, and yawned. "Well, I don't think anyone here will try to arrest you."

Gwynn took a long, yellow-grey cigarette and a box of matches out of his waistcoat pocket. He struck a match on the metal wall, lit up and inhaled deeply. "A pity," he said, "to have to leave this place . . . "

"I don't know. I think I'm ready for somewhere quieter."

"I know of a nice graveyard."

Raule gave a little smile. The grave would come soon enough. She asked which way Gwynn was going. He said east. She told him she was going west and south.

He pointed his cigarette at the buildings over the street. "There's no work for you here, then?"

Raule shrugged. "I saw a dog in need of a wooden leg." She cocked her head towards the doorway. "Who were those men, anyway?"

"Some fellows I travelled with for a few days. They weren't the best company."

Gwynn moved away and took the four camels off the rail and around to the back. Raule lifted her mount's saddle off its hump, then sat down on the porch and stretched her legs out. The three-legged dog appeared again and trekked back over the street. Raule fanned flies away. It crossed her mind that the bodies indoors ought to be buried. They would spread disease.

That might be good for business.

She felt torpid, and not just because of the heat. She thought about getting up and seeing if she could, in fact, find some work in the town. With such an elderly population, it would be strange if there was no ill health. Or she could ride on. Probably Gwynn expected her to. But her body wouldn't move, and she drifted off into sleep, and a dream. She was back in her home town, a place larger than Proof Rock but otherwise not unlike it. Everything was normal except for the people, who had no heads. They walked up and down the dry streets, and worked in the languishing beanfields, with their upper vertebrae poking up from the stumps of their necks.

Gwynn woke her. The broiling jaw of the day hung slack. The sky was darkening. The dead men smelled fulsome, and all the flies in the world seemed to be at the inn. Gwynn was veiled again and wore a bulky overcoat. He had roped the riderless camels behind his own, and looked ready to depart. He asked Raule if she would consider backtracking east for a short way. She asked why. With his whip he gestured back at the dead men's camels. "I'm reduced to a vagrant salesman's existence. I have a contact at the Yellow Clay souk, to whom I can sell these beasts and the considerable property which I inherited from my late colleagues today, including three dozen excellent firearms. However, I'd rather avoid the eyes of the crowd. If you'd care to come and do the trading, half the profits are yours."

"No."

"No?"

"It's not a bad offer. But I'm afraid I don't care for the provenance of your generosity."

Gwynn gave her a long look. "Have you taken up martyrdom to pious ideals, Doctor?"

"Not martyrdom, I hope. But maybe I've taken up an ideal or two," Raule replied. She stretched her legs out again and folded her arms in front of her. "Even if those men weren't worth much, whom did they kill to get all that gear in the first place?"

"Others who were worth less, no doubt. How many worthy people out here have any money?"

"None, since the worthless never stop robbing them."

Gwynn shrugged. "Well, do as you like." He made his camel kneel, got onto its back and urged it up. He kicked it into a walk. "Take care of yourself," he said over his shoulder.

While he rode away, Raule looked in the other direction. The town was deserted. The palm tree rustled in the first night breeze.

"Well, now it's just thee and me," Raule said to her camel. She got up and made ready to go.

While she buckled saddle girths and checked stirrup leathers, she thought about how badly she needed some money. Riding west through the town, past the silent houses with their dark windows and now deserted porches, she struggled with the faculty which she thought of as her phantom conscience.

Being only a phantom, it had little strength. "Damn you," she muttered, not really sure whom she addressed. She turned around, rode back and caught up with the miniature caravan and its diplomatically silent owner.

Down the dark road, jolting and creaking, a line of wagons rolled. There were fifteen all counted, drawn by mule teams and accompanied by some bone-thin cattle and dogs. Some of the people under the big canvas hoods waved at the two riders. Raule waved back. She might have been inclined to linger and talk, but Gwynn was looking straight ahead, plainly not keen to be sociable to the strangers. Most of the time, however, he was a talkative companion. He had numerous stories of recent adventure and suffering—specifically, his adventures and other people's suffering, almost invariably connected—that he told with the air of an amiable ghoul. Since the life of an itinerant doctor provided its own share of macabrely amusing moments, Raule fell easily into a pattern of swapping grisly anecdotes with her old comrade. This was now their second night of travelling east. In accordance with Gwynn's preferences, they rested during the hottest hours of the day. When they weren't talking, Raule frequently looked up and studied the constellations pinned around the sky. The Manticore arched his tail above the Crown, while the Rider Queen stood forever ready to fling her lasso; the Running Boys chased the Hopping Girl; the Vulture harried the Seven Guests out of the Inn; the Tortoise trudged with the Cup on its back, trying to reach the Old Woman on the other side of the sky; the Lizard led her children homeward, following the wily Bat. Raule wondered if, in millions of years, the stars would shift into positions that showed how the stories ended.

"So which of you robbed the innkeeper?" she ventured to ask Gwynn at one point.

"The fellow who killed him," he answered. "I'd won it all by the time I killed *him*, mind you. That might make it clean money now, depending on how you look at it."

"I've been trying to get away from the old life," Raule said.

The period of history which had caught them both up in its turbulence was over. The war was lost. Three years had gone by since General Anforth won the victory that ended the revolution and saw its leaders sent to the lime kilns. The Army of Heroes, under Anforth still, hunted its old enemies across every territory in the Copper Country. Sometimes a ballad telling of someone's heroic death against overwhelming odds could be heard; but betrayal by erstwhile allies, followed by trial and execution or just a quick lynching, was the more usual reality.

"So what waits at the end of your itinerary, Doctor?" Gwynn said. "What's your desideratum, the mirage in your eye?"

Raule shrugged. "I've been thinking of heading across to the Teleute Shelf."

"No doubt a good choice. I've heard life's quite civilised there."

"So I believe."

In truth, Raule had no serious intentions. Like Gwynn, she had a price on her head, but it was a comparatively small one, and as a native of the land she had the advantage of being ordinary. No one ever noticed one more small, thin dark woman among the rest in a market or saloon crowd. Moreover, the people who dwelled in the hamlets out in the wilderness were, as a rule, glad to have a doctor come by, and if any of them had ever matched her face with that of Raule the brigand, malign witchdoctor and associate of murderers, none had ever betrayed her. She was drifting, numbly content to go to bed alive and wake up alive, letting days and weeks and months slide past.

"And you, my gunslinger riding towards the sunrise; are you going to the prairies?"

"No. I've got my sights on the real Orient. Sarban, Ambashan, Icthiliki where the girls are pretty . . . "

"Ah, an eastern paradise. One with gardens and shady terraces where you can laze all the lotus-eating day, and beautiful servants bring you more wine than you can drink, and you can get filthy rich without lifting a finger?"

"All that goes without saying, doesn't it?"

"Indeed it does." Raule drifted off into a reverie about the sweet life in such a place.

Later that night, they came to a ghost town huddled around an abandoned mine. They didn't bother stopping. Anything worth scavenging would be long gone.

An hour past dawn the next morning they reached Yellow Clay.

Looking through their spyglasses, they saw many sky-blue uniforms in the crowd at the souk. The soldiers weren't just idling. They were asking questions and checking papers. A group of unlucky people stood roped together under guard. More soldiers were setting up a camp at the edge of the town.

Gwynn quietly uttered a curse.

Raule shrugged her shoulders. "Well, we can go on. There'll be another place somewhere."

"We?"

"Now I've come this far, I want to collect my share."

And so they continued to go east. They reached the other end of the wall. Where it finished, the road forked into two tracks diverging across a flat, reddish-brown plain. Raule pointed to the track on the right. "That was the way I came," she told Gwynn. "There wasn't much down there."

"Then we'll go this way," Gwynn said, taking the left-hand path.

Four hours of riding in climbing heat brought them to a range of broad, fissured red-rock hills with thin bushland on top. The road went up the first hill in steep switchbacks, then followed a dry gorge through the bush. Acacias and spindly blackpod trees made up most of the taller vegetation, with nail grass and tough, tangled succulents growing over the ground. The camels pulled towards the blackpods and tore off leaves. Something had already thoroughly chewed the lower branches. The culprits presently became visible: some skinny goats, with bells and brands proclaiming them to be someone's property.

A mile further on, the trail passed through a group of shacks. A painted board nailed to an acacia read: PATIENCE.

Patience, if that was the hamlet's name, had no inn; but one shack bore a sign proclaiming that guests were welcome. Raule and Gwynn stopped outside it and dismounted. A lot of knocking finally brought a man to the door. He was sleepy-eyed and surly. He pointed at the dirt floor to indicate that this was the bed, and named an exorbitant price. Raule haggled him down to half of it. There was nowhere for the camels. The man flatly refused to have them inside; was his house a shitting-place for livestock now? They would have to be left out in the open. He beckoned a girl-child out of the shack. At some time, she had been horrifically burned: below a soiled mobcap, her face was a red, one-eyed mask of dense scar tissue. "My daughter," the man said with a mean laugh, "will keep an eye on your animals."

Raule suggested they take watches. Gwynn agreed, and offered to take the first, so Raule brought her bedding into the shack and fell into her usual troubled sleep. Gwynn woke her in the afternoon, and took his turn to stretch out on the floor with his hat over his face. Their host was ostensibly sleeping too, sprawled on an old coach seat serving as a divan, but now and then his eyes opened and darted around. Was he afraid they would steal the dirt from his floor, the spiderwebs from his ceiling?

To pass the time Raule took some cards off a shelf and played hands of solitaire. When she was too bored to shuffle the cards again, she opened one of her saddlebags and brought out an old journal. Once upon a time she had kept copious medical records. She had thrown away all but this one book of notes, which dated from one of the last, hardest months of the war. She knew it by heart, and skimmed through it without having to do more than glance at each entry, her eyes travelling along the close lines of writing, which contained not only useful information, but personal memories. For many of the men and women whose bodies' travails were detailed in the book, the jottings about their bones, muscles, organs, temperatures, excreta, vomits, fits and deaths were the only written record that they had ever lived. Gwynn's name never appeared, for while calamity had regularly brushed near him, it had just as regularly failed to strike a noteworthy blow. His was a lucky litany of close shaves and narrow scrapes.

Halfway through the journal, Raule stopped reading and put it away. From the same bag she pulled out the one other piece of reading material she owned. It was a traveller's guide to the Teleute Shelf that she had bought as a curiosity some six months ago.

A map inside the front cover showed the vast Salt Desert spreading southwest of the Copper Country, crossing the belly of the world. Further west, the Teleute Shelf was a curved line, meeting the desert on its outward swell. From the book Raule had learned that the escarpment rose over a thousand yards high and held a whole other world of countries, cities, mountains and rivers on its top. In a past age, said the introductory essay, the Teleute Shelf had been the edge of a continent and the Salt Desert a sea. Now, however, the desert was a completely waterless place. Raule knew something of it. Mercantile concerns held power there, maintaining fortified mining compounds which operated like miniature provinces. For water and everything else these were dependent on the vital artery of the railroad. But the book described an opposite climate on the highlands of the Shelf. The lines fell over themselves with depictions of fertility: emerald-green mountains, unpenetrated jungles, huge rivers teeming with fish, and rain that fell for

21

weeks upon weeks. Raule couldn't imagine so much water. There were also sections on twenty-odd major cities, from which she received a vivid impression of places that were old, big and full of history. While she was not so naive as to imagine that any of them would be paradise, she could not help but be somewhat beguiled by the descriptions of architecture, gardens, palaces, universities, theatres, fashions and the other features and trappings of a well-established material civilisation.

She glanced at Gwynn, who lay as still and quiet as a stone. His native country of Anvall was a land where the only seasons were degrees of winter. A place as white as the moon and colder than a thousand graves, was how he had once described it. In summer its borders melted, like morning ice crystals on the top of a cistern, and fell into a heaving black sea; in winter the sea returned them. Did he dream of water? she wondered. Of the cities he had sometimes spoken of, fastnesses built half of rock, half of ice? Was he called back at night to that strange cold top of the world, or did he dream of pleasure in Icthiliki's flowery towns?

When he woke, she asked him. He replied, with a laugh, that he was rarely able to remember his dreams.

The failed revolutionary war had attracted numerous foreigners. Professional mercenaries, the bad and the crooked, idealists and romantics wanting a cause, opportunistic wanderers, and sundry adventurous flotsam had flocked to the rebel army. Gwynn was one of several dozen outlanders who had joined the company to which Raule was attached as a surgeon. The revolutionaries had initially enjoyed popular support, but as the war dragged on, conditions in the Copper Country inevitably became hungry and dangerous, and the wind of opinion changed. The people began looking to the Army of Heroes to restore the status quo and peace. The revolutionaries found themselves suddenly unwanted, and when it was all over they found themselves wanted in the wrong way. For the sake of survival many companies turned to banditry. Raule's was one such. By that stage Gwynn had become their leader. For a wild couple of years they lived as highway pirates in the comparatively populous north of the Copper Country, robbing banks and trains to support a prodigious lifestyle, while still fighting the army wherever they encountered them. But the will of the people prevailed. Aided by

General Anforth, the towns formed militias, and from then on the wages of crime came less in gold and more in lead. Former fellows turned coat in droves, becoming informers and bounty hunters. The proud and the mad, and those who were simply unable to think of anything else to do, marauded their way into shallow graves. Gwynn, to his credit, disbanded the gang, giving everyone a chance to disappear and survive. That was over a year ago. Raule had managed to fade away, but in more ways than one, and more than she had intended to.

The revolution had been an important dream of hers. After the war she had come to wonder why. Now she didn't wonder. All her thoughts of politics and great affairs and history had become like sand blowing around in a very distant wind.

Their host had gone outside earlier, carrying some traps. Gwynn had moved to the coach seat and was cleaning his guns. He had several pistols, a pair of shotguns, and a fine Speer repeater rifle that normally lived beside his saddle in a calfskin case. He hummed softly while he made them all immaculate. The scarred child came into the room with two tin bowls of soup. She left them on the floor and hurried away. Raule picked a chunk of meat out of one bowl and tasted it. It had the familiar flavour of goat. She didn't think it was too bad, but Gwynn only ate a mouthful of his, then pushed it away and made his own repast of a cigarette and a few swallows of liquid from an unlabelled bottle. Raule finished her soup and reached for Gwynn's.

"Mind?" she asked.

"Go ahead."

While she ate and Gwynn went on with his cleaning, Raule thought her situation over. As a doctor, a native and someone whom Gwynn had cause to trust, he no doubt considered her an asset worth hanging on to. If she was useful to him, she could expect to profit. Such pragmatism had always informed his notion of friendship to a considerable degree. This suited Raule, as it allowed her to maintain an equally self-interested detachment in her dealings with him, without any dishonour.

Their way was taking them towards the Saint Kaseem Crack, a massive trench in the earth that split the Copper Country from north to south. There would certainly be guards at the bridge, plenty of them. No doubt she could help Gwynn smuggle himself past them. But if subterfuge failed and it came to a fight, she was at best an ordinary shot, and didn't fancy her chances. Gwynn's good luck had never protected anyone but himself. She owed him no debts. If they found a souk before the bridge, she could take her money and go. But if they didn't, was it worth tempting fate? She decided it wasn't.

"If we don't find a market before the Crack, I'll be going back west," she said. Gwynn made an acknowledging grunt while he squinted down the Speer's barrel.

They left Patience that evening when the shadows were stretched out long and violet. The road wound down out of the hills and continued on across the arid plain. The light of a half moon showed small islands of nail grass separated by channels of sand. To Raule's eyes the grass and sand archipelago looked like one small area of ground repeated over and over, as though it had been made by a lazy god with a stamp. She imagined herself riding around that land in circles, never leaving it until she came to grief or grew old.

When they had ridden for some three hours without coming across any other sign of human presence, she remarked, "At least the Army of Heroes doesn't seem interested in this territory."

"There wouldn't be much for a hero to do here," Gwynn said.

Later on in the night they reached a mining town that had several streets and was actually on their maps. Dozens of people, mostly men of hardbitten aspect, were out and about. A building with red-curtained windows and GENTLEMEN'S CLUB painted in scrolling letters across its verandah looked to be the queen of the main street. Next door to it was a saloon from which a loud noise of piano and singing came. At the end of the street there was a gallows and a graveyard, and, along with these amenities, a water cistern and a trough. After they had filled up their canteens and let the camels drink, Raule leaned against the cistern and studied her map. She estimated that they were three or four days away from the Saint Kaseem Crack. The only other bridge marked on the map was the one on the Ghan Highway, two hundred miles to the north, virtually next door to General Anforth's headquarters in Glory City.

Raule asked Gwynn how he planned to get over the trench.

"How?" he echoed the question. "Don't you know camels can fly?"

He was drinking from the unlabelled bottle again, holding it under his veil. To Raule's nose it had a bouquet of brass cleaner.

"That's the drunken answer," she said. "What's the sober one?"

"The sober answer," he replied, "is possibly not available at the moment. But I shall try. I plan to approach our little abyss at midday. I plan that our friends garrisoned there will be disinclined to come out of their nice cool bunker. In fact, I plan that they will be asleep."

"And if they're not asleep, what's your plan?"

"To shoot better than they do."

"I see. So as long as you grow enough arms to use all your guns at once, you'll smoke the opposition? If you'll forgive an agnostic's scepticism, I'd say you're going to die."

"Care to wager?"

"Not a chance. If I win, you'll be dead, so who'll pay me?"

"Plenty of people, if you can salvage my head to show them." Gwynn threw the bottle over the road, into the graveyard. "Are you still going back?"

"Yes."

"Perhaps you should stop here, then."

"There's supposed to be a place called Gravel up ahead," Raule said. "I'll ride till there."

They mounted and went on. The moonlight dimly showed country that became more desolate with every mile. The clumps of nail grass grew sparser, and occasional brown, pebbly sandhills appeared.

The dawn broke over true desert. Dramatic outcrops of black rock rose from a plain of hardpan. The coarse brown sand formed steep ramps where prevailing winds had blown it up against the rocks. Faint wagon ruts and the usual bones and garbage served to mark the trail. Raule and Gwynn followed it for two nights, looking out for Gravel.

On the third night a strong wind rose. It worsened through the night and as the sky paled, scooping up sand from the slopes and flinging it wildly around. Such sandstorms could suffocate you, and a very bad one could even lift you into the air and drop you, breaking your bones on hard ground or burying you in a dune. This one wasn't like that, at least not yet, but it wasn't a pleasant thing to be riding through. Gwynn tied his domino around his face for extra cover, and Raule tied a scarf of her own likewise. Though they rode with their heads down, the sand, which was as fine as dust, still got into their eyes and nostrils and lodged in every part of their clothing. The camels became restive, bellowing their displeasure at being forced to continue. It became hard to see the road.

"Gwynn!" Raule shouted. "How about waiting this out?"

The wind snatched away his answer, but she saw him raise his whip in assent. They took shelter on the leeward side of the next outcrop of rock, and huddled down next to the camels. With shrieks and shrill moans, the wind churned the sand up into spinning clouds that blotted out the dawn. Now that the camels had nothing to do, they took the opportunity to show their annoyance with the situation by spitting. The wind picked up the reeking slime and cast it around liberally, smattering it back over the animals and the two humans.

The storm blew for several hours. Meanwhile, the sun grew into an afrit wielding a scourge of heat. Gwynn slept. Raule couldn't do more than doze fitfully.

When the wind finally abated, the sun was well past its zenith. Raule lifted her head. Brown grit covered her and Gwynn and the camels. The land might have expelled them out of its deepest reservoirs of dirt. While the heavier grains of sand had fallen back to the ground, the finer grains remained suspended in the air, covering the sky with an umber pall. She shook Gwynn awake, and they dusted off their clothes and their gear as well as they could. Gwynn assiduously stripped and cleaned all his guns. Raule, too, went to work with reamers and oil on her scattergun and the old carbine that she kept for shooting occasional game. When they were done at last, Gwynn favoured moving further off the road to camp. It occurred to Raule that if Gravel was any distance from the road, they easily might have passed it during the sandstorm and not seen it. She suggested looking around, and pointed out a high rock with a sand ramp half a mile down the road, which would give them a good view.

The slope brought them some eighty feet above the road. At that height, they found themselves above the thickest layer of dust in the air, and could see past the area where the storm had been. Raule took her spyglass out of its case and scanned the horizons. The search yielded nothing in any direction but the ubiquitous sand and rock.

Nothing. Or, perhaps not. Back the way they'd come, flickering in the brown, heat-warped distance, there was a row of dots that she had at first taken for small rock spurs; but it struck her that their spacing was unusually regular. Possibly it was a row of shacks or tents.

Or smaller, closer objects.

She turned to Gwynn. He was gazing down the road the other way. "Gwynn, give me your glass for a minute." His had a better lens than hers did.

"What is it?" he asked, handing it to her.

Looking through the stronger lens, Raule was able to ascertain what the dots were.

"Trouble," she said.

It was a line of camel-mounted figures. She estimated at least two dozen, riding at a brisk jog. They lacked the animal herds that nomads would have had with them. She did some calculations, and judged that they were less than ten miles away.

"Looks like Heroes." Raule gave the glass back to Gwynn. He looked through it, and nodded.

"It seems so." He didn't sound particularly surprised. He lowered the glass quickly. "That was a flash off a lens. I'm afraid they've seen us. The Crack can't be far. We'd better not dally." He kicked his camel into a run. Raule lost no time in following suit.

As she bounced in her saddle alongside Gwynn, she said, "I doubt they came out here just for the scenery. Would they, by any remote chance, happen to be on your trail?"

"I ran into some trouble about a month ago," he answered, sounding uncomfortable. "I thought I'd shaken them."

"Did you really?"

"I should have told you. I apologise."

"Has it occurred to you that if you didn't leave little piles of corpses everywhere you go, you'd be harder to track?"

"I've tried, but things always seem to snowball."

They reached the bottom of the slope. After dismounting with haste, Raule spat over her shoulder. "Whatever your head's worth, it's overpriced! Does Anforth know he's searching for an empty vessel?"

"We'd better travel light," Gwynn said as if he hadn't heard her, and started pulling bags off his camels' humps and throwing them onto the ground.

Raule imagined what he would look like with a dagger between his shoulder blades. But her anger dissipated with a speed that surprised her. In its place she felt a sense of fatalism, as if death had already drawn a bead on her. She couldn't see an escape route. If she went her own way now and the soldiers decided to split up and chase her, she didn't envision surviving long. Having little of her own to get rid of, she helped Gwynn. She was about to cut the ropes securing a sturdy leather pack on one of the spare camels, when he stopped her. "Not that one," he said. "It's a bit too valuable." She shrugged and moved on to the next pack. As she climbed into her saddle, she spared a glance at the pile of discarded luggage, which included the guns from Proof Rock. It would be good salvage for someone.

They took off down the road, kicking up clouds of dust, the spare camels following behind on their ropes.

After several minutes, Gwynn spoke:

"Do you want to know what I traded my poor sword's beauty for? It's in that pack."

Raule looked askance at him.

"Dynamite."

Raule allowed a pause of some length to elapse. At last she said, "That's splendid. How much?"

"Enough to take out a guard bunker. And that bridge."

"That was your plan?"

"Yes. I was going to tell you."

Raule thought about the heat, and how rough the going was now that they weren't just walking, and how big the bang would be if the explosives ignited. Then she thought about how, if they lived long enough to cross the bridge and blow it up, she was going to be stranded on the far side of the chasm.

"It occurs to me," she said, "that you're an arrogant, ridiculous, piss-eyed, mullock-brained, dung-engendered bastard, and you deserve to be forgotten by the world."

In reply Gwynn only shrugged, not disputing the matter.

TWO

GWYNN STOOD IN his stirrups with his spyglass to his eye, and leaned forward. He did this twice. He was keeping the lookout ahead, Raule behind.

They were nearing the Saint Kaseem Crack. It was in sight now, a thin black line, wavering in the silver mirage on the horizon.

They had been riding for something over an hour at the fastest canter the camels could sustain. It didn't seem fast enough; and even so, the animals were showing fatigue. Down at the level of the road the pursuers had not yet appeared on the horizon, but they surely couldn't be far behind.

"What can you see?" Raule said.

"Nothing at all, which may be a problem."

"What are you talking about?"

"The bridge. It looks like a landslide."

Raule looked to the fore and scanned the road where it intersected with the black trench in the distance ahead. The bridge that should have spanned the crack wasn't there.

"Perhaps someone else blew it up first?" she suggested. The luck seemed too bad to credit.

They reined their mounts to a halt.

"Damn amateur engineering," Gwynn muttered.

"Damn you," Raule snapped.

Without reacting, Gwynn reached inside his waistcoat and brought out a map. Raule followed suit, but already knew what she would see: an expanse of white paper with nothing at all printed on it, save for the Saint Kaseem Crack's line, for a very long way in all directions.

29

Gwynn's map displayed an identical void, with beautifully lettered labels: Eastern Desert, Southern Desert, Marginal Desert, Desert of Heats, Desert of Humours.

Raule looked around. The rocks had grown fewer and smaller, and were concentrated in the north. To the south, there stretched a too-familiar vista of flat, nearly featureless hardpan. She glanced down at the road. There was little sand on the surface now, and their tracks were faint. It wouldn't take much wind to erase them.

"At the moment they can only see us if they climb like we did," she said. She pointed southwards. "If we can draw them out onto that flat ground and keep this far ahead, we should be able to lose them."

Gwynn nodded assent. "And once it's dark, we can loop back to the road."

Raule shaded her eyes. "We should still head towards the Crack. Enough towns and oases never find their way onto a map. There could be an uncharted bridge."

"That's the spirit," Gwynn said.

The Saint Kaseem Crack was a hundred yards wide and said to be as deep as ignorance. Its walls of dark, rugged stone dropped through fathoms of shadow that thickened in gradual degrees, to eventually become one with a river of pure, permanent night.

Raule and Gwynn followed it, stopping periodically to change mounts. The camels were now able to go no faster than a slouching jog. Raule kept looking behind, expecting to see the troops, but her vigilance only brought an unchanging view of empty dun-coloured horizons. When she was not gazing back, the depths of the chasm often drew her eyes down.

The sun seemed not to move at all. Raule had a sense of being pitted against an inimical force that was keeping the day in place and preventing the night from arriving.

"Like being chased by phantoms, is it not?" Gwynn said at one point. Raule made no reply.

The sun did, eventually, dawdle down the sky. When full night had fallen, they risked stopping to give the camels a brief rest. Checking their water situation, they calculated that they had a week's worth.

The subject of a bridge didn't arise again. In that empty vastness the very idea of a bridge was contrary, as strange as the idea of rain. They agreed to ride in a wide arc that would not bring them back to the road too soon. Navigating by the position of the Lizard, they left the Saint Kaseem Crack and rode southwest.

To Raule the night felt even longer than the day. At times she was sure she sensed riders behind them in the darkness. Her heart pounded every time she turned around to check. But the moonlight always showed her a view of solitude.

Dawn brought nothing new. Now steering by the sun, they turned west. Gwynn chain-smoked, dropping the butts into an empty canteen. Later in the morning they passed through several miles marked by low hillocks of pale stony rubble, strewn around as if a celestial kiln-shelf full of giant unfired clay pots had been hurled down upon the earth by a choleric brother of the lazy god who had made the plain of nail grass. At noon they rested briefly, then continued in the hammering, shimmering heat, taking turns to doze in their saddles.

Raule dreamed she was a stage magician's assistant. This caped conjurer killed her and brought her back to life in all sorts of ways, until he finally led her to a gallows.

"You don't know how dead you are," he said.

"That's where you're wrong," she answered, whereupon she woke.

The hillocks fell behind them, and the hardpan continued. It was a land as empty and dry as a thousand-year-old skull. There wasn't a nub of cactus or a single fly, not a bone or a scrap of refuse; life had no embassy in that whole country. It was strange to think that this alien territory was still her home.

The sun went down. They kept riding west, intending to turn back towards the road the next day.

Early in the morning they saw the riders on the horizon behind them. They were four miles away at most.

"How?" Raule breathed, trembling.

"When heroes turn hunter, they're the best in the world," was Gwynn's reply. In his voice there was a rancour that Raule had never heard before.

They could not run. The camels were too tired to go faster than a jog, no matter how many times they felt the whip.

Raule had once seen a giant land snail pursue and kill a smaller snail. The hunt began on one side of a yard and ended on the other side, and took three hours. She wondered if this chase would last that long.

At first she didn't think it would, as the troops put on a burst of speed. But they fell back; they had ridden too hard, too soon. In a few minutes they were dots on the horizon again.

This pattern was to repeat itself over and over. Each time the pursuers tried to close the tiny final distance, they failed. It occurred to Raule that the situation would have been amusing, had it not been a matter of life and death. As it was, she had no doubt about the final outcome, and she felt the exhaustion of someone labouring at their own grave. Raule felt the wasteland mocking her. *You too will be exhausted and broken and rendered down to dust,* it seemed to taunt.

Looking back, she judged that the troops were closer. She told Gwynn they had to go faster. They whipped their mounts furiously, but could not get more speed out of them. As the enemy closed, Raule realised that she had badly underestimated their numbers. There were at least forty of them. They came close enough that she could see the blue colour of their uniforms. Then, yet again, they fell back and diminished in size.

Miles came and went and came, bringing more of the same desert, and worsening exhaustion. Raule poured water down her throat; her skin squandered it in sweat. A hammer pounded an anvil in her head; her stomach heaved, and she nearly lost all the water. She kept her mouth closed and breathed through her nose, trying to conserve moisture. She felt her fear age and settle; it lost its acuteness and became ordinary, a part of her like her organs and limbs. She remembered the feeling well, from other times when she had been sure she was going to die. She tried to draw hope from the fact that on those other occasions she had survived, but she could raise nothing except a feeling of caustic self-mockery.

At around noon, Gwynn's camel collapsed. He wasted no time trying to make it stand, but shot it between the eyes, and changed mounts. The death seemed to put fear into the other camels, and they ran harder; but only for a short while, and the troops kept pace, bobbing relentlessly at the hazy edge of the world.

An hour later, Gwynn halted.

"What?" Raule rasped, stopping beside him. She thought he must have spotted something.

He said, with what seemed the resolution of despair, "I'm not of a mind to keep running like this. I'd rather fight before I'm too far gone to aim straight." His voice, like hers, was raw and slurred.

"There are too many of them. We'll die."

He said nothing.

Raule made a scornful spitting noise, without wasting water on actual spit, and kicked her camel on. In a little while, Gwynn came up on her right side and drew level with her. He said nothing, nor did he offer any glance her way, but from then on he stayed abreast of her. He might have decided he was more willing to trust his fate to her judgement than his own.

But Raule only knew that she wanted to die later rather than sooner.

She imagined that when she died, her ghost would ride on across the land forever; for she could hardly remember doing anything else. It was as if the rest of her life had served no purpose other than to lead to this ludicrous finale.

Time seemed to stop moving, as it had done the day before. Minutes lasted interminably. Raule wondered whether they had, in fact, died already.

A hoarse noise roused her. She jolted in her saddle. Surely she hadn't been asleep? She realised Gwynn had called her name. He had his hand raised, pointing unsteadily south. Something large and dark quavered in the haze. It looked like an isolated mesa.

"A good place for a last stand," Raule heard herself croak. Without further exchange of words, they veered towards it.

As they were coming near to it, Gwynn laughed like a raven. Raule wondered what in the world could be funny. Gwynn had his spyglass to his eye. With another hoarse laugh he said, "See what has found us!"

Raule focused her own glass on the blocky shape. The lens showed the truth of it. It was a wall. It heaved up like the flank of a leviathan lying on the torrid earth. From end to end it had to be five miles long. It appeared to be perfectly intact. A single tall arch, set between two square watchtowers, pierced its centre.

Raule could not at first make herself believe that it was real. The Copper Country didn't lack for tall tales of lost cities in the deserts. She expected it to be a mirage, a last joke played by the mocking country before it killed her. And so she only shook her head slowly. But the wall didn't disappear. It stayed steadily there as they approached it, until at last they stood near enough to see its smoothly joined stones. Raule felt her parched lips cracking and reluctantly pulling away from her gums, to which they had become firmly glued, as they stretched in a grin.

The wall stood seventy feet high. Its shadow blackened the ground in front of it, and the glare of the sun behind concealed whatever lay beyond the arch, which was narrow, built for defence. While Raule strained to see details, her mind conjured up an entire ancient metropolis, with buildings of marble and antique wells still brimming with water. She imagined that the city went deep underground, down to the shores of a cool black secret sea, the very opposite of the desert above. A place of rest and safety, governed by beneficent influences, where the desire for violence died: she went so far as to imagine such a haven beyond the wall, and could not discard the fantasy, despite the vigorous objections of her intellect.

Under the arch they rode. The wall was built massively for its height, with a thickness of some twenty-five feet.

They emerged, blinking, into the glare of the sun, and into an open area of the same perished land that lay behind them. A hundred yards ahead there was indeed a small city, but it was ruined to the point of being little more than a pile of rubble. Of the outer wall, only the one side stood. The other three were as ruined as the rest of the city.

Raule's spirits plummeted down from the poetic heights of false hope. But Gwynn stayed in a good mood.

"In this place we can win," he declared. He dismounted, took a long drink, and started unstrapping the leather pack. "This should nicely ruin their day."

"Or bring that wall tumbling down on us," Raule muttered listlessly. But she listened to the simple plan he proposed, and conceded that it was worth trying.

Forty-three soldiers. It was ridiculous overkill, Raule thought, watching the blue uniforms come nearer.

She nervously rubbed her carbine's stock. Her heart was going like a mine battery. She stood at the top of the watchtower on the west side of the arch. Gwynn was in the east tower. Both towers had crenellated parapets that were in almost perfectly sound condition, spiral stairs within, and intact chambers at the bottom, where they had hobbled the camels. It was as though whatever force had destroyed the rest of the city had left the single wall as a monument to the greatness of the conquered foe—and hence to the greatness of the conqueror.

For extra company, Raule had most of the dynamite, about thirty sticks. There had barely been time to cut fuses and get them packed into the explosive. Adrenaline had driven some of the exhaustion out of her. If she and Gwynn weren't in superb form, she reasoned to herself, neither would their attackers be.

As the troops approached within a mile of the wall, a rifle shot cracked from Gwynn's tower. No one among the enemy fell. Gwynn's plan was to simply make their position known, without inflicting early casualties that might make the opposition cautious. He had expressed confidence that the captain of the pursuing band would simply order his troops through the arch and up the towers. Raule was less convinced; she thought they might try approaching in small parties, in which case the advantage of surprise with the dynamite would be lost; but Gwynn seemed certain. "They won't bother," he had stated. "Remember, they're heroes. All their instincts will tell them to do the simplest thing, especially if it involves a rousing charge through a front door."

And it looked as if he was correct. The troops closed up into a column and gathered speed. Their captain rode out in front on a tall white camel, blue plumes nodding on his hat. Gwynn fired off-mark again. Raule followed suit. She eyed the dynamite set out and ready beside her, and the matches that she had neatly lined up. She wiped sweating palms on the back of her pants, and got ready to move.

The captain lifted his hand and barked an order. And the enemy came in, charging at a hot gallop.

At the very last instant before they reached the wall, Gwynn's shooting suddenly became accurate, and three riders went down. The rest swept on through the arch.

As they cleared it and entered the open space, Raule lit two sticks of dynamite and threw them through a crenel. One hit the first rank, and a soldier and his mount burst apart redly. All the ammunition the man was carrying exploded at once, so that bullets flew every which way out of the eruption. The other blast went off on the ground just behind the third rank, throwing up a huge cloud of dirt and sending camels lurching and stumbling, several throwing their riders. Raule hurled another two sticks down.

Within seconds the charge broke down into a confused magic lantern show of bucking and flailing shapes engulfed in a devil-cloud of smoke and dust. Human screams and animal bellows rose up to Raule's ears. The wall shook with each explosion, and she hoped it was as solid as it appeared to be.

Gwynn was firing steadily into the melee. Working methodically, he shot the captain first, then chose targets among the other riders. He seemed to be taking care not to shoot the valuable camels. Several without riders bolted for the ruins. On the ground inside the wall, blue figures fell down in rapid succession. Calm now, and smiling with grim satisfaction, Raule kept dropping down her rain of fire.

Her smile vanished when a bullet hit the parapet in front of her head. She ducked down, swearing. More bullets smacked into the stone. Gripping the matches too hard, she broke three before she managed to light another fuse. She blindly threw the dynamite over the parapet.

After the blast the bullets stopped, and Raule risked sticking her head up. She saw Gwynn leaning dangerously out of a crenel, aiming the Speer at the arch. In the shadow and the smoke, Raule couldn't see anything, and doubted that Gwynn could see either.

He pulled back to reload, and the firing immediately started again. It was definitely coming from under the arch. Meanwhile, three men had got their mounts under control and were galloping away towards the ruins. Raule ran across the top of the tower and threw one stick down at the arch. It was an awkward angle and she failed to get it in, but the explosion filled the arch with smoke. She ran back, in time to catch two men who came staggering out. They looked up at her and were aiming their guns as the dynamite fell towards them. It hit them directly, blowing them to pieces, with the firecracker effect again.

Gwynn had turned his attention to the fleeing trio. He took two down quickly, then his aim went off and it looked as though the third would escape; but at last he had success, and the man fell at the edge of the ruins.

Soldiers were still alive on the ground. Several limped for the towers, but their slow, injured movements made them easy prey for Gwynn, who showed off by shooting each of them neatly through the skull.

A last soldier, lying on the ground below, sat up and started firing a pistol, but he had only one arm, which wavered, and he shot nothing but empty sky. As suddenly as he had started shooting, he stopped, dead, his arm pointing up, steady at last. After that, nothing moved but the dust, and that too eventually settled to stillness around motionless men and camels and small mounds of gory, smoking meat.

Gwynn got up from his crouch and gave Raule a salute. She returned it. The whole fight couldn't have lasted more than two minutes. The world was still very much as it had been beforehand, but now she felt great love for it. That feeling would fade, she knew well enough; but it was something to be enjoyed while it lasted.

By pointing down and drawing a line across his throat, Gwynn signalled that he was going below to check for wounded to finish off. Raule gathered up the unused dynamite and climbed with care down her tower's inner staircase.

In the room at the base, it was dark and almost cool. The camels, Raule was surprised to discover, showed no signs of distress. All four were kneeling on the floor, chewing cud with an air of sleepy dignity, as if they cared about nothing but the sweetness of rest. Raule's own feelings could not have been more in agreement. She put her dangerous burden down carefully in a corner and collapsed at the bottom of the stairs. She slaked her thirst, then lay on her back, resting her worn-out body and savouring the lightness of mind that came with perfect and easy victory. When the enemy was dead and you were alive and whole it was a fine thing. Her phantom conscience raised no objections to her indulging in this sentiment.

In a short while Gwynn came to the doorway, unveiled, hand resting on his sword, a cigarette dangling from his lips.

"Feel up to looting?" he said.

"Not really. Is there anything left?"

"No idea, Doctor. But finding out should provide quite a diversion." He made a sweeping gesture towards the mess outside.

Raule squinted at him. "You're very restless. You might have worms."

Gwynn looked awry at her. "From this jocund mood, should I assume—"

"No," she said, "you shouldn't. You should never assume." She heaved herself up off the floor.

"Dear woman, you're wisdom in the flesh," Gwynn said, stepping back. Raule gave him a hard look as she went past.

"It's merely that I'm not completely careless."

Outside, she skirted a charred foot and stepped over a kidney.

Scavenging the spoils of battle was a messy and tedious business. Very little was in a salvageable state. Many of the camels were wounded, and had to be shot. In the end they were able to save a mere eight army beasts, and took a modest haul of guns in working order. In food and water, however, they gained greatly. When they counted up the number of canteens and tins, there proved enough to let them avoid settlements for a fortnight. There was, as well, sundry gear in the way of blankets, utensils and the like, which replaced much of what they had discarded.

The yield of cash was small, and there was only one trinket of value. On the captain's body they found a watch, marked solid silver, still ticking. If it told the right time, it was nineteen minutes past two. Inside his wallet Raule found another thing, a piece of paper with a list of phrases written on it. They seemed to be pass-codes, as they had consecutive weekly dates next to them. Whoever wrote them appeared to have a wistful way of thinking. One read:

You went yesterday; today the watchdog barks so loudly.

Another—

Old seedpods on the ground, hardly worth the wind's trouble.

There was also evidence of a whimsical sense of humour:

You and I, gecko—the moonlit road's ours tonight . . .

Raule found herself hoping that the author was a bored staff officer living behind a desk somewhere, and not one of the present day's casualties. She folded the paper away, thinking it might be a useful thing to keep. It never proved so, but she kept it for a long time anyway.

Raule opened her eyes and saw stars and a bright moon, now slightly gibbous. She lay in her blankets on a small stone floor within the ruins, next to the cold ashes of a fire. The moonlight shone brightly on the shapes of Gwynn and the camels nearby, and cast sharp black shadows across the uneven contours of the stones. The corpses were far enough away that the air reaching Raule's nostrils carried only a faint whiff of death.

She felt fragile. She couldn't remember falling asleep.

It must have been the cold that had woken her. Her body was freezing. She couldn't be bothered trying to get the fire going again. Struggling to her feet, she walked over to her camel and huddled next to it, intending to go back to sleep. But as she warmed up, she stayed wide awake.

The moonlit wall drew her eye. The arch seemed to be looking back at her. She felt compelled to get up again. She walked past Gwynn, who woke at the sound of her footsteps. Seeing her, he closed his eyes again. Raule walked across the bare ground, towards the wall. She held her breath as she went past the corpses, and returned to the watchtower. Taking care on the pitch-dark stairs, she climbed up to the top and looked south over the ruins.

The city was a damaged puzzle that would forever tease the inquisitive, she mused. In the time when it was built there must have been a water supply either above the ground or accessible below it, but the water was long gone. The ruins were devoid of information about the city's past and its people; not a single surface yielded even a fragment of an image or inscription. The watchtower's stairs were granite, and the hard stone was deeply scooped, evidence of the passage of many feet over many generations. The city's active life must have been as long as the period of its desuetude. Beyond that, Raule could glean nothing.

A hollow, uneasy emotion grew in her, as old dreams visited her mind. She recalled her childhood wish to become an eminent physician, and remembered imagining the discoveries she would make about sickness and health, life and death. She identified the hollow feeling: it was mourning, for the loss of time and the loss of something of herself, perhaps a great deal of herself.

She stood for a long time. The night breeze swelled into a dry, cold, booming wind. The edges of the world were black, so that ground could only be differentiated from sky by the stars populating the latter. The leagues of empty space seemed to tug at her, pulling her in all directions, making her nebulous, insubstantial. At last, standing exposed to the dark and the wind, she suddenly and deeply regretted joining the revolution and choosing a violent way of living that had never had anything to do with her true aspirations. She felt as though she didn't exist, and it was a relief.

Like a sleepwalker, she went back down the stairs and returned to her bed among the broken walls.

Gwynn reached inside his coat and drew out a thick roll of notes, which he handed to her. It was the middle of the night and they were preparing to leave.

"What's this?"

"Yours. Call it danger money, if you like."

She took it with a nod.

They were back where they had been before, in need of a market. Gwynn showed indifference regarding which way they should ride, so on Raule's instigation they kept to their westerly heading.

As they led their small caravan out of the ruins and back into the desert, Raule often looked back. By moonlight the wall was a white, straight banner. When it at last disappeared below the horizon her heart became a little heavier. It would have been pleasant to have a similar bright image for a cynosure ahead.

The going was hard and dull, with their route taking them first across a great deal more of the same featureless dry earth, then over a gibber plain that took three nights to cross, then into hilly badlands through which they wound for another four nights, after which the monotony of hardpan resumed. They continued to be vigilant, but the cycles of daylight and darkness brought no sight of more enemies, or, for that matter, of any human beings. Other life reappeared, occasionally and at random, in the form of patchy tracts of grass and succulents with small populations of reptiles, rodents and insects. Nowhere was there water on the ground. Occasionally a solitary eagle or vulture cruised overhead in the sky, at a great height. Once only, in the light of the second daybreak on the gibber, an eagle spiralled down to the ground: it grabbed something, a lizard or a rat, then returned to the heights of the open sky.

One night Raule counted the money Gwynn had given her. It was a lot. He had been unusually silent, even taciturn, since they had left the ruins. She guessed he was preoccupied with the question of where he could run to next.

The settlement wasn't on their maps. It wasn't a town, just a handful of sheds beside a waterhole, but around it there was a large camp of tents and shelters, and lamps strung on wires illumined a sprawling souk on the eastern side of the camp. They came to it in the small hours of their tenth night of riding. The moon, now rounded almost to a full disk, gave plenty of light to see by. They made a wary approach, riding a circuit around the camp, looking for uniforms and army flags. This reconnaissance yielded a happy negative.

"And even in My desert shall ye be provided for," Raule quoted the old Verse of the Promising Afrit, adding the next line under her breath: "Though dullard all ye stoop and lag anigh the Garden Door." And, indeed, a small but dense garden of plants surrounded the waterhole. They rode up and dismounted to let the camels drink and graze.

They put up their tents as dawn was breaking, filled up all their canteens, and retired to rest. Gwynn stayed sequestered for the whole day, never emerging from his tent. Raule napped in short stretches and went outside often, partly to keep a lookout and partly for the pleasure of being among people again. The market remained constantly busy, and Raule found herself eagerly listening to the noise, as though her ears had grown thirsty for sound in the silence of the desert. She noticed a lot of Harutaim in the crowd. At sunset a new, large group of them arrived from the south, with some pageantry, riding in orderly double file, beating drums and singing melodiously to announce themselves. Raule observed that most of the nomads, including the new arrivals, were heavily armed. Harutaim parties always had a few members riding shotgun, but in these groups every adult and most of the children over the age of eight or so carried a gun of some sort.

Gwynn emerged with the first stars of the night. Raule pointed out the warlike nomads.

"They might be our buyers," she said, adding, "They won't care who we are, and they'll forget us after we're gone."

"If you think so," Gwynn said passively.

The Harutaim parties were camped in circular and semicircular clusters of tents, with their animals in rope enclosures beside them. Raule set out across the ground towards the nearest group, leading the camel that was carrying the guns, wrapped up in saddle blankets. Gwynn followed behind her, in his domino and veil with his hat pulled down low.

A fire burned in a shallow pit in the middle of the camp, with about two dozen Harutaim sitting around it. Raule approached the circle, uttered greetings, and announced that she had weapons to sell. Before she finished speaking, the nomads began to laugh. Some made the sharp trilling noises that were a ruder expression of mirth. "When so many of our enemies are generous enough to die and let us take their guns, we don't need to trade with jackals," guffawed one man.

It was the same with the second and third groups. But at last, at the fourth camp, some of the people made laconic gestures of interest. One of their old women took charge of the conversation, and she agreed that perhaps some trading could be done. Gwynn lifted down the guns and the nomads inspected them, making a good show of disappointment as they did so. Shaking her head, the old woman said she was sorry, but the arms were in very poor condition. The haggling then commenced. The matriarch bargained as though she was fighting a battle then and there. Gwynn was silent, leaving Raule to fight the mercantile duel. After half an hour of to-ing and fro-ing, she and the Harutaim woman had still not negotiated a mutually tolerable price. She decided to try another camp, and started packing up. That did the trick. The woman thrust her hips out and laughed, said she had only been joking before, and made a more reasonable offer. Raule felt too weary to face going through the same rigmarole again with another group; and she knew the woman had guessed as much, and she didn't care. She clapped her hands, palm to fist, to show they were agreed.

The matriarch made the same gesture, then called out something over her shoulder. In a few moments a teenage boy came running up with a carpet bag, out of which bundles of dog-eared cash were brought and payment counted. The old woman's belligerent manner completely evaporated. While two men gathered up the guns and carried them into a tent, she looked so happy that Raule regretted her capitulation.

With many elegant phrases of hospitality, the woman invited Raule and Gwynn to sit and share tea with her family. Raule accepted on behalf of them both, and room was made for them in the circle around the fire, over which a large iron kettle of water was boiling. Soon the Hurutaim and their two guests were drinking pungently spiced tea from tin cups and chewing on squares of sweet, oily candy. While Gwynn sat mute, holding his cup underneath his veil, Raule spoke with their hosts. The nomads proved to be eloquent talkers, but behind their loquacious front there was plainly a barrier beyond which they didn't permit outsiders to approach. Nor were they averse to making, or at least implying, criticisms. After listening to one of Raule's stories of the war, one of the young men asked her pardon for his forwardness, then told her that in his people's eyes the differences between the revolutionaries and the Army of Heroes were of no more importance than the different colours of flowers.

"The affairs of those who settle in houses are not our affairs. We have affairs enough of our own, which is why we must buy your guns," he said, with a gently self-mocking smile. And then a young woman joined the conversation, saying to Raule that if the world was a paved road, the Harutaim walked in the cracks where older dirt lay. Then she laughed and said:

"May you who walk on roads have steady feet."

"We haven't been walking on roads too much lately," Raule said. "I'm afraid we're not entirely certain where we are."

The young woman laughed again. "You have a map? Show it to

43

me."

Raule brought her map out, and after perusing it for a few seconds the woman pointed to a location only about a week's ride away from the Copper Country's southwestern border. The Salt Desert lay beyond. If there was a time to head away to the Teleute Shelf, this was it, Raule told herself. She wondered what Gwynn was planning to do now, but there was something in his quietness that discouraged her from asking. When she tried to put her finger on what it was, she could only think of the ghosts that visited her dreams, and of the barrier between the living and the dead.

A short while later they took their leave of the Harutaim and wandered through the souk, buying provisions, a little apart from each other. To Raule the souk seemed rather less real than the ruined city had. The crowd was diverse, their wares varied. Where could they all have come from? Had a wind gathered them all up and blown them to the one spot?

She felt a sudden sense of comradeship with everyone in the motley gathering, as though she was a member—for however short a duration—of a secret society.

As they were walking, and these thoughts were going through Raule's mind, something brought Gwynn to a stop. Raule looked in the direction his head was turned, and saw what had caught his attention. Among all the livestock, contraband and junk straggling over the sand there was a piano, of all things. By its looks it had seen service as a battering ram. Five very dirty, gaunt children were gathered around it. The tallest, a girl, was making an address to passers-by, while the younger ones stood silently with impassive faces.

In the old days, Gwynn's fondness for the piano had been nearly as legendary as his fondness for rapine and slaughter. Whenever the bandit company relaxed in a saloon or inn with an instrument, he would play it at all hours. Now he was moving slowly towards the dilapidated upright with its attendant youngsters. Raule followed him. As they came nearer the girl's voice reached their ears:

"We are five brothers and sisters, alone in the world, for our parents are dead as doornails, and our grandmother too. This was her piano, and we have hauled it ourselves on its castors from her house sixty miles away yonder." Then she spread little scarecrow arms wide and cater-wauled like a seasoned carny barker: "No beggars or scabs are we! To Wild Hog Ridge we go! To Wild Hog Ridge where the gold is! Anyone with eyes and ears can tell this fine instrument is worth ten times what you can buy it for here! Five hundred dinar, a piano for a song!"

Up close, the instrument's condition looked even more lamentable. Nevertheless, Gwynn approached its custodians.

"Might I try it out for sound?" he asked, making his voice very gentle.

The children looked at each other. "All right, mister," the older girl said. "Just mind you take care with it. It's a delicate antique."

"So I see, honoured miss," said Gwynn, his expression hidden behind the veil.

He flexed his gloved fingers—he wouldn't remove the gloves and show his distinctive light skin, thought Raule—and bent over the worn out keyboard. He played a few bars of a simple, pensive prelude. Surprisingly, the piano proved to be in better tune than its appearance suggested. However, Gwynn let the notes fade and lifted his hands off the keys. "I'm rusty," he murmured, looking down as though addressing the instrument itself rather than any person present.

A fat woman selling brassware on the next patch of ground overheard. "Not a bit of it, love," she said, shaking her head slowly. "That was pretty. Go on, play us the rest." She stood, picked up the folding chair she had been sitting on and waddled over with it. "Here, put your backside on that." She plunked the chair down in front of the piano and gave Gwynn a motherly pat on his rear.

He started, and Raule tensed. But then he smoothly took the woman's hand and lifted it up to the level of his lips, and inclined his head. He appeared to be suddenly enjoying hamming up the part of a gentleman. He sat down and began the piece again. This time he played with a surer touch. Raule remembered the tune well. It was one he had often played when everyone was drunk, and night was giving way to day and revelry to stupor. A few people who were walking by stopped and stood to listen. But in the middle of the music the girl stretched her hands out and hit the lower keys, making a deep jangling discord.

"Stop," she said. "You can't just keep playing it."

A younger girl nudged her. "Maybe he hasn't made up his mind yet."

The older one shook her head. "He doesn't mean to buy it. Do you, mister?"

"No, honoured miss, I do not," Gwynn admitted, spreading his hands in a gesture of surrender. "I'm obliged to travel light, and I fear this piano wouldn't fit in a saddlebag. However, I should like to rent it for a while, if that might be possible." He fished in his hip pocket and produced a fifty-dinar coin, which he proffered to the girl. "Would this be sufficient to purchase an hour?"

"Take it, quick!" hissed the smallest boy.

The girl hesitated for a fraction of a moment, then took the coin and squirreled it away inside her clothes. Then she said, "We don't have a watch."

"Ah, then, it is just as well that I do, isn't it?" Gwynn said, bringing out the dead captain's silver timepiece. The small boy rushed in front of the girl and took it from Gwynn's hand, his eyes wide with admiration.

"It's half past eight," the boy announced. "I can tell the time," he added proudly.

Then at a gesture from the girl the children stepped back, and Gwynn resumed playing. He finished the prelude, then moved on to the livelier measures of the Moonlight Drinking Song. More people stopped to listen. He played the Caravan Ballad, Binzairaba's Dance, So Long Angel Eyes, The Hangman's Apology and other popular tunes of the Copper Country, to the delight of his audience, who were soon clapping the rhythms and singing the well-known words.

Then Gwynn played two pieces of a different sort, complicated and melancholy compositions that, Raule knew, were music from his own country. She could hardly believe what he was doing. Anyone in the crowd might identify him, and they would certainly remember him later if they were questioned. She watched faces closely, looking for signs of incipient trouble. But oblivion seemed to have descended on everyone but her. Gwynn launched into another whisky tune, and the audience once more struck up loud clapping and singing.

At the end of the last chorus the boy jumped up, shouting out in his high voice that it was now half past nine. Gwynn bowed to the onlookers and retrieved his watch, and the boy followed its path of disappearance with depressed eyes. There was applause. Some people threw coins, which the children pounced on.

"That was a good show, love!" shouted the fat woman.

After Gwynn had relinquished the piano back to its vendors, and he and Raule were walking away, Raule smiled wryly and said, "Well, I don't know what to make of you tonight. You walk around covered up like a harem girl on the eve of her deflowering, and then you go and do that."

"Music is one of the finer things in life," he replied with a shrug.

"Was that little concert intended to be a swansong, or a premature wake?" she said, unsure of what she was trying to provoke.

"Neither."

"Then what?"

"Just a dalliance with an interesting moment."

Raule laughed. "Well, comrade, it's your neck."

No, he isn't one of the dead, she thought. *Nor am I.*

He said he was going back to check on the camels and make a fire. She nodded. "All right. I'm going to do some shopping. I spotted an apothecary of sorts back there."

Gwynn handed her some money. "I need bullets, gun oil and soap, if soap persists in these dark times."

The apothecary had his wares out in handsome wooden boxes and he himself was a dapper person with a gold monocle. Raule stood in front of him, trying to bargain. Among his jars and boxes and bottles of brightly coloured fake cure-alls were some genuine medicines that she was running low on. However, he wouldn't budge on his steep prices, pointing out that she could try to do better elsewhere if she wished. She said she did wish.

As she wandered around, looking at the stuff spread out on mats and tables, she thought about the children with the piano. If they ever made it to Wild Hog Ridge, wherever that was, she doubted the place would be kind to them. "But at least they're going somewhere," she muttered to herself.

The first tune Gwynn had played came back to her. And while the slow melody repeated in her head, something shifted inside her, as though a key had at last been fitted to a waiting lock. The door of regret opened, and she found that on the other side was desire. It was a thing like a shard of glass, clear and painfully sharp. She felt it physically, so that she had to stop and breathe deeply. She knew what she wanted, and why it meant she had to leave the Copper Country and travel far away. She wished to bind herself inextricably into a place where she could become a civilised person, and remain so for the rest of her life. In the space of no more than a minute this intention established itself in her mind with implacable authority.

In some way she felt herself standing again in the watchtower in the ruined city, with vertiginous black space around her again. Only now, instead of there being merely the stale winds of memory and remorse flailing around in the darkness, Raule felt a fresh wind blowing at last, a wind that carried the seeds of her old plans, still unsown, and miraculously dropped them back into her hands.

Among the market tents and tables, her imagination placed streets and walls, and in her mind's eye the crowd turned into citizens. She saw the faces of shopkeepers, labourers, scholars, priests, artists, bankers; she imagined, elaborately, that such streets and walls, and such an orderly civilian population, might provide a mould into which she could pour herself, and become the distinguished physician she had once dreamed of being. It did not seem an entirely ridiculous idea, even when her mind returned to the present and to practicalities; for now, at last, and with the best timing imaginable, she had money. She would not arrive destitute in the far west. She would have a chance to establish herself. Remembering how she had felt sure that death had marked her, she smiled, realising that the joke was on her. She could hardly have been expected to see the long-lost face of good fortune lurking behind all the hazard and bother.

It occurred to her that she might try to bring Gwynn with her, and give the gentleman in him a fighting chance. Even if it might also be something like taking a wolf into a fold and hoping it would turn into a sheepdog, her phantom conscience suggested that it would be the proper thing to do.

The railroad across the Salt Desert began at the town of Oudnata. The Army of Heroes kept a large garrison there, but trying to cross the immense desert by any means other than the train would be a venture even more dangerous than walking into the enemy's camp. In theory it might be possible to ride to the first compound; but they could hardly do so invisibly, and it was almost certain that they would be chased. As a final deterrent, the mining authorities were not known for their hospitality to vagrants.

The train it had to be. Having Gwynn in tow would certainly narrow her chances of getting through, but she was willing to take the risk. And it wouldn't hurt if Gwynn ended up owing her a favour. Soon Raule had formulated something that to her mind passed for a plan. To carry it off, certain props would be necessary. She searched the souk and eventually found what she needed, scrounging most of it from a rag-and-bone cart. There was no other apothecary, however, so she returned to fork out for the monocled one's goods. Raule headed back towards the water and looked for Gwynn. She found him at the end of a line of tents. He had made a fire and was squatting beside it with a griddle, cooking pancakes. She tossed him a bottle of gun oil, the only thing on his list that she had been able to find. "No soap, no bullets. You'll just have to shoot fewer people."

He caught the oil with his free hand. "And join the great unwashed too. I really love this country of yours."

Raule sat down on the sandy ground. A stack of cooked pancakes rested on a tin plate to one side of the fire. She speared the top one with her knife, rolled it up and bit into it.

"And if I told you that you don't have to stay here learning meekness and getting on the nose?"

She described her plan, and showed him the things she had bought. It made him laugh, as she had thought it might. As far as any kind of serious reply went, he only said that he'd sleep on it. Raule decided that she had satisfied the requirements of courtesy. She turned the conversation to the mundane matter of selling some of the camels. Gwynn agreed that they might as well. They decided to sell six of the army beasts and keep two for carrying extra water. The camel market was at the end of the souk. They spent most of the night there, waiting around, since none of the buyers were in a hurry. But the army camels stood out as well-trained mounts, in good condition, and eventually they sold them for an adequate price.

They returned to the waterhole as the early light was breaking. Gwynn promptly retreated into his tent. Raule stayed out in the open for a while, enjoying the atmosphere as she had the day before. With the morning sun, a flock of ibis came from the north and landed at the water's edge, lining up to drink, probing the mud for insects with their long, curved bills.

As the sun climbed and the day grew hot, she took shelter. For the thousandth time, she perused the Teleute Shelf guidebook. She read the description of the rack-and-pinion rail that took the train in a zigzag up the shelf's face at the other end of the desert. The book recommended the view to passengers of stout constitution. Of the places the book described, a city-state named Ashamoil particularly captured her fancy. The writer made much of the river on which the city was situated. She read over and again about the deep slow water, the myriad boats that plied it, the houses with front stairs plunging right into it.

Raule dozed, and dreamed of a street full of balconies where the dead crowded, all gazing down at something she was never able to see.

When she woke, she more than half expected Gwynn to be gone. But the afternoon light showed him to still be there. Already dressed, he sat cross-legged at the water's edge, hazardously smoking a cigarette under his veil.

He had saddled his camel and her own. When she shot him an inquiring look, he only shrugged, and when she mounted up and started out of the souk he followed her.

An hour later, she was riding south under a darkened sky and he was still abreast of her.

"One thing," she said to him. "Is anyone else chasing you?"

He seemed to consider that for a while. "There was a woman in Quanut who claimed I was responsible for one of her children," he said eventually. "I had a hard time escaping her. She might still be after me."

"Could it have been yours?" she asked.

"Well, the lady was about your colour," the reply came, after another pause, "and the little girl was as black as my hat, so I think I can assume I'm not leaving family here."

Some time later, Raule took a look back. The oasis was gone from view. She set her gaze firmly towards the front, following the Lizard who followed the Bat.

On the lip of the plateau above Oudnata, two figures on camels were silhouetted against the stars. The settlement around the railhead was booming. The extension of the railroad, which had stopped during the war, was now under way again. A construction gang worked by lantern light, laying tracks. Several big engines loomed in the yards. There was a high stockade around the town, and half a dozen blue-uniformed figures at the gate.

The riders started their animals along the steep track that wound down the plateau's face. They rode slowly, and it was an hour before they reached the gate of the town. Women, both were swathed in ragged black mourning weeds. One was small. The other looked tall, but her spine was hunched. Dirty bandages were wrapped around her eyes, and her camel was roped to the other woman's. She wore a veil over her mouth, leaving only her nose visible. Her skin was dark, coloured a shade of brown that a shoeshiner's eye might have recognised as Holden's 'Cinnamon Snake' boot polish. Her fingers, covered by a filthy pair of grey gloves, constantly rubbed the beads of a rosary, while her husky voice muttered words in a strange language that might have been a holy tongue.

The women stopped at the gate, and a guard wearing a corporal's insignia asked them their business.

The small woman spoke. "My mother and I are going south. She has lost both her eyes, and both her sons, my two brothers. She can no longer bear to live in this land."

There was pity in the guard's look. "I'm sorry for you both, but beggars aren't permitted into the town."

"Of course not. But we have money for the train." The woman dug inside her rags and pulled out a few notes.

"You misunderstood me," said the guard sternly. "I don't care for bribes. Show that you've enough to pay for a ticket, or leave."

The woman hesitated, but at last she opened a saddlebag and brought out a smaller cloth bag, from which she extracted several rolls of money, tied with string. The corporal grunted, jutting his chin out, as he took them. He untied the notes and went through them, scrutinising and counting. At length, he bundled the money up again, tying the strings neatly, and handed it all back to her.

"Welcome to Oudnata," he said.

Three days later, the weekly train that plied the Salt Desert departed from the town. The women took a private compartment. Troops from the garrison went around the carriages while the train was getting up steam, checking for felonious types on the run from justice. When they reached the compartment where the pair sat they glanced at the mumbling spectre of age, loss and death hunched in the corner seat and hurried on, discomfited.

As the train steamed out, peals of hyena-like laughter escaped through the door of that compartment.

PART TWO

THREE

HE NEEDED OPHIDIAN scales on his throat and jaw to match that tranquilly unkind smile, she decided.

He stood with a group of a dozen or so men, loitering under an amber-coloured gas lamp below the Crane Stair. By the martial luxury of their attire—elaborate silk coats, with sides cut to expose the guns and other ironmongery they toted on their hips, polished riding boots with long spurs, jewelled gloves—they were undertakers, cavaliers of some grandee's household.

Rice-white skin marked him as foreign, one of the river quarter's throng of outlanders. His unbound black hair was as long as a woman's. Embroidered peacock feathers scrolled down the back of his coat and around the collar and cuffs.

With those looks, was he a passionate libertine or an impassive, merely picturesque dandy? Did the outer appearance explain the inner man, or did it exist in lieu of him?

He stood very still, only the ends of his hair moving, tugged by a draft from somewhere. The woman who watched him also stood still, in the shadows inside the Viol Arcade, where the shops were locked behind iron grilles for the night and the horn lanterns under the corbels were dark. The men seemed intent on their conversation. None of them looked in her direction. They were certainly an evil-looking lot. It could be imagined that they were devils, possibly attracted to the city by the sulphurous light. But even if not supernatural, they were indubitably men of the underworld.

The woman had migrated from the other direction, a year ago, from the heights of the city, leaving a house where fourteen generations of

55

her family had lived, turning her back on wealth, order and tradition, in order to become another foreigner in the riverside district. When a girl, her teachers had attempted to instil certain fears in her, but she had developed antithetical fears. She knew she was of a different mould to those around her. As she grew up it became plain to see, as the coppery curls that adorned her head in childhood thickened in texture and deepened in colour, becoming a rose-red mane; her pale brown skin turned dark gold, so that her breasts, when they grew, resembled those of a gilded pirate figurehead, or of some brazen she-beast, on whose milk infant tyrants would hope to suckle. Finally, on her sixteenth birthday, her eyes had darkened from brown to the black of burnished iron.

She fixed those eyes on the man in the peacock coat. His calm demeanour stirred something in her. She focused her will on him, trying to compel him to detach himself from the others and come walking her way. But if he sensed he was being watched he gave no sign of it, and he stayed with his fellows. A short while later the men moved away, out of the light and up the Crane Stair's narrow zigzag, where they were soon lost to view behind outcrops of cantilevered shacks.

During the following weeks she kept an eye out for him, but never saw him or any of the other men in the group. Her classical education equipped her to imagine a reason for this. Certain philosophers of the late antique period had proposed the theory that every person functioned as the centre of a universe, a permeable world—the individual being likened to the eye of a storm or whirlpool—which could intersect with the realms carried by other people, or spin far away from them. According to one of the antique sources, this theory had been proposed in response to the question of why, when two philosophers who were old friends had a bad falling out that both were too proud or too genuinely offended to try to mend, they suddenly ceased to see each other even in passing, even though they lived in neighbouring streets. As much as she believed in anything, she was inclined to believe in this conception of existence.

Perhaps her world had briefly passed through that foreign man's. Perhaps he had taken a riverboat out of the city, or had met his death, or had gone back to hell.

In the end, she put him in an etching.

"God will thank you even if no one else does," the nun had said.

It was the dry season in the city, the season of brickdust and droning flies. It was the time when Ashamoil's climate was most like that of the Copper Country. It was also the season of festivals and parades. The gongs, drums and firecrackers of a celebration reached Raule's ears as she sat up late in the tiny room she had converted from a private kitchen to a laboratory of sorts, completing her notes on her latest acquisition: a male foetus, stillborn at five months, lacking a skeleton.

If she looked up she was faced by the others, arranged in jars on shelves. Of those directly in front of her, one of the larger jars contained twins joined through the head, a circumstance which had created a single broad face made of two profiles turned slightly towards each other. This face was reposeful and unalarming, the eyes shut, the mouth smiling serenely. The specimen next to it was more conventionally freakish: lacking cranium, cerebellum and scalp, its head was a hollow bowl, its upper face radically distorted with the eyes sitting huge and toad-like on top of the brow. On the shelf above, a mockery of childhood was bottled. It was about four inches long, with a doughy torso and head and thin sprout-like limbs. The puffy distortion of the face resembled the faces of those soft rag baby-dolls that were supposed to portray ideal infantile sweetness. That one had been another kind of twin, superficially attached to the chest of an otherwise normal newborn girl. A midwife had brought the girl to the hospital and Raule had done the necessary cutting. The odd little humanoid blob was waste matter, lacking a brain or heart, Raule discovered when she dissected it afterwards. Its neighbour, in contrast, was all fragile, emaciated bone. Most of its internal organs floated outside it, moored by membranes extending through the defective abdominal wall. The foetus in the next jar had a deformity of the facial bones that caused it to look like a fish.

The strangest of all, to Raule's eyes, was a conjoined twin with an axis of symmetry running horizontally through its pelvis. The upper and lower halves were perfect mirrors of each other. There were two fully formed pairs of arms, and the autopsy had revealed two sets of female reproductive organs inside the elongated body. For days after she interred this *corpus vile* in its jar, Raule had suffered nightmares in which she watched it floating in a sea, slowly rotating end over end, flip-flopping towards her. Her dreaming self was always sure that the thing had a malicious intent, and she invariably woke from the dreams with a pounding heart and sweating brow. She was very much relieved when the dreams stopped.

She downed her pen, placed the boneless child at the end of one row of jars, put the autopsy notes into a file, then sat and contemplated the total array of specimens. She learned from the midwives, and recorded in her notes, the details of the age, health and occupation of each infant's mother, and of the father when he was known. No single parental characteristic, nor any particular adverse condition among the many under which Limewood's denizens laboured to live, predominated in this data. Raule had no access to the stillbirths of high- and middle-born women, by which she might at least have made some comparisons. She had learned nothing from her autopsies. After three years of study, she simply had no idea what caused the aberrations. By now, her teratological research had effectively ceased to be medical. She supposed it was more philosophical than anything. She acknowledged that it was at least a little voyeuristic.

When she was still a journeyman surgeon, she had observed that in the view of the healthy, the sick often appeared as monsters. When the monstrosity was too extreme, whether in the form of disease, old age, madness or deformity, the sufferer would be shunned regardless of whether their condition was contagious or not. She had concluded that it was human nature to superstitiously fear the transferral of misfortune via some imagined, intangible but highly conductive medium. Now she knew that her urge to study the frailties and failures of the flesh, and to understand their causes, was born of a desire to immunise herself against them. She was no different from the unthinking crowd in that her deepest motivation was fear.

She had learned this truth during the time which had passed since the early dashing of her hopes, when the city's College of Physicians refused her application for membership. She had pleaded her case to no avail. Through bribing a succession of lackeys, and in the process bringing her finances almost to nought, she had succeeded in obtaining a farce of an interview with the College board. As she gave a summary of her years of apprenticeship and further years of experience as a field surgeon, a number of the black-gowned men and women of the board had smiled tolerantly while others had glared as though affronted by a bad smell.

The chairman was in the camp of the amused. "Madam," he had drawled, "were this College to admit every stray witchdoctor and fairground tooth-puller who turns up on its doorstep, you would not be seeking to join an association of skilled medical practitioners, but instead, a conclave of quacks! And if you are not intelligent enough to see this, then, frankly, I cannot believe that you are intelligent enough to have achieved even the basic attainments of medical study."

Raule had kept her temper as laughter followed, and asked what those basic attainments might be, in the board's view.

"A six-year academic novitiate at a university approved by this College, followed by a two-year internship at an approved hospital. That is the minimum," said the chairman.

"And the fees I might expect to pay for such study?"

"Twenty-three thousand florins per annum, plus expenses. Scholarships may be awarded to worthy students after the third year."

Raule was moved to pronounce: "Sir, it seems I have wasted my time here. It only remains for me to recommend that you take your learned opinion, insert it into your sphincter ani and manoeuvre it past the sphincter interior into the sigmoid, where, it might be hoped, its weighty gravity will precipitate an intussusception."

This display of insider knowledge only resulted in the chairman summoning a pair of burly footmen, who escorted Raule out in a far from ceremonious way.

Following that, she had researched other options. She learned that although it was impossible for her to work in private practice or a municipal hospital without College membership, not of all Ashamoil's hospitals were administered by the city's secular authorities. Sundry religions ran small sanatoriums, all in poor districts. She approached one of these churches.

Could she deliver a child? Clean and stitch a wound? Determine cause of death? asked the dour nun to whom she spoke. To Raule's affirmative replies the nun responded with an offer of a position at the parish hospital in Limewood, which had been without a resident doctor since the previous incumbent died of blood poisoning. The pay would be low, the conditions primitive, and the only gratitude would come from a deity Raule didn't believe in. She said she'd take the job.

The man wearing one diamond earring was making a fuss. "Look at it! See what your bitch did!"

The overseer, an orchidaceous foreigner who was seated in a chair under an awning in front of the tightly packed slave pen, opened his half-closed eyes a degree wider and raised the angle of his gaze to observe the cause of the man's ire. The man turned his head to display his unadorned ear, which was bleeding profusely from the lobe. In his hand he held the earring that the slave woman's teeth had torn out of it.

"Yes, I see it," the overseer said, yawning behind a lace-cuffed hand.

Another foreigner lay in a hammock under the same awning. He was of the same breed as the first, with skin as white as boiled fish and hair as black as tar, and was similarly overdressed. However, where his companion was slim, he was thickly built. His face was glum. He lay staring at the broad river which flowed past the steps of a ghat below the slave market, and seemed to be paying the situation no heed at all.

The man addressed the one in front of him loudly. "Did you hear me, you son of worms? What are you going to do about it?"

The overseer sighed. "Nothing, I fancy," he replied with extreme languor.

"You fancy?" the man spluttered. "*You fancy?* Well, I think I fancy seeing you flogged! Does your boss pay you to do *nothing* when your so-called merchandise bites, assaults and maims me? I don't think so, white worm. I think you really want to pay me some suitable compensation for my suffering. Otherwise, I'll see that your boss hears about this. And then you, my worm, oh, you'll be the one who bleeds, won't you?"

He took a step closer to the overseer, who said, "By all means, make your report. Don't omit to mention why she bit you. No doubt my employer will be most sympathetic. He might be so touched that he won't send someone around to cut your hands off."

The man in the hammock roused himself. He pointed to a curtained booth next to the slave pen. "You want to check if the temple gate's been unlocked, you ask and we take you and the lady in there. Then we make sure you look but don't touch. We can't sell a virgin who's had half your fingers inside her, can we?"

"It would be unprincipled," said his companion, standing up.

"*Virgin?*" The bitten man's voice rose an octave. "The slut's *gate* was as wide as a *mare's*!"

"I'm afraid I don't know such details about mares," the slim overseer said with a delicate smile, then he shrugged. "As it happens, we've sold all the virgins in this lot."

"So we don't have to avenge her virtue," the big one added.

"Luckily for you." The slim one stretched out his hand and flicked the man's remaining earring.

"You'll both be maggot-meat," the man spat. "You've made a very serious mistake, my white worms. I'll see you stripped, birched and buggered!" Spittle flecking his chin, he spun around and strode away, thrusting himself through the crowd.

The big overseer lay back down in his hammock. The other swatted a mosquito on his sleeve, cracked his knuckles, then walked up to the side of the pen, where he spoke quietly to a bronze colossus of a man who stood there, in leather clothes despite the heat, holding a huge whip in his hand. The overseer stood back and folded his arms as the giant tapped one of the chained women on the back of her neck with the handle of the whip.

The woman turned around. Her face showed fear, but she stood still without flinching and spat on the ground between her feet. The whip-man stepped back and let his weapon fly. The long lash struck the woman on the thigh. She stumbled back and a cry escaped her. She straightened, and screamed a volley of words in her own language. The whip cracked a second time, striking her arm. She stumbled again, this time in silence, with gritted teeth. After she got her balance back she stood like a trapped storm, snarling and glaring at the whip-man and the overseer. Blood ran down her arm and leg. The whip-man prepared to strike again. As he was readying his arm the woman's ferocious expression faltered slightly.

"Enough," said the overseer. Leaving the pen, he went back to his chair. The whip-man returned to his post. Meanwhile the other slaves all moved away from the woman, as though she was bad luck.

Gwynn had rooms at the top of the Corozo, an old six-storeyed place on the river in a once-fashionable suburb which had literally gone to seed. Returning home at a late hour, he rode his horse over pavements that were bumpy and broken, undermined by the roots of flame trees and the buttressed trunks of kapoks and figs. Behind fences above the street, grandly conceived mansions tottered with cracked walls and fallen pillars. In the river-rich dirt, liberated where stone and macadam had split, ferns and moss sprang forth like stuffing from frayed uphol-stery, and vines and ivies hung over sagging verandahs in dense, trailing ropes and curtains. The vegetation was accompanied by animal life: a yellow and blue parrot might be seen perched in an old guelder rose, a python curled up under a public water-spout, a colony of bats hanging like tear-shaped fruit in the high branches of a jacaranda.

The suburb was walled in by the sheer faces of two granite spurs jutting out into the river from the steep hillsides, up which Ashamoil's buildings climbed in tier upon tier of walled terraces. The windy para-pet of Tourbillion Parade's less glamorous end made a third bound-ary above. This enclosed district kept caged, as well as the wildlife, a population of the ancient lords and mistresses of noble families that had failed to produce new generations. Gwynn had observed the extraor-dinary tenacity with which these venerables clung to life. They fought Time as a matter of honour, it appeared. The newly respectable would succeed them, and would pull down the caried mansions and put up narrow house-rows; the trees would be lopped, their roots extracted and fresh macadam laid down; there would be an exodus of beasts, soon followed by a bustle of humanity everywhere; but not yet. For now, the streets were still innocent of perambulators and piemen, and life in the wild gardens burgeoned without interference.

The Corozo had across its front a terrace laid on top of walls that dropped down into the river. The terrace was shaded with potted palm trees, and it was always littered with their fallen leaves. The front door was permanently locked. Residents, visitors, messengers and servants alike came and went through a yard at the back, where there were stables, disused kennels, and a slimy fountain in which mosquitoes and leeches bred in abundance. Walking past this fertile bowl, Gwynn reached the back door and let himself in. He carried a flat package under his arm. The lamps in the rear lobby were dark, and there was no light under the door of the janitor's cubby-room beneath the stairs. The city's night-time glow, produced by its amber gas lamps reflecting off a permanent smog, seeped through the fanlight and dimly filled the lobby, but the staircase going up to the apartments was as dark as the inside of an executioner's hood. On a table next to the door there were candles of the tall, white, long-lived ecclesiastical kind, kept for general use. Gwynn kindled one of these with his cigarette lighter, and started climbing the stairs. The candle flame showed carved banisters inlaid with heavy dust and a carpet with a threadbare acanthus pattern. From the ceiling hung dark green silk lanterns in which large tropical spiders dwelled.

The stairwell had a permanent odour of furniture polish and charred toast. This smell infallibly invoked memories of the boarding school he had attended in the winter months of each year during his childhood. As they existed in his memory, those months seemed to have been lived by a different boy than the boy who lived in the long days of the summer, hunting mammoths on the tundra and fighting in skirmishes with rival clans. The odour on the stairs summoned the winter boy's ghost, and at the second or third landing it often seemed that a young voice began speaking, conjugating the verbs of dead languages, and reciting rote-learned passages from the ancient writers. That night, as he climbed, it recited from the oldest poems, which gave account of ancient oddities and monstrosities. In fragments, it described visions of Ifrinn beyond the north, where the sun never rose and the ice never thawed and dead clansmen awaited their living kin. It chanted of the eighty arms and eighty mouths of the Kraken, and it whispered, in a voice full of both childish fear and childish longing, of the diamond crown and steel sword-teeth of the Coldrake. When he unlocked his door the voice faded away.

His rooms were furnished when he took them, and apart from having heavier drapes hung and kerosene lamps installed in the sconces where there had only been tallow flambeaux, he had made no changes to them. He ate his meals out and made his ablutions at a bathhouse. He owned few books, since when he wished to read he preferred to use the city library, which had well-appointed reading rooms and an agreeable atmosphere of quiet scholarly comradeship. As far as personal accommodation went, Gwynn relaxed best in an atmosphere of transience.

He put the package down on a desk, lit an Auto-da-fé and went out onto his balcony. The Skamander river below was five hundred yards wide, slow-moving, and dirty on a grand scale. Seven bridges crossed the water, on which a multitude of boats jostled back and forth at all hours. What could be seen now, in the tawny half-dark of the night, was a slowly moving parade of silhouettes, attended by the lights, white, turquoise, yellow and cinder-red, of lanterns and engine chimneys, all darkened and smudged by steam and smoke, giving the scene an edgeless, otherworldly appearance; meanwhile the noises drifting up were raucously terrestrial: horns and steam whistles blowing, livestock lowing on the decks of transport barges, and boatmen shouting curses at each other. The water was never calm; the motion and noise were perpetual.

Around the iron railings of the balcony a vine twisted. Its leaves were variegated and fleshy, and in the dry season it produced stiff, waxy, mottled brown and cream trumpets. These flowers were like nothing organic to look at or to touch, but resembled celluloid blooms from a factory, as though the vine was an automaton that brilliantly mimicked the processes of life; and their fragrance, a satiny brew of aromatic notes, was more redolent of modern perfumery than of nature's work. It could be conjectured that the vine had evolved in order to attract human noses, and have its pollen carried by men and women rather than insects. It was now the warm and dusty, breezeless month in which the flowers appeared, and the small green spheres of their buds were just beginning to erupt among the leaves.

Gwynn finished the cigarette, went back inside and sat down at the desk where he had left the package. He removed the wrapping paper, revealing an etching in a cardboard mount. It was titled *The Sphinx and Basilisk Converse* and was marked as the fifteenth print out of fifty. The sphinx in the picture had the hind body and front legs of a lion, the wings of an eagle, and a woman's muscular naked torso and beguiling face. Her expression was proud, subtle, amused, conspiratorial, inquisitive, frightening, carelessly erotic, and a thousand other interesting things, all suggested at once through a prodigious sleight of artistry. The basilisk was a crested serpent, depicted in profile, with an armoured hide, his long narrow body coiled, a shit-eating grin stretching his scaly jaws. The etching was printed in red and black, with the basilisk mostly black and the sphinx mostly red, her hair like a torrent of wine. The encounter between the two monsters was taking place in a condensed version of Ashamoil. All seven bridges were in the image, along with the Viol Arcade, the Crane Stair and several other places that Gwynn recognised. Much of the architecture was decorated with graffiti-like fragments of maps, both terrestrial and celestial. The basilisk lay on the ground, rearing his head towards the sphinx, who dominated the top of the image, crouching on top of a trapezoid building unfamiliar to Gwynn. A female monster, a male monster. Despite the title, no conversation appeared to be taking place between them. Perhaps the title was meant to be ironic: a basilisk's gaze would turn any would-be interlocutor to stone, and sphinxes were famous for speaking riddles which no one could safely hear. And finally, the basilisk's evil eye was the eye of a peacock feather; and in the middle of the paper, disappearing behind a shanty on the stair, were the distinctive peacock-plumed tails of Gwynn's own favourite coat.

The artist's name, signed in a fine hand, was Beth Constanzin. The owner of the gallery had possessed no contact details for her and said that she had only brought in the one print. She had no reputation, he had added. Gwynn had found himself paying the cheap price for the etching. Though the mere fact that it happened to be he whose clothing had caught her eye meant very little, he was nevertheless intrigued by the possibility that an invitation had been made, or possibly a challenge laid down. The suggestion of badinage in the sphinx's expression didn't escape him. The whole image itself seemed to be a riddle or a joke, in which the artist had involved him, but for what purpose? If she wanted to contact him, he was easy enough to find. For lack of a better answer, he told himself that it was the nature of a sphinx to deal in enigmas.

He felt compelled to look for Beth Constanzin. He would have liked to ask the man at the gallery whether her face resembled the sphinx's, but had been unable to think of a way to pose the question without looking foolish. He began keeping an eye out for that face on the streets and in bars. He looked around other galleries, but found no more of her work. At the same time, he tried to locate the trapezoid building. It was on the Crane Stair in the etching, but there was no such building on the stair in actuality. For several days he spent much of his free time searching for it elsewhere without success. Of course, the artist might have invented it; but if it was a pure whimsy and referred to nothing concrete, then there was really no elegant riddle to solve; there would only remain the comparatively clumsy process of searching for a woman with that face. Gwynn pored over the picture looking for other clues, but found none. It happened that after this failure he became busy with his work. There were weeks of late nights, early mornings and long trips up and down the river. When he had the time to look for the building again he found that he had lost interest in the search. The right time for it seemed to have passed. Strong perfume flooded his rooms and receded again as the trumpet flowers bloomed and died. Half a season passed, during which he occasionally unwrapped the etching and looked at it, but he always wrapped it again, and never thought of hanging it up.

FOUR

THE SKAMANDER RAN from the mountains near the centre of the Teleute Shelf to the city of Musenda on the southwestern edge, where it poured over and cascaded into the sea. For most of its great length it moved slowly, carrying an enormous load of silt, which it deposited in muddy embankments. The flamingo was the river's handsome prince, beloved of the people, and the crocodile was its terrible king. Between the one above and the other below, humans took their boats.

Ashamoil was built along a straight stretch of the river, in tropical hills almost exactly halfway between the mountains and the Musenda cataract, filling some twenty miles of valley. The upper reaches of the city, in the airy sphere of the pink flamingos, belonged to the wealthy. Their mansions had walls of marble and mosaic, towers with stained glass minarets, and around them huge park-gardens, with lakes that mirrored swans, artificial islands and boating parties. But going down the hillsides, the city descended by degrees into a stew of heat, dirt, noise and bad odours: the mouth of the crocodile. Next to the main wharf, on the south bank, was an older stone quay that served as a repository for all manner of refuse, from broken, rusting boiler pipes and propeller screws to household trash that rag men collected from the city and traded to water-gypsies, who took some of it away to a mysterious fate while the rest stayed and rotted until somebody bothered to push it into the water. East and west of the wharves were massed rows of mills and foundries, whose chimneys ceaselessly excreted columns of black smoke, which spread across the lower parts of the city and didn't budge for anything less than a typhoon. The moon was never more than vaguely visible in the yellow nocturnal sky, and the stars and planets were permanently occulted. When she missed the desert stars too strongly, Raule rode the hospital's mule up to the heights, above the smog, and reacquainted herself with the constellations, using her old spyglass to get a better view of dim stars and the spotted surface of the moon.

Flowers and leaves floated down from the pleasure-gardens when strong winds blew, and sometimes a man or woman would leap from a grove of palms on some scenic ledge, to drop down into the river or onto one of the seven bridges.

The poor had one advantage: if they wanted to jump, it wasn't so far. Hundreds of tiny slum streets behind the waterfront factories were the living space for a labouring underclass. Of these overpopulated labyrinths of misery and indignity, the area called Limewood was a typical wretched example. The faces you saw were variously frightened, vicious, cunning, mad, or heart-tearingly sad, but all were hungry. Each new day opened with a scene of streets littered with the corpses of those who had died in the night—the old and sick who had been turned out of doors, unwanted infants, and the murdered. A great deal of casual killing went on, but the number of people packed into the tenements and shanties was so great that no appreciable extra room was created by the deaths. Raule had seen worse, but only at the height of the war.

The parish hospital was a narrow two-storeyed building wedged between a sawmill and a soap factory. In return for a minimal stipend and a cheerless little flat inside the hospital, she did what she could to treat the malnourished, sick and injured. In the crowded conditions, abetted by the tropical climate, diseases and infections flourished. The church sent nuns trained to serve as nursing staff and novices to do the hospital's domestic work. Sometimes there was enough of this help, sometimes not, and then Raule changed bandages, emptied bedpans and scrubbed floors herself. Her experience in treating wounds was useful with the many children injured by factory machines, and with the older youths, amongst whom knife-fighting wasn't so much a pastime as a way of life, and, all too frequently, of death.

The only other permanent staff member was a priest employed to attend to the patients' spiritual needs. An unkempt man with well-known bibulous and prurient habits, this cleric spoke of God to the patients with feverish intensity and kept vigil beside the dying with an air less of sanctity than ghoulish fascination.

Limewood had drawn Raule into itself, to some extent. She had come to know many of its families. She had soon learned that the numbers of working poor were equalled if not surpassed by the unemployable insane and mentally deficient, the elderly destitute, and orphaned and abandoned children, all existing like dirt in the slum's interstices. Her phantom conscience—that odd, purely intellectual and unemotional organ which had grown, like scar tissue, to replace her original conscience, lost in the war—didn't inflict her with actual feelings for any of this suffering humanity, but she felt an aesthetic objection to the squalor and the lowering of human dignity, and this if anything made her cling all the more rigorously to the principles of virtuous living that she had learned before the war. After all, civilised behaviour didn't require actual compassion, only the ability to follow compassionate rules. Raule conscientiously played the role she had chosen, and as a result had gained a reputation as a trustworthy human being as well as a good physician. The business with the stillbirths didn't bother anyone. It might have been looked at askance elsewhere, but in Limewood it was considered an extremely benign eccentricity.

It had started with a single awry birth, of a girl with limbs like flippers. Raule had seen such occurrences before, in both human and animal newborn, but the sheer numbers of people in Limewood even if no other condition in the district could be implicated—gave her occasion to see many more such deviations of nature. They had begun to arouse her curiosity. The local midwives disposed of the corpses of these infants, who were customarily killed if they did not die naturally, so she approached one of these women and found out that pig swill makers paid five farthings a pound for the scrap meat. Raule made it known that she would offer ten pence a pound. Word got around like the clap, and soon no woman birthed a monster that didn't end up in a swaddled bundle outside Raule's office door.

In the early days, when she was still occasionally meeting Gwynn for meals, he expressed concern about her situation, and ventured that she might do better in another place. He might have been right, but the truth was that she was tired of travelling. Moreover, if her more ambitious dreams had come to nothing, she had still restored herself. She was not discontent. She refused the money he offered her.

Raule was doing the round of the wards that she always made at night before going to bed. A ratta-tatta-tat in the corridor outside made her look up. A night-sister, an older woman upon whose calm capability Raule had come to rely, came hurrying into the ward from the one next door, a look of inquiry on her face.

"It's all right, I'll get it," Raule told her. "I know that knock. Can you finish up in here for me?"

The sister nodded. "Of course. Be careful out there." Obviously she recognised that particular urgent knock too.

"Don't worry, I will be," Raule said over her shoulder as she went out. She walked briskly down the corridor, lifted a ring of keys off a hook and unlocked the hospital's front door, which she had only locked for the night half an hour ago. Two half-naked urchins stood outside, both panting hard.

"There's going to be a fight at the Orchard," one gasped. "Bellor Vargey and Scarletino Quai this time. They're both hot for a deading. You'll be needed."

Within minutes Raule was driving the ambulance mule-cart through the hot, foggy twists and turns of Limewood, along streets that were sometimes red brick and sometimes unpaved mud, with the urchins riding on the seat beside her. It was only a trip of a mile, but the crowds shuffling on and off the graveyard shift held up her progress, so that it was a slow quarter-hour before she halted the cart at the small brick square known as the Orchard (local history had it that there had indeed been lime and orange trees growing there, in people's grandparents' grandparents' days). Wedged at the back of some high tenements near Lumen Street, a flashy, raucous strip that ran parallel to the river through the districts of the poor like an imitation gold thread through sacking, the square was favoured by the local kids as a field of honour.

When Raule arrived the preliminaries were still going on. The sides of the yard were crowded with youths wearing bright-coloured shirts and tight breeches. Most were barefoot. All were openly armed with knives and coshes. At one end, the Esplanaders had marked their territory with red paper lanterns. The green lanterns at the other end belonged to the Limewood Push. Kids who belonged to neither gang stood along the walls between them, making something of a buffer zone.

In the middle, two teenage boys wielding long knives were circling each other. They weren't crouched to fight yet. They were standing straight with their shoulders held back, strutting, whirling their knives around, showing off their dexterity. Raule recognised Bellor Vargey from the Limewood Push and Scarletino Quai from the Esplanaders. The two gangs were long-standing rivals.

To Raule's eye the Esplanaders looked particularly tense and ready for violence. Among the waterfront gangs they were the most criminal lot. They specialised in kidnapping young girls and selling their flesh in alleys and cellars, ran a large and particularly brutal protection racket, and into the bargain they had a penchant for arson. The Limewood Push operated at a much lower level; ordinary muggings and break-ins were about their limit.

But the youths and boys on both sides were playing up—shouting obscenities, twirling their knives and truncheons like the two in the middle, and striking theatrically aggressive poses. This display was not just for each other, but also for the girls leaning out of windows above to watch. And, especially, it was for the horsemen. Of these there were a dozen or so, in a group beside the neutrals on the side Raule entered, dressed to the nines and armed to the teeth, astride splendid mounts. They were drinking from fancy flasks, smoking tobacco and joss, and bantering among themselves in a relaxed way. They were household cavalry, out slumming.

At the Orchard they could watch bloodsport that wasn't fixed or faked. They could also keep eyes out for potential recruits. There wasn't a coshboy who didn't want in. Though the risks to life and limb were considerable in the lower echelons of the great houses, the risks were almost identical in the factories and foundries, and factory wages wouldn't buy a hundredth part of the high life that the cavaliers flaunt-ed. It could be argued, not entirely speciously, that the boys trying to attract the notice of these men of rank were doing the most intelligent thing they possibly could.

Gwynn was there, mounted on a fine-boned black horse. He had landed lightly on his feet in Ashamoil. Within days of arriving in the city he had met by chance a man called Marriott, a countryman and old companion of his. Marriott worked for a south-bank grandee called Elm, a famous man in the city, with interests in many businesses, the slave trade being the chief one. A seemingly perpetual war in one of the small nations in the wild jungle territories that lay along the Skamander, not a great distance from Ashamoil, kept a steady supply of defeated and captured people coming into the city's slave markets. The slave trade was legal, but that did not make it safe. Elm had need of fast, reliable guns, and via Marriott's good word Gwynn had been accepted into the employ of Elm's business house, the Society of the Horn Fan. Word on the street kept Raule in touch with Gwynn's doings. She knew of how a few fights had thinned Elm's ranks, helping Gwynn to rise quickly. Now he was a senior cavalier, one of Elm's trusted men about town.

Raule hadn't been able to keep a neutral view. For Gwynn to be so undiscriminating in his choice of master made her think the less of him. While she had never openly expressed her disappointment, she hadn't tried to conceal it either. They'd made fewer and fewer calls on each other, until the present situation was reached, where their only encounters were chance ones. Gwynn had, however, struck up a friendship—based on mutual antagonism, it seemed—with the hospital's peculiar priest. Raule shrugged her shoulders about it, thinking they were welcome to each other.

Upon hearing her cart arrive, he turned his head around. He looked well, and in good spirits. His coat, of figured black and oyster damask with double rows of crystal buttons, hung open to display a silver-sprigged waistcoat and an elegantly long, lace-trimmed white cravat. Steel-toed boots on his feet provided a thuggish touch that countered the ladylike effect of the rest. He wore his customary two guns and Gol'achab, its hilt refurbished with ivory and jade. On an oversized horse next to him was the glum-featured Marriott, whose big pale head loomed like the globe of the moon over a thorny mass of gilt lace gathered at his throat. As Raule brought the mule to a stop, Marriott eyed her expressionlessly, while Gwynn bowed from his saddle and bade her good evening in friendly fashion. He had never stopped being cordial to her, and usually she was somewhat amused to think of him worrying that he might need her services one day. But nothing could amuse her right now.

"For some it might be," she scowled. With no more words, she climbed down from the cracked leather seat, carrying her bag, and pushed her way to the front of the crowd, or rather followed the pair of urchins while they did the pushing, shrilling: "Make way for the surgeon!" On the way they'd told her that the dispute concerned an insult and a girl. A coshboy had to be willing to die over insults and girls.

As Raule reached the front the onlookers on both sides were settling. The prancing had gone on long enough and it was just about over. Soon the two youths dropped into low stances and closed, as if on a silent signal. Neither of them showed any flashy moves now; there was only fast and deadly serious fighting. Both gangs raised the name of their man as a chant. The girls above shouted words encouraging one or the other fighter to be brave. They dropped flower petals down, and envelopes in which there would be notes of invitation to the winner.

Knife fights were usually fast and short, and this one was particularly so. In no more than a minute, Scarletino Quai had Bellor Vargey in a grapple-hold on the ground. The Esplanader boy jerked his arm once, and everyone heard Bellor Vargey's scream of pain. The Esplanaders cheered, and hoisted up their lanterns, while the Limewood Push howled a sore chorus of curses and threats.

The winner spread his arms wide, accepting his comrades' embraces and praise. The loser, lying on the ground, curled up, clutching his stomach. Raule stepped forward and went to his side. He swore at her, tried to elbow her away, then went quiet as he lapsed into shock. It was a deep gut wound. Two from the Limewood Push came out and lifted him into the ambulance cart. One looked as if he was blinking away tears. "He won't make it, will he?" said the other.

"No, probably not. I'm sorry," Raule answered. Death might well dawdle for days, during which the wounded youth's existence would be unrelenting agony. She saw Scarletino Quai's smug face, and guessed he knew very well that he'd done his opponent no favours by omitting to kill him.

The Limewood Push were already slinking away. Despite their verbal show of defiance, their dejected spirits weren't up to a fight with the victory-charged Esplanaders. There wouldn't be a brawl tonight. Raule saw money passing around among the cavaliers. It looked like there had been some heavy betting. Out of the corner of her eye, she saw Gwynn smiling. She was sorry for having rescued him.

Tiredly, she climbed up onto the cart and cracked the whip. On the return journey people got out of her way as if she was the boatman of the dead.

It was the Rev's job to attend to the dying: to hear final confessions, offer bedside comfort and administer last rites. He had done the latter already for Bellor Vargey. Raule had served as witness to the perfunctory ceremony. Bellor's condition had deteriorated badly. Looking at him, Raule could only keep thinking that because of her efforts, he had taken three days to die instead of just one. She eyed the Rev, slouched on a stool next to the hospital cot. The priest's face was a soggy facade on a rough block of a head. His jowls were unshaven, his thin grey hair uncombed and greasy, his eyes glaucous. No one would have chosen him to be the last human being their eyes saw. As for who Bellor Vargey would want to see—a girl, a friend, Scarletino Quai with a rope around his neck? Not the foreign doctor who was responsible for prolonging his pain, at any rate; that seemed a safe thing to assume.

"I'll leave him to you," Raule said to the Rev, who nodded without looking up.

The Rev heard the doctor leave the ward. He straightened up for a moment to stretch his back, then resumed slouching. His stomach rumbled. It was past seven. He wanted to eat, and he wanted to drink, but his whisky flask was empty, and one of the pious sisters was hanging around, praying beside the beds. He couldn't very well leave while she was there to observe him deserting his post.

"Consideration for others will help you get into heaven, so have some consideration for me, and die quickly," he muttered, using an ancient tongue in case the nun had sharp ears.

Suffering had refined and ennobled Bellor Vargey's loutish features. He would make a good-looking corpse. That state would likely be the most gracious one that he attained on earth, the Rev suspected.

He tugged at his stiff collar, cursing the rules that made him wear such a thing, and a three-piece grey woollen suit, here in the tropics. In his old wandering days he had worn white robes, which were not only the uniform of living saints since time immemorial, but also the only really sensible clothing for hot climates. However, the modern Church preferred to keep the dust of the wilderness confined to history, and frowned upon her modern clergy bringing it onto her porches with sandalled feet.

I mourn you, old beldame Church, glorious courtesan of singularly corruptible gold! If I had a drop in my flask I would drink to you, even though your weak-blooded latterday bishops have succeeded in making you respectable!

So the Rev addressed the church of the past in his mind.

Long gone were the days when a priest could openly walk around with a wineskin or a woman, a cardinal run a casino in his palace, a pope make fat, cherubic babies with his own sister. But it was minds belonging to the present century that had made the most forceful push for the religious life to be a dull one, given over to pursuing a notion of perfection conceived as a sort of blamelessness, with purity being lifted up to the place where excellence had once sat as the acknowledged crown of the soul. Practically every day something went onto the Out list. Anything that gave off a whiff of heathen practices in foreign lands or bore the stamp of disorderly times was expunged from religious services. Antique language was discarded, oneiromancy abandoned, the burning of incense frowned upon. Relics were condemned wholesale for their association with idolatry and the graveyard, and were locked away out of sight or donated to museums. The entire host of angels had been banished from the prayer book, out of prudence, since scriptural example showed that they delivered trouble as often as they delivered anyone from it, and in appearance were, by all accounts, bizarre creatures that might have been designed for the purpose of scaring modern congregations out of their wits. The eccentric lives and dramatic deaths of the martyrs, the writings of the ancient monastics with their hot-house odours of ardent lust for God, and even those parts of the holy scriptures themselves that were not as safe as milk pudding or else as dry as dust, had all been shoved into the cupboard that held the skeletons of the old swashbuckling warrior monks and rakehell pontiffs.

Outside that cupboard, religious practice was rapidly becoming a matter of white elephant stalls and teas with the vicar. It was in condemnation of this trend that the Rev silently offered an elegy for the old Madam Church and damned the prudish new Matron.

For himself, he mourned much else that he had lost. Inevitably he came to thinking of the girls, the desert flowers. He dipped into memories of their cascading hair, tinkling anklets and hennaed breasts, their stealthy ways and their soft delights. Thinking of them was not only pleasant in itself in a bittersweet way, but it helped him not to think too much about the other, entirely bitter absence in his life.

Bellor Vargey stirred. The nearly-dead sometimes did, as if the departing spirit had a fierce will to experience earthly consciousness once more. He half-opened his eyes, licked his lips, then mumbled, "Where's Mother?"

"She's at the factory, Bellor," the Rev told him.

The youth looked confused. "What's she doing there?"

"Working. She's working."

"Oh. Well then, where's Jacope? He should be here."

The Rev extemporised. "He's surely making trouble somewhere. In memory of you. This very moment, he's almost certainly getting drunk, for your sake."

Bellor Vargey smiled crookedly. "That's my fine brother. What a turd! He should be here, to see me off. But he pikes out of everything. Look after Emila, and pray for God to strike Quai, give it to that bastard, waste him good . . . hey, Padre, I always said I wanted to die in bed, but not like this, you know what I mean . . . ?"

And with that his mouth went slack. His eyes remained glassily open, so the Rev closed them. From a bottle that he took out of his breast pocket he daubed oil on the corpse's brow, and muttered the required prayers for the departed soul.

Not that the soul was actually gone. Not properly, not yet. Few people understood death's workings. The moment when a life ended was as mysterious as the moment when it began. A corpse not cold was like a child in the womb: a golem-thing, neither truly alive nor truly un-alive. The body, going through its after-death changes, continued to hold onto the soul, in whole or in part, for an unpredictable duration.

In olden times the last rites had been meant as banishments to expel the spirit, less to assist the dead to heaven than to protect the living from any remnants of will and desire that might be stuck in the flesh and could thus remain, lost, half-sentient, and potentially troublesome. No one liked ghosts or walking corpses. But modern prayers weren't worth much. They were hack jobs, leavings from the feast of language, the work of bad translators and worse poetasters. It was no wonder that the daily newspapers were full of ghost sightings. Shreds of the dead were surely lingering like unwashed clothes in corners and under beds. The Rev therefore customarily added an older formula to the end of his prayers.

"Aroint thee, soul of Bellor Vargey, and trouble this earth no more. Worms will have thy flesh; it is the worms' due. Do not linger in this corpse, no longer thine, or thou must feel them gnawing; do not tarry, or thou wilt feel the vile pains of rot in every part of thee. There is nothing here for thee; so fleet-foot go to thy afterlife, and leave nothing of thee here."

No one else was dying right then, so after telling the nun that there was a corpse to be removed from the ward, the Rev went out and walked down to the river to visit the Yellow House where Calila lived: Calila, who was fifteen and smooth and sweet, and performed all the arts of love with precocious mastery. She welcomed him with a faultless imitation of delight. He wanted very much to be young again so that he could have reason to hope she wasn't being so nice just for the money. She made him forget himself; small, soft, perfectly formed oblivion she was.

After their session, while he was lying quietly, just holding her—an extra pleasure which he also paid for—he started crying. When she asked him why, he thought, *I am vile*, and for a moment imagined having the money to buy her from her keepers and set her free. But the fact was, that was the last thing he'd do.

Raule went out to inform Mrs Vargey of her elder son's death. While there was still a little daylight in the sky she left the hospital on the mule and rode to the street where the family lived. She passed a lamplighter treading loudly in hobnailed boots, carrying his lighting pole over his shoulder. There was little work for him to do in Limewood, where only a few corners had gas lamps. Shadowed by six- and seven-storey tenements, often facing each other across alleys so narrow that a person leaning out of a window in one could lean into their neighbour's window in the building opposite, the streets received little of the lute-ous night-glow, and after dark there were long distances of coalsack blackness, interrupted only by an occasional naphtha flare or a rack of saint-candles. Not knowing how long she was going to be out, Raule took a kerosene lamp with her.

Her way took her past the Orchard. A few youthful figures strut-ted around a barrelfire in the centre of the yard. It wasn't a fight, only a gathering. It still felt strange, sometimes, to be watching them as a member of the law-abiding world. Her wary observation kept company with a ghostly nostalgia. She suspected it would always be that way.

The Vargeys dwelt in a grey block with iron stairs outside. The pavement in front was crowded with chicken coops, crates, a mangle, and ragged people of various ages lying on blankets and sacks, some asleep, some awake. Some of them greeted Raule, and a few held out their hands.

Raule returned the greetings and fished in her pockets for change to put in the outstretched fingers, which closed around the coins like rat traps, while she said, "If you'll keep an eye on my mule." The build-ing had two bent spikes embedded between the bricks in the front wall for the purpose of tethering animals, and Raule tied the mule's reins around the nearest one.

"Don't worry, Missus," said a boy. "If anyone tries to nick her, we'll kill 'em and eat 'em."

"Thank you very much," Raule said. Then she went up the stairs, stepping over more sleepers, to the third floor. The door was open, as always. Beyond it was an evil-smelling, deserted hall. Raul walked nearly to the end and knocked on the Vargeys' door.

Emila, the family's little girl, answered Raule's knock. She was eight, too thin, and already wearing lip and cheek rouge. She went to school, Raule knew, whenever her mother could find the money to pay the weekly fees.

Inside the single room that Mrs Vargey and her children occupied,

Bellor's younger brother Jacope was leaning against a wall, polishing a set of brass knuckles, pouting sullenly with a lip on which fuzzy hair was starting to grow. He gave Raule a cursory glance, then went back to polishing his weapon, rubbing the chamois against the metal with violent force. Mrs Vargey was washing beans in a wooden tub in the middle of the room. She looked up, and instantly her haggard features grew clouded by a pall so dark and bitter that Raule had to force herself to not look away. She might have been calling with news that Bellor had recovered, but either her face gave the truth away, or Mrs Vargey instinctively knew it.

Mrs Vargey got up and ran, stumbled past Raule and slammed the door.

Raule waited by the door while Jacope kept pushing the chamois back and forth, never looking up, and Emila played with some blue sequins. The girl arranged them in lines, circles and zigzags. She made a spiral on the floor, then the outline of a bird. It occurred to Raule that all children were monsters in the world and were instinctively aware of it. They were reminded of their anomalous nature by adults, whom they failed to resemble, and with whose habitations and tools their bodies were at odds. This was surely why the little girl played with the sequins so solemnly and with such intense concentration. She was doing nothing less than conjuring, out of pattern and colour, a world which conformed to her desires and obeyed her will. The boy, on the other hand, showed with the whole attitude of his being that he knew there was only the one world and he would kill it if he could.

When it seemed that Mrs Vargey wasn't likely to return soon, Raule went to look for her. She found her outside, sitting under the stairs with her arms wrapped around her knees.

Mrs Vargey spoke hollowly: "I've always been so afraid of my sons. I always feared Bellor, and I still fear Jacope."

"You have a daughter," Raule said.

"She'll learn to fear. Bellor died because he was too brave. Women die because we're too frightened." Mrs Vargey grabbed the hem of her skirt and beat her bony legs with her fists.

Raule could think of nothing appropriate to say.

"I am terribly sorry. Your son's body is at the hospital. The church will pay for his burial. If there is anything I can do, please tell me."

"Take me to your hospital and cut out my womb, Doctor. It is a foul sack that drops only rotten fruit. What am I?" Mrs Vargey thumped her knees, her eyes squeezed shut. "I am a bottle of reeking slops. And I am wormwood, I am wormwood. I was an apple with a worm born inside. Wormwood!" she screamed, and thrust her arm into her mouth and bit a gash in her meagre flesh.

"Help over here!" Raule called out.

Two of the men on the pavement dragged themselves up. Raule told them to hold Mrs Vargey still, which they did, long enough for Raule get laudanum out of her bag and force a liberal dose into Mrs Vargey's mouth.

She became quiet and slack-jawed almost immediately, and in a few minutes was stone asleep. Raule gave the men a florin each, and they gently carried Mrs Vargey back up the stairs.

FIVE

AT LEAST IT was Croalday, so he didn't have to get drunk alone.

In Ashamoil, the days of the week were called after seven famous traitors; or, rather, seven traitors who had been famous but were now forgotten. For it had been part of their punishment, in addition to being executed, to have the weekdays named after them, so that through countless repetitions their names would become devoid of meaning. It had come to pass exactly as those who meted out this punishment wished: in the present day, all knowledge of the traitors was gone, and not a single person knew why the days were called by the odd words Wale, Hiver, Croal, Voil, Obys, Rabber and Sorn.

On Croaldays, the Rev had a standing date with Gwynn at Feni's bistro down by the Prison Bridge.

He drew aside the curtain of dusty orange glass beads that hung in Feni's doorway. As usual there was almost no one in there, only a couple of soused journalists propping up the bar, and Feni's sister and her friends, a coven of thirteen, who were sewing clothes and telling tarot over gin and cheroots at the biggest table. Gwynn was up the back, playing a soft aubade on the piano that Feni had installed years ago when business was brisker and he could afford to pay entertainers.

The Rev put money on the bar. "A half-bottle of the Black Sack, thank you, Feni."

"A whole bottle's better value," said Feni. This was a ritual. The drink, which was not sack at all, but a rough, cheap medlar liqueur, had ecclesiastical origins, its recipe having been invented by a hermit monk who lived in a cave in the inland region of the Teleute Shelf, well over a thousand years ago. The Rev drank it because it reminded him of the

81

vigorous and hardy adolescence of religion; the days, as he sometimes liked to think of them, when God had been much younger. He also drank it because it was terrifically alcoholic.

"But I want a half," said the Rev.

"Why? You'll want another half by and by."

"Why are you arguing? I want a half-bottle, and you can make a bit of extra profit if I want another."

"As you like, Reverend," Feni shrugged, and uncorked a half-bottle.

The Rev took a swig, then walked over to Gwynn. "That tune's for a bar full of lovers, not this place."

"Are things going badly with your heart?" Gwynn kept playing the piece, with his eyes dreamily half-closed.

"Badly with my soul. I've sinned again."

"With the delectable Calila?"

"The very minx. No, not a minx; a precious girl. But how they wear out! They get the pox, they get with child, they die. But ah, while they live . . . she's life itself, I swear! Four times I sinned with her last night. Four!"

"Four? That's hardly a sin; more like a miracle, for a man of your age. I only hope such sins will warm the nights of my autumn years."

The Rev snorted. "Autumn years, what a joke! Your kind don't last that long."

"Sometimes we do. And we hate to be caught without contingency plans. I plan to ripen into an old rake. My pastimes will consist of getting schoolgirls into trouble, fighting duels with irate fathers and brothers, and giving witty oratories in the courthouse. And if I survive into the winter of life, I'll get myself into a comfortable prison and write my memoirs."

"My son, the only way you'll get old enough to write your memoirs is if you get yourself into prison now, quickly, and stay there. But don't expect anyone to read them. After you're dead no one'll give a shit, mark my words." The Rev tilted his head back and poured drink down his throat. Gwynn only shrugged, and played on.

"Vanity, all is vanity," burped the Rev, "and grasping for the wind." He picked at a spot where the piano's dark-stained wood was chipped, and made it bigger. "You get a little life, a few years of feeling important, or of feeling as if you ought to be important. Then, long before you're ready, it's all over. Judgement time. Wheat or chaff, sheep or goat, fair or foul. No second chances; no appeal. You, my son, cheat yourself with your indifference. You should be terrified, when instead you're arrogant!"

Gwynn smiled and took his hands off the keys. "If I am, so are you, Father, to assume that the judge, if one exists, shares your opinion of what is worthy."

The Rev snorted again. He operated out of a belief that Gwynn was always wrong when it came to moral questions, and that if his arguments convinced, it was because of clever phrasing alone and not because of any actual merit in their content.

"Don't you ever feel the slightest fear that you might be terribly wrong and that you'll suffer for having so wretchedly misused your intellect?"

Gwynn appeared to consider the question. "No, I don't," he finally said, as he closed the piano's lid. "I doubt I'd really enjoy paradise, anyway. And as for you, you'd hate it. So much of your god's breast, but so little of any others, if your literature is to be believed . . . "

The mention of breasts distracted the Rev. "Calila only has little breasts, but they're very nice. No, perfect. She reminds me of Nessima. Did I ever tell you about that girl?"

"Skin of burnished copper, pretty ankles, willing and able?"

"No. That was Eriune. Lovely girl. But Nessima . . . ah, she was something else. She had a smile like the sun when it first comes up over the dunes. Hips that swayed like a boat on the ocean. A belly like a soft little pillow." A gleam came into the Rev's weary eyes. "Her breath was of frankincense and cloves. She was the fountain in the dry land. The grapes on the vine. The desert breeds beautiful girls the way it breeds flowers after rain, but they're too much like the flowers: they don't last long. Middle-aged at twenty-five, and old and hating men by thirty. And who can blame 'em? For we do crush 'em when they're young, don't we?"

"Yes, sometimes we do."

"Ah, well, my son . . . ah, well . . . what are we without our regrets?"

The Rev quaffed the rest of the bottle. "I'm hungry. Let's eat."

It was their habit to dine whilst contending. They took their usual seats at a small table against the back wall. Feni was a good cook, and he always did his best for the only two customers who actually came to his place to eat. He had prepared a feast, which he now brought out and set in front of the Rev and Gwynn. There were dishes of cod rissoles, fried and honeyed locusts, red rice dumplings, turtle sausages, eel smoked with peat and stuffed with pork mousse, a tureen of seasonal vegetables drowned in a dark oxblood and plum gravy, and a basket of pastries stuffed with Feni's own recipe of brandied lamb sweetbreads, almonds and cream. Feni brought the Rev his second half-bottle, and set a silver teapot and a lacquered bowl—other relics of better days past—in front of Gwynn. Gwynn filled the bowl with tea for himself. It was a smoked type called Nine Blessings, and it gave off an aroma not unlike asphalt. From his waistcoat pocket he took out a small oval flask of milky agate carved with mandragoras, and measured three drops of liquid from it into the tea bowl. He took a sip of the tea, then set it aside to cool a little. The Rev tucked a napkin under his chin, picked up his cutlery, speared a dumpling, then made his first earnest sortie:

"You're a true musician, and therefore of God's party, even if you won't admit it."

Gwynn picked up a locust and delicately bit off its head. "Music is certainly one of the finer things in life, old man; that much I'd never contest. But I see no reason to attribute its existence to a god."

"Reason!" The Rev uttered the word as if it tasted odious on his tongue. "You're being deliberately obtuse! You know—you've said you accept it, many times—that to comprehend the God I speak of is beyond the capabilities of reason. While I must always argue from a position of faith, you're not bound by any such constraint, yet you persist in refusing yourself any modus operandi but the single one that makes you feel cosy: mere reason, a method every mundane man with half an education can use. You're like a child afraid to try a new food!"

"Without experience of faith, I'm afraid I can't argue except by the rules of reason," Gwynn countered reasonably.

They had never confined their argument to a particular topic, but had always allowed it to wander, like some knight errant of bygone times on a quest that had been explained to him sketchily or not at all, over a range of theological, philosophical, spiritual and ethical themes. Nevertheless, the Rev had a purpose; he wished to save Gwynn's soul. He had sworn to do so, since he believed his own salvation depended upon it.

Gwynn also had a purpose. He wished to prolong their argument for as long as he continued to enjoy the intellectual exercise and reap amusement from watching the Rev torment himself. It had been nearly three years and he wasn't bored yet. He was still entertained—indeed, sometimes almost enchanted—by the strangeness of the priest's thoughts.

At the argument's beginning the Rev, deep in liquor, had talked of a superhuman presence which he'd loved and which had loved him, and then of falling from its favour, of anguish and of longing for reunion. He spoke of needing a gift to give, to make amends:

"The soul of a human being. Nothing less will suffice. And not just any soul will do. It must be a soul which has waded far into the sewers of sin. To turn such a soul to the ways of righteousness and faith—return it to its source, turn lead into gold—such great and good labour would be an offering acceptable to God. I know it in my marrow. There can be no glory without sacrifice; in this case, the sacrifice of my labour and your soul. It's the only way. The barriers erected by the mind around the soul must be worn down to a thinness through which grace can break. Therefore will you be my subject, sir?"

Thus the Rev had begged Gwynn, whose past and present life he had learned something of.

Gwynn had refused at first.

"Ah, it seems you're afraid. Very well: I dare you!"

"Priest, you wish to corrupt my heart; to violate and ruin my essential nature," Gwynn had resisted. "I might reasonably object on grounds of propriety. There's also the matter of tradition; in certain ways I'm still a dutiful son of my land. At my mother's knee I learned to view religious worship as a practice which lures people away from their duties and pleasures on earth, and breeds in them a thirst for impossible things, the chasing of which can bring no honour or delight but only bewilderment, disappointment and insanity. While it's some time since

I've resided among my people, I still have no stomach for theism. You'd be wasting your time."

"Your race worships nothing?"

"Our clans revere their ancestors and value their children. We see no reason to worship one part of a continuum of which we are another part."

The Rev, by then exceedingly drunk and almost in tears, spoke of the Singular Infinite, the Power Sublime and the Comfort Incomparable. Gwynn, who was somewhat drunk himself, had been unsettled. He had allowed himself to consider for a moment the possibility that such an ultimate power existed. If it did, he would have to suborn himself to it; to do anything else would be naive. He would be compelled to live with the knowledge of absolute truth existing, all alternatives not even illusions but outright lies, no possible escape from it. His mind strenuously rejected the concept, and he had incredulously asked the Rev whether he actually desired such a reality.

The Rev claimed that he did, more than anything. "With respect, your understanding is not comprehensive, sir," he told Gwynn.

The sense of something to be fought caused Gwynn to accept the Rev's challenge at last. And when, not much later, he realised that he was in no danger of losing the battle, curiosity kept him interested.

While he could in no way identify with a state of spiritual crisis, it was still obvious to him that the Rev had lost something which had been of great value. He felt a certain measure of compassion for the priest, who as an adversary was agreeably unthreatening.

"Have I ever claimed to be anything other than a mundane man?" Gwynn continued, selecting a portion of eel. "I think not. But if we're to talk of reason, no doubt you can explain why your god has given us great powers of reasoning with which to fail to comprehend him. It seems either perverse or very careless on his part."

The Rev looked at Gwynn with profound sadness. "What are you so afraid of? No, don't trouble to answer, it's self-evident. You fear simplicity. You fear losing all your vain complexities. You think the loss would make you into something you'd despise. But once it was done, there'd be no pain; quite the opposite. And you'd be astonished to find yourself far stronger than you are now."

"I have no ambition to be anything more than what I am. You can decide whether that's a sign of vanity. Whatever the case, you'll have to lure me with something more attractive than the opportunity to become a simpleton, if you want a chance of winning me over through temptation."

"What could I tempt you with, then?" the Rev mumbled around a mouthful of sausage. "What do you desire?"

Gwynn smiled opaquely. "Despite your contemptible purpose, I admire your dauntless persistence."

"And I occasionally admire the force of your pride, until I remember that it's the offspring of your fear. Believe me, the parent is stronger than the child."

"Perhaps. I claim to be fearless no more than I claim to be extraordinary. But you were speaking of music before. Say what you would have said had I not sidetracked you."

"As you wish. Scripture tells us that this world—the whole universe—is the manifestation of God which is tangible to the physical senses; the body of the divine spirit, created by that spirit for a purpose. Do you follow?"

"I'm acquainted with that theory."

"The music of man is the voice of God speaking through man. When you play that piano, you're so close to God, if only you knew it! When you play, don't you feel, in your heart, a growing, an expansion, joy?"

"Certainly, but you've said nothing sensible. Music brings me pleasure, but so does strangling the breath out of an opponent, or putting my sword through him. If the one joy is sacred, why not the other?" Gwynn bit another locust in half and chewed its body. "If I hit a wrong note, do I cause a divine voice to utter nonsense or a lie? If a lunatic escapes from his cell, comes in here and pounds on the piano with his fists, making a random noise, but believes, with joy, that he is playing a beautiful sonata, is the cacophony, which causes pain to all who hear it, an utterance of your god? If I whistle a happy tune after slicing some poor bastard, is your god whistling?"

"Yes and no."

"And no? Then your god must have somehow given elbow room in his universe to phenomena which exist at odds with his omnipresent self. But I dare say that sort of thing happens when reason is ignored."

"Actually, I think you'd find the reasoning quite rigorous. The explanation was worked out during a period when the Church was dallying with Classical Philosophy—near the end of that affair, as I recall, shortly before she went off on a fling with Ancient Fertility Rites."

"And?"

"Eh?"

"The explanation?"

"It's one of the esoteric secrets."

"But you obviously want to tell it to me."

"I wasn't going to. I just wanted to tell you that it was logical."

"You're lying. But never mind, go on."

The Rev downed another lengthy draught of the Black Sack. "Even without esoteric knowledge, we're still well-armed with our sensibility, which in its original state is infallible. The heart is capable of unerring judgement. Whether we cultivate that faculty, ignore it and let it atrophy, or wilfully debase and pervert it, is our choice. And by the agency of this natural wisdom I can tell you that the lunatic's playing partakes of God's nature and your hypothetical whistling does not. It's you, my son, who'd be making the senseless noise, while the lunatic would be making music. No healthy person would think otherwise."

"Interesting," Gwynn said. "But, as I think you're mad, I can't believe you."

The Rev waved his hand and a cigarette appeared in his fingers, as though out of thin air. A second wave produced a box of matches. He kindled the cigarette then made the matches disappear again. He glared at Gwynn. "We'll see who's mad on the Last Day."

Gwynn lit an Auto-da-fé in the conventional manner. For some minutes they sat and breathed smoke over each other. The Rev tried to burn into Gwynn's eyes with his own. It was like trying to burn into water. Gwynn did look away first, but the Rev couldn't feel even a minor sense of victory; Gwynn simply gave the impression of having lost interest in whatever he saw in the Rev's eyes.

The Rev took a deep breath and a long drink, and dredged his passion up again. "Conscience, my son, is nothing less than the divine in man. You, for example—you kill another man, but if you were strong in

God, the divine in yourself would recognise the divine in the other man, and love would stay your hand. If you'd dare to see God's splendour in your victims, you'd know what a thing your violence desecrates. You'd weep for what you've done, and then you'd sin no more. Thus the illusion is destroyed, the poison neutralised, and love reigns."

"I doubt that."

"Love reigns supreme," the Rev insisted. "Nothing is stronger than love, and nothing is more sacred. Through loving, we come close to God."

"But you call it a sin to enjoy the company of a pretty girl, which is love of a sort," Gwynn said mischievously.

"Now you're just being facetious," the Rev mumbled, swallowing pastry. "If you never reach heaven, don't say I didn't warn you. You're a dreadful creature."

"I'll pay that," Gwynn said, apparently without rancour. "Perhaps that's why this world suits me well. Certainly, if there's another past death, I'd wish it to be no different, suffering and all."

The Rev snorted stickily. "Whatever you know of suffering, I can promise you that I know more. And I'd be happy to do without it. But, unfortunately, just as ore must be smelted to make gold, suffering ennobles us."

"I'll believe you've suffered. But can you honestly say you've been ennobled? No offence intended, but . . . " Gwynn spread his hands.

The Rev tipped the dregs of the Black Sack down his throat. "I probably haven't suffered enough yet. Though you've certainly helped me towards meeting my quota."

"I do what I can," Gwynn said modestly.

The Rev gave a rueful smile. He raised his hand to catch Feni's attention. "Another half, Feni!"

Feni shuffled over with an opened bottle. Gwynn refilled his tea bowl and again supplemented it with three drops from the agate flask. For a while there was silence, as they drank. Then Gwynn spoke words that almost caused the Rev to jump out of his seat.

"Father, perhaps there's a god after all."

There had to be a catch, the Rev thought, his surprise plunging into scepticism. He waited to find out what it would be this time.

"The theories of evolution and creation agree that plants appeared first of living things, yes?"

"Of living things, yes," the Rev agreed cautiously.

"Very well. The pageant of life commences with plants; not at all aggressive, a handful of carnivorous species excepted. But then beasts appear; and all of them, by their nature, must devote their energies to killing and eating plants and each other. And for a finale there's man, a creature who hurts and maims and kills not only when he must in order to survive, but whenever it pleases him; and it pleases him often. True, he has a great capacity for virtue; but his capacity for vice is time and again shown to more than match it. People are always complaining in the newspapers that the world has become a more wicked, violent place; they're right. I might be willing to believe that a god is indeed at work, carrying out a divine plan of destroying the meek. I might even approve of him, although I wouldn't care to meet him alone in a dark alley," Gwynn finished with a smile that showed his satisfaction with the neatness of his argument.

The Rev didn't try to argue back directly. He couldn't. Instead he made another essay of his own. "It's sad when we wilfully debase ourselves; when we're so at odds with our hearts that we despise what they long for."

"Which is what?" Gwynn continued to look pleased with himself.

The Rev took a deep breath. "*God!* We long for God! God, who we've been talking about for three years!"

"Who you've been talking about. I've been talking about humankind."

The Rev tugged at his collar. "Let us get this as clear as gin. We are, are we not, talking about filling the terrible abyss, the unspoken and nameless longing in the human heart?"

Gwynn shrugged his shoulders. "I know no such abyss."

The Rev jabbed the air with his laden fork, dripping sauce on the tablecloth. "That's because you're spiritually senseless! If you could observe the vacuum in your soul, you'd scream out in horror for something to fill it. And only God's infinity would suffice. You would have to submit, or go mad!"

"Ah, then your god is like an infinite tub of putty. I begin to see how you sell your cult to the gullible. A life without design? A heart lacking hope, love or honour? Take one deity, apply according to directions and leave to set. Guaranteed to fill any gap with cheap yet resilient lies. Sold by the pint at the small price of your soul."

"I wish," the Rev said with a wistful look, "that this was a hundred years ago. I could have you roasted over coals for blasphemy, and then I'd win."

"I thought you only won if you converted me," Gwynn said, looking closely at the Rev.

"Your agonies would purify your soul. You'd love God before you died, and then God would bless me for my efforts. I'd win."

"Really? Well, if we were having this conversation in my homeland, I could have you sewn up alive in the belly of a dead mammoth for being a polluting agent of religion; in fact I'd be obliged to do so by law. But since we're both stuck here in this tolerant place and time, bragging about the torments we might inflict on each other under different circumstances is pointless. Unless, of course, you want to try to kill me yourself?"

"Just enjoying the comforts of nostalgia," the Rev muttered.

Gwynn saw his opponent tiring. He pursued the earlier train of his argument. "Whatever this thing is that you think is missing, you seem to have decided *a priori* that it's a god. In fact, you could almost say that your god is absent by definition. Absent and unknowable, and therefore impossible to believe in with any accuracy."

The Rev was getting muzzy-headed and finding it harder to think of points to make. He slumped back in his chair and glared blearily at his adversary. "You're doing it again. Using reason to argue faith. Can't be done. Like playing croquet with a crochet hook. Sounds something like the right tool for the job, but isn't. All right, tonight I'm going to lose. But therefore so will you."

"No. You're trying to win paradise. I'm not trying to win anything. I'm just passing time."

"What is it that you hate so much?"

Gwynn was caught by surprise. "Hate?" He laughed, "Nothing in this world. As I've said, I'm fond of it. And, were I to believe in a god, I'd admire that god for his cruel beasts, his earthquakes and the villainy manifest in man, as much as I'd admire him for his haphazard gentleness. But I would not love him; and if he demanded that I did, I could only think the less of him for having such a childish need."

The Rev gathered himself for a final effort. "You belittle God because you fear what God might be. If you were God's ally you'd have to fear nothing—fear to have nothing—have nothing to fear," he finally got his words in order. He rubbed his stomach and belched. A mosquito appeared near his chin and buzzed across the table.

"If I were at all inclined towards religion, I'd say it's less important that we believe in any god than that somewhere there's a god who believes in us," Gwynn said, and swatted the mosquito.

"Ah, Calila, Calila," the Rev mumbled. "God punishes faithlessness, and I am a whoreson of a roué. Do you fancy the future title of rake for yourself? Take a good look. You should be afraid. I certainly am. But still, but still . . . I visit the ladies, because they are the flowers growing around the jakes of my heart. I pressed my eye against a frosted rose-pink pane, and thou wert moving there, an adumbration . . . A man can't live without love, can he?"

"Oh, he can. But he can't love what he fears," Gwynn said. He sipped his tea, waiting to see whether the Rev would rally again, but the priest had turned his full attention to his bottle.

"I believe this round is mine, Father."

The Rev acknowledged it with a grunt.

That night the Rev suffered a nightmare in which a woman of surpassing loveliness dismembered herself in front of his eyes. She explained to him that she sought the location of the distemper that had caused suffering to be a fundamental principle of her own existence and the universe's, but the search was proving to be like looking for a needle in a haystack. She handed him a tomahawk and a small saw, and asked whether he would like to help.

SIX

HER STAGE NAME was Tareda Forever. At nineteen she was lissome and doe-eyed. She sang torch songs at Elm's club on Lumen Street, the Diamantene, where she was the star attraction. When she ascended the stage, her slight frame wrapped in bare-sleeved gold or silver lamé, satin or net gloves up to the elbows of her thin brown arms, conversation in the club hushed. She wrote the sad, wry tunes and melodramatic lyrics of her songs herself. It was her genius that she could convincingly sing both the outward and the inward lives of every cutthroat, fancy woman, gambler and defeated lover in her audience.

Elm had engineered her rise to fame, and now he managed her image carefully. However many jewels and fine gowns he bought for her, she wasn't permitted to wear them onstage. Her public finery was always flashy but cheap, expressing the pathos of imitation luxury. Her voice never seemed far from the verge of tears, but it never entirely succumbed to them. It was an ideal instrument for telling, over and over, a tale of compromised pride and tragic regret.

The band began to play, and she lifted her head:

"He was the prince of bad luck," she sang. "He broke everything he touched, he was the worst joke of the street, but once he had a lifelike love . . . "

Marriott had his eyes fixed on her yearningly. Too yearningly. Gwynn discreetly kicked his foot. Marriott wrenched his attention away from Tareda and anchored it on the blue leadlight lamp on their table, where Elm was entertaining the Superintendent of Customs and his wife. In a show of force, which conveniently doubled as a gesture of respect, those cavaliers of the Society of the Horn Fan who could close

93

their mouths while chewing and open them without cursing were in attendance with their boss.

On either side of Elm sat his stubble-skulled twin bodyguards Tack and Snapper, drinking no alcohol, only cordial in small glasses which they held with odd delicacy in their huge hands. There was also a yellow-skinned man known as Elbows because he had a fetish for breaking that part of the human anatomy; Sharp Jasper, a handsome black man with a grin of filed teeth studded with little twinkling jewels; Screw-'Em-Down Sam, whose eight-and-a-half fingers constantly groomed his long moustache; and Biscay the Chef, an obese and oily man who kept the Horn Fan's well-cooked financial figures under his pomaded topknot. They were an ugly lot by anyone's reckoning, Gwynn thought privately, but he acknowledged with equanimity that many people would consider him an equally ugly character.

Elm was middle-aged, of indeterminate brown-skinned stock, slim, grey-haired, aristocratic when he wished to be. His eyes were the colour of dark amber and as sharp as broken glass. They never missed seeing the slight tremble of a hand, a tense jaw, a too eager leaning forwards or a falsely relaxed slouch. It was impossible to believe they had not seen Marriott's desire for Tareda. Gwynn didn't like the situation one bit, but he hadn't been able to persuade Marriott to choose a less dangerous object of devotion.

To the Superintendent and his wife the mood of their host's men seemed relaxed. This was far from the case in reality, however. As of the previous night the Horn Fan's number was down by one. They had taken a man called Orley down the river, bound to a chair with his feet in a block of concrete, his hands beaten into mealy pulp. The Horn Fan had for a long time been fighting the Five Winds Family, and had finally defeated its rival in a single night of carefully organised murder. Only a handful of low-ranking members who were out of the city at the time had escaped the massacre. But Orley had owed a debt to a man who belonged to Five Winds, and had attempted to pay it by sheltering him and his family, and trying to help them escape Ashamoil. Orley's courage deserted him on his last day, and he screamed through his gag all the way to the swampy bayou where Tack and Snapper had thrown him overboard. Gwynn had been glad to be in the wheel room with the practicalities of navigation to occupy his attention.

Orley's execution had set every other man's nerves on edge. No one liked to be reminded of his own expendability.

Elm regularly entertained the Superintendent, and on every second full moon paid him regards in cash. Ashamoil's city authorities were in most ways liberal, imposing little rule upon the citizens' lives, but they took a dim view of tax evasion. Elm's main ship, the *Golden Flamingo*, carried a small number of slaves openly, in order to maintain a respectable front of honest, licensed trade in human cargo. The bulk of this cargo, however, was smuggled into port in a secret hold. Elm's generosity towards the Superintendent ensured that customs inspectors boarding the *Flamingo* never investigated the discrepancy between her outer and apparent inner dimensions.

The Superintendent was telling a story about a pirate he had repeatedly crossed swords with in his youth. Gwynn thought there were too many beautiful women in the tale for it to be entirely true, but the Superintendent told it with vigour and plenty of humour at his own expense, making it worth the listening. When it ended—with the pirate dead at last, property donated to charity and the pirate's own daughter wooed and won ("This was long before I met you, my dear," the man assured his amiable wife)—Gwynn excused himself from the table and headed for the bar. He realised he was resting his hand on his sword hilt, as he was wont to do whenever he felt uneasy. He forced his hand away from the weapon.

As he negotiated the narrow spaces between tables, things crunched in the carpet under his feet. The Diamantene was in a basement near the river and was therefore perpetually damp. Bugs thrived in the moisture, as did mould, which grew upon the red flock wallpaper in huge grey and brown colonies. But Elm didn't have to worry about losing customers. From all over the city Tareda drew a crowd which no squalor could deter.

While Gwynn waited for his drink, a woman in a beaded headdress lowered her fan and smiled at him. The group she was with looked like well-to-do bourgeois. The man beside her glared. Gwynn winked slyly at the woman. He knew what she saw. For every woman or man who gave him dirty looks or wouldn't look at him at all, there was one who looked with desire—lust, envy or both. It wasn't necessarily personal, or even anything to do with the fairly easy money he made. He knew, even if they didn't, that what they saw was pain and death, and that unlike those who openly feared suffering, or those who scorned to fear it, they were the ones who feared but hoped to avoid suffering by getting on evil's good side. He was happy enough to play the part; it was no trouble, at any rate. He bought his drink and returned to the table, wearing a confident expression, conscious of the eyes on him.

The Superintendent and his wife took their leave at around midnight. When they were gone Elm began talking finances with Biscay. Tareda finished her set and came over to the table to sit on Elm's lap. Elm petted her and she regarded him with a calculating kind of affection. Marriott continued to hide his emotions poorly. Gwynn was concerned, and a little embarrassed for his friend's sake.

Sharp Jasper brought cards out and looked around at the rest of the party. "You all in?" Everyone said yes and put money down. Marriott seemed to wrest his attention away from Tareda at last.

After an hour, Elm got up to leave. Before he went he gave out orders. To Gwynn and Marriott he said, "See the Colonel tomorrow. Deal with our little problem. Biscay calculates the full particulars at one-ten. Now, listen to what I'm telling you. For the sake of business I must be generous, over the objections of my heart. To replace him at the present time would be irksome and onerous. So don't get carried away. Just persuade him of his error. If he won't cough up, bring him back. Nothing more. Understood?"

They nodded.

"Tack, the box," said Elm. Tack produced a slim wooden box and handed it to Elm, who handed it to Marriott. "Show this to the Colonel. I expect he'll find it quite inspiring."

Marriott pocketed the box, and Elm looked around at his men. There were no questions, and he left with his arm around Tareda's waist, Tack and Snapper lumbering in tow.

The gambling went on until four in the morning when the Diamantene closed. It was a seedy-looking group that filed out of the club and around the side lane to the mews house. Marriott had finished well up, but he wore the look of a man who had lost everything and held out no hope of getting it back.

"He doesn't care about her."

Gwynn closed his eyes and let his head sink underwater for a few seconds. When he surfaced he said, "He does, in his way."

They were sweating out the previous night's alcohol in the hot pool at the Corinthian bathhouse prior to going out on the river. The early morning bathers were mostly gone and the luxurious bathhouse was quiet. Female attendants had brought them fruit juice, and tea made with herbs that were good for easing headaches and bringing refreshment to the tired.

"The way of a man who keeps a caged bird. He doesn't care the way she deserves," Marriott said softly but vehemently.

"And what, my friend, do you believe she deserves?"

"Better."

"She mightn't agree with you. She seems to be happy enough with her situation."

"She seems. But she's got scars. It's obvious. She needs a lover with a good heart."

"Marriott," Gwynn sighed, "scratch her soft young skin and I'd wager my eyes that there's a heart underneath which declines to love anything so worthless as another heart. She has her eye on the money, just like the rest of us. He's given her jewels worth a fortune. She's using him as much as he's using her. When he discards her for some younger beauty, she'll be a wealthy woman with a lot of time left in which to do as she pleases. That's what she wants. *That* is obvious."

Marriott shook his head. "You wrong her, Gwynn. She's in pain."

"No, you're in pain," Gwynn said a bit impatiently.

Marriott's expression hardened, and he said nothing more. They finished their ablutions in silence, and afterwards rode down to the docks where Elm's two launches were moored. Gwynn could see that Marriott was still sulking. He could stay in a bad mood for days, sometimes weeks. Gwynn left him to himself and enjoyed the morning, which was unusually clear, with even a bit of pure blue sky visible. The sun would be fierce out on the river.

As they were riding along the Esplanade a boy leapt down from a terrace wall onto the road in front of their horses. He was perhaps four-teen and was decked in black pantaloons and a sequined red vest, open to show a skinny, scarred chest. He drew two long knives and twirled them around in a dexterous display of shadowfighting. Gwynn recog-nised the victor from the recent fight at the Orchard. Far from con-stituting a challenge, the boy's blade-waving was a kind of courtship overture, a bid to be noticed and remembered. Gwynn wasn't going to pay him any attention, but Marriott jumped down from his horse.

"Is it a fight you want, then?" he growled.

The boy looked confused. He licked his lips. The faces of several other youths had now appeared over the top of the same wall above the street. Gwynn halted his horse and watched, amused.

The boy drew himself up and looked Marriott in the chest. "Yes, I do, sir!" he shouted, since he could hardly back down.

Marriott moved at speed. Roaring, he grabbed the boy, punched him, efficiently disarmed him of both knives, then proceeded to give him a bare-handed thrashing. Gwynn thought he might have to inter-vene to stop his friend from committing murder right there, but Mar-riott marshalled himself and stepped back. The boy started spitting blood, but it seemed he'd only bitten his tongue. He wiped his mouth as he stared nonplussed at Marriott, who calmly remounted his horse.

"Feel better?" Gwynn asked when they had ridden on a bit.

"Somewhat," said Marriott.

The Horn Fan's three small steam launches were berthed at a private wharf beside a rock spur at the far end of the Esplanade. Tarfid the stoker had one of them steamed up and ready to go. Gwynn took the wheel and headed them upriver. As they left Ashamoil the air became clear, and the sun was indeed hot. Gwynn took off his coat, then his waistcoat. He steered through the river traffic with one hand, shading his eyes with the other.

Marriott was quiet while they were still within the city's bounds, but when rice paddies started appearing on the riverbanks he began to talk about Orley. He spoke in Anvallic, quietly, as if Tarfid could some-how hear from the engine room.

"Orley was a straight arrow. He did what he had to do. He did the honourable thing. I don't like to think about what we did."

Gwynn steered towards the middle of the river to avoid a tug pulling a flotilla of barges. "So don't think about it. It's done."

Marriott wouldn't be deterred. "Orley spoke for me. No matter what, I should have said something to defend him, but I paid him back with silence, because I was afraid. I don't know if there's a good enough excuse for that. I don't know anymore, Gwynn."

It seemed that the mildly restorative effect gained from beating up the coshboy was already wearing off, and that he was again falling prey to the depression and self-loathing which had increasingly afflicted his mood of late.

Gwynn believed that either there were no excuses for any act, or the fact of being human was a fully satisfactory excuse for all human behaviour, in the same way that the fact of a crocodile being a crocodile provided all necessary justification for that beast's habits. He could see no viable middle ground. Nor could he see how Marriott would ever regain happiness while he continued to court suffering. He himself had never been tempted to play the tragic part, but he'd known enough people who chose to, and had become addicted to it, to recognise the symptoms, of which a painful vulnerability of the soul was one.

"I don't know," Marriott repeated. "Do you think I'm mad? Am I mad? Perhaps I am. Ha!" He shook his head vigorously. "Tell me, have I always been as I am now?"

Gwynn felt helpless. "You're tired," he said. "You had a lot of drink and joss last night. Why not get some shut-eye?"

"I don't need to sleep," Marriott muttered. He lit up a black cigarette and dragged on it aggressively while glaring ahead.

Gwynn also looked to the fore, taking in the view. The tiered paddy fields and small villages on the hills were picturesque, and the sage-green mountains in the distance were elegant. It was all very easy on the eyes. These days he was nearly always in a good mood. His life had never been so easy and comfortable as it was in Ashamoil. He often felt like a storm-tossed ship that had arrived at last in a congenial port. And now, with the end of Five Winds, the Horn Fan, along with Elm's business allies the Astute Trading Co. and the Golden Square Society, together held the lion's share of power among the great households.

Treachery could be expected in the future, but Gwynn refused to worry about that until it occurred.

Even Marriott's silently agitated, brooding presence could not dislodge his feelings of contentment. He hummed the tune of a sea shanty.

The Majestic Hotel came into sight shortly after midday. It was a grand wedding-cake confection from the previous century, three storeys of whitewashed stone, festooned with white iron lace which was in turn festooned with white wisteria, set back from the river with lawns and lush gardens around it. Beyond the hotel, within half a mile, the scenery on the Skamander's banks became dark green jungle.

The border with Lusa, where the war was, lay another thirty miles downriver. The Majestic was the turning point for all the party boats that came up from Ashamoil. So far the war hadn't disrupted river commerce; nevertheless, it was now common to see large commercial vessels with cannon mounted, and Ashamoil's authorities offered an armed escort to any shipmaster willing to pay. The hotel had its own well-disciplined security force, employed to keep the peace and protect patrons. It took no interest in what those patrons did quietly behind closed doors.

Gwynn pulled in at the hotel's landing and cut off steam. Marriott went out and moored them. Gwynn put his dress back in order, then he and glum-faced Marriott walked up to the front door along a path lined with magnolias and rose bushes. Two flunkies in white linen uniforms ushered them into the spacious lobby, where another two hurried forth, one to buff their boots and the other to offer scented cloths for wiping their hands and faces. Then they went up the great staircase, and a short time later were ensconced in leather armchairs in the lounge room of Colonel Veelam Bright's suite, drinking liqueurs out of ruby glasses while listening to their host enumerate the physical, mental and spiritual dangers of the tropical latitudes.

"You need to take care, you know," the Colonel was saying. A lean, louche man with heavy-lidded eyes, he acted the part of a military officer with a slightly sardonic air. "Down here a man can go native like—" he snapped his fingers—"like that! Goes to bed a gentleman, and in the morning he wakes up wanting to wear feathers and beat drums and put other fellows in cooking-pots. Eh, Join?"

"Sir! Yes, sir!" said Corporal Join, Bright's batman.

Both wore white, red and gold uniforms, the Colonel's distinguished by heavier and fancier gold epaulettes, buttons and braid. The uniforms had a home-made look. The Colonel's white jacket was sweat-stained under the arms, and only half done up, showing a soiled shirt underneath. On the other hand, Join's appearance and manner suggested that at every hour on the hour someone washed, starched and ironed him, cut his hair and tightened his shoelaces.

"You young men, take some advice from an old dog," the Colonel said, leaning forwards. "Remember your homes. Remember your mothers. Remember the taste of their breasts, if you can." He regarded his drink with a lascivious expression, as if the red glass showed him faraway vistas in which sensual memories played.

The shutters on the windows were closed to keep the heat out, and the room was lit by gas chandeliers that hissed like modern gorgons. A square gilded clock ticked loudly on the mantelpiece, and the strains of a dance band playing in one of the reception rooms downstairs floated up through the floor. Beyond these sounds, the chittering and squawking ruckus of the jungle was distantly but perpetually audible.

An oil painting above the clock showed a young, stately woman on a gold-draped throne, with a man in plate armour of ceremonial rather than practical design kneeling before her, holding a bunch of lilies in an outstretched gauntlet. The woman was leaning slightly forward, her hand beginning to extend. Gwynn found it interesting that the artist had chosen to freeze in time the moment when the outcome of the encounter was still uncertain. He had sometimes wondered what plans would be completed or spoiled, what disasters occur or be averted, if the woman refused the flowers.

The Colonel straightened his shoulders, and raised his glass. "To home, gentlemen!"

"Home," Gwynn and Marriott repeated dutifully.

"Sirs! Home, sirs!" Join chimed.

The four expatriates drank. The Colonel snapped his fingers. "Brandy, Join."

"Yes, sir." Join brought a decanter out of a marble-topped cabinet and poured glasses. Taking his glass from Join's hand, the Colonel leaned back, half-closing his eyes, as though to convey the impression that he was entirely unconcerned about his visitors' purpose.

"This is very good," Gwynn remarked.

"I'm glad you think so," the Colonel said. "It isn't always easy to live well down here. But good grog is one of life's essentials."

"The other four being memory and forgetfulness, evil friends and honourable enemies," Gwynn quoted.

"So they are! Jashien Sath's exact words, if I'm not mistaken," Colonel Bright talked on. "Now there was a canny woman for you; not that all women can't be canny when they want something from you, eh? It's a pleasure to find a properly educated man in these parts. I hope you still make time to read the classics. They guard against rot of the brain."

"I can't imagine that my education was of the same standard as yours, Colonel," Gwynn said, wearing a sincere expression. "Sath's maxims are popular reading material in the north, as are her treatises on warfare."

The Colonel cocked an eyebrow. "Are they? The warfare stuff's interesting reading, of course, but a bit old-fashioned to be worth learning nowadays, I'd have thought."

"She's held up as an example of an honourable enemy," Gwynn smiled.

The Colonel laughed loudly. "A reputation is ever the plaything of history."

"So it is, at least for as long as history cares to play with it."

"Nothing lasts forever," the Colonel said with a shrug.

"Which serves to remind me," said Gwynn, bringing the conversation around to business. "How goes the war?"

"Going quite well, still nicely enough balanced. No sign of it stopping." Colonel Bright leered rancidly, while his eyes became chilly and alert.

"It isn't running too fast either, I hope?"

"No, no. The population's keeping up."

"Tell me if it's true that the locals make head counting easy, or is that just a gruesome story?"

"Oh, it's true all right. On spikes, like toffee apples, my dear fellow. Both sides. They're all completely savage. It's the heat; it turns them mad in the womb."

"We understand the difficulty of keeping the situation under control," Gwynn said. "We appreciate your efforts. The Horn Fan values this partnership highly."

"Thank you. Naturally, it's my pleasure to do business with you people. Join's indispensable of course. Join!"

"Sir!"

"Go and take a mess break. Be back here at thirteen hundred."

"Sir." Join saluted, turned around smartly and marched out of the room. Gwynn listened. The sound of crisply striding footsteps stopped well before it should have. About five yards from the door, he guessed; far enough that the Colonel's batman couldn't overhear anything said in ordinary voices, but near enough for a shout to bring him running.

Long books would be written about the war in which the Society of the Horn Fan had involved itself, but none of these books would mention the Horn Fan in so much as a footnote, the war's inordinate length being instead attributed solely to the savage temperament of its known participants, the Ikoi and the Siba tribes. If a complete and accurate record had been made, it would have included the following facts:

At the time of Gwynn and Marriott's visit to Colonel Bright, the war in Lusa had been going on for some thirty years. It began when the Ikoi people of the country's eastern part invaded the territory of the Siba people in the west. Having equipped themselves with modern weapons, the Ikoi were successful conquerors. But the Siba, in their most desperate hour, had received a visitor in the person of Colonel Bright, who offered to supply them with guns to equal those possessed by the Ikoi. The Siba leaders explained that while they would be delighted to accept, they were now extremely poor and could not pay for such guns. The Colonel responded by offering them the first shipment on credit. This gamble paid off. Within days of getting themselves armed, the revenge-hungry Siba began destroying and looting Ikoi settlements. They kept buying the Colonel's guns, and gradually forced the Ikoi back into the east.

It was at this point that Elm became interested in Lusa. Seeing profit to be made, he formed a plan and launched the Horn Fan into international affairs.

For ten years since then, the war had been running like a precision model. The Siba, fearing the Ikoi would multiply and conceivably grow aggressive again, were delighted to raid Ikoi territory, kidnap their old enemies and sell them to the Colonel, who sold them to Elm, who sold them to buyers in Ashamoil. Elm made part of his payment to the Colonel in munitions, which in turn continued to make up a large part of the Colonel's trade with the Siba. The Ikoi, meanwhile, had found a new, cheaper arms supplier and were fighting back well enough to hold their own. They, too, traded their prisoners of war to an agent, a man who claimed to be a merchant from the inland town of Enjiran. In fact, he was employed by none other than the Colonel; and the guns he supplied, of course, came from Elm, whose munitions factory in Ashamoil was able to operate at a highly efficient cost by employing the labour of the smuggled slaves. Children, being more easily controlled than adults, were preferred for the work; and as they were also easier to capture at the Lusan end, a smooth harmony of supply and demand existed.

The Colonel kept a monopoly on his end of the business. Elm had negotiated with him to keep a corresponding monopoly for the Horn Fan at the other end. The delicate act, for which the Colonel was responsible and at which he was adept, lay in controlling the distribution of arms in order to keep the conflict evenly balanced and constantly smouldering, without allowing it to ignite into a blaze that would overly consume the small nation's populace.

Over the years, the Horn Fan had become heavily reliant upon the war. Gwynn had not viewed the figures, but he was aware of the practical facts. If the Horn Fan lost the Lusan trade, not only would the financial blow be severe, but Elm's house would suffer a serious loss of face. Old enemies would, without doubt, seize the chance to attack, and allied houses would find an opportunity for profitable betrayal. Gwynn hoped the Colonel did not possess a full awareness of the situation.

"We were concerned that you might be experiencing some problems," he said. "The last two cargoes didn't reach the standard we've been used to getting from you. To be honest, we were embarrassed to sell them. Can you explain why they were in such poor condition?"

The Colonel scowled at Gwynn. "Now, sir, a man could take that the wrong way!" He pointed a finger and wagged it emphatically. "War makes everyone a bit threadbare after a while, even savages. I'd have credited you with knowing that, and I'd have thought your boss would know it too." He inflected 'boss' with a note of distaste, as though Gwynn's situation as an employee of a company affronted him.

On a couple of previous occasions, Gwynn had received the impression that the Colonel assumed there was some sort of kinship of social class between them. This belief seemed to be one article of a larger faith, of which his view of himself as a civilised man, and the Lusans as savages, was another article. Gwynn could have enlightened him on both counts. As they shared no ties of blood or of fellowship in battle, there was no sense in which they were kin, and the only significant trait they shared was savagery as robust as any cannibal's.

"There is an alternative explanation," Gwynn said. "Recently, one of our competitors attempted to smuggle Ikoi into Ashamoil. A customs boat intercepted them. Apparently your name was mentioned when the crew was questioned."

"I'm afraid I'm not sure what you're suggesting. It sounds rather insolent to me," the Colonel drawled. "If you don't want to deal with me, find someone else to harvest your live meat."

"A party offered you a very attractive payment," Gwynn continued unperturbed, "in return for which you supplied them with the cream from your last haul, and encumbered us with the remaining third-rate goods. The party with whom you dealt is known to us. They don't intend to keep paying you at that tempting price. In fact, they're no longer in a position to."

The Colonel continued to resist, smiling cynically. "I might see no reason to believe you."

"Forgive me, but from our point of view that doesn't matter. However," Gwynn shrugged, "the evidence is easily supplied."

Marriott reached into a pocket in his coat, took out the wooden box and passed it to the Colonel. The Colonel opened it and glanced at its contents. To his credit, his expression didn't change. What he was looking at, wrapped in oiled paper, were several ears, soft from boiling, with large jagged shreds of scalp attached. He recognised the long lobes of one ear and the square, fleshy shape of another. In addition, the box contained three identifiable noses, and some bits of baggy, rugose flesh with which the Colonel had no personal acquaintance.

"Are you trying to impress me with the means you customarily employ to deal with 'situations', sir? Very little of that nature can impress me, nor has it impressed me for some time longer than you've been alive." The Colonel tossed the box onto the marble-topped cabinet. An ear fell onto the floor.

Gwynn swirled his brandy. "Colonel, be assured I'm not here to make threats. But there's an outstanding matter to be resolved. Shall we be amicable? We understand that any man can fall prey to temptation. From a valued partner we'd only ask some recompense. This is what I have been instructed to tell you."

He said nothing further, while Colonel Bright appeared to be trying to destroy the mantel clock with his gaze. Gwynn didn't feel hopeful. In fact, he expected it all to go bottom-up. He tried to get Marriott's eye, but Marriott was utterly absorbed in the painting.

But at length the Colonel gave a small, tight cough. Gwynn took it as an admission of defeat. "We estimate our loss, along with sundry expenses incurred in dealing with this affair, at a total of one hundred and ten thousand florins. I must ask that payment be made within the week, in gold."

After a second round of futile visual combat with the clock, the Colonel nodded stiffly. "It will be arranged. Now get out of this room."

While the conversation was going on, Marriott's mind was distant. The noise of the band, the jungle, the clock, Gwynn's and the Colonel's voices, all scraped on his nerves. He concentrated on the painting, drawn by the lilies, which seemed to glow with a light of their own and hover, somehow, in a separate space, not fixed to the canvas with the rest of the painting, but merely resting on it. In their unfurling whiteness and their floating isolation, they made him think of the arctic geese that had flown overhead while he lay alone on the deep snow. And in a moment he was gone from the hotel, and was there in the past again, hearing only the geese honking above his own ragged breath. The midsummer sun was still glowing on the horizon in the depth of night, an ember that wouldn't go out. The snow had been red, dark red with black shadows in the undulating dips, like a velvet cloak to look at, wet and cold to lie on.

They'd given him a chance. The beating wasn't meant to be fatal. Sixty lashes, enough to injure but not kill. He had furs on, and he was strong; he could have walked and tried to find shelter, but he'd already made up his mind to let life go, for he hadn't experienced anything to fuel him with love of living. Thievery alone gave him satisfaction, and he was forever finding ways to take what wasn't his.

The village had tolerated him because he never took very much, and in other ways he was useful, a youth strong enough to do two men's labour, whether it was digging peat or skinning deer or working the bellows and lugging iron in the forge. He was tolerated until he did a stupid thing, and an ugly one: taking her, the saga-singer's daughter, she of the rare golden hair and the honey-voice, who everyone loved, who no one would forgive him for taking. He had known better than to try to tell them that in that moment of possession he'd believed she was truly his. He knew this thinking was no good, and he felt painful remorse for having hurt the one thing he desired above all else. He hated himself. But even as he lay on the snow, devoid of volition, he hated his kin for discarding him. The flogging would have been enough; he wouldn't have done it again. He'd have gone back to stealing deer meat and worthless brass cloak pins, and he would have endured the looks of mistrust and contempt, and he would never have dared to raise his eyes to look at hers.

But who would have taken a chance on it? No one had spoken for him. His parents and brothers had been as silent as they would have been were he a stranger.

Even he had surprised himself with how easy it was to decide to die. He lacked whatever it took for a man to kill himself—he'd poked at his arm with a knife, but couldn't make his hand cut deeply enough—but he could let the world kill him. That he could certainly do.

But the world had other plans. On the night they banished him, fate crossed his path with that of a recklessly speeding dogsled. He played dead at first, closing his eyes while the dogs sniffed at him and licked him. Then he heard human footsteps crunching on the snow, and felt warm fingers on his neck.

And then laughter, and a youthful voice: "You'd better get up, or I might let them eat you. I might eat you myself. You've got plenty of meat on your bones, and I'm hungry."

Marriott had managed to let a few seconds go by, but then he lost the resolve to let the world kill him. He opened his eyes and saw a boy of about his own age, dressed in leathers and thick furs, with a sword at his side.

At that point a thing like a large hairy snowball bounded out of the sled. Marriott shortly found his nose being energetically licked by a young hound pup.

"Meet Dormarth," said the smiling boy. "He has no manners, but out in this uncivilised world that might stand him in good stead. I am Gwynn, lately of Falias, currently of no fixed address."

Marriott got up from the ground. He felt extremely wary, but tried not to show it. Here was a chance to make a new start. He sensed in front of him a clear, wide road and a different version of himself walking along it.

The boy called Gwynn asked no direct questions. He said his team had been excited about something, and, being curious, he'd given them rein to follow their noses. Marriott supposed the dogs had smelled the blood seeping out of his cuts, but he said nothing about the flogging, or his pathetic self-wounding. No one needed to know about his old self.

After that the memory became patchy. He remembered riding in the sled, thawing, drowsing, wrapped in furs. And he remembered Gwynn giving him a bottle of distilled metheglin, and him drinking it all, and telling everything, and then being sick over the side of the sled. The new road had gone crooked, it seemed, as soon as he stepped onto it.

Nevertheless, in the years of hectic adventure which followed his meeting with Gwynn, it was true that as Marriott acquired fame he also acquired a reputation for chivalry towards women. However, women themselves avoided him as if he bore a brand that was clearly visible to their eyes. He hoped for happiness, often fell in love, and was without exception met with indifference, fear or scorn. He came to believe that he'd cursed himself with his brutal act.

When he first saw Tareda Forever he immediately adored her, but it had long gone beyond that. Lacking the option to flee from her presence, he could only stay and become, nightly, more deeply in love with her. She had become the centre of his world and, he believed, the only possible agent of his true rescue. He knew he was captivated by the illusion that she sang to him alone and understood and accepted everything in his heart; meanwhile, a hundred other men and women in the same room believed she sang to them alone and accepted their hearts with her undivided attention.

He had convinced himself that if she would just once smile at him, genuinely, at some time and place away from the stage, his guilt would be washed out and he would be forgiven, the curse lifted, and the door to love unlocked; he would be able to make her desire him.

Giving in to fantasies, Marriott imagined that he lay on the snow again, but in the sled it was Tareda, wearing white mink, who found him, and he took her hand and she smiled and drew him close.

Inevitably, the woman to whom the knight offered flowers also took on Tareda's form in his mind's eye. He kept looking at the painting, although it filled him with anxiety, until he heard Colonel Bright tell them to leave.

SEVEN

AS FOR GWYNN, the image of the woman and the knight made him recall the crouching sphinx and scaly basilisk. His dormant-lying curiosity about the etching's elusive artist began to stir, and the mood took him to search for Beth Constanzin again.

It was a convenient time to try, at any rate. He found himself with more leisure than he'd had for months, for after his and Marriott's visit to Colonel Bright things had gone quiet on all fronts. The Colonel sent his cargoes down the river punctually, and they were all young, strong and beautiful. The Horn Fan enjoyed a time of prosperity and peace.

Gwynn approached his self-appointed task systematically. It occurred to him that the trapezoid building in the engraving might be an enlarged representation of a smaller structure, such as a folly in a private garden, or a burial vault; some sort of chamber in which a further clue might be waiting. Liking this idea, he took a large map of Ashamoil and ruled a grid of sixty squares on it in red ink, then cut up the map along the red lines. He made a tracing of the sphinx's building, took the tracing to a printer and paid for sixty copies. Then, over the course of several days, he contacted sixty people who had good standing in the trade of eyes and ears for hire. All boasted that they could find anything they were paid to find. Gwynn gave them each one of the prints showing the building, a square of the map for a search area, half-pay in advance, and the promise of a generous bonus to the lucky one whose assigned area turned out to contain the object of the quest, whatever it actually turned out to be.

And then he waited.

One month later, Gwynn sat on his bed, unclothed, and considered the results of his efforts. He poured himself another glass of wine.

Nothing.

The infallible spies had returned, all of them, without success.

He considered sending them out again to look for a woman with that face. But as he had already decided, if that was the only game it was a crude and tedious one. Gwynn felt disappointed in the artist. He chided himself for being irrational.

He drained the glass, and closed his eyes. With sight gone his other senses sharpened. Over the clamour of the river and the background rumble of the city he heard a voice speaking in the room below. It sounded like an actor rehearsing a soliloquy.

"I was born human, but horror and the griping ache of the wound to my pride caused me to seek and find alternatives at a young age. I was happiest as a hog, when a mattress of manure pleased me more than a divan of silk, and I esteemed a bucket of slops as equal to burgundy and stuffed figs. After returning to bipedal form I never succeeded in becoming a hog again, but I did become a goat, which would have been a satisfactory condition, save that there was an undeniable beauty in my yellow eyes, with their elegant horizontal pupils, so that when I saw myself in a stream I felt a longing which caused me pain. I found refuge in the earth and blindness. You who see birds every day, and wish for their wings, have never imagined the happiness of the earthworm: he has only one desire, which is to fill his interior with dirt, and that desire is perpetually satisfied. It is only because of the range and voluptuousness of his senses that the sublime hog is able to say he is greater than the royal worm . . .

"I delight in turbid images, my friend. You must not have forgotten my warning on the subject of winged octopi who will, any day now, bring messages of stern admonishment to the cities of the world. Did you observe the flight of these gloomy, coruscating molluscs when you stood with your face pressed to the window, shocking passers-by with the sight of your hollow cheeks and wild hair? Your strigiform eyes never blinked. But though you observed the murderer and the pederast giving each other confident nods in the street, perhaps you noted nothing else amiss. Octopi possess superior powers of camouflage, despite being colour-blind . . . "

The voice talked on in this vein, but Gwynn stopped listening. He smelled the season changing. The dry months were almost over. It was now coming to the time when the air began to moisten and to carry the earthy, metallic smell that foreshadowed the approaching monsoon.

His days had fallen into a comfortable routine. In the mornings he slept late, read, or dallied in cafés. Most afternoons found him at the Mimosa Tier Sporting Club with his colleagues, shooting, fencing and riding, followed by an hour or two in the club bar, and then a bath at the Corinthian. Evenings he spent either with the same colleagues or with wider society in a round of other activities that were indispensable to an elegant life: card games, billiards, dances, dinners, the theatre, strolling for no other purpose than to be seen, and, of course, buying clothes. That day he'd had himself fitted for three new suits. After two hours of having fabric samples spread in front of him by his tailor—a man passionate about the materials he worked with, whose discourses upon weave, drape, colour and pattern were nearly ekphrastic—Gwynn had made his selections from among the panoply of light and heavy silks, jacquards, damasks, crêpes, moires, eye-abducting brocades, sculpted brocatelles and matellassés, dyed leathers and metal-threaded broideries. Then there was another hour of perusing patterns for coats, waistcoats, trousers and shirts. The new fashion for the latter was plain, with a high wing collar and no lace. And lace cravats, the tailor had informed him, were about to become items of attire strictly for ladies. If a gentleman did not wish to make a fool of himself, he would wear plain silk only.

Gwynn thought the dedicated, skilled tailor one of the best of men.

At night he worked. An hour ago he'd come back from going with Sharp Jasper to visit a quartet of young would-have-been operators who had managed to get themselves into a staggering amount of debt with Elm. Their rich parents had refused to bail them out. The four had proved unexpectedly hardy, to the point where Gwynn and Jasper had needed to exert themselves somewhat in order to make their point. Eventually, however, they had brought the youngsters to a state of misery sufficient to be an incentive for their parents to repent of their parsimony.

And now it seemed he was going to sit in bed, naked, alone, and drink the wine he had planned to drink with Beth Constanzin. The thought, when he phrased it like that to himself, was enough to make him put the bottle down. He grimaced in the dark.

He was contemplating simply going to sleep when he heard light footsteps coming up the corridor outside his rooms. He recognised them as belonging to Mrs Petris from the fourth floor. They stopped, and then he heard the bell in his sitting room jangle.

He thought of pretending to be asleep already. It was late enough. However, a call from Mrs Petris always meant an invitation to a party. Of his several neighbours, she was the only one with whom he had much in the way of social relations. She had social relations with everybody; if a block of stone had taken up residence in the building she would have pressed it into coming to her suppers and soirées.

He got off the bed, threw on a dressing-gown and answered the door.

"Hello, Gwynn dear!"

Mrs Petris' head came up to his chest. Smiling, she showed teeth still painted with indigo in the fashion of her youth. Decades ago she had been a showgirl. She still had a dancer's upright figure, and a face which, though gaunt as an ancient bird's and marzipaned with ceruse, exuded tireless vivacity. She wore a black beaded gown that was probably fifty years old, and a coronet of crystal stones and black feathers on her short white hair. As usual she smelled of champagne, and as always she spoke in a girlish, excited way that, Gwynn thought, must once have been a fashion too.

"Hello, Mrs P.," he greeted her. "To what do I owe the pleasure?"

"I'm so glad you're in! I know I never have to worry about waking *you*, you night-owl! I've got Madam Enoch and some other people downstairs for a little session with the spirits. We would be so delighted if you could join us. Do say you will! I was hoping that you might agree to play something. Last time it had such a stimulating effect. We feel so very lucky to have a musician in the building—and such a handsome one, too!"

Gwynn's hands were sore from beating up the kids, but he couldn't very well explain that.

He couldn't help being a little fond of Mrs Petris. His own grand-

mothers had been grim, militant women who wielded swords and po-
litical power with an equal ease of long custom. The other old women
in the clan were similar, or else they were sibyls: witches, speakers with
the dead, women to be wary of. Yet all of them put all their might into
serving the clan. Theirs was the grandeur of great links in a great chain.
Gwynn had come around to thinking that Mrs Petris showed a greater
strength of character in having stayed as frivolous as a butterfly all her
life.

She had once told him that he reminded her of her late son, who had
died in a boating accident. She frequently professed a wish to surround
herself with interesting young people. Since she had first coaxed him to
one of her séances he had attended several. The mediums she invited
were uniformly atrocious old vaudevillians, but he'd had good con-
versations with some of the other guests, who were usually people he
wouldn't have been likely to meet in the course of his normal activities.
The women invariably outnumbered the men at such gatherings. In his
homeland, perhaps, they were women who would have become sibyls.

"Of course, I should be happy to," he told her.

"Oh, wonderful!" Beaming, she gripped his arm. "Now, you'll get
dressed up, won't you? Something suggestive of the mystical, for atmosphere. The spirits are dreadfully sensitive about such things."

"I shall consult my wardrobe, Mrs P.—though I fear I've little
knowledge of mystical matters, or the sartorial tastes of spirits."

Mrs Petris giggled. "You're a treasure, my dear boy. Go on, find
something from your box of costumes."

Gwynn excused himself and returned to his bedroom. An ensemble
came readily to his mind. He wasn't entirely ignorant of esoteric symbolism. He came back to the door shortly, attired all in black, with his
many-eyed peacock coat. A cameo brooch, a memento mori depicting
a skull in a noose—one of the few things he'd kept from his bandit
days—pinned his funereal black linen cravat.

Mrs Petris immediately gushed: "Oh, so perfect! The dead will love
it." She nodded many times, smiling her blue smile. "Thank you, my
dear." She put her hand on his sleeve again. "Come down, the others
are waiting for us."

Leaning on his arm a little as they went along the corridor and down

114

the stairs, she said, "And have you been thinking about the matter we discussed last month?"

"I have very faithfully thought about it, as I promised," he replied.

"But, you have taken no action?"

"There hasn't been anyone for whom I'd wish to take any action. Perhaps I am too fussy—or perhaps women are too fussy. Then again, one wouldn't wish to be chosen by someone who wasn't fussy."

"Love is terribly important, dear Gwynn. One needs it."

"I know, Mrs P."

"I'm glad you do. To live properly, one needs a few certainties, even if they're not based entirely upon truth." She gave an ironic little laugh.

"I shall take your advice to heart, then."

"You'll find the right woman to be your wife, my dear. One does exist for you. There's someone for all of us." They had reached her door. "I've invited two young ladies tonight. Perhaps it will be one of them. Well, you never know, do you?"

No, you never did, Gwynn agreed.

Mrs Petris opened the door just enough to let him in, and shut it quickly. This, he knew from prior occasions, was to prevent the spiritual ethers in the room from escaping through the doorway.

The parlour into which they stepped was draped with lengths of dark purple gauze. The only light came from candles burning inside peculiar brass holders shaped like naked men and women, with their heads upturned and their mouths opened enormously wide; the gaping mouths held the candles. Incense hung heavy in the air.

Around a table covered in a black cloth were six people. Mrs Petris introduced Gwynn to them.

"Baira and Onex Ghiralfi." She gestured towards two handsome, elegant women sitting next to each other. They both smiled and inclined their heads. "And this is Lieutenant Cutter." A man in a Halacian hussar's uniform got up and bowed stiffly. "The lieutenant's cousin Marcon." A frail-looking youth of about eighteen, who would have been exquisitely beautiful had his eyes not been so dead, made a copy of Cutter's bow. "Mrs Yanein you've met before, I think."

The heavy, but very beautiful, middle-aged woman in widow's black and rubies smiled and nodded. "At your birthday party, dear. He was brave enough to dance with me."

And prudent enough to do no more than that, Gwynn refrained from saying. The previous year two elderly, wealthy counts had fought a duel over Mrs Yanein. The survivor married her, becoming her fourth husband. A month later he was dead. Of heart failure, it was said, at least by the tactful.

After Mrs Petris introduced him and said that he would be providing a musical accompaniment to the session, Gwynn bowed. "My pleasure to meet you all, and you again, Mrs Yanein. I am only an amateur, but I shall do my best for you."

The last person's face was obscured by a shawl covering her head like a deep hood. A crystal ball rested on a silver stand in front of her.

Mrs Petris turned towards this figure. "And it is my pride and pleasure to introduce you to Madam Enoch, who will be channelling the spirits for us tonight."

Gwynn hadn't heard of this particular medium before. He was surprised, when she drew back her shawl, to recognise her. She was from the Copper Country, one of its many itinerants. He'd run into her from time to time. She'd been a whore, an arms trader, a cattle-thief, a card-cheat and an actress. He could see that she recognised him, too.

Kohl-rimmed eyes fixed upon him with a look of distinct amusement. "They say the devil has all the best tunes. They're right, don't you think, young man?"

Gwynn smiled. "Madam, I have been told that musicians are of a certain god's party."

Lieutenant Cutter interrupted. "We're not going to rattle up anything too diabolical tonight, I hope!" He laughed a bit too hard.

"Oh, I think we already have," said Mrs Yanein, raising a hand to touch her plump throat, while looking at Gwynn intently.

"I might agree, Widow Yanein," Gwynn retorted.

Mrs Yanein only laughed, more comfortably than Cutter had. Mrs Petris followed with a blithe giggle. "Gwynn dear," she plucked at his sleeve, "go to the piano and play something for us. Play an overture! We'll talk to the spirits first, then have a party. One kind of spirits, then the other." She always made that joke. Everyone smiled or laughed, except for young Marcon, who plainly saw no reason to be agreeable.

A piano, draped with more of the purple gauze, stood against the wall near the table. Gwynn sat down on the tapestry-covered stool.

"Play something celestial for us," Madam Enoch commanded dryly. "We do not want infernal powers to intrude and disturb Lieutenant Cutter's sensibilities. Give us music befitting sacred mysteries."

"If you don't mind," Cutter interjected.

Gwynn began an inoffensive minor-key sonatina that didn't tax his tired hands overly much. After he had played a few bars, Madam Enoch ordered those around the table to link hands and close their eyes. She began to moan, and to shake, and presently, a sharp jerk of her head announced the arrival of the first spirit. This was Mrs Petris' son. He spoke words of comfort to his mother through Madam Enoch's mouth, assuring her that he was still in paradise. He asked after his mother's health, and she replied that she was well.

"And are you also well?" Mrs Petris asked her dead son.

An affirmative reply was returned.

Gwynn heard a small noise, quickly stifled. Someone, he couldn't tell who, had almost laughed.

Madam Enoch then produced the ghost of a fallen comrade for Cutter, to whom the hussar spoke bluff, awkward apologies.

When that was concluded Madam Enoch droned, "Is there a spirit for Marcon?"

"No," the boy said quickly. "I don't want a turn."

Mrs Yanein did want a turn. Hers took the longest, as she wished to speak to each of her late husbands. Madam Enoch made a good show of giving them different voices, while Mrs Yanein put on an equally good performance of expressing her love to each ostensible shade.

When she had bid the last, the count, farewell, Madam Enoch began to make growling sounds. Taking this to mean that the 'spirits' were leaving her and she was 'coming back to herself', Gwynn ceased playing and turned around.

Madam Enoch jolted in her seat. Her hands shook, then grasped the crystal. She slumped, took deep shuddering breaths, then slowly appeared to recover herself.

"I am drained," she announced in a husky voice. "We will have a recess. Mrs Petris, let's have some shandy."

"Eight shandies, Isobel!" Mrs Petris called out towards the kitchen.

The séancers moved to the lounge chairs at the other end of the room. Gwynn joined them. Invited by the smiles of Baira and Onex Ghiralfi, he took a seat between them. Out of the corner of his eye he saw Mrs Yanein sitting close to Lieutenant Cutter. Marcon sat by himself. Mrs Petris began conversing with Madam Enoch, asking earnest questions about the afterlife, to which the other, shrewder old showgirl gave reassuring replies.

"The world beyond is very *convivial*, Mrs Petris," she said firmly. "The dead are always at leisure; they may do as they wish."

"And do they feel any unhappiness?"

"Only enough to lend their existence the poignancy of life; but they cannot suffer excessively, or lengthily, and of course they cannot die."

"Tell me, do they always know that they are dead?"

"They do not always," said Madam Enoch, "know how dead they are."

Gwynn turned his full attention to the two younger women.

Baira told him she was a mathematician; Onex, that she was an astronomer. He didn't volunteer an occupation for himself, and neither woman asked.

Isobel, Mrs Petris's housemaid, brought in the drinks on a tray.

Gwynn waited for the sisters to take theirs, then reached for one. "It will be your turn next, ladies. Who in the beyond do you wish to speak to, if I may ask?"

"Our sister," they spoke together.

"There was a third," said Onex.

"She was an architect," said Baira. "She died in an accident on a building site."

"I'm sorry." Gwynn wondered why they didn't see that Madam Enoch was a fraud. Or perhaps they did, and like him had really only come along to socialise.

Onex smiled sadly.

"Now that we've answered you, you must answer us," said Baira. "With whose spirit do you wish to talk?"

"Oh no, I'm just part of the decoration. I don't intend to take a turn."

Onex reached out to take his hand. He let her. Her thumb lightly stroked the underneath side of his wrist. She looked into his eyes, frowned quizzically, and said, "Why don't you hurry up and find your lady?"

"I've lost no lady lately," he replied. He was a little unnerved and tried not to show it. Then he remembered Mrs Petris's hopes for him. She'd no doubt said something to the sisters. Amused now, he relaxed.

The astronomer shook her head. "I see a lot of things in the stars. Their patterns are a language. My sister sees even more in the numbers. What are you doing here?"

"Playing music, talking to you, obliging a neighbour," Gwynn said lightly.

The sisters both raised one eyebrow at the same time.

Onex spoke. "In the mornings, when I wake, I look into my mirror and talk to it, and learn who I've become while asleep." Her finger brushed his cuff where square-cut diopsides winked among the embroidered threads. "You look as if you're fond of your mirror."

"But I don't talk to it."

"Then perhaps you should. Or, at least, you might think on this: when a star is reflected in a river, you can pick up the water and the light in your hand, and be holding part of the star itself. Unless you can tell me how a star and its light can be different things?"

Whatever he might have thought of saying next was forestalled by a ragged, shuddering gasp from Madam Enoch. As everyone's eyes focused on her, she dropped her glass into Mrs Petris' lap, clutched her chest, opened her mouth wide, and fell face down on the floor.

Gwynn thought at first that it might just be another act. But Mrs Petris was swift to kneel down and turn Madam Enoch over onto her back. It then became apparent that she was dead.

"Her heart," Mrs Petris muttered. "Poor woman."

Mrs Yanein gazed at the corpse with an expression of vague approval.

"Time is the only predator not ultimately on the side of life, don't you think?" said Marcon, in a serious and cold voice.

119

Cutter cleared his throat. "Should I, ehrm, fetch a porter?"

"Oh . . . oh, well, yes, I suppose someone should," Mrs Petris said.

Cutter strode off quickly, taking the dead-eyed boy with him.

The sisters put their glasses down, rose together, expressed condolences, then followed the hussar. They gave Gwynn odd, knowing looks as they left, as if they and he had shared a secret.

Gwynn was left alone with Mrs Petris. When she saw he wasn't going to go with the others, she rushed over to him, collapsed against his chest and burst into tears. He led her to a settee, then called Isobel to sit with her until the porter turned up. Not wishing Mrs Petris to be left with the porter's bill for removing the body, he gave the housemaid money for it, in case Cutter didn't.

Before leaving, he looked down at the late Madam Enoch. She was lucky not to have ended up in a shallow sand-grave years ago, lucky to have made a new life, however ludicrous. He couldn't very well avoid seeing the parallels.

He went down to the terrace.

A light breeze carried frangipani down the hill to challenge the Skamander's reek of engine smoke and putrid mud. The night was mild.

He lit an Auto-da-fé. He wasn't tired. He was restless.

After inhaling a few times he flicked the cigarette into the river. He wanted something a bit more festive. It was a while since he'd really indulged himself. Checking his pocket watch, he saw that the hour was scarcely half past midnight. He decided to pay a call on Uncle Vanbutchell. He went around to the stable to saddle his horse.

Vanbutchell lived in the old Ghetto of the Doctors on the other side of the river. Gwynn rode up through the streets above the Corozo, turned east onto Tourbillion Parade and rode for a mile, coming to the fashionable end, where party crowds milled in street-bars out the front of cabarets, under awnings and tasselled umbrellas, and danced inside open-walled ballrooms with names like Abandoned Hours and Rumour of Delight. Music came out of every door, all the tunes colliding in the street like drunkards.

Gwynn rode through the whirl without taking it in. His thoughts were with the past. He was visited by his last memories of the clan citadel in Falias, with its grey and black stone all iced over and snow covering the roofs and domes. The streets outside, rarely hospitable, were deserted; the people were inside, in the great hall deep within the fortress, hundreds sitting on cushions around blue gas fires set in concentric circles on the floor, cooking and drinking and talking. Ambassadors, petitioners and entertainers came and went in the blue light. On one night each month, at a late hour, the major domo would strike a gong, and the sibyls would file in to prophesy the future and curse the clan's enemies. The sibyls spoke of legends as truth, the dance of the stars as a key to knowledge, and the north wind as a song from the land of the dead. Their prophecies were often accurate.

Anvallic society's entrenched atheism had never adversely affected its equally entrenched respect for the ancestors and their powers. When a clan's dead members were seen to be aiding the living ones it always made the ruling family look good. In years when the ancestors seemed to be withholding assistance, the high and mighty watched their backs.

It was said that the sibyls could send their souls back and forth between the quotidian world and the beyond. Distance and time had drained Gwynn's youthful belief in that other world, the icy and starry land of spirits, away to indifference. Yet he hadn't lost all his credulity. Fake as Madam Enoch had been, he wasn't entirely able to dismiss Onex Ghiralfi. He was half sorry that he hadn't asked her what she saw in the stars.

And he was going to Vanbutchell's because he felt strange and wanted to have a reason for it.

Gwynn followed the bright street until he came to the Bridge of Fire, guarded by two brass giants, a male and a female, with raised arms that had once held torches and now held gas lamps. He rode onto the bridge and joined the throng of other riders, pedestrians, sedan chairs and coaches going across. At the other end, he rode west to the Tusk Stair, up past the Small Towers, and west again to the Omphale Gate in the wall of the ghetto. He heard a clock strike one. After a few twists and turns through courtyards and black underpassages he rode into Vanbutchell's street, a narrow and very steep one of wooden houses, with no paving. Vanbutchell's house had mahogany gargoyles under its eaves, and, on a small patio in the front yard, a mosaic depicting an alchemical allegory. An oil lamp was alight outside, and Gwynn pulled on the bell-rope beside the front door; but there was no answer. He rang several more times to no avail. Either Vanbutchell was out, or out for the count on one of his own elixirs. Gwynn gave up and considered other options. He wasn't far from the Crane Stair. Between there and Lumen Street was the city's main nightmarket, where he knew a few dealers. He headed that way.

Below the Crane Stair he took a shortcut through the Viol Arcade, where his horse's hooves echoed hollowly on the tiled floor, and emerged at the other end in the nightmarket, in an alley of glassblowers. The market was crowded and he was obliged to slow down to an idling walk. While he nudged his way through the people, his eyes were entertained by the sight of balls of molten glass being spun on long rods and inflated into glowing translucent spheres. Turning left into a street of lapidaries, he viewed arrays of beaded and inlaid fans, slippers, gloves, cutlery, writing sets and all else that could be bejewelled, including, in glass tanks, live tortoises with stones set in patterns on their shells. Next he followed an alley of confectioners, then one of nail makers, then one of letter writers, and then crossed a small square occupied by makers of cages for birds and insects. These artisans shared their space with a man selling brightly painted crocodile eggs, and with two teenaged girls selling a teary-eyed boy.

This route took Gwynn to the corner of the street of weavers, which wound through the market, looping and doubling back on itself many times. All along this street, and above it, fabrics and carpets were hung on poles and wires, lit up by hanging candles to show their colours and designs, so that the street was like one long multicoloured tent, or the moulted skin of a patterned snake. He followed it a short way, then left it to enter a minor maze of alleys at the market's edge, where the pharmacopolists were. He looked for, and found, a booth with bright blue curtains. A young girl stood next to it. She stepped forward and asked if he would be leaving his horse. He told her that he would, and handed over the reins. He went into the booth, and emerged again a minute later.

Nearby were several lanes that weren't part of the market. They were dark, but not deserted. Gwynn went down one of these, found himself an unoccupied doorstep and took out his purchase: two corked phials, one marked with a dab of silver paint. He poured the liquid from the marked one into the other, and lifted it to his lips. A vapour filled the bottle as the chemicals reacted. Gwynn inhaled it, and leaned back against the door.

Fast stitches of prickling heat ran down his spine. His mouth and throat dried out and itched madly. His bones ached as though huge hands were trying to break them and his eyes felt swollen and dusty.

After about five minutes of this discomfort, much more pleasant feelings started to pulse through him.

Soon he felt too happy and full of wellbeing to move.

The euphoria lasted for somewhat more than an hour, and then began to ease away gently. Gwynn was able to open his eyes and walk light-headedly out of the alley, still in an extremely good mood. He pressed a generous tip into the girl's hand, and mounted up again.

In this buoyant state, Gwynn rode along with his mind at play.

"Something in the stars; what do you think of that?" he said to the horse.

"What stars?" said the horse, tossing its head at the yellow fog above. "The stars exist in a state of being or non-being, depending on whether I can see them. I can't see them; therefore, no stars. Stars, nay."

"Wrong, horse. The stars are there."

"You've got a lot of faith," the horse said. "Will there be daylight tomorrow?"

"I will look for that lady tonight," said Gwynn. "My elusive imago of a woman." An idea had come into his head, an idea as simple and as powerful as a perfect circle. He would return to the street of the weavers and follow it, and by magical association the street would become a thread of gnosis leading him to the thing he desired to meet; that which, riddle or senseless riddle or no riddle, he had seen in the face of the sphinx. He was aware that it was generally the world's role to impose difficult and absurd tasks on humans, and not vice versa; but he saw no reason why that should be a rule, especially in this age when humans were showing a capacity to rule the world.

"I must still be on the wing," he said.

"You are," said the horse.

"This adventure will test the nature of the world."

"You missed the street, gunslinger."

"Easy, horse, we'll catch up with it."

Gwynn rode on until the street of weavers crossed his path again, and went into the tunnel of fabrics, feeling mirthful and masterful.

As he followed the street, the drug in his system made it easy for a particular type of pleasure to come to him: that nocturnal enchantment or glamour in which the heart, seeking mystery, and the eye, loving obscurity, collude against the survival instinct's desire to see everything clearly. Conflicting with his mood of wanting the world to alter in accordance with his whim came a reckless desire for exactly the opposite thing: to be bewitched, worked upon, altered by something stronger than himself.

To be corroded?

Infected?

Fed?

It was a wish he could not name.

Back and forth, up and down, the picturesque tunnel wound. On went Gwynn on his horse, seeing each face as a mask, each woven pattern as a lock awaiting a key or a pick, each black shadow as the reverse of a surface facing a clandestine light.

The sphinx was surely the most sophisticated of fabulous beasts. It killed not out of brute hunger or blind rage, but judiciously, destroying the witless who failed to amuse it. By speaking to its victims it appeared to seek relief from solitude—for solitary it had to be, having no equals—a trait which suggested that if the monster possessed the same self-knowledge that it offered as a prize for answering its riddles, such knowledge wasn't enough to keep ennui away. It could perhaps be considered the heraldic totem of the chattering classes. As for the basilisk, however, Gwynn couldn't be sure that it had any purpose beyond being a brash sort of menace, a gutter relative of the lofty dragon, to be briefly admired and feared, then exterminated without regret.

At that moment something literally caught his eye. Blinking, Gwynn removed the foreign matter.

It was a long hair.

A hair of a dark red hue that called to mind wine and blood and the unperishing midnight sun. And, also, a particular shade of red ink. The hair was caught in the weave of a heavy brocade cloth. Gwynn gently pulled it free and looked at it in the light of the nearest lamp.

Lit by the dancing candle flame it shone, vitreously bright. Volcanic, brave red. Royal red, lying naked in his left hand, one line of brilliant clarity.

A smile of astonished, utterly innocent delight passed across Gwynn's face, without the sanction of his mind, which was unaware of it. Then he accosted the owner of the stall where the brocade hung, showed him the hair and asked whether he knew of the person to whom it belonged. The man looked at Gwynn as if he were mad, said that he knew nothing, but told Gwynn that if he visited the woman who sat on the corner of the street of weavers and the alley of scribes and paid her twice the sum she asked for, she would perhaps be able to enlighten him.

Gwynn coiled the hair around his index finger, inside his glove, to keep it safe. But he did not ride directly to the alley of scribes. To do so would be, he felt, to move too fast. He wanted to linger with the moment of discovery, stretch it out and see what became of it, before going on to the next stage.

He detoured down a narrow alley of leadsmiths, which took him to the edge of the market. Across the street was a bar he knew, a place called the Carrefour. Leaving his horse at a hitching rail under the eye of a doorman outside, he went in and ordered an ale. The bar was crowded, and he took the last place at a table where three other men sat. Feeling invisible to their eyes, he removed his glove and kept looking at the hair bound to his skin while he sipped his drink. He was trying to decide what his discovery meant, but the degree of cognitive effort required to do so posed a challenge which his mind, in its current state, was incapable of answering. His thoughts behaved like highly volatile liquids.

He was surprised when the man next to him spoke:

"If you don't mind me saying, you look like some kind of mad poet."

The man's voice was rough and dry; he had a long sharp thorn of a face, half buried in a black muffler. He was drinking whisky.

Gwynn gave him a measured look, then shook his head. "No. I am like you."

"I figured so," the man said. "Otherwise there would have been no cause for me to comment on your mien. So what's that . . . hair?"

"A favour. A present."

"You get presents often?"

"No."

"I figured that, too." The man sounded satisfied. "So it's a lucky day for you."

"Apparently so."

"Yeah, well, one day, years ago, I was sitting in a place by the sea, turning a glass around like I'm turning this one," the man said. "My thoughts were interrupted by a huge shadow passing across the street. I looked up to see what it was. It was a ship, a steamer, the biggest I've ever seen. Built for crossing oceans. At the moment I saw her, my whole life changed. I learned about everything I didn't have, all in one instant. I knew she was there for me. I was supposed to go on board. Don't ask me how I knew. Sometimes you just understand things like that. But I stayed where I was. I was too full of hate at the time, you see? I even hated that ship. So I cursed her, and cursed her shadow and her captain and every soul on board her. Sometimes I feel I'm still there, looking up and seeing that ship, swearing at her like the biggest fool on earth. But if I'd found a red hair like the one you're holding, I think I would have found my way on board. You know why? Her name was the *Rosie Hare*. I'd have known it for a sign. Sometimes that's all a man needs, just a sign, then he can get his courage up. I reckon I'd be prince of my own country by now, if I'd found that hair you've got on your finger-bone. Yeah," he nodded, "I'd be a man of no small consequence."

The man across from him smiled bitterly. He was younger, and was dressed head to toe in black velvet. "Sirs, I'm a musician. Curiously, I once dreamed that I found a red lute string, a filament similar enough to a hair for the purpose of this conversation. I strung it onto my lute, and in my dream I played music unheard before on earth. But when I woke I could not remember it. I can only tell you that it was the music of a life lived valiantly and poignantly and beautifully, music of a soul enchanted. My soul. Ever since, I have struggled to find that music. I have always failed." He looked at Gwynn. "But now I am coming to think that you are holding the thread of my genius. It can be of no use to you, sir, and therefore I ask that you give it to me. Come, I can see by your fingers that you play an instrument. You must realise what I've suffered." His chin started to tremble, and he looked on the verge of tears.

Then the third man, who was old and deathly gaunt, spoke up:

"I can tell you all of a minotaur. This monster was born in the old black town of the ivory hunters. It seemed a savage but simple place, in which anyone could fear being murdered for their teeth, which was bad enough; but the town's wickedness was not simple. There were fig and cypress trees whose leaves stirred violently at night when no wind was blowing; and the skulls of apes were found hanging from the branches in the morning. Children disappeared from padlocked rooms with no windows. All families lost one or two out of each generation in this way. As for the survivors, they were all crooked, bad people.

"No one ever spoke to the minotaur, save to mock him. No one touched him, save to beat him with clubs. When he reached the age of ten he ran out of the town. No one had told him that there was anything better out in the wide world, but he had at times smelled strange, wonderful odours on the wind, and he had followed the path of the sun across the sky with his eyes, and desired to follow it beyond the horizon.

"Escape failed to bring about any sweetening of his circumstances. On the contrary, he experienced blight upon blight, suffering pains familiar and new: aching loneliness, illness, deprivation, freak shows, bad fortunes with women, bullfights in poor villages where they couldn't afford a real bull, stretches in prison. His life enraged, horrified and bewildered him. He never received a name. After a long time, he at last found a job as an assistant to a gravedigger, a cruel man who flogged him morning and night. After a few weeks of this treatment the minotaur crushed the gravedigger's skull with a shovel.

"A militia captured him and tried to hang him, but instead of his neck breaking the rope did. Charging with his horns, he managed to escape, and ran alone into some mountains. Finally he had done something that human beings, certain human beings at least, could respect. A gang of bandits accepted him. These men gave him a name at last: 'Bully'. His human side didn't appeal to them much: they liked the bull.

"He killed many more men. He looted, burned, pillaged and did everything else the bandits did. He learned to walk without stooping, despite his heavy head; he learned to swagger. To gratify his lust, sometimes he chose women, sometimes cows. His desires were confused. He had an instinctive and pure love for certain things—rotten hay, the full moon, guitar music—but those things weren't going to change his fate.

"One year, a war broke out. The minotaur joined the army. Of course his heart wasn't fired with patriotism; he simply thought it would be a fine lark to do what he did every day and be paid a steady wage for it. In this way he came into his own at last. Half-beast as he was, both less and more than a human being, he was a natural soldier. Bullets never touched him; it was as though magic protected him. His fellow soldiers soon came to value him. To them, he meant good luck. They learned his lowing speech and the simple sign language with which he supplemented it. He rose up the ranks like an eagle ascending in the sky. He won victories and medals. He became a hero. Women made themselves available to him, and he forgot about cows. He was made a general. There was even talk of marrying him to a royal princess. A splendid place in the world was prepared for him after all.

"Or so he thought. But most unfortunately, the enemy won. The people were bitter and wanted a scapegoat. The minotaur was thrown into a dungeon. Soldiers of his own army took him to a yard and, using pliers, tore off his epaulets and then his testicles. They blindfolded him, threw him in a cart, drove him to a labyrinth and installed him in it. The frightened buggers encrypted him. They fed him on rotten apples and onions, dropped down long shafts too high for him to climb.

"After that, all his long life was a disastrous repetition of deepening darkness, narrowing walls, desolate loathing of himself and the world, head crashing into walls and hoofed feet slipping on dung. Sometimes the minotaur dreamed of a red thread guiding him to an exit. But even if there had been such a thread, he would not have been able to find it in the dark.

"But that is only the beginning of the story," the old man said quickly. "The reason bullets could not hit the minotaur was because he was not real. He was the protagonist of a dream. The dreamer was a man locked up alone in prison. This man did not know what his crime had been, or what his sentence was. He had no trial. The only openings in his cell were one window, too high to see out of, and a drain in the floor.

"After the first month of his imprisonment, when he was sure that he was going mad, a sheaf of paper was poked into his cell with his morning meal tray, along with a pen, nibs and ink. He counted the paper. There were exactly one hundred sheets. For a moment he was less miserable; but the moment only lasted briefly. Then he felt sicker with anxiety than he had felt at any time during his incarceration. He knew that he had to decipher the purpose of the paper. Any sign of lenience in his captors was worth something. And it was impossible not to hope, too, for something else, something crazy: that he had been given an opportunity to save himself, if he wrote the right things. He could write a confession, leaving a space blank for someone to insert the name of his crime; alternatively, he could write a denial, an abject plea, a plausible alibi, or a raging tract that would demonstrate his courage and perhaps therefore his right to live; or he could try to write something so profound or beautiful or witty that his captors would judge him worthy to live in freedom.

"He would have to be very lucky, he thought. He had never been a good gambler. Then it occurred to him that perhaps the paper was meant as an instrument of torture. He could assume that he would be dead or mad the next day and take the opportunity to write furiously on every sheet, immediately, to try for the jackpot of salvation or at least leave something of himself behind that might be filed away and found in the future. On the other hand, he could assume that he was going to be kept locked up alone for years, or decades, in which case he would want to use the paper very sparingly, only a little each day, and meditate at length about what he would write, in order to occupy his mind and thus stave off the advancing baboon of madness. It wasn't inconceivable that if he endured long enough, more paper or some other amusement would be given to him. But he would have to choose what to do, and make the same choice the next day, and the next, and every day after. Each day the matter of deciding what and how much to write would be momentous, a matter of life or death, madness or sanity. True, it wasn't difficult to think of more painful and injurious torments; but he was in no state to be able to count his blessings.

"All that day he lay like a log, unable to pick up the pen or do anything at all. He greeted the night with the whimper of an exhausted child. He tried to tell himself that every mortal creature lives every day under many restrictions, and that in fact he had always been ignorant, confused, distant from his fellow human beings and helpless before the whims of fate, and that therefore his situation was little different from his life before his imprisonment. But his own sophistry did not impress him at all.

"It was during that night that he suffered the long and unpleasant dream about the minotaur, a dream which lasted far longer than the hours of his slumber. He lived the minotaur's life, day by day, for decades, until the light levered his eyes open. 'O Minotaur!' he groaned, wiping tears from his face. 'Your heavy head droops like the narcissus at the brink of the waterfall. The wound between your thighs has gone bad. For a count of years equal to the period of the sixth planet's long circuit around the sun, you have heard nothing but your own lamenting roar. You didn't think of using your horns to open the artery in your thigh and end your life, which proves that you were more beast than man after all. The clearest point of distinction between a sentient being and a brute is that the former is capable of suicide while the latter is not. While I was you, I couldn't think of killing myself, and had to suffer until the light woke me. I suppose my waking killed you. Powers of mercy, I've served a sentence strict enough to compensate for any crime! Since I was in prison for so long, and suffered so much, and went so mad, I should be set free this instant! Indeed, I believe I should be paid some compensation!' As he moved, during this speech, from the language of dream to the language of the waking world, he spoke all the more indignantly because he knew how ludicrous he sounded. To be dealt with fairly was his earnest wish, but he knew of no reason why he should be singled out among human beings for such treatment.

"The dream of the minotaur haunted him all through the day, following his thoughts like the black hound that follows travellers on lonely roads. He could think of nothing else. At nightfall he sat down on his bed and accused himself of wasting the day in profitless re-viewing of the same images. He imagined darkness waiting impatiently during the cold indigo twilight in the world outside the prison, eager to disgorge the rind of the eaten day. He was full of trepidation about the night.

"But when he closed his eyes he found himself inside a dream as charming as the dream of the minotaur had been wretched. This time he was a green bird who befriended a princess, who fled her castle and took to the seas on a sailing boat, and the green bird sailed with her and shared her adventures. At the end of the dream the princess turned into a red bird, and the red bird and the green bird flew away to the summer stars together. This dream, too, covered a span of many years. It was as though his mind was creating time. Even if he was executed in the morning, he had already lived longer than a human lifespan, albeit half in a hell of body and spirit.

"The answer to the difficult question of what to do with the paper then became clear to him. He vowed to himself: 'I hold my captors in stern contempt. I have no interest in them or their world. I disown my waking hours in this prison. I claim only my sleep, and only to the events of my sleep will I bear witness. I shall use as much or as little paper as seems right to me. Whatever game my captors are playing, I do not know its rules, therefore I cannot play and will not attempt to.' He sat down, took a sheet of the paper, and wrote out as much as he could remember of the two long dreams. As he did not wish to stoop to communicating with his captors, even by accident, when he had finished writing he tore up the paper and dropped it down the drain hole. Already he felt brave, as though he had begun working undercover for a vital cause.

"Days went by. He dreamed every night, and his dreams continued to last for years and to be extraordinary. Some of the lives he lived were good, some bad. He played the parts of hero, villain, victim, lover, betrayer and clown. The questions of what his crime might have been, and how he might avoid punishment, ceased to matter to him. They were hypothetical. The prisoner almost ceased to exist as himself. His nightly lives overwhelmed him. He existed only when his eyes were closed. When the paper ran out he was glad, for it belonged to his old, despised life.

"The first night after all the paper was gone, he had a dream of ordinary length. He dreamed he was in his cell, and a jovial man visited him and told him that his whole ordeal had been a test, one to which he had voluntarily submitted and for which he was being paid handsomely.

"When he woke, he felt unwell, and his right hand was sore. He looked and saw that his fingers had been cut off. The hand was neatly bandaged. His meal tray had been delivered, along with a new stack of paper.

"He was faced with the question of whether the removal of his fingers was a terrible punishment or a lenient one. Soon, with shame and disgust, he realised that he was thinking like his old self. By taking away part of his body, his captors had succeeded in getting his attention. He swore that he would continue with his oneiric life. But he was unable to believe himself. He was too badly shaken by the mutilation of his hand, and no matter how he tried he couldn't regain his indifference.

"Each night after that, he dreamed that he was in his cell, alone, exactly as he was during the day, down to the detail of his missing digits. Naturally he went mad. One day, in his madness, he did a grotesque thing. He thrust his left hand down into the drain, for the smell of the filth in it had started to interest him. He found nothing down there but foul moisture. If only he had found a red thread, gentlemen! A long, long red thread with a key tied to the other end, a key that had lain all along in unknown waters, in seas beyond the sewers of the world, only needing to be reeled in and hauled up. He could have slipped the key under the door, and the ones he called his jailers would at last have had the means to let him out!"

His story finished, the old man threw himself forward upon the table and wept. "I have tried!" he sobbed. "I have tried so hard. I have done everything." He threw a look of towering wrath at Gwynn. "What right do you have, you wretch, to keep that divine filament?"

"He's right," said the man in the muffler, speaking to Gwynn. "I think that hair might be worth something. More to us than it is to you."

"We should play for it," stated the young man in velvet. He slapped his hand on the table. "What's your game, sir? Poker, dice?"

Gwynn stood up. He felt his curiosity was more than satisfied. As time could ripen, so it visibly could rot, and a prolonged moment deteriorate badly.

From a pouch on his gunbelt, he freed one of the spare loaded cylinders he customarily kept handy. He slipped three bullets out and placed them on the table.

"If your burdens are too heavy, there is the solution," he said. "Were we in a less public place, I could do more to help you. As it is," he shrugged, "that is the most charity I can spare."

"You are of low character," the man in velvet said coldly. "Clearly, you must have cheated. Everything you win, you will lose."

The man in the muffler snorted. "Big deal, kid. That happens to everyone some day."

"I can do better!" cried the old man, a wild, sick look in his eyes. "In my youth I was a puppeteer; I had one daughter, a little girl like an angel, but she died of the shaking fever, for she was a golden child and too good for this world. To console myself, I made an exquisite marionette, a child of porcelain and carved wood and stuffed silk. That was the body I made; it only awaited a soul. With the many threads I tied to her joints, I could make her imitate life. But if I had found a red thread, if the gods had given me a red thread to go into the place set aside for her heart—"

Gwynn walked outside, hearing the old man's voice retreat into the general hubbub of the crowd.

"Time, gentlemen," he murmured. He got on his horse, which neighed loudly, and he rode back to the street of weavers.

A woman indeed sat on the corner of the alley of scribes; she was old and evil-looking, with a bald yellow head like a melon.

"Honoured Aunt," Gwynn spoke to her from his horse, "I'm told you can sell me the answer to a question. From whom did this come?" He leaned down from his saddle, taking his glove off and holding out his hand so that she could see the hair wrapped around his finger.

He knew he was being irrational, but right now that didn't matter at all. Perhaps he was still in the alley, drugged and dreaming; perhaps there was such a thing as magic in the world and he was ensorcelled as he had toyed with wishing to be; perhaps he had lost his mind. The truth didn't concern him. He had a track to follow at last, and he would decide what he believed once he found what he was looking for.

"Fifty florins," said the beldame.

He counted out a hundred and passed it down to her.

"And the hair," she said.

He unwound it and held it out. She pinched the end of it between her fingers. He let it go.

She rolled it up into a ball. She blew on it, spat on it, sniffed it; then she put it in her mouth, chewed upon it, and slowly drew it out again. "Rare tasty," she mumbled. Her melon-head drooped on its thin stalk of neck. "There are tracks. The lair on the stair." She looked up. "You will find your desire on the Crane Stair."

"Impossible," Gwynn said flatly. He had made a thorough search of the stair in his first search for Beth Constanzin, and he knew every building on it.

"Go and see for yourself," she shrugged, and held up the hair, now glistening with saliva.

Gwynn drew his sword and picked up the hair on the end of it. "If you're wrong, I'll be back here for my money, hag."

The witch laughed like a little girl.

After wiping the red filament and returning it to his finger, Gwynn put his misgivings aside and rode all the way back to the Crane Stair. It occurred to him that perhaps the witch had not been talking about the building but had meant that he would meet the red-haired artist herself.

He dismounted and led his horse up the long, steep and winding climb. He didn't meet anyone. He went back down. The horse was showing signs of impatience, though it had said nothing.

Gwynn tried to get his mind together.

To connect with the right moment, he thought, was to be like a weft thread intersecting with a warp thread at a precise point. He was pleased with the fit of the metaphor. It followed that he had possibly dallied too long in the Carrefour, and now had arrived too late. He sneered at himself, while at the same time half admiring the absurdity of his situation, as though he was an outside spectator as much as a protagonist in the rigmarole.

What would be more absurd—to continue, or to give up? At first thinking the former, he ripped his glove off, unravelled the hair from his finger and cast it away, not watching where it fell. He told himself he would go home and write the whole night off as a hallucination. But having resolved this in his mind, he found his body automatically walking up the stair again, the horse plodding alongside with its head down in an attitude of weary resignation.

And when he was almost back at the top, he saw the shape made of light. A quadrilateral with two sloping sides.

He caught his breath. The trapezoid shape was a recessed attic window in a house, an ancient three-storeyed wooden firetrap enmeshed in creepers, which hung over the window, concealing it. Previously, he had only seen the two ordinary dormer windows beside it. Only now, with the light in the room, was the trapezium visible. Gwynn could see the top of an interior wall covered in unframed pictures. It couldn't be a coincidence. It had to be her studio.

Musing over whether there really had been a supernatural force at work, Gwynn let the idea sit in his mind, and found that he didn't particularly like it after all. He put his finding of the house in his largest metaphysical folder, the one he mentally marked 'dumb chance'.

And then, because he couldn't turn up at her door empty-handed, he rode in haste all the way back to the market, bought a gift, and rode back again to the house on the stair. While he was making this trip, he considered the significance of the relationship between the building in the engraving and the window in the house. The window's space could be considered the inverse of a solid, much in the way that an engraved plate was the inverse of the prints made from it: the inverse was the original. Perhaps that had been a subtle clue, which he had missed— and which, in any case, had been spoiled by a simple matter of a light being on or off.

The light was still on when he returned. A side gate without a lock led him down a path to a tiny rock-strewn yard with a crabapple tree. Three flights of iron stairs climbed the back wall of the house. Leaving his horse tethered to the tree, Gwynn went up the stairs to the topmost landing, which faced a flaked white door. On the architrave was a brass name-plate, decorated with elaborate scrollwork: **BETHIZE CON-STANZIN, ENGRAVER.** Gwynn raised his hand to knock, then had a moment of hesitation. He had imagined the sphinx in the picture to be a literal projection of its maker, but imagination had served its purpose, and if he proceeded he would swap mystery for knowledge. Possibly he would be disappointed, or she would be.

Nothing ventured, nothing gained, he shrugged to himself. He knocked.

EIGHT

THE WOMAN WITH ink-stained fingers answered the knock at her
door. She immediately recognised the fetching peacock coat, and its
wearer, who bowed from the waist, very decorously, then straightened
up wearing the smile of an evildoer.

For his part he saw more than he had hoped for: a woman as tall
as he, she was well-built, an image of muscular grace. Her flesh was of
a dark gold tint, smooth as tumbled amber, her hair the now familiar
shade of rose-red, wound in a coronet above the subtle, beguiling face
of the sphinx. Her eyes, for which he had never settled on a colour,
imagining sultry topaz, simmering green or even red to match her hair,
showed themselves to be intensely black. If they were windows, they
looked onto an unilluminated place.

She wore an olive-green dressing-jacket with a pattern of yellow
birds over maroon pyjama trousers. Her feet were bare, and Gwynn
noticed that her toenails were painted, like a river-woman's, with ver-
milion lacquer.

Her smile became wily.

"You're very late, sir," she said. It surprised Gwynn to hear her
voice, speaking in educated tones, with Ashamoil's accent. He had
thought she must have been from some place as far away as his own
homeland. She curled her fingers under her chin. "And would you be
death or the devil?"

"I would not be either, madam, given a choice," he said.

"But tall dark gentlemen calling late at night are traditionally one
or the other."

"Then I must flaunt tradition. Far from being any such distinguished

137

person, I am not, I fear, even a gentleman."

"Well, that may be no bad thing," she said. "What name do you go by?"

He bowed again slightly, fingertips to his chest. "Gwynn, of Falias; and it would please me to be at your service."

She stretched out a hand, which was lean and calloused and stained with black ink under the nails: Gwynn brought it to his lips and placed a decorous kiss on it. He smelled aromatic, slightly bitter chemicals on her skin. He felt a certain wish to linger there beyond the brief contact dictated by proper courtesy, but ruled himself and made the kiss a merely amicable one.

"I know of Falias," she said. "You are from the eternal ice under the Pole Star. A foreign devil, indeed." She inclined her head. "You have won my game; now we shall see if there is another to play. The next move is yours, whatever you may be."

She winked at Gwynn.

Damn, he thought, *but she's fetching.*

He brought out the small parcel which was his gift for her. "This is but a lagging appendage," he said, "to the elaborate amusement you devised."

While they stood in the doorway she unwrapped it, and laughed when she held it in her hand. It was a leathery egg, painted with a maze-like geometric red and black pattern.

"It is a very apt and pretty finial," she said, turning it around in her fingers. "What creature should I expect it to hatch?"

"I venture no claims, madam, but perhaps if kept warm it will hatch a basilisk."

"Then I hope it does," she stated. "There are too few apocryphal curiosities at large in the world. I shall put it by a window where the sun will shine on it often. And now," she said, lifting her chin, "since you have arrived at this eyrie after a long journey, will you come and drink wine with the mistress? Though be forewarned, this place is con-secrated to Art and the only wine is the cheaper sort of red."

"No one has yet accused me of being precious about wine," Gwynn said.

She smiled and showed him in.

The room he stepped into was her studio, a large space in a state of orderly clutter. The trapezoid window, with a lamp and a vase of dried flowers on its sill, was by the far right wall. Three presses occupied the middle of the floor, and under the windows there were several sinks and tubs. One wall was covered in shelves, which held tins of ink and various other cans and bottles, and a bench with cupboards under it ran around the other walls. Above the bench, hundreds of sketches and etching proofs were pinned on cork-boards. It looked as though she did a lot of work.

She placed the egg on the sill of the trapezoid window. "It will be incubated by sun, moon and paraffin," she said, striking a match to light the lamp.

She invited him to look at the pictures, while she went into a room next door and came back with two glasses of wine.

Gwynn looked at the art, occasionally asking questions, which Beth answered with a manner less arch and more serious than she had shown at the door. He understood that she wanted him to become acquainted with her first in this way, through her work. The images on the walls were arranged thematically. Occupying the first wall were botanical, zoological and technical engravings, all with beautifully executed detail. The next wall was divided between landscapes—again exquisitely rendered—and portraits, mostly of actors and singers, including several of Tareda Forever. A section of the wall was devoted to illustrations for 'gentlemen's curiosa', in Beth's words: pictures of models, both notorious and anonymous, posed in various stages of undress and debauch. Some were straightforward erotica, others more like caricatures, populated by fat femmes fatales, and odalisques with retinues of priapic dwarves, satyrs and dog-men.

When Gwynn came to the last wall Beth said, "And here is my own work, done for my own pleasure."

They were bizarre pictures, fantasies like the image of the sphinx and basilisk, but stranger. In most a similar mood of narrative or theatre was present, but the sceneries were entirely imagined: queer, outlandishly opulent gardens, grottoes, pavilions, courts and chambers, in which whimsy and savagery were closely partnered in a thick amalgam of details. All the actors in these baroque fairylands were prodigies: not legendary creatures, these ones, but beings straight—or crookedly—out of private hallucination: men, women and hermaphrodites with attributes of flora, fauna and even machines. A man in a morning suit had a tall, smoking chimney growing on top of his head; a multi-armed hookah had the faces of women and apes in place of its mouthpieces; a man with the lower body of a leopard cradled a snail's shell containing a slender arm; in one with a written title, *The Ways We Adorn Ourselves*, a woman lying on a feather-strewn couch held open a door in her stomach, disclosing a garden inside her body. It was much as if Beth had taken all her other works and thrown them onto a carousel of exchange and metamorphosis.

It was a carnival world: upside down, inside out, parodic and overfull, with themes of lust and gluttony in many of the pictures. The erotic tableaux ranged from pairs to orgiastic dozens, all interpenetrating each other with strange pieces of equipment. Freakish though these images were, the participants were nevertheless alive with festive wit and grace, as though a single hectic but entirely joyful spirit animated them all. Elsewhere the protean creatures were shown feasting, on lavish dishes of food, and also on each other, using animal jaws, the sticky pads of carnivorous plants and metal limbs equipped with saws, blades and hooks. The eaters and the eaten showed equal pleasure. To call it a theatre of the carnal was too narrow a definition: it was a comedic romp of all matter.

"What does it all mean?" Gwynn asked, intrigued.

"An unnatural history of existence in a state of flux," she said. "The midden of an old world, surfacing after a frost. A new world in a nymph-state, before its mature form is decided."

"And how will it be decided?"

"With inspiration and passion, and perhaps a little tragedy. Or perhaps cynically, in back rooms, behind closed doors," she answered. "Time will tell." She reached up and touched his throat, running her fingers lightly under his sharp jaw.

And she's lecherous, too, he thought. He felt pretty lecherous himself.

"I liked the look of you," she said. "That's why I put you in the picture. I'm glad you came. I dare say I'll want to put you in other pictures now."

"To squire your genius would give me joy," he said, and raised his glass to her.

Her smile moth-like, she beckoned.

Gwynn found it hard to pull his eyes away from her iron-black ones. She led him through the door, into a bedroom. This was smaller than the studio, and comparatively impersonal. The furniture was all hand-some and well matched, but the ornamental touches were few: a silver censer hanging over a small fireplace, a bowl of clove-spiked oranges on top of an escritoire, another vase of dried flowers.

Very casual now, Beth sat on the bed, while Gwynn lay back in an armchair, and they finished the bottle of wine. Then she slipped down and stood behind him. Her hands went around his neck, and his cravat and collar came away in her fingers. Gwynn remembered he had been lying in a none-too-clean alley only a short while ago. But if she could smell the streets on him, it didn't seem to bother her.

They adjourned to the bed.

He anticipated an interesting encounter, and he was not disappoint-ed. He found all the old familiar sensations transformed into something he could not explain in words, even to himself. His eyes were opened to beauty as they had never been before, so that it was not the minor novelties of a stranger's flesh that he saw, but art brought to life in the long line of her flank and the bold rise of her breasts, the sweep of her back and the smooth swell of her hip, and in the red ace of diamonds ornamenting her sex. And when she touched him, he sensed an intent to which pleasure was incidental, something that he could only think of as fascinatingly sinister. As his enjoyment mounted, so did his curiosity; but when the former crested, the latter continued to rise, tantalisingly unsatisfied.

"So, Gwynn of Falias: why did it take you so long to find me?" Beth said in a teasing, familiar tone that he found very winsome. Exhausted at last, they were lying on her bed, sharing another bottle of wine.

Partial truth would do, Gwynn decided. "Things got in the way. Work."

"Oh, you work?"

"You see how it gets worse? I'm not the devil, not a gentleman, and not even a rich idler."

Beth regarded him. Naked, the layers of his anatomy were starkly visible: muscle, tendons, skeleton. Scars all over his white skin. His body hid no secrets; it was all there to read.

"I was joking," she said. "I can see that you're a man of action."

Gwynn smiled languidly. "By trade, that's so. But a man of inaction by nature. Not so much your basilisk as a lounge lizard manqué." He closed his pale eyes.

Under Beth's red mane her brain was busy. She had to think of what to do with him. She had been curious. A part of her curiosity was now well satisfied—but only a part. She had always taken lovers as it pleased her; but all of them, after the first night, she had put down again.

It was fundamentally a matter of them being the wrong species.

. This one in her bed was, of course, not of her own kind either, but for the first time she felt a sense of compatibility.

With a long finger, she stroked the smooth, sensitive skin below the ridge of his hip. "Not on my time, you're not, white man."

"And what am I on your time, madam?" he mumbled.

"A clever talking beast. A redoubtable snake . . . " Laughing lightly, she continued her caresses.

He sighed. "Snakes," he observed with a mock frown, "have no respect for the dignified lassitude of men."

"They are incorrigible beasts," she agreed. "They should be shut up tightly in dark places. Given to hungry bitches."

He laughed, and kissed her. Then he unexpectedly took her hand away. "Listen, I've got no wish to deceive you. I might not be the devil, but I do work for him. For a slaver."

Beth's eyebrows went up. She looked amused. "And so?"

"That doesn't offend you?"

"Why should it?" she shrugged. "No great civilisation has ever risen and survived without some form of slavery in its foundations. I'm not sure how wise it is to try to knock away the base on which everything else stands." She propped herself up on one elbow. "Do you imagine that I'm a soft creature, ruled by emotion?"

"Perish the thought, madam. I've dared to hope that you're ruled by your appetites."

"As you are ruled by yours?"

"I'd consent to be ruled by yours—now and again."

She slid her body on top of his. Like gold, she was heavy. She was very warm, too. He closed his eyes and felt her simply as heat and pressure. Those words would do well enough, he thought, to describe what he'd gone looking for that night. Transformative forces.

Was he bored with being the man he was? It was a difficult question. Certainly he was content, and comfortable, so perhaps he was looking for danger again. The thought flitted in and out, then he stopped thinking and ardently concentrated all his attention on her.

When they were lying slothful again, now in hot morning light, he drowsily brought up the matter of his occupation a second time. "If we remain lovers, or even simply friends, you will be in danger. I have unpleasant enemies, and unpleasant confrères. Felons, mohocks, deviants . . . "

She stretched her arms. "You can be unpleasant too, no doubt, and I took you into my bed."

"But I can be banished." He rolled away, making space between their bodies. "Certain others aren't so easily rid of, and they outlive everyone."

She pulled him back to her. "We've let the sun come up on us," she said. "Stay here. Sleep."

Gwynn soon discovered that Beth had a high appetite for low company. She was partial to sculling around pool halls and gambling with boatmen and gypsies in the riverside cellars: drinking with the lowest of the low at the Folly of Men and the Chlorine Star, betting on cockfights, trading dirty jokes with dirty men in dirty rooms—these were the ways in which she liked to spend her nights. When Gwynn joined her in these pursuits, he observed that she was quite fearless in the company of ruffians. And Gwynn was amazed to see that none of the ugly and dangerous types whom she casually befriended ever directed so much as a hint of a threat of violence her way. It seemed that no man could conceive of her as prey.

He tried doing so. It was impossible. In every scene he tried to visualise, her image effortlessly turned the tables and killed his.

Sometimes he had wondered at the reason for his own good luck—the luck that had spoiled death's aim so many times, keeping him safe. Perhaps she was gifted with a similar sort of luck.

Nevertheless, he had no intention of introducing her to his colleagues.

She loved to go to the wharf fair, showing an unflagging interest in the snake charmers, the tumbling dwarves, the bearded women, the hairless brothers, the cyclops, Modomo the escapologist, Hart the strongman who bent iron bars and juggled axes and small cannonballs, the contortionists, conjurers, puppeteers, old Bibbar and his flea circus, vast Palee the Glutton who ate anything given to her—even swollen dead rats and broken bottles—and all the other knockabout human oddities. She said they were her greatest inspiration.

Gwynn wondered why he had never seen her until the night on the Crane Stair. She frequented the same parts of the city that he did. It really was as though something had spoiled his sense of aim.

When he and she were together alone they exchanged, gradually and in small pieces, pictures of the past. She spoke of a small family, a quiet house, a younger sister who died, lengthy silences at meals between retellings of the same handful of old stories.

"At some point new things stopped happening to those people," she said.

The only relative of whom she spoke with affection was her maternal grandfather. He had been court cartographer to the Princess-Governor of Phaience, and when he could be roused from dozing or reading he would take his old maps out of their folios and tell her what he knew of the beautifully drawn and coloured countries, repeating tales that explorers had brought back to him.

Beth spoke of her wish, dating from then, to take a long ocean voyage and perhaps never return. "Everything came out of the ocean. That's where all possibilities are, symbolically, at least," she stated. "Perhaps even physically."

One night, when they were drinking cocktails in a bar on the Blue Bridge, she said to him, "Your part of the world was always coloured white. There were only ever a couple of cities marked, and, I think, a sea."

He nodded. "That would have been the Nas Urla. That means 'grey tide.' It's a sea that claims a lot of ships. We use the same phrase for the feeling of life passing away. Old people say that they hear the grey tide coming in, or they'll tell you to get a blanket to keep the grey tide off them. I don't know whether the expression or the name of the sea came first."

"My grandfather never met anyone who'd gone further than the Dividing Mountains," she said. "I imagined you northern people all being pure white, with white hair and pearl-white eyes, living in castles of ice."

Gwynn smiled. "White and green and transparent ice, carved into towers and colonnades and flying buttresses. There were ice statues, and even carved ice gardens, for it was too cold for real trees to grow."

"Ice birds too?"

"Snow geese."

"What was it really like?"

"In Falias? Busy and dirty, like here, only cold enough to freeze kerosene. Ice did get used for building, but it was always black with oil and soot. You could say it was atmospheric."

"Is that the truth?"

"I'd hate to disappoint you," he said, "so please believe what you like. I left a long time ago; I have no idea what the place is like now."

"I know a place like paradise," she said. "Before the monsoon comes I'll show it to you."

NINE

THE BOY HAD the distorted knock-kneed legs that were common in children who had worked in factories from a young age. He was thirteen, and had begun when he was six. The condition was caused by the young, soft skeleton being kept standing for prolonged periods—fourteen to eighteen hour days were the norm—in front of the machines. The distortion caused imperfect circulation of blood, which, in turn, resulted in the drying up of the bone marrow. This condition could occur in any of the bones, and was most obviously present in the boy's right wrist, which was swollen to a circumference of nine inches, and was causing him agony.

Limbs so affected invariably had to be amputated; it was a case of losing a limb or a life. When the operation was over, Raule examined the bones. They presented the appearance she was accustomed to seeing, like dry coral, completely empty of marrow. If the boy survived, another job might be found for him. Something he could do with one hand.

The factories maimed and killed their indentured child labourers every hour of every day. All, like the boy, were slowly crippled, and many were injured horrifically in accidents with unguarded machinery. It was not uncommon to hear of a boy or girl getting caught on a piece of moving equipment and dragged completely inside it, and being torn or crushed to death. The indentured children, bought from orphanages and poor-houses and contracted to work for a fraction of an adult wage until they were twenty, if they survived, were scarcely better off than the slaves from the jungle. Some families sold their children into such labour as an alternative to starving, while some did so to pay debts or support addictions.

Raule had sedated the boy heavily with poppy syrup. By the smile on his face she could tell that he was dreaming opium dreams. Sometimes people woke up after those dreams with a taste for the drug. The irony was hardly lost on her.

It was late. She put her head around the door to the next ward and spoke to the night-sister who was keeping vigil beside one of the beds. "Sister, I'm turning in for the night. Would you keep a special eye on the lad in bed seventeen?"

The sister nodded. "Of course. Good—"

Ratta-tat. Thud-thud thud.

Raule felt her shoulders droop. She had very much wanted to go to bed. Even though the mocking horse of dream would collect her as usual and carry her on a tour of familiar awful frights, at least her body would get to rest.

The night-sister aimed a cold look in the direction of the corridor. "You're tired, Doctor," she said firmly, as she might have spoken to a patient. "Let me deal with them."

Raule smiled wanly. "Let's see who they are first. It doesn't sound like the kids this time." There was at least one woman's voice yelling imprecations and curses that were quite distinct, even at the distance and through the intervening walls.

The nun shrugged. "It's up to you." She hesitated, then said with a shake of her head, "I fear that people here have noted your good nature. They're shamelessly taking advantage of you."

I want them to, Raule thought.

"Shame's a luxury. Like a good nature," she said. The nun looked at her strangely. Feeling uncomfortable and annoyed, she went out into the corridor, picked up the door keys and marched to the door. It had a square peep-hole, which she opened and peered through.

Her eye met another eye. It was dark, thickly painted with kohl and coloured powders, and furious. It was the eye of Madam Elavora from the Saffron Terrace Gentlemen's Club, the fanciest brothel in Limewood.

The eye blinked. Raule realised that she had been wrong. The fierce expression in the eyeball between the frescoed lids wasn't anger, it was terror.

The teenager lying on the threadbare satin bed screamed obscenities. She bucked and thrashed, while four women held her limbs down. About a dozen other women and girls, and two painted boys, were in the room when Raule and the madam got there. They were all crying nearly as wildly as the girl on the bed.

She had olive skin, straight black hair, blue eyes. She was Lusan. Ikoi, Madam Elavora had said. The birth had come on suddenly, and it was breech.

And why had Elavora not shouted down a midwife's door instead of the hospital's? The answer was very obvious: the woman was hoping to make a sale to the doctor who was known to be interested in such things as that which now had its lower limbs outside the girl's badly torn vagina.

For the first few seconds, Raule thought she was looking at the result of a scarcely credible sexual game, or even a ghastly practical joke. But the membrane encasing the thing between the girl's legs made the truth impossible to deny. Through the membrane, the body could clearly be seen: dark, scaly limbs, with a small tail between them. The size of a human infant, it was a young crocodile.

Raule ordered everyone out of the room. Madam Elavora left voluntarily, but she would no doubt be waiting outside the door. Once she was alone and no longer pinned to the bed, the Lusan girl became calmer. She gripped the sheets in her fists, and bore down. Not screaming now, she snarled rhythmically, the sounds of her pain breaking short against her clenched teeth.

Raule didn't let herself think. She simply helped the girl to get the thing out of her body.

When the head came there was another shock, for it was human.

The girl surprised Raule. "Give it to me," she whispered.

It breathed, and it bawled like an ordinary, healthy baby. It fed at its mother's breast, tiny claws pressed together.

Doing what had to be done, Raule set to cleaning and stitching the girl's wounds. Despite having lost no small amount of blood, she remained conscious; and, seemingly oblivious to her body's pain, she calmly talked to her infant in her own language.

Then she spoke to Raule. "I know you were brought here to buy my child, Doctor. How much do you think he's worth?"

Raule understood that it was a rhetorical question.

"His father was a god," the girl said. "The god of the river. I called him into a dream, and I laid down with him in his kingdom of water. He told me I would bear his child, and that the child would be the saviour of our people. My child was going to have the river's power."

Raule listened, beginning to think that she was dreaming.

"The god told me my son would look like him."

Raule kept stitching. When she was finished she looked up at the girl, who had fallen silent. The newborn monster was silent too. The girl held it out to Raule.

It was dead.

"The river god has the head of a crocodile and the body of a man," the girl said calmly. "I failed. Perhaps the magic went awry in my womb, or perhaps the god tricked me. They say you collect monsters. Take this one."

Moving like an automaton, Raule took it.

Outside, Madam Elavora was waiting, and moved to accost her, but Raule held the crocodile baby's body up like a talisman and Madam Elavora shrank back.

Raule sat inert until very late that night, sunk in a whirlpool of thoughts. Eventually she took the tiny monster's corpse to her laboratory to dissect it. There was no obvious abnormality in the crocodilian part. Its sex was male. The human head and the brain inside were likewise normal, showing no physical defects. It had blue eyes like its mother. Where head and body joined, the scales smoothed gradually into soft human baby skin.

After writing detailed notes and sketching numerous diagrams of the exterior and interior anatomy, Raule prepared a jar and placed the child in it. She could draw any number of theories from the aberrant corpse, but no conclusions.

Nor did she feel excitement, wonder, awe or fear, or even horror.

She felt sad.

Reckoning that it might be a matter of shock that would need time to wear off, she allowed days to go by while she waited expectantly for some sort of fire to ignite inside her.

How could I witness this and not be profoundly changed in some way?

This was a question she asked herself so many times that it became almost a constantly repeating murmur in her mind. She spent much of her scant spare time staring at the monster in the jar. But it might as well have been a jar of pickled onions for all that it was capable of affecting her. She began to wonder if it wasn't only her conscience she'd lost, but if, like some wind-eroded stone in the Copper Country, she was gradually losing more of herself to a force of attrition which she understood no better than the stone understood the wind.

Raule had no one to whom she could talk. She had not sought love in Ashamoil. There were liaisons, but none of any significant length or substance, and respected though she was, she had not found any friendships in Limewood. She almost missed Gwynn's company.

She did not expect any change in these cheerless circumstances. She certainly did not expect to find intimacy with Jacope Vargey.

The unlikely affair had begun when Mrs Vargey died of rabies one Hiverday morning, two weeks after the birth of the crocodile baby. Raule was able to ascertain the cause of the infection: the bite of a monkey, the pet of an organ grinder who lived in the same building. When he was told what had happened, the poor man smothered the monkey with a pillow, weeping floods of tears. But it was too late for Mrs Vargey. Raule thought it a surreal way for her to die, when so many mundane diseases and accidents could have killed her.

Three days after Mrs Vargey died in the hospital, Raule took it on herself to have words with Jacope.

"Emila should keep on going to school," she said gently and firmly to the youth. "Will you do that for your sister?"

Jacope, slouched against a wall polishing the blade of a new stiletto, shrugged. "With what money, Doctor?"

"With the money you make. The money that pays for pretty cutlery like that knife, and for those new boots you've got on. I know you steal.

That doesn't matter to me. But your sister needs you to think of her. School doesn't cost that much. Why not do something for her with your gains?"

Jacope smirked. "So, are you telling me I should keep doing evil and damn myself so that my little sister can grow up to think she's better than me?"

Raule smirked back. "Should I really say to you, 'Jacope Vargey, go and get a proper job, and no one will think they're better than you'?"

That made him toss his head back and laugh raucously. Raule found herself laughing too, in exactly the same way.

She made herself be serious again. "Jacope, it would be a good thing if you stopped robbing people. If you get arrested, you'll be hung. Then you can imagine what will happen to Emila."

"I'm overwhelmed by your concern for her, Doctor." He spoke with bitter sarcasm.

Raule was immediately ashamed. "Jacope, I'm sorry," she said. "Shall we begin this conversation again?"

"I don't want to talk."

After he said that there was a long, uncomfortable while in which Raule stood silently in the room, feeling stupid, and angry at herself.

Then she walked over to Jacope and put her arms around him.

The urgency of his response surprised her. Her own enthusiasm surprised her even more.

In large part the enjoyment came from the long-denied thrill of the illicit. He was a thug, perhaps a murderer, and he was half her age. With that thrill also came the indulgence of nostalgia.

This lust wasn't the sort of fire she had imagined being lit in her, but at least it was human passion. She slept with Jacope again after that day, and often. Sometimes she went to the room that he continued to rent, and sometimes he came to the hospital.

Jacope rarely talked, preferring communication by touch. Whether burnishing his weapons or caressing her, his hands spoke eloquently, while his mouth stayed in an aloof, mannered pout, and his eyes glared their message of universal condemnation. His lovemaking was precocious, that of an experienced man; but in every other respect he was a boy.

Raule took pleasure in being the much older partner. It came to her that perhaps she'd never been very good at being young, but might one day be better at being old. She hurt no one by spending nights with the youth, and therefore her phantom conscience shrugged its shoulders and permitted her to enjoy the rather sleazy and greasy pleasures of Jacope's company for what they were.

And he did keep Emila at her school. Raule found out that he actually loved his sister deeply. Emila became quiet after her mother's death, but she was too tough a child to languish for long. As for Jacope's ways of making money, though, he didn't change them.

"I want to be a rich man," he said. "I want a horse and fine clothes. And those things not just for me, but for Emila too. Don't tell me about the risks. I'm not my stupid dead brother; I don't pick fights I can't win."

Raule saw that it would be useless to try to persuade him to think differently.

"It's in the jungle," Beth said.

Gwynn thought of the black swamp into which they'd thrown Orley. "Where in the jungle?"

"South. Not far."

It was a pleasant morning, with a mellow sun above Ashamoil's bridges, a mild breeze whispering down the river and a slight humidity softening the air, the breath of the approaching wet season. Their hired caique was a pretty vessel painted dark blue with silver-leafed flourishes of carved wood around the gunwales, and slightly shabby but comfortable pale blue silk bench seats.

They rowed, both pulling oars, west down the Skamander for about two miles, coming into lowland hills. At Beth's direction, they then turned south down one of the ancient irrigation canals that branched off both banks of the river. The narrow canal ran in a perfectly straight, green and shady line through the jungle.

After leaving the river-trunk and its congested traffic behind they met no other vessel. Their only visible company in the water were large brightly coloured snakes which, though poisonous, were no threat, for they stayed in their element and avoided the boat. Crocodiles were the only possible menace, as a big one would capsize the boat if it attacked, and Gwynn had brought a shotgun; but while they occasionally saw long dark heads lying half-submerged in the water, none of the reptiles showed the slightest interest in them.

With the dense jungle blocking much of the sun it was almost cool down the canal, but the work of rowing kept them warm. In the filtered, dimmed light they saw green and yellow boas coiled in great heavy loops around the moisture-darkened branches of trees. Reptiles weren't the only giants they saw: rowing past derelict temples, they came within feet of tigers lounging on creeper-grown ghats, and what at first glance seemed a band of robbers' masks, sans wearers, flying across the water, proved to be a flock of enormous black moths with white eye-like markings on their wings. From all directions there issued a hooting and screeching and fluting of animal throats. Birds were flashes of startling orange, lime, magenta, yellow and azure.

When the sun came overhead the temperature on the canal rose sharply, and Beth suggested that they rest oars until the noon heat passed. Under a towering mahogany they stopped, and opened the bottle of wine and the jars of brandied melon and figs they had brought along for refreshments.

They had spoken very little during the trip. It was a companionable silence, and it continued as they ate and drank.

Then, "Look," said Beth, who sat facing back the way they'd come. She pointed at something, smiling. Gwynn turned to see a round object bobbing up the canal. It was a glass float from a fishing net, a bluish ball nearly the size of a person's head. When this traveller caught up with the boat, Beth leaned over and took it out of the water.

She examined it admiringly, then tossed it across to Gwynn. He turned it around in his hands. The glass was crudely blown, but the bubbles and irregularities in it made it more interesting to look at. Playfully, he lifted it up to the level of his head and peered through it.

Beth laughed. "The world on your shoulders?"

"In your hands," he said, and tossed it back to her.

She caught it gracefully. Balancing it on her fingertips, she held it out in front of her, like a trophy. Then she bent over the gunwale again and rolled it back into the water, sending it on its way.

Gwynn leaned back in the stern. "So," he said, "this is your paradise?"

"I think it's close. You don't agree?"

"It's a paradise without much of a place for humans in it."

A sly smile crossed her face.

"That's right," she said. She stretched out her arms and legs. She was wearing green silk pantaloons that came halfway down her calves. She had taken her boots off, and she rubbed her bare feet together slowly.

The sun had moved, and shadows were floating on the water again. Gwynn asked what lay further down the canal.

"More canals. They go on for miles," Beth told him. "But unless you want to sleep out here in the boat we should be going back."

He didn't, so they turned the caique around and started rowing again. When they came back to the ruined temples, however, she said, "Let's stop here a while. The tigers seem to have gone."

Gwynn felt less confident about that, but he had his guns, and he didn't think something as large as a tiger could sneak up silently through so much vegetation. They disembarked, and sat down together on the vine-draped stone of an ancient quay.

Gwynn took a moment to look at Beth. Even with little light shining on her, the red and gold of her hair and skin were vivid. She was a brilliance in the wet oozing world, something from the sun's domain.

Her eyes, however, were chthonic. Their darkness couldn't have been more opaque. He felt he was dealing with only the tip of her soul; that the rest was submerged.

She pressed his shoulders down onto the stone.

After their lovemaking they lay half-naked and mute, resting their heads on each other's bodies, dozing while the jungle darkened. Only when sounds like soft thunder began to rumble in the strengthening shadows, and the boas began to wake and stir, stretching along the black tree-limbs, did they rouse themselves and step into the caique.

In the dark, they came back to the river and joined the Ashamoil-bound traffic, slowly losing the tropical stars as they entered the environs of the city.

TEN

A FLOCK OF masked ibis rose into the air after feeding on the fish-guts left on the dockside from the cleaning of the morning catch. They flew over the bottom steps of the ghat, where a crowd of women scoured laundry, and children dangled fishing lines in the water. At the top of the steps, the slave market was opening for business.

The day was already hot. Gwynn sat under the awning with a glass of chilled punch and that morning's *Dawn Chorus*. Marriott lay in his hammock cleaning his fingernails with a knife. Two bare-chested boys waved big flamingo-feather fans over them both.

Three of the Horn Fan's salesmen were standing beside the pen, supervising the servants who were oiling up the chained slaves. They were attended by a trio of youngsters holding parasols above them. Even Gwynn and Marriott's horses, tethered nearby under another awning, had a boy fanning them.

Gwynn put his drink down on the wide, carved arm of his chair and rubbed lingering sleep from his eyes. He was in shirtsleeves and had a hat on for shade. He picked up his drink again and went back to half reading the paper, half keeping a lookout.

They had been tipped off.

A few earlybird customers turned up. Gwynn watched them. They were all just ordinary shoppers. He yawned.

About an hour later he felt the skin at the back of his neck tighten. He looked over the top of the paper, and saw the group approaching.

"Ah, here they come," he said to Marriott.

Marriott sat up a bit more alertly in the hammock. He spun the knife around in his fingers like a coshboy.

Out of an archway between two buildings on the right had emerged the man with the diamond earring. He lacked not only the other earring, but the other ear. He had nine mean-looking, armed companions with him. On their foreheads they all wore a painted or tattooed red glyph. The man with the earring sported one too.

Gwynn drained his glass, folded the paper and put both down on the ground. He rested his elbows on the chair's arms and waited while Earring Man and his posse approached.

They stopped in front of the awning. Earring Man spat between Gwynn's feet. The others stood behind their leader.

"Hello, cockmaggot," said Earring Man.

"That's Mr Cockmaggot to you," said Gwynn pleasantly.

"I'll call you whatever I please, fool. Arsehole. Manbitch."

Gwynn ignored the insults. "What happened to your ear?" he asked.

"It turned septic. I had to have it cut off. I got blood poisoning. All because of what your slave bitch did to me." The man took a step forward. "So now," he grinned, "I've come for compensation."

"I see," said Gwynn. He waved his hand at the posse. "And these other fellows with painted heads are your friends who are going to help you, I suppose?"

"The gentlemen behind me are my brothers. I have joined the Order of the Blood Ghost. They're here to help me rip both your ears off, and your lips, and your . . . "

He went on at some length. By the time he'd finished a few people had stopped and were watching.

"Well, get on with it then," Gwynn said.

"What?"

"Remember he's half deaf," Marriott prompted.

Gwynn raised his voice. "I said, get on with it. As you can see, my colleague and I are exceedingly busy."

Earring Man sneered. "You're going to be exceedingly dead."

There was a soft, swift whir in the air. Some of the Blood Ghosts turned their heads, but not in time.

While they were distracted, Gwynn took the opportunity to fire a few rounds.

The five Blood Ghosts at whom he had aimed fell to the ground.

Meanwhile, Earring Man opened and closed his mouth. Marriott's knife was sticking out of his neck. Arcs of blood pumped out of the wound. Then he fell down as well.

The remaining Blood Ghosts stood uncertainly. They looked at Marriott, who had produced a carbine, and at Gwynn, who hadn't moved from his chair, and sat with his smoking pistol raised, the fingers of his left hand tapping the handle of its mate. They looked down at their fellows. Each had been shot through the middle of the symbol on his forehead.

Gwynn wagged the long-barrelled gun at the five men standing. "There's still a bullet in here. Which of you would like it?"

One of the Blood Ghosts snarled, and reached for his holstered gun.

The others went for theirs an instant later. With the advantage of surprise lost, and the five of them standing there, Gwynn had already decided that the range was too close for comfort. He fired at the legs of the man nearest him, and leapt out of his chair, dropping his right-hand gun and drawing the loaded left one as he jumped. The man he had shot at dropped with a scream, clutching his knee. Gwynn landed on top of him, causing him to scream again. And, as he had hoped, the others hesitated to fire, afraid of hitting their own man, who was thrashing, trying to dislodge Gwynn. Marriott, now kneeling on the ground under the hammock, shot one, and the others belatedly remembered him. While two turned to deal with Marriott, one struggled with a jammed gun. Gwynn shot his prisoner at point blank in the back, then aimed at one of the two turning, and shot him through the jaw. Marriott took the other down. Then Gwynn heard a gun go off again, and felt a hot, sharp shock in his right shoulder. The last Blood Ghost was still struggling with the jam. Gwynn fired, and heard Marriott shoot at the same time. The Blood Ghost jerked and dropped.

Examining his shoulder, Gwynn ascertained that he had a negligible half-inch graze and a ruined shirt. He straightened, dusted himself off, and looked back at Marriott.

Marriott looked unhappy.

"Sorry. That first one I got wasn't quite dead."

Gwynn picked up his dropped pistol, and shrugged. The pain was minimal and already easing. "Never mind, my friend," he said. "*Yche'ire faudhan bihat.* No one can kill all the people all the time."

Marriott gave a gruel-thin smile, then shook his head, and climbed back into the hammock.

Gwynn returned to his chair, and picked up his drink and paper—all three necessities of his repose having survived, unharmed and undisturbed, as though some invisible guardian of life's modest pleasures had protected them. He snapped his fingers, and the boys emerged from behind the awning, where they had been hiding, and presently resumed their work of stirring the air.

Gwynn sipped his drink, and breathed out a contemplative sigh. "Blood Ghosts! Have you ever heard of them?"

"No. You're the one who keeps up with social news."

"Probably just hired bums with a gimmick." Gwynn lit an Auto-da-fé and offered the packet to Marriott.

Marriott reached down and took one, and eyed the corpses. "Just blood and ghosts now, anyway." He spat on the ground.

Gwynn laughed, but Marriott didn't seem amused by his own joke.

The slow morning business had already resumed at the pens. The passers-by moved on. In a short while a band of urchins appeared, seemingly out of nowhere, and ran to the bodies. They worked efficiently. Within two minutes they had stripped the corpses completely naked. One of them had a wheelbarrow. They piled everything into it and ran off down the side of a shed.

That wasn't the end of it. Figures larger than the urchins now began making entrances. They walked with awkward gaits, and wore dark rags that completely hid their faces and bodies from the light and from anyone's view. Working in pairs and threes, they hauled the ten dead men away into nearby dark lanes.

One of them threw a coin at Gwynn's feet.

The scavengers were in every part of the city, he had learned. They weren't fussy—he'd seen them take the dead, the dying, the crippled—and no one who they took away was seen again. Some said they were ghouls, some that they were servants of black magicians, and others that the city authorities employed them.

No other incidents occurred that morning, and at midday Sharp Jasper and Elbows arrived to take their shift.

Elbows poked the toe of his boot into some of the blood on the ground. "Did we miss a party?" he said, looking a bit disappointed.

"You did," Gwynn said.

"So what happened?" Jasper asked. "Looks like you could have used some help," he added, pointing at Gwynn's sleeve.

Gwynn shrugged. "A disgruntled customer came by with some friends."

"What customer?" Elbows wanted to know.

Gwynn shrugged again. "Some boat boss from Phaience." He wasn't about to say he'd been shot by followers of a one-eared pimp.

"Yeah, who?" Jasper took up the question. "I've got cousins who run boats down there."

"We didn't exchange family histories," Gwynn said, folding his paper and rising to his feet. Stepping past Jasper, he clapped the dark man's shoulder. "It's too bad you missed the action, cannibal. You could have had a steaming hot fresh breakfast."

Whatever Jasper's riposte might have been, Marriott silenced it. He swung down from his hammock and strode past, with a terrible, bitter look on his face. He untethered his horse, swung into the saddle and departed at a canter, leaving Gwynn and the other two to stand uncomfortably, avoiding each other's eyes.

That night, Marriott sat at the Diamantene. Tareda Forever was singing, sheathed in a dress of tiny silver mirrors. It was weeks since he had taken interest in any amusement other than watching her. On nights when she didn't sing—nights when she belonged to Elm alone—black depression visited him. Tonight she was being minded by Tack and a spiky-haired junior called Kingscomb. Tack and Kingscomb sat together at a front table. Marriott had taken a seat well back, hoping they wouldn't see him.

He was trying to forget what had happened at the slave market.

Many times Tareda made a motion of embracing herself, as if by that delicate enclosure she held herself together. Marriott gave himself up to imagining how he might hold her. He wanted her to stop singing, look at him, and turn dream into truth. When she finished her set and was escorted backstage by Tack and Kingscomb, he lit up some joss of the strongly numbing kind.

Elm had never allotted him the task of minding her. Elm must have seen what he felt, right at the beginning. He wondered how long Elm would keep her. Surely it wouldn't be long before he tired of her, as he always did with his women. Then, perhaps, there would be an opportunity.

When he'd finished the joss he left the Diamantene by the back door and walked into the first brothel he saw. The madam brought girls out, and he chose the one who looked the least unlike Tareda.

Afterwards, as he rode through the amber-soaked night streets towards his lodgings, he brooded over his old predicament.

Because she is near but untouchable I suffer. But to leave this city and be unable to see her would be worse.

Wouldn't it?

I'm a weak man, he concluded for the millionth time.

What could he do? He could only stay put and hope and suffer. Who would think there was a kind of dignity or honour in that?

I'm a stupid man.

As he rode down a steep, quiet backstreet near the Burnt Bridge, absorbed in his misery, Marriott heard a sudden commotion behind him. He looked around and saw a cart careening into the street, taking the corner on two wheels. It looked as if it would capsize, but it righted itself and came flying down the hill. He hastily nudged his horse back against the houses.

The cart was flimsy, the load that swayed on top of it far too large and ill-balanced. The brake had obviously failed, and now the cart was gathering speed rapidly. A donkey, still harnessed to it, galloped madly in front, hopelessly trying to escape. The driver was teetering half off the seat, hauling on the reins with one hand, his other arm clutched around the brake lever. "*Clear the way!*" he screamed as the cart hurtled downhill. "*All clear the way!*" Part of the load fell as the cart bumped and slewed. The paper-wrapped parcels of goods broke open instantly, shattering with a volley of loud brittle bangs. Bright glass shards of all colours spilled down the street.

Marriott had a moment of vaguely wondering what sort of idiot piled a cart so precariously with glassware.

The cart ran past him, and as it did so it overtook the donkey. The poor animal went down under the front wheels, and the cart, as it hit the donkey, flipped over, pitching the driver off and launching the rest of the load into the air. Polychrome bombs exploded across the ground with crash after crash.

When the cascading noise surrendered to silence, Marriott rode out onto the street. He dismounted and cursorily examined the driver, then the donkey. Both were dead. A long stretch of the street was covered in scrambled millefiori brilliance. Marriott stared at this rainbow, to which there was no living witness but himself. He knew better than to dare believe it was a good sign.

As he rode on, he found that even his thoughts about Tareda could not completely drive the memory of the skirmish at the slave market from his mind. He saw, again, the Blood Ghost struggling with his jammed gun, and saw himself aim. Again he felt the spasm shake his hand at the moment when he squeezed the trigger, and he saw Gwynn flinch (and he imagined the bullet going a few inches to the right, through Gwynn's head). He saw himself shoot at a dead man, when he should have been shooting at the one still alive, and he heard himself tell the lie afterwards. He didn't think he had lied well, but Gwynn had believed him.

Marriott imagined telling Gwynn what had really happened, while knowing he was going to do no such thing.

He was going to make himself forget.

By the time Marriott arrived back at the rooms he rented in a lane off Lumen Street, he had nearly managed to convince himself that his lie was true, and that it was the Order of the Blood Ghost, and not himself, who owed Gwynn a new shirt.

But when he was unlacing his boots his right hand spasmed, and then kept trembling so badly that he had to finish undressing using only his left.

"Promise you won't tell anyone else?"

"You overestimate the interest this kind of thing has for most people. But I promise. Cross my heart."

It was the Croalday after the incident at the slave market. The Rev had drunk a lot and he was talking about esoteric secrets again. This time the potent Black Sack had loosened his tongue a great deal, and he had come to the point of telling Gwynn certain things that were supposed to be reserved for the ears of initiates.

"Try to listen with some kind of respect for the sanctity of what you're going to hear: God is infinite, and an infinite presence must logically contain all things, including all potentials. Therefore, God contains the potential for that-which-is-not-God. When God made the universe that potential became manifest. This manifestation of the not-divine, we call the infernal. Its nature is completely paradoxical. That, my son, is how phenomena which are not divine can exist in a divine universe."

Gwynn sipped his tea. "And that," he said, "is it?"

"Over your head?" The Rev looked pleased. "I'm not surprised. No doubt it's just as well. I shouldn't be speaking of such matters to an atheist."

"Well, you can be assured I shan't be telling another soul. But let's hypothetically suppose the theory is correct, for argument's sake. This 'infernal' would manifest as a fellow like me, for instance, would it?"

"Yes—"

"Excellent. Even in that scheme of things, I am what I would wish to be."

"—though only in your vices and crimes. Some part of you—perhaps even more than half—is quite perfect. You're a good candidate for redemption. Your wickedness is deep, but not broad."

Gwynn took a piece of the turtle and quince pie that was the main dish that day. "Could your god and this infernal be called enemies, then?"

"It's more complicated than that. God knew what was going to happen, of course. The divine has a plan for the infernal. Because all is of God and nothing of God can truly be destroyed, the infernal must instead be transmuted. It must realise its error, comprehend the illogicality of its existence, and choose to become part of the divine. When all is converted, that erroneous potential will no longer exist. Perfection will be achieved. We are all subjects, substances, in this greatest alchemy, the Great Work of God."

"Very stirring. And your hell, how does it fit into this efficient scheme?"

"Think of a potter taking a misshapen bowl from his wheel and pounding it back into the tub of clay. A soul suffers while it is being pounded in this way, and suffers until it ceases to be. You are pounded down, and that which was you gets put into something else. God tries again, and tries until the Work is complete. Meanwhile you, my son, are long gone."

"Beautiful," Gwynn said admiringly

"Beautiful?"

"Absolutely. Such a strange and tragic tale has to be beautiful."

The Rev snorted. "No doubt you think your mockery is sophisticated, but it's juvenile. Will you not try—will you not *dare* to question the foundations of your incredulity?"

Gwynn lifted an eyebrow. "I hardly think that I'm obliged to make efforts on behalf of your plans, Father."

"Fair enough," the Rev sighed grudgingly. He sought comfort in his bottle.

"Nevertheless, I should like to discuss this matter of your imaginary god's imaginary aberration, which he's going to such pains to eliminate. Am I correct in assuming that violence belongs in the province of this infernal?"

"Violence, cruelty and every kind of wickedness, my son," the Rev said in between swallows of his drink. "They are not part of divine nature. I'm sorry to disappoint you. I know you liked your notion of a vicious god."

Gwynn made a dismissive gesture with his knife. "I'd still vastly prefer no god. But I admit to being puzzled. Why is this particular cranny of your doctrine kept secret—don't you want your flock to believe that virtue alone is divine?"

The Rev shook his head emphatically. "The masses might accept it, but mischievous intellectuals would argue that it proves God to be imperfect and limited. They would seize on the idea of God toiling, God sweating out impurities, God striving for betterment, like any ordinary person—even of God being ill. It's happened before. It leads to dualism. People start thinking evil is a power in its own right, as strong as good. Can't have that."

"But even if we only consider the human species, it would appear that this little blot of the infernal easily rivals its divine progenitor in size."

"You are wicked, but don't let that cause you to underestimate the goodness of other men," the Rev lectured.

Ignoring him, Gwynn said, "And what of the overwhelming wickedness in nature? We don't know whether the beasts enjoy their cruelty as we enjoy ours; but even if theirs is less sophisticated, it's certainly abundant and varied. Animals display all types of viciousness, from the crocodile's simple brutality to the shrike who pecks open the skull of its prey and eats the living brain, to the ichneumon fly who deposits her eggs in the living caterpillars of other insects, where in due course they hatch and eat the caterpillars alive from within. Or, less cruel but certainly no saint, the female scuttle fly, born without wings or legs, who contrives to be nursed by ants throughout her life; her whole kind is compelled to an existence of deceit and sloth. And we should also include all the vectors of disease, which science now tells us are tiny animals."

Gwynn made this speech with enthusiasm for his subject. Having spent most of his life in lands where species were few, he was fascinated by the abundance of life in the tropics and kept up to date with the zoology journals in the library.

"Mischief," he concluded, "appears to be flourishing in the world."

"Are you quite finished? Because you've done nothing but show that you see the world with cack-eyed vision. You ignore the grandeur and tenderness in nature like an idiot jester playing with cockroaches in the corner of a great throne room; by your words you mar what has been made; it's an unworthy aim."

"Have you ever considered that your infernal can fight, and is winning, and has been winning for a long time?"

The Rev wasn't about to be sidetracked. "We can't know," he insisted, "the intentions of the infinite, the boundless." He drank deeply. "He has made everything beautiful in its time. How beautiful, you can't imagine."

That was the last coherent thing the Rev said before the drink, which had been quietly waiting in the backwaters of his blood, made a sudden all-out assault and overcame its host.

The Rev woke up the next day in a fancy hotel. His clothes had been cleaned and were laid out for him, and someone had thoughtfully left a packet of headache powders beside his bed. It was good that they had, because he needed to be at the hospital. Not that he thought the doctor or any of the nuns would particularly miss him if he failed to appear, but he knew for a fact that one of the female patients was dying, and he hated missing deaths.

When he got there she was still alive, though barely. She had no particular illness; she was merely old, and fading. He sat down by her bed and settled himself to watching her bony, still face.

How many times had he seen death? Thousands, certainly. At each of those times he'd looked for the same thing: something in the face, in the eyes, to tell him that the dying person beheld God. He had never yet seen this sign. Its perpetual absence disturbed him badly, so much that he'd lately taken to actually asking, quietly but fervently, as he did now:

"What do you see? What do you feel?"

"I see nothing," the woman rasped irritably, not opening her eyes. "I feel as tired as an old bone rolling around in the wind."

Guiltily, the Rev pressed on, "Don't you hear anything? Please, try and listen."

"I hear you babbling, priest," she groaned, "and it's a heavy burden to my ears. Be silent, or go away where I can't hear you."

"Sorry," muttered the Rev. He gave up and sat in silence by her bed, scrutinising her. There was nothing for him to see. As she was dying her eyes opened, but if they saw anything more numinous than the ceiling nothing in her countenance betrayed it. Another vigil wasted.

Looking around furtively to make sure there were no nuns to observe him—there weren't—he fished out his whisky flask from inside his jacket and took a hasty pull on it.

The Rev was well aware that most people were content either to be ignorant of what lay beyond the door of death, or to faithfully believe what his religion or another told them to believe. It was part of his guilt that he, though he argued the case of faith, had never actually possessed true faith at all. He had never needed it, for he'd always had certain knowledge of God—or so he'd believed at the time.

This was the point at which his thoughts always took hold of each other's tails and began to gnaw fractiously each upon the other.

In the Rev's memory—the veracity of which he had ceased to be certain—he had known God, felt God, heard God, had even seen God. The divine presence—or a phenomenon which had seemed to be a presence, and divine because of a greatness that far outstripped all greatness he had ever perceived in humankind or nature—had been beside, above, around and within him all his life.

He had never been without it, and therefore had only understood its enormity on the day it vanished. Its departure was abrupt, unheralded as the flight of a capricious lover.

The Rev knew no words with which he could have adequately described the presence itself. Its absence was the void, the heartache of lack and loss which was nameless but could most closely be described as a sense of exile, from which he had latterly come to believe all human beings suffered, whether they realised it or—like Gwynn—did not.

More than he spoke to the dying, even, the Rev had a habit of speaking to, or at, the dead. Their silence always made him want to talk. He addressed the dead woman now:

"Time steals from us the capacity to be smitten, does it not? It slowly but surely washes away all our enthusiasm and deposits uncertainty in its place. In my youth I was smitten with God, and went to preach divine love in the deserts. I had an enthusiasm for deserts. Every day I beheld God in the terrible sun, the scorched earth and scouring wind, and every night I beheld God in the fluctuating moon, the fires outside the tents and in the silence of sleep. But above all, I confess to you, madam, and I'm sorry if I offend your matronly ears, I beheld God in the women; their glorious bodies and gazelle eyes, their sweet and tempestuous tempers! Fasting, I had visions of a veil in the sky and understood that it hid beauty beyond beauty, sweetness beyond sweetness, tempest beyond tempest, infinite grace and glory!

"Ironically, it was because of a girl, in the end, that I lost God. The veil remained, but I could discern nothing behind it. That veil might have been all that there was or had ever been of holiness. When I close my eyes I still see that terrible veil!

"My soul longs for God, but a man is not just his soul, is he? Terrible to say, my clay lusts after the clay of nubile girls. To soothe my guilt, and please forgive my indelicacy, I've half convinced myself that I seek to find God again in their arms and their unmentionable places. Thank you, madam, for your attention."

He pulled the sheet over the dead woman's head. Then he went to the Yellow House.

Bad news awaited him. When he asked for Calila, the proprietress told him another man had bought her and taken her away for his private use. She suggested another girl, but the Rev felt cheated and robbed, and he lost all desire for pleasure. He went away, and sat under a naphtha flare on a stretch of rubbly ground where a row of houses on the riverbank had been demolished. He found bits of broken brick and tile around him, and tossed them one after another into the water.

When he was tired of that, he grew cocoons on the palms of his hands.

He never knew what would hatch when he did this. Often it was wasps; but he had also produced scarab beetles, scorpions and even hummingbirds. This time, when the cocoons split, it was large luna moths that emerged onto his palms, where they sat fluttering their diaphanous pale green wings. When their wings were dry they flew away and up, climbing quickly through the air. The Rev watched them. Although he didn't want to like them, he couldn't help but think how beautiful they were.

However, they were doomed. Attracted by the light shining above, the moths flew up to the iron cresset in which the flare burned. They circled it twice, then flew directly into the flame, expiring with two tiny pops.

Tears of frustration stung the Rev's eyes. Refusing to give up, he grew another two cocoons, from which hatched a pair of superb blue dragonflies.

They, too, ascended to the flame, and fell back to the ground as shrivelled black sticks of charcoal, like spent matches. Breathing heavily, the Rev made cocoons grow a third time. He got moths again, drab brown ones this time, hairy and not beautiful at all. The Rev tried to shoo them across the water, but they followed their predecessors straight up to the flare.

He gave up and made the wounds in his hands close, and shoved his knuckles in his mouth to stop himself from howling like a madman.

ELEVEN

THE WET SEASON arrived in Ashamoil, bringing air like hot glue, thunderstorms, and swarms of mosquitoes and midges, flies and cicadas. Moisture-trapped smoke and coal dust clotted the air above the Skamander and along the lower terraces; fabric rotted, plaster crumbled and metal rusted. The whole city sweltered, and stank of overflowing drains, every whiff an omen of dysentery and cholera.

The onset of the change in the year was traditionally a time for odd fashions, as people who had the means to distract themselves from the physical discomfort attempted to do so, trying to remove their minds from their suffering bodies. The previous year's fad had been for science, with many a kitchen being converted into a laboratory for the duration of the season. It followed that numerous souls had blown themselves up, suffocated in clouds of poison gas, started fires, and caught diseases from animals on which they were experimenting. As a reactionary consequence the present year witnessed a craze for a romanticised medieval past, saturated with magic, sans any technology whatsoever. A man called Durn Limment, who had made a large fortune in chemical dyestuffs, paint and ink, saw an opportunity to unite fantastic pageant with commerce, and commissioned Beth to create illustrations for a bestiary. It was to be an opulent limited edition—"a modern incunabulum," in Limment's words, printed in his inks and bound in leather coloured with his ultramarine and gold dyes. He had told Beth that she was at liberty to do as she liked with the pictures, as long as the work fully showed off his range of colours, and was completed quickly, to take advantage of the season's mood.

Gwynn was present to see the illustrations Beth began producing

169

for the book. It seemed to him that they partially organised her world of undecided-upon forms into something more codified. She grouped certain elements and gave names to the results: a beast with the body of an owl, wings of fire and the head of a laughing black child, she called Rambukul; to one with the body of a ship, the necks of nine swans and the heads of nine lilies she gave the name Lalgorma. The oddest thing she designed was a smooth red stone with a beard of white grass, which she named Ombelex. Though it seemed an inert thing, she depicted it locked up in a heavy cage. She also created interpretations of traditional monsters, including a new basilisk with a sharp-featured male face, a cobra-like hood made of peacock feathers, and a thorned tongue. The sphinx she drew was of the traditional lion-eagle-woman type, though it was whimsically playing with a glass fishing-float.

While occupied on this project, she kept up with the work that provided her regular income. In particular, she laboured long hours to meet a steadily growing demand for her erotic portraits. In these, her new lover's influence showed. She told Gwynn that as he was linear and monochromatic, he was ideally suited to the engraver's medium. Faces and figures in her work became sparer, their beauty more martial; they acquired something of their prototype's tranquil mien, and also something of the current of malice that could be observed in his habitual gestures and expressions. Their model said little about them, only offering aloof smiles when he and they faced each other. He understood the behaviour required of him in the role of her muse.

Her private art took an even more pronounced change in direction. Stating that the bestiary was satisfying her interest in extreme appearances, she ceased making the prodigious carnival images and commenced a series of dark-toned aquatints in which the ornate sensational jumble of the previous work was replaced by its near opposite. Within architectural enclosures, either oppressively narrow or oppressively vast, indistinct human figures stood in ones and twos. Partially hidden in shadow, or standing at a distance, they seemed caught on the verge of vanishing. In these scenes Gwynn received a sense of secret life, in an unrevealed world existing past the walls, hinted at by the furtiveness of the figures, or by some unfamiliar, intricate object lying in a street as if discarded.

Inevitably it became common knowledge in the Horn Fan that he had a new ladylove, one who was very easy on the eyes. The others needled him, wanting to know when they'd meet her. Only Marriott said nothing. He withdrew into himself more and more. Meanwhile Gwynn spent ever less time socialising with his colleagues and ever more alone with Beth. Sometimes he watched her at her work. She could turn herself from a creator of dreams into a machine of production. When he first saw her sweating over the base chores of the engraving process, from filing the edges of the metal plates to cleaning the bitumen and ink off them with lakes of turpentine and reams of paper, he asked why she did not take on an assistant. She replied that the manual labour exercised her body while allowing her mind and spirit to rest, adding that she believed there was value in the discipline of ordinariness, provided that it was only a discipline and not an unvarying state of being.

She, in turn, watched him train with his sword, which he often did for a short time in the mornings, directly after waking and washing. One day, she told him that she envied his martial skills. It was only under dangerous circumstances, she asserted, that anyone could find out their worth. He made a noncommittal reply, inwardly wondering what sort of circumstances would prove dangerous to her. In the uncouth places they frequented, it had never yet been necessary for him to protect her.

He felt unable to ask her why she had sought him out, but he often posed the question to himself. He understood that theirs was in certain ways an attraction of opposites that weren't truly complementaries. She had spoken a second time of voyaging abroad on a ship for years, going from port to port without stopping, or imagining an end. Whether she had meant to or not, she said "I" and not "we" when she talked thus of departing the Teleute Shelf. It wasn't hard to envision her travelling like that, on and on without fear, always seeking and finding new phenomena and yoking their essences to her invented worlds.

Made wary by Marriott's condition, Gwynn scrutinised his own temperament for signs of melancholia. He noted that he felt a slightly increased, vaguely poignant fondness for the romantic hours of dawn and twilight, and a marginally heightened sense of life's brevity and essential loneliness, but he was familiar with these mild symptoms from certain previous affairs, and therefore saw no reason to start fearing for his health—at least, not for the health of his mind. During the wet season, like everyone in the city, he feared physical sickness. The humidity succoured parasites and plagues, and corpse carts went around twice daily, picking up the dead to be dumped in the river, a practice which attracted scores of crocodiles. They learned the times when the carts came, and in the hour after sunrise and the hour after sunset the water along Ashamoil's quays filled up with hungry saurians. At these times small boats kept out to the middle of the river, away from the aggressive primeval traffic in the edgewaters. No boats whatsoever went near the feeding frenzies that occurred at the dumping spots.

Beth and Gwynn made twice-weekly excursions to the canal in the jungle. The atmosphere there was no less oppressive than that in the city, but it was cleaner. On one of these trips, on a day when the sky was completely covered in hot white clouds and musky-smelling steam filled the air, Beth sat in the prow of the caique, wearing an old shirt, rolled-up breeches and sandals, and even Gwynn had abandoned his usual sartorial standards and was in shirtsleeves, with his hair in a boatman's queue. A portable burner on the floor of the boat released fumes from a camphorous oil to repel mosquitoes. They had also brought a folding gauze shade with three sides and a roof, for protection both from heat and from insects, especially the large spiders that bred in the wet season and were not known to be the slightest bit offended by camphor or any other odour (that they were big enough to be easily shot was at best an ambiguous comfort).

In the middle of the day they stopped at a ghat and opened the shade out. There, while they idly played dice after lunch, Gwynn learned something more about Beth's fascination with the ocean.

"I've never been to the ocean, but I have a memory of flying there," she said. "I remember all the ships, and the curve of the horizon. I sat on a cliff, watching the port. Would you believe me if I said the memory doesn't seem like a dream?"

"I'd believe that; though if you insisted it actually wasn't a dream, my credulity might fail."

"Yes, I suppose it would have to, wouldn't it? I can't remember how old I was when I dreamed that. I was young. But before I dreamed it,

I was good, and afterwards I took to playing truant and telling lies. People were always finding fault with me, but it seemed they were angry with someone else. They were angry with the good child I'd been. They didn't understand that that child was dead, lost somewhere, and that another creature had woken up in her bed. I sometimes think that little girl went out on the ocean, and I'm the only part of her that stayed behind; conceivably, nothing more than a sediment of her memory or fancy, caught in the dustbin of a perpetual past. Or I'm something she met that agreed to swap places with her. Or perhaps I forced her to swap places."

"And which of those possibilities would you have as the truth, if you could choose?"

"The second to last, I think."

"Then you'd like to be a monster, but not a cruel one?"

"Not too cruel. A monster, not a brute. Do you know the story of the man and the heavy box?"

"I'm fairly sure I don't."

"A man acquires a small casket. In some versions he buys it, in other versions it's given to him as a reward for doing a good deed; it doesn't matter. The story really begins when the person who gives him the box tells him that the longer he keeps it without opening it, the more valuable the thing it contains will become. The man believes this, so he carries the box around for a few months. Gradually it gets heavier. Finally, one day, it's so heavy that he can't carry it anymore. He thinks about buying a donkey, but he realises the box will soon be too heavy even for a donkey to carry. One day he'll need a horse to carry it, and eventually an elephant, and by then he'll be an old man with no time left to enjoy whatever the box holds. He decides that the wisest thing to do is to open the box up."

"And what's in it?"

"An imp. He's always a buffoon who tells scurrilous jokes. At first the man is furious that he got nothing better from the box, but the imp turns out to be both cunning and kind, and in the end he helps the man to win the heart of a woman who he's had his eye on throughout the story. Of course, he'd hoped that he would find her in the box."

Gwynn guessed, "And he always wondered whether, if he'd left the box unopened for a little while longer, she would have been in it by then?"

"In some tellings, but usually he thinks he's done exactly the right thing, since he gets both the woman of his dreams and a useful friend in the imp. There's a rarer version where he finds out that the box only ever contained the imp, who would always lead him to his heart's desire, whatever that happened to be. Then he begins to regret having desired nothing more than a woman, and the story ends less happily."

"But you prefer that version?" Gwynn guessed again.

"I do, it's true. One of the old inland schools of philosophers asserted that that we always find our heart's desire. They admonished people to therefore be bold and desire great things."

"Did your philosophers ever mention what *they* wished for?"

"Never outright. They wished for power, but always used euphemisms."

Then she cried out: "Ha!" in triumph, because she had won the game. "I've told you a story; now you shall tell me one."

Gwynn agreed that this was fair, and asked what sort of story she would like to hear.

"The truth about you," she said. "What drew you so far away from your origin? What were you seeking?"

Lighting a cigarette, he inhaled slowly before beginning. "To live," he answered her. "My people have a saying that when a family isn't occupied with killing its enemies, it must kill something, so it kills itself. One night, in order not to be killed, I found it expedient to steal a dogsled and leave Falias. I was quite young. Before I'd gone far I met up with another boy, who became my friend. He and I followed sunrises as far as a small dukedom called Brumaya. Unfortunately, while we were sojourning there, war broke out. As it happened, my clan were the aggressors. I was recognised, arrested and put in the duke's prison under suspicion of being a spy.

"Naturally I tried to tell them that I wasn't very popular at home, and just as naturally they didn't believe me. Conveniently, my friend had managed not to get arrested, and he hired some people to help him rescue me. However, he'd had to sell nearly everything we owned to pay them. We were left with the clothes on our backs and a young hound pup of mine—so there were three mouths to feed. To avoid getting arrested again, or starving, we joined a mercenary army who were— you'll like the irony—contracted by the duke of Brumaya. So I was soon fighting my own people. I exacted enough revenge to satisfy even the pride of an adolescent boy. That was when I acquired this sword, too." Gwynn tapped Gol'achab's scabbard.

"Anyway, to cut a long story short, in Brumaya we had to sign with the army for three years. After that, various contracts took us south and west. When our three years were up, we'd come to the Copper Country. My friend called it quits and went his own way. I stayed. Things were good for a while, then not so good. Then they were terrible, and I was lucky to get out alive. Another friend helped me. Or perhaps I shouldn't call her a friend; she mightn't agree. A woman of high principles, though; that definitely."

He stopped. Beth was giving him a strange look.

No, not him, he realised. Something behind him.

"Gwynn . . . " she whispered. Whatever was there, she didn't sound afraid. The tone of her voice, and the way she was looking, evinced ad-miration, even awe. He felt a small, ridiculous pang of jealousy.

Slowly she lifted her hand and pointed at a place over his shoulder. "We have distinguished company."

Gwynn was about to say that while dramatic tension was all very well, clear communication also had its merits. But then he caught a whiff of the new arrival's smell, and his heart lurched in his chest.

Tiger.

Beth's face glowed.

By very careful degrees, Gwynn freed his right-hand pistol from its holster, and turned his head.

Through the transparent fabric of the shade, he saw the beast. It was no more than two yards away, sitting on a stone. Gwynn levelled the pistol at it. He was afraid of its strength, its sheer mass. He almost phys-ically itched to shoot it. He cocked the hammer back. Not to squeeze the trigger took all his self-control.

While he waited with his heart in his mouth, he sensed how calm Beth was.

Eventually the tiger moved. It came around the side of the shade, padded down the ghat and splashed heavily into the water. Rocked, the caique banged hard against the ghat's bottom platform.

Gwynn exhaled slowly. He eyed Beth. She was watching the black and gold head moving across the river.

"Thank you," she said.

He shrugged. "I don't think you'd have forgiven me."

She gave him one of her enigmatic looks, then held out the dice shaker. Sighing, he put his gun away.

He won the next game. Beth sportingly asked him what he wanted.

"I want to know the truth of why you don't fear that which merits fear," he replied, regarding her levelly.

"The answer's simple," she said. "You can't guess?"

"I'm a soldier, madam. I was taught to read everything in an opponent's eyes. First one learns to see intentions. Then one starts to see souls. People become brightly lit. Nobody can surprise you. That's the theory. But your quintessence is occult to me, I confess. If you were an enemy I'd have to start worrying. As it is, I'm intrigued."

"Well, perhaps I don't have a soul. Perhaps that was the part of me that went away on the night I had the dream of flying to the ocean. Perhaps the thing I am doesn't fear a tiger because it is much stronger than a tiger. And the tiger comprehends."

Her words didn't strike him as idle nonsense. Those senses of his that could pick up subtle things were sure of a great mystery behind her surface, like the unrevealed world in her new engravings.

"We should become wise when we're old." She looked past him into the jungle and the water. "We should become fathomless richness."

He held out the dice to her. "Another game?"

"Last one."

"All right."

They both cheated, and Beth won by a narrow margin. She said she had no more questions, but still insisted on a token of victory, so Gwynn wound a wreath of creepers, and crowned her with it. Then he knelt, and magnanimously offered her his throat.

When they came back into Ashamoil that night, Beth wanted to take a turn around the wharf fair, so after returning the caique to the hiring station they strolled the few blocks along the river towards the fair's torchlight and bunting.

Beth was delighted to find a new arrival, occupying a space near Modomo's shackle-draped podium. This attraction, which did not advertise itself under any name, was a middle-aged man, lying on his back on a small mattress, wearing only a loincloth. He was of average size, appeared sound in body, and he and his mattress were clean. His skin was nearly as light as Gwynn's, but had a pink tinge. His eyes were closed, his lips curved in a gentle smile.

He was freakish only in that a lotus was sticking up from his navel. It was a large, perfect flower, pale pink like the man himself.

Beth went up and examined the flower. The man didn't move. Beth stroked a petal.

"A shilling a tug," the man said, not opening his eyes. "If you can pull it out, you win a prize."

"What prize?"

"It doesn't matter," he said, "because you won't be able to pull it out. No one ever has, and no one ever will. But you can try, if you like."

Beth fished in a trouser pocket and found a shilling coin. The man took it from her and poked it under the mattress. Beth gripped the stalk of the lotus and pulled—without success. She tugged a second time with all her strength. But as the man had said, the flower would not come out. It seemed to have the roots of a mountain.

The man had a rather deep navel and it was impossible to see exactly how the lotus was attached to him. Beth stepped back.

"Gwynn, you try," she said.

Gwynn crossed his arms and looked down his nose at the lotus man. "No, thank you, my dear. This sort of exhibitionist fantasy isn't to my taste."

"Dour creature. You could cut it off. You'd enjoy that."

"It will grow back," the man interrupted. "The roots are inside me, and they will put out another flower."

"How long are the roots?" Beth asked.

The man let out a long, drowsy-sounding sigh. "Longer than you could conceive."

"Does it hurt?"

"No."

"Then why do you want it pulled out? It's rather beautiful. Don't you like it?"

"I do not dislike it. But most people share your companion's view; they find it distasteful. Except by my parents, I have never been loved."

"I think it really is growing in there," Beth said to Gwynn. "It doesn't feel glued."

"Put him in your bestiary," Gwynn suggested.

They walked on.

"You wouldn't even think about believing that it's actually growing in him, would you?"

"Indeed not, sweetheart," he said, not with full candour; but something in that moment made him want to set himself apart from her.

"You want too little from the world, Gwynn," she said, shaking her head.

Alone in his apartments, he contemplated the meaning of love.

Many as the moments were when he'd have liked to believe that what he and Beth felt for each other was true love, he knew it wasn't. It was not the emotion, or rather the situation, which he knew in Anvallic as *cariah*. Though he had quickly grown to like the speech of Ashamoil, which was essentially a skeleton of elegant Halacian grammar generously fleshed with the vocabulary of a dozen other tongues, it was his view that his native language offered more precise tools for defining certain concepts and emotional states, of which love happened to be one. In Beth's language he could, if he wished, say, "I love you." In Anvallic this phrase was impossible, for *cariah*, loving, had no form in the singular person, but could only be expressed in the plural. It was understood to be something that existed as a mutual sentiment or not at all, and it implied a voluntary blending of identities. When one person wished to affirm *cariah* with another, the expression most often used was, "We love as water loves water and fire loves fire."

To say precisely, "*I* love *you*," he would have needed to use *naithul*, which had the meaning of turning or leaning towards the object of the verb. It variously implied fond feelings, admiration, carnal desire or even fervent devotion, but held no implication of reciprocal sentiment.

Marriott's obsession with Tareda Forever was a case of *naithul* at its worst. Equals rarely used the term towards each other.

There was another word, *suhath,* denoting a person met at a cross-roads. The sense was of two travellers meeting, enjoying each other's company, then parting and moving on. Gwynn believed Beth and he were of this kind. He refrained from hoping for more, except for one thing: to understand her before they parted.

It had not escaped him that he was missing something obvious—that he was seeing the stripes but failing to recognise the tiger, as it were. For this reason he had made up his mind to visit Uncle Vanbutchell. This time he'd taken the precaution of making an appointment, to avoid a wasted excursion.

At the hour of Gwynn's appointment Uncle Vanbutchell came to an-swer his door looking like a very old, vague and kindly angel, wearing a gold smoking jacket over striped pyjamas, and a beaded brimless cap that was falling over his forehead. The alchemist welcomed Gwynn with warm familiarity and ushered him in, down a hall and into a dim den furnished with couches. Gwynn sat down on a couch next to a wall case displaying a collection of antique hookahs.

"It seems a long time since I last saw you," said Vanbutchell, folding his hands in his sleeves.

"You've had competition for my time, I'm afraid, Uncle."

"Now I'll be offended, if you're speaking of those lowlifes in the nightmarket!"

"I've been reduced to visiting them, when you've been visiting other planes of consciousness. And in all honesty, the last time wasn't bad at all. You should be careful not to let your game slip." As Vanbutchell looked deeply chagrined, Gwynn smiled. "No need to worry. Your rival is something else. Something that doesn't come in a bottle."

"Ah, a lady, is it? Or if not a lady, a boy?"

"Uncle," Gwynn shook his head and crossed his arms, "I'm not go-ing to tell you what it is. I'm only going to tell you that I require insight on an unclear matter. What can you sell me?"

"For the clarifying of perceptions," Vanbutchell said, going to a cabinet containing many small glass-fronted drawers, "it happens that

I have something quite good. Most fortunately for you, I can currently offer it at a reasonable price." He opened a drawer and took out a glass phial that he handed to Gwynn. "Its name is Seas of the Moon. A lovely name for a lovely little soup, in my opinion."

Holding the phial between his thumb and forefinger, Gwynn examined the liquid it contained. It was pale reddish brown, watery and slightly cloudy. "It gets you rather high, then, does it?" he inquired.

Vanbutchell beamed. "The hallucination's total. You'll trip the light fantastic."

Gwynn held the phial out for Vanbutchell to take back. "If I only wanted to go day-tripping I'd have said so. I'm looking for information, not illusions."

"Ah, no, no, you misunderstand!" Vanbutchell said in haste, holding his hands up in a placating gesture. "That tincture will take you to a vantage point from which you'll be able to see everything that you need to. It bypasses the illusion of linear time. I've used it on many an occasion, and can say I've never been disappointed. What it gives you is not so much insight as outsight," Vanbutchell chuckled at his own joke, "which is surely more useful to anyone but a mystic—and you, if I may be so forward as to make a personal comment, don't strike me as a mystic. However, for a rational and inquisitive bon viveur's purposes, it's just beautiful."

"When you flog it like that, I feel sceptical."

Vanbutchell spread his hands and spoke obligingly. "You know I don't expect anyone to buy a product without an introduction to it. What say you sample a little now, gratis?"

Gwynn turned the phial around in his fingers. "Any side effects?"

"None, though I wouldn't mix it with anything. And I can't vouch for your safety if you over-use it, of course. It can be taken straight, or diluted."

"All right, I'll try it. Put the kettle on, if you will, Uncle."

"Incomparable woman," Colonel Bright remarked approvingly. "Fine haunches!"

"Very fine, sir!" Corporal Join saluted.

"A goddess!" exclaimed the Rev.

"A star," smiled the astronomer.

"I'd trade Tareda for her," Elm commented with a wink.

Above a collar of green feathers, Tareda Forever's lush mouth pouted angrily. Her expression changed to a smile as she leaned forward and whispered, "What would *you* trade for her, Gwynn?"

He looked at the beast they were speaking of, a sphinx which prowled up and down on the beach in front of the hotel terrace where they were all sitting under a bamboo awning. Champagne, and white grapes in a crystal bowl, were on the table. Enamelled sky and sea stretched out to the horizon, where a line of steamships was visible.

"I think we're shortly about to find out," he answered.

Everyone at the table eyed the ships, which were crossing the sea very quickly.

While the others stayed at the table he went down to the beach. The sphinx stopped her pacing and padded along the shore towards him. Her breath was furnace-hot, and smelled of roses and freshly killed game. Her eyes were iron balls.

Then she turned and walked away a little distance. When he looked back at the sea the ships had put down anchor.

General Anforth, wearing a bright blue coat and even more gold braid than Colonel Bright, stepped down from the biggest ship and marched over the water, treading on top of the rolling waves like a saint. He held a leash, at the end of which was Marriott, naked, crawling over the water on hands and knees. Anforth stopped at the edge of the sand. Marriott strained at the leash, snarling and drooling.

"Heel!" Anforth snapped, and Marriott squatted down on the sand, looking up with mad, murderous eyes.

"I always knew I'd catch you, Gwynn," Anforth said. "It was only ever a matter of patience." He drew a sword.

Knowing how it was bound to end, Gwynn nevertheless gave it his best. While the sphinx engaged Marriott with riddles, he fought General Anforth. The old man's swordsmanship was incomparable; Gwynn, outclassed, dazzled, was cut and cut again. He felt no pain, only boundless humiliation.

The sphinx had better fortune. She bit Marriott's head off, and spat it out into the water, where it stayed afloat, bobbing up and down on the waves. Then she turned her attention to Anforth. She grabbed his shoulder with one huge, razor-clawed foot, pulled him to the ground and pinned him there with her weight. Anforth struggled to no avail: the sphinx extended the claws of her other forefoot and gutted him like a fish.

Gwynn wanted to applaud her, but when he tried to clap, he saw with surprise that Anforth had cut his right hand off. It lay at his feet, holding not Gol'achab but only a piece of red string, which disappeared into the stump of his wrist.

He fell down into the water, onto sharp shells that dug into his flesh. Beseeching, he looked up into the sphinx's blank iron eyes. The mingled sweet and pungent odour filled his nostrils. The monster growled deep in her chest. Gwynn saw that the iron eyes were only lids; there was a seam running horizontally through the centre of each, with tiny latches holding them shut. Putting out his last strength, he raised his left hand, straining his fingers towards the nearest latch.

Gwynn opened his eyes. He was disoriented for a moment, then the room at Vanbutchell's came into focus. He softly swore.

"Not good?" Vanbutchell asked, hovering. "Are you all right?"

"Fine."

He got up from the couch immediately and straightened his clothes. He noted that Vanbutchell had at least told the truth about there being no side effects. Or no immediate ones, anyway. There was nothing to tell him he'd been in a chemical haze for—he checked his watch—half an hour.

"It was deeper and truer than the common run of dreams, I trust?" Vanbutchell enquired.

"I'm not one to judge depth or truth," Gwynn said, tweaking a mutinous cuff into line.

"Be that as it may, can I interest you in further journeys to the lunar seas?"

With the vision gone, Gwynn's initial scepticism returned to him. He had hoped the drug's chemical eyes, looking into his memory, would be able to decode hidden aspects of Beth through those enigmatic images of her which his own eyes had observed, and recorded like scribes taking down dictation in a language they didn't know, syllable by mysterious syllable. However, as he recalled the vision, it acquired the aura of a sham. If it had lasted long enough for him to open the iron lids, he believed he would have been shown a lie.

"No, I don't think so. Just make it the usual. Four drachms will suffice."

"If you wish," Vanbutchell shrugged. He went and obtained a small bottle from the cabinet with the drawers. "May I ask, why do you like this one so much?"

"It assuages the fear of absolute truth," Gwynn said, and counted out payment. "Good night, Uncle."

"Ah, yes; it would do that. Good night, and sweet dreams," Vanbutchell said.

TWELVE

IN THE DIAMANTENE, a type of torch-eye beetle had found a habitat that suited it. On the floor, wherever you looked, pairs of little fiery red dots twinkled and darted. The effect was pretty to look at, but the smell of the beetles when stepped on was, unfortunately, putrid. To rid his establishment of them, Elm had introduced several yellow pythons, which were known to have a great appetite for beetles of all species. One of the pythons had climbed up Gwynn's chair, and Sharp Jasper enticed it to lap at the foam on a mug of beer, though all Gwynn's attempts to make it try a cigarette met with implacable resistance.

Elm had gathered his lieutenants at the club in order to make an announcement:

"Gentlemen, as you all know, my youngest son, Elei, has been staying this past year at my sister's household in Musenda. I'm pleased to tell you that this morning he arrived back here in Ashamoil. Tomorrow night, to welcome him, I will be holding a party at my villa."

Gwynn clapped with the others, while listening with only half an ear. Marriott, seated on his left, was fidgeting. It was one of Tareda's nights off, and without her there Marriott didn't seem to know what to do with himself other than drink like a fish. His eyes were bloodshot, his complexion the hue of pissed-upon snow, his expression haggard and desperate. He folded and unfolded his table napkin, loosened and tightened his cravat, picked his teeth with his fingernails and then his fingernails with his teeth; it was a pitiful spectacle. During the evening Gwynn had attempted to speak to him, but getting only monosyllables and tormented stares in reply, he had abandoned the effort. The others had simply ignored Marriott from the start, obviously not wishing to

184

be dragged down with a falling man. Even Elm had ignored him, which made Gwynn nervous, since Elm never ignored anything. Was Elm going to wait for Marriott to go completely mad?

Then he heard his name. "Gwynn, I want you to bring that lady of yours. I think you've been hiding her away for quite long enough."

"I certainly will if I can, but she may already have made other plans. She has a very independent nature," Gwynn said, innocently.

Elm leaned forwards, showing some tooth in his smile. "You don't think you could convince her that a night of wining, dining and dancing at my villa would be better amusement than socialising with the shit of this city at the riverside sumps?"

Gwynn made a suffering face. "Elm, she's a woman. I'm just the male of the species. I couldn't convince her that the sun rises in the east if she preferred it to rise in the west," he said, getting laughter from some of the others.

"Gwynn, you girl's blouse, what are you afraid of?" Elm mocked. "Do you think someone at this table will snatch her from you?" This drew louder mirth.

"If she should have the poor judgement to attach herself to any of these ugly lowlifes, I'd have to consider myself well rid of her," Gwynn answered with a lazy air. The others, except Marriott, started up a chorus of answering insults. The noise alarmed the python so much that it dropped down from Gwynn's chair and slithered under the next table (some would say, later, that they saw it sipping from the beer taps at the bar). Sharp Jasper challenged Gwynn to a contest of beauty and nobility, Tack and Snapper proposed a contest of strength, and Elbows fancied a reckoning of virility.

"Any time, you poor dogs," Gwynn smiled with equanimity.

"In that case, Gwynn, why not at the party?" The jeer came from Biscay the Chef.

"Why, Biscay, you rascal; do you intend to thrill my lady with an adventurous bit of accounting?"

"Financial acumen has been known to win the favours of many a sweet young body," the fat man said.

"Many a body must seem young in the dark of a whorehouse, and sweet to a man who must live with the aroma of his own sweating lard,

185

I dare say."

Biscay only threw back his head and laughed. "Sticks and stones! He throws sticks and stones at me!"

"All right, gentlemen, enough," said Elm. "Gwynn, bring her. Don't be selfish. Ornament my son's homecoming." Despite the playfulness of his speech, it held a tone of command.

Knowing he couldn't press it any further, Gwynn lifted his hands in a resigned gesture. "Whatever you wish, I shall naturally endeavour to do."

Later, reviewing the conversation in his head, he winced at how it had demeaned Beth. Yet there was no other way he could have spoken of her to his colleagues.

Beth answered his apologetic explanation of Elm's demand with laughter. "But I want to go! I believe the high life wouldn't disagree with me at all." She spun away from him to lean against the wheel of a press in the studio, striking an elegant pose. "I shall buy a gown tomorrow, and Rose Ragged shall go to the bad men's ball—" she sauntered back and slipped her arms around his waist—"with her black knight."

Eyeing his less than happy look, she returned an archly challenging one. "What are you afraid of?"

If he was to be honest, he no longer feared for her safety in the company of his fellows. Elm was right. He did fear losing her to one of the others.

"Of hearing that question one more time, for starters, my dear!" was the answer he gave.

Gwynn remembered little of the party. He assumed it had been an excessive debauch, as he was taken poorly for a full two days afterwards, but the details were somewhere down a dark drain, irretrievable except for a scant few that floated up like bubbles during his sickbed sojourn.

Nearly all these memories were of Beth. If Elm's son, who Gwynn couldn't recall in the slightest, had been the ostensible star of the party, Beth had been the actual star, outshining even Tareda Forever. She had transformed the men of the Horn Fan as even Tareda at her most tragic had never done. Gwynn's mind replayed, in flickering fashion, moments where each of his colleagues, in Beth's company, was entirely charming, noble in manner, gracious and thoughtful in speech. In one fragment of memory, he and Beth were embraced by Elm who said, apparently with utter sincerity: "Marry each other. I wish you only the best."

Of his own behaviour he could dredge up nothing; there wasn't a shred of recall to tell him whether he had partaken of the bizarre grace or not. He did remember that Marriott had not. He had a recollection of Marriott kneeling in a corner, clutching his head, weeping, "My hands shake, my hands shake, I can't look."

Gwynn found his thoughts going along unaccustomed lines: *To truly win her, what would I have to give up?*

By Croalday he was well enough to make his usual date with the Rev.

The Rev noticed that Gwynn was looking even paler than usual, and eating little. Abandoning the point he was arguing—he'd been making a dog's breakfast of it anyway—he poked his knife towards his adversary's almost untouched plate. "What's wrong? Are you sick?"

"Just a little tired."

"Well, you look sick to me. Come on, my son, what's the matter?"

Gwynn found himself speaking his thoughts: "It's conceivably a slight case of . . . " He trailed off as he hastily recovered his discretion, making a vague gesture in lieu of the unsaid word.

"Pox?" the Rev guessed. "My son, I hope you haven't been too coy to see a doctor!"

"Thank you, but I am in satisfactory health," Gwynn said. "I was going to say 'overwork'."

"No, you weren't," the Rev said, shaking his head. "I recognise the manner of a man who has suffered a mishap of intimacy. If not pox, then that lady of yours—the one you never talk about—you've got her pregnant? Well?"

"No."

"Then," the Rev pressed, "perhaps someone else has got her pregnant, and she's blaming you? Or is it simply that her lust's inexhaustible and you're feeling . . . wilted?" He jiggled a limp noodle on his fork for emphasis.

Gwynn suddenly lost his temper. "Joke at my expense as you wish, but speak of Beth with disrespect again, and I'll kill you, you old fool!"

The Rev let out a low whistle. "Dear me, dear me. Something's obviously amiss. You should understand my concern. You know I need you intact for my purposes, and therefore I'm interested in your health."

"I hope you don't imagine you're amusing me."

"I fear, my son, that I've never imagined I was your personal jester!"

Gwynn collected himself. He found his sense of humour again. "Isn't the position a reciprocal one? I leaven your bleak existence, do I not, Father? And we both get to ham it up a little . . . " He lit an Auto-da-fé, inhaled deeply and blew smoke rings at the Rev.

"You know what I think?" said the Rev. "I think you're lovesick. Or, rather, you fancy yourself so."

"If I am, what of it?"

The Rev did his trick of producing a cigarette and matches out of nowhere. He blew smoke rings back, and sent one of his through the centre of one of Gwynn's. "My son, believe me, there's not a chance you're in love. There are men who are capable of love—true, earnest and profound love—and men who simply are not, and never can be. It's unthinkable that a fellow like you could be anything but the latter."

"Specious words—I doubt you really believe them."

"Then, pray, suggest what I do believe?"

"The opposite. But I'd hazard that you're jealous. You don't want me to be happy. You would prefer to imagine that I suffer, in order to feel reassured that you're not alone in doing so. Well, Father?"

After a moment of self-interrogation, the Rev concluded that it was indeed a spirit of jealousy and malice that had taken hold of him. He also concluded that he didn't care. If Gwynn was a friend, he was equally an enemy; one whom fate should have made to suffer, but instead had treated with unfair generosity. The Rev thought of all his own lost loves, from God to Calila, and interest in saving either Gwynn's soul or his own slipped away from him as the vindictive spirit strengthened its grip. He couldn't stop himself from speaking further mischievous words.

"You hurt me—and when I'm making such an effort to see things from your side! I'm only thinking that a man like you, a man of the world, a boulevardier, surely must enjoy life while absolutely forbidding it to enjoy him. Haven't you proofed yourself from sentiment, mutilated your soul to protect your vanity? How then can you imagine yourself in a love-swoon? Whatever's wrong with you, a case of love it surely isn't!"

Gwynn's mien became thoughtful. In a tone of rare gentleness and rarer candour he said, "Do you think so? I hear you appealing to a perverse pride, which you seem to think me ruled by, striving to tempt me into denying my better sensibilities. By doing so, you're slipping badly. Even I can see it. Do you want to cut your own throat for the mere sake of scoring a cheap and spiteful point against me, and do you really think I'll let you score it, when I'm now the one with something worthwhile at stake?"

With even more dignity he continued, "I find the rarest enjoyment and challenge in Beth's company. She kindles in me a far from ordinary flame. I believe I'd never tire of being with her. And while it would be unwise to hope that we have a future in common, only a fool would allow that to forbid happiness in the present. I won't dishonour her by being anything less than sincere in what I say about her. However my thoughts may err, they will not be mocking. When she is the subject, you will find me completely serious."

The Rev hung his head. His moment of malice was over. He was equally ashamed and bewildered. Yet from the confusion a sense of wonderment grew, as he realised that he had at last struck a telling blow. How paradoxical and ironic it was, that in his outburst of spleen, his moment of failure, he had driven out into the open something which had been deeply buried in his adversary. His clumsy barb had found an undefended place and sunk in deep enough to draw a drop of virtue.

"I'm sorry," the Rev said, raising his eyes. "Will you forgive me?"

"Either nothing can be forgiven or there's nothing to forgive. I've said words to that effect many times, but as far as I know, no one has ever listened."

After several minutes that passed in silence, the Rev spoke again. He had returned to his old form. "My son, your affection for this lady is only a symptom of your real longing for union with God, it goes without saying. But I've made progress with you! Yes, I have. I'm winning now, because you admit to feeling this true and profound affection, and long for some kind of decent life with your beloved."

"You misunderstand me entirely, as usual, if you believe decency is what I long for."

"To hell with decent, then; it doesn't matter. Some kind of life with her. As God is my witness, I'm winning!" The Rev thumped the table, making all the dishes rattle.

"Believe what you wish. It matters nothing to me."

"Then I believe I've won this round, whether you concede it or not."

"I do not concede it. But it was an interesting round. Therefore you have my thanks. But, as I said, I am tired. I am going to bid you good-night." Gwynn left payment for his meal, and pushed his chair out. With a nod to the Rev, he got up and left.

Outside, Gwynn whistled softly as he swung onto his horse, and set off along the street at a trot.

He felt a flower of delight unfurling silently inside him. This sensation had begun as he spoke of the sincerity of his feelings for Beth.

"Whether you've won anything or not, Father, I undoubtedly have won something," he thought aloud.

The small instrument—resembling a miniature, delicate pickaxe—went easily into the eye socket of the young man lying prone on the demonstration table. The tall, spry man calling himself Doctor Lone gave a deft twist of his wrist, then pulled the little pick out. His patient's displaced eyeball returned to its rightful position.

"There, ladies and gentlemen!" Doctor Lone addressed the audience packed into the new brick hall of the Society for Civic Hygiene. "With the smallest expenditure of money, time and effort, our wolf is made into a lamb! When he wakes up, no longer will he feel the urge to beat, rape, kill or otherwise abuse or injure any human being! Your venerable mothers, your tender daughters, no longer need fear him in the night. He is meek. He is mild. Should you wish to see the proof of this, return tomorrow; he will be awake, and fit to be examined and tested by any of your good selves!"

Lone raised his hands to quiet the ensuing applause. "Ladies and gentlemen, we stand poised on the brink of a new, humane era. No longer will any such as this man, poor victims of their own worst nature, crowd in prisons and asylums. Never more will they menace orderly persons! Nor will these former criminals and lunatics, in their new state of peace, burden the hardworking man and woman, for they will labour as reliably as oxen at the simple and menial tasks for which we currently employ weak children and dangerous savages. In a nutshell— a golden nutshell with a marvel for a kernel, ladies and gentlemen—evil shall be turned to good, and most efficiently."

Raule, standing towards the back with the general public—the front seats being taken up by members of the Society, among whom were several physicians of the College, sombrely conspicuous in black gowns—half-listened to the spiel.

Early on in her time as the doctor of Limewood she had conscientiously made an effort to keep up with medical advances, reading journals and attending public lectures when she could find the time to. However, the volume of quackery had been so gross, and that of useful science so miniscule, that after a few months she had stopped bothering. She had only responded to Doctor Lone's advertising poster out of ghoulish curiosity.

"Now, to all of you, my esteemed colleagues in our great human search for a perfect world, it is my honour to present examples of what you will see tomorrow. My daughter Opal will show them to you now!"

A well-groomed teenager came forward, leading a group of six men and women onto the stage. Lone announced that these were former patients on whom he had performed the same operation. All, he claimed, had been violent, insane or deeply troubled. Now, in front of the audience, the personalities they exhibited were, all alike, stolid and slow. Lone slapped one of the men; the man cringed. He shouted at a young woman; she returned a dull stare. Meanwhile, Lone's daughter carried tubs of potatoes onto the stage. She set them in front of the six, and handed out peelers.

"All of you, peel the potatoes!" Doctor Lone ordered. His patients all squatted down and began doing so obediently.

At this point Raule turned and left, her scientific curiosity having found a natural limit. She did not care to know how the young man whose brain had just been sliced up inside his skull would fare. She rode on the mule through warm drizzle, back to the hospital, to do her afternoon rounds of the wards. The hospital was busy, as it always was in the wet. Unsanitary Limewood was an especially fertile incubator of disease, and the wards were full of the old, the young, the weak, the tired and the plain unlucky who had succumbed to fevers and infections.

On her way back she happened to notice a boy and a girl embracing in a doorway. The girl she didn't know, but the boy was Jacope Vargey. Raule felt a little regret.

THIRTEEN

THE USURER'S HEAD near the wharf fair was crowded with drinkers as usual, and by midnight was getting rowdy. The clientele were mostly night-shift workers, and traders and performers from the fair. Hart, Modomo and huge Palee were at a table, sharing a tureen of food. Also there were Gwynn, Biscay, Elbows, Kingscomb and another junior, newish to the Horn Fan, called Whelt. They were at the Usurer's Head because Biscay liked the place. The fat figures-man had announced that he needed money, and suggested cards. Unfortunately, luck wasn't with him; instead it was with Whelt, who seemed unable to lose. A small, talkative, excitable youth, he became more voluble as his pile of cash grew. The drinking at the table was heavy. Elbows brought out a pipe, started chasing the dragon, and was soon losing almost as badly as Biscay. Gwynn, for his part, kept reasonably sober and played tight, resigning himself to the fact that it was simply someone else's night.

But as the early hours of the morning turned, so did Fortune's wheel. Whelt and Kingscomb went out to relieve themselves, and when they returned indoors Whelt started losing. Kingscomb joked that he'd pissed his luck away. Biscay ruthlessly took advantage, and soon recouped his losses. As Whelt came to the bottom of his money, Biscay offered to loan him some more.

"Have a care, he isn't friendly," Gwynn warned the junior. He shrugged in reply to the dirty look Biscay threw him. Whelt declined Biscay's offer, and sat out the rest of the game.

From then on Biscay won monotonously. Gwynn watched the fat man, sure he was cheating, but couldn't catch him out. Elbows ascended to paradise on the dragon's wings, careless of how much money he was losing, while Kingscomb looked ready to explode with fury, and Whelt just looked pathetically sorry for himself. Gwynn almost sighed with relief when the bartender called for last drinks.

He had begun to doubt the veracity of his memories from the party. Since that night none of his colleagues had mentioned Beth, and moreover none of the effect she'd seemed to have on them had lingered in any way.

The next evening, while he and Beth were having night caps in the bar on the Blue Bridge, he broached the subject.

"Any memories of that party are bound to be less than reliable, I think. I certainly don't trust mine," she said. "But there is a theory that the world is not truly one place, shared by all people, but has a manifold form—a world for every person—and that like liquids, all our worlds pass through each other when they meet, though unlike liquids their substances are as easily separated as mingled. Perhaps something of that sort occurred."

"You give this theory credence?"

"I find it appealing. And that which appeals to us, we tend to believe in, yes?"

Gwynn thought the idea interesting, but was indifferent as to its possible merit. Truly, it was somewhat as if a world imbued with her particular enchantment had met with and overpowered a world shared by the Horn Fan's members, and had then swiftly withdrawn. But as she said, the memories of the encounter couldn't be relied upon.

One thing, though, was certain: he was undergoing a change. He felt different, even when he wasn't thinking about her. He didn't pretend to entirely understand the alteration; he assumed he would understand it when time had passed and he could look back. He had no doubt that Beth would change him further, if he allowed it; how much further, or how permanently, he couldn't guess.

He did not seriously consider retreating. The idea of something transforming him remained a seductive one. It appealed, he realised, to his antipathy towards absolutes and permanent things.

This, it turned out, was the last philosophical thinking Gwynn did for a while. Work, which had been so agreeably uneventful, returned to the main stage of his life with a vengeance.

He had been working a graveyard shift, overseeing the loading of a cargo of weapons for the Colonel, and was still asleep at mid-morning. The noise of someone shouting and banging on his door woke him up. It was Kingscomb. He wore the look of a man who had been forced to eat live spiders.

"The *Golden Flamingo*'s been impounded. The boss is in a hell of a mood. There's a meeting at the villa, right now."

Gwynn swore a weary oath and told Kingscomb to wait while he got dressed.

"Hurry, then."

"Who else do you have to get?"

"Marriott, Elbows and Jasper."

Gwynn dragged clothes on and jammed a hat over his sleep-tousled hair. Preceded by Kingscomb, he jogged down the stairs and out to the stable, fastening his gunbelt as he went.

It had been raining, and the sun burned through oyster-coloured clouds that hung low, obscuring the upper city. Steam rose off the wet pavements, drifting up to re-join the clouds. Leaves, mud and dead cicadas lay in the gutters. As Gwynn rode through the streets with Kingscomb, he asked for details. Kingscomb seemed to know very few.

"The ship was boarded when it came in this morning. Afterwards there was some sort of coup at Customs and Excise. The sonofabitch who took the *Flamingo* is the new Superintendent now."

"Who is he?"

"Udo Nanid."

Gwynn didn't know the name, not that there was any reason why he should.

They went around to raise the other three, who were all at home, it being morning and none of them skylarks. While they rode through the streets, Gwynn kept an eye on Kingscomb. Something in the younger man's manner struck him as surreptitious, as though Kingscomb wasn't telling him everything, a thought which made Gwynn's nerves tighten. Elm's mood would certainly be inclement this morning, and Elm in an inclement mood was capable of suspecting anyone of anything. Gwynn didn't relish the thought of an interrogation before breakfast. He allowed that Kingscomb's furtive air might be due to the same apprehension.

An hour later the senior cavaliers and the higher-ranking juniors were all assembled at Elm's villa on Palmetum Terrace, in a long, windowless mahogany room used for meetings. Elei was present, seated next to his father, in a black and silver coat, with brand new pistols and crossed bandoliers. At fourteen, the boy had a delicate air which the swashbuckling outfit only accentuated.

Elm began by glaring down the polished table at his cohorts. When he spoke, his voice was calm enough.

"Gentlemen, some time last night our ship the *Golden Flamingo* was attacked, disabled and boarded by a customs squad under the supervision of one Udo Nanid. The second hold was opened, the cargo therein confiscated and the crew arrested. At five o'clock this morning, our friend the Superintendent of Customs was arrested on charges of corruption. At six o'clock Nanid was sworn in as the new Superintendent. At seven o'clock a notice was delivered to my hands, giving me the news that Mr Nanid intends to make his first task a thorough investigation and audit of the Society of the Horn Fan. At seven thirty I read all about it in the papers."

Elm paused—perhaps allowing time, it crossed Gwynn's mind, for the facts to sink into the denser skulls present. He sipped from a glass at his elbow, then continued. "Since this is all over the front pages, the option of killing Nanid is sadly closed to us, at least as an immediate course of action. Blackmail is unfortunately another closed avenue. The bastard appears to be clean-living, and we don't have time to set anything up. Even were he open to an honourable arrangement, which is unlikely, to offer one at this juncture would make us appear weak. This is the kind of thing I've always tried to avoid, gentlemen." Elm bared his teeth in a chilling smile. "Have I slackened the reins too much, perhaps? Allowed you all to take my money for not doing very much at all, when I should have been requiring you to keep constant vigilance?"

No one seemed very interested in answering the question.

"Among you lazy dogs there's obviously a busy rat. I shall find out who that man is, and he will die. As for the rest of you, you will not be lazy anymore. In these comfortable times, we don't challenge ourselves enough. It's a failing of the modern citizen and no doubt it will prove his downfall. There should come a time in every man's life when he must step into the fire and either be burnt to ash or forged into a stronger man. I've decided to make that step now, and therefore so will all of you. I'll put my faith in you and you'll prove yourselves to me, or die trying."

"Boss, what are you saying?" It was Jasper who dared speak.

"I say that I have extended a hand of enmity. You will all be tried by ordeal. Thank providence for quaint old traditions. I've already sent word of our intent to the Customs Office. I expect an affirmative reply soon."

"What are the terms?" Biscay asked.

"One of us to three of them, on Memorial Bridge. Testing odds, I know. Nanid mustn't be tempted to refuse. Gentlemen, you will prove yourselves with a victory so splendid that the tax collectors will not bother us again, or you will go to your graves in the attempt. And, with you, so will I. You are mine; how can I not take some of the blame for your failings?"

A mood of stillness settled over the Horn Fan's cavaliers. All were aware of the antique custom in the city, dating from before the rule of legal courts. From time to time over the centuries, Memorial Bridge had been to Ashamoil's grandees what the Orchard was to the Limewood gangs. Anyone with a dispute, and with enough finances to pay the large fee required by the municipal authorities, was entitled to challenge their opposition to a trial by combat on the bridge's span. The birth of the tradition was lost in distant history, along with the bridge's original name, its present title being a reference to the huge effigies of ancient heroes erected along its parapets. It was a full fifty years since the last fight, but the by-laws had not been changed. If Nanid refused the challenge, he would be obliged to drop the charge of smuggling and discontinue all investigations stemming from it.

"This Nanid animal is bold. I doubt he will decline," Elm said. "Perhaps he hopes I will pursue this course. Let him be broken upon that hope, then. We are going to war. Prepare yourselves. Dismissed."

All rose from the table and exited the room in silence. As Gwynn walked out through the villa's marble corridors with his fellows, he studied their faces. He saw some stoic expressions, and some happy.

Not one man looked discontent or afraid. It was only in himself that he could discern the emotions he was looking for in the others.

Particularly, he observed Kingscomb. Throughout Elm's speech the spiky-haired junior had been wearing a faint smile, and he was still wearing it now. Gwynn couldn't shake the feeling of there being something odd, and decided to act on his gut instinct.

As they emerged into the garden, he fell in with Marriott, Jasper and Elbows. All three—even Marriott—looked alert and bright-eyed. Gwynn remembered that long ago Marriott had enjoyed being a soldier in a real army, far more so than he had himself.

The men all rode down from the villa in a group. Presently Gwynn left the others, discreetly following Kingscomb, who was riding some way ahead. Kingscomb took a straight route downhill, into the lower city. The tighter quarters forced Gwynn to close the gap or risk losing his quarry in the bends of the streets. He was taken past the Corinthian, so he jumped off his horse and threw the reins to the bathhouse porter, and continued on foot with the morning crowds to hide him.

Kingscomb eventually rode into a street in a run-down area near the Prison Bridge, not very far from Feni's, where he went into a dingy brick building with a sign advertising rooms for rent. Entering half a minute later, Gwynn found himself in a lobby that smelled of mice. Behind the concierge's desk, a female dwarf perched in an infant's wooden high-chair.

"The man who just came in, where did he go?" Gwynn put coins down on the chair's tray.

"Second floor, room twelve," the dwarf said.

"The key."

"He took the spare." She pointed to a door behind Gwynn. "Stairs in there. Don't leave *mess*, or *bodies*. Janitor *hates* bodies."

Gwynn went up to the second floor and turned left into a wooden corridor. Hearing sounds of violent contest, he hurried. The noise was coming out of twelve.

Gwynn found the door unlocked, and kicked it open. On the floor of an untidy room, Kingscomb and Whelt were grappling. Kingscomb had a gun, which Whelt was trying to push away from his face. At the crash of the door, they sprang apart; Kingscomb fired, the shot going through the floor. The next instant, Gwynn shot the gun out of Kingscomb's hand.

Kingscomb froze and stared at Gwynn in the doorway, appalled. Whelt started to giggle hysterically.

Then swift footsteps came along the corridor. Gwynn slid sideways into the room, turning his head to see who was coming.

It was Sharp Jasper and Elbows. They stopped in the doorway. They, too, had weapons out. Elbows waved his in Gwynn's direction.

"What the fuck," said Gwynn, "are you two doing?"

"We thought you were looking strange, Gwynn, so we followed you," Jasper said.

Gwynn lifted an eyebrow, very slowly.

"So what the fuck are *you* doing?" Elbows said.

"Following him," Gwynn nodded towards Kingscomb, "because he was looking strange." He smiled. "And I thought today was going to be devoid of all amusement."

Elbows lowered the gun. He rubbed his nose. "Sorry," he said.

"Forget about it," Gwynn shrugged.

"What was he doing?"

"Trying to kill Whelt."

Kingscomb started to speak.

"Shut up!" Elbows barked.

"Who spoke for him?" Jasper wanted to know. Elbows grunted in reply.

"Oh. Well, shouldn't you take care of this, then?"

"I know his mother," said Elbows. "I promised her I'd look after him. I can't go back on my word."

"Shit on that," said Jasper.

"It's all right." Gwynn walked up to Kingscomb and Whelt, and ordered them to kneel with their heads down. As they complied, Whelt, who had stopped laughing, started to scream. Gwynn hit him hard on the back of the skull with the butt of his pistol, rendering him unconscious and silent, and a second later did the same to Kingscomb. "Call it my good deed for the day," he said, walking past Elbows.

"You're a decent man, Gwynn," Elbows said.

"Shit on that," said Gwynn.

The launch's propellers churned the stagnant water in the bayou. Gwynn brought the boat to a stop. Leaning against the wheel, he had a cigarette while he watched the afternoon sun glistening on the water. Over the simmering of the engine and the opera of birdcalls in the jungle canopy, the splashes off the bow came faintly to his ears. Presently Elm came past the wheel room.

"Take us home," he ordered.

Gwynn turned the launch around, letting the bayou return to its boggy pastoral peace.

Whelt's testimony was thus: when he and Kingscomb had gone outside to make use of the gutter during the gambling at the Usurer's Head, he had asked Kingscomb how Elm got so many slaves past the nose of the customs authorities, and Kingscomb had told him about the *Flamingo*'s second hold—a fact about which Whelt, being new, hadn't yet been informed. Whelt swore that he didn't pass the information to Nanid, insisting a third party must have overheard. He avowed that Kingscomb, not trusting him to keep quiet about the slip-up if he was questioned, had been trying to silence him when Gwynn appeared. Kingscomb, when interrogated separately, had naturally protested his innocence, saying the fight with Whelt was something private, over a woman. The woman was found, and said yes, she had been seeing both men, Whelt behind Kingscomb's back; but this meant little, as even if her story was true, it didn't prove that Kingscomb's was. And there remained the question of how Whelt knew about the second hold, if Kingscomb hadn't told him.

It was Sharp Jasper who suggested that a soothsayer be consulted, and Gwynn who vouched for the abilities of the hag at the nightmarket.

Elm agreed to it, and the hag was duly brought to the villa.

Kingscomb and Whelt were shown to her. She examined them both by staring into their eyes, sniffing their palms, and licking their fingertips. After carrying out these procedures, she announced that both men were guilty of stupidity and verbal incontinence. But she pronounced Whelt to be an honest idiot, and Kingscomb the liar. There had indeed been a third party who was within earshot, and who had passed the information to Nanid.

Elm asked her who this third party was.

"You are not fated to know that, my lord," she said.

She resisted all Elm's attempts to get the information out of her. Finally Elm lost his temper, and cut her throat himself.

He gave his men orders to find the third party, after they had made the trip up the river to dispose of Kingscomb, and Whelt, whose honesty had not moved a disgusted Elm to spare him.

Half an hour after the launch left the bayou, Elm came back to the wheel room door. His manner was easy, almost amicable, but his words were strange:

"Gwynn, last night, before all this, I had a vision of an albino crocodile. The beast spoke to me and told me there can be no glory without sacrifice. What do you think?"

Gwynn recognised the Rev's words and felt a sense of vertigo. He opened his mouth to agree, which seemed to him the wisest thing to do, but before he spoke Elm cut in, shaking his head. "You're not the one I should be asking. Some fighting men are like short-lived flowers, others are like weeds that no one can uproot. You're one of the weeds. You don't believe in sacrifice, do you?"

"It is merely an opinion," Gwynn said cautiously, "but I believe the mindset which demands sacrifice is essentially tragic in its type of nobility. Tragedy finds glory in losing bravely, but loss is still the outcome. Comedy finds glory in a happy victory. I prefer comedy."

Elm laughed. "When you put it like that, so do I, most certainly." He slapped Gwynn on the back, then walked out of the wheel room, leaving Gwynn to wonder.

The Customs Office's reply arrived. It was an acceptance. The contest on Memorial Bridge would take place in three days' time, on Sornday.

The response was an enthusiasm that Gwynn could work out no reason for. Most ludicrous in his view was Elbows. Having spoken for Kingscomb, Elbows had lost face. Now he swore to redeem himself in battle.

Gwynn wondered whether Beth had, after all, created a lasting effect on his colleagues. Was their odd mood of heroism something that had been lying latent since the party? But Marriott, he remembered, had been unhappy at the party—and Marriott was now in better spirits than Gwynn had seen him show for a long time.

In the end, he asked Jasper.

"Why am I happy?" Jasper drew his head back, looking astonished. "We're going to go out and kill the tax collectors, and you're *not* happy?"

"I would be happier if the odds stood a little more in our favour," Gwynn said.

Jasper punched him lightly on the shoulder. "Better get your balls out of hock," he chuckled.

Word came that the Customs Office would have help from allies in order to boost its numbers to the needed size. Gwynn wondered if the Astute Trading Co. or the Golden Square Society would betray the Horn Fan, or if Five Winds might rise from the grave. But apparently the Customs Office had been joined by assorted anti-slaving groups. It was an odd alliance, since the city made a lot of money from taxes on slaves, and in no way did its authorities want the trade stopped; but war often brought strange bedfellows together.

Evening had come, inauspicious, armoured in brass clouds. Raule was eating a meal of rice in her office when one of the young novices came to her door to tell her, "There's a man outside, ma'am, asking to see you. He says you and he are acquainted." The girl wore a look of doubt. "He wears the apparel of an undertaker . . . "

Raule hadn't so much as exchanged a greeting with Gwynn since the night when Scarletino Quai killed Bellor Vargey. She'd avoided him, and he'd never come seeking her out. Having read about the Horn Fan's upcoming battle with the Customs Office in the papers, Raule guessed this visit had something to do with that. She was tempted to tell the novice to send him away. However, it was unlikely that he'd accept an offhand dismissal; and besides, if she was honest, she had to admit to a modicum of curiosity.

"He'll behave himself. Let him in."

"Yes, ma'am." The girl was too well-schooled to speak with anything but deference, but her look made it obvious that she thought the visitor to be a man whom the doctor had no business knowing. Stiff-backed, she went out. Shortly Gwynn presented himself at Raule's door.

"Doctor," he greeted her with a slight formal bow.

"Slaver's henchman," she greeted him in reply.

He sighed. "Do we have to?"

"No, but I like to. Sit down." There was a chair by the window. Gwynn sat and lit up a cigarette. Raule seated herself behind her desk.

"Shall I guess," she said, "that this is about the casualties you're expecting on Sornday?"

"It is. I don't have to tell you that most doctors in this city don't know battlefield surgery from a dog's hindquarters."

"Insulting my enemies won't get me on your side. You work for a filthy cause, Gwynn."

Gwynn spread his hands wide. "I'm certainly not suggesting that you side with us, only asking whether you'd consider treating wounded here. Memorial Bridge is close enough that they could easily be transported."

"No doubt. But this hospital is for the parishioners of Limewood. I have a copy of the parish registry. If any of your men are on it, they'll be most welcome to a bed."

Gwynn leaned forward a little. "Speaking of beds, I couldn't help noticing the wards as I came in. This place looks rather in need of a cash injection."

"An injection of what size?"

"Ten thousand florins or thereabouts, I'd say."

Raule felt she might be going to laugh. "I could almost be touched that your boss cares so much about his bully-boys."

Gwynn shrugged his shoulders. "Good staff are hard to come by. I've told him that if lives need saving, you're the best person for the job. He's willing to make a donation to this hospital in return for a guarantee of your help. I took the liberty of saying you probably wouldn't accept a personal bribe."

Raule picked up a pen and tapped the end of it on her desk. Then she shook her head. "I have to confess, when I think of you all lined up and charging at each other on a bridge, I wonder whether the predictable result mightn't be rather good for this city."

"You're entitled to your views," Gwynn said mildly. "Believe it or not, even though you've clearly lost all respect and affection for me, I haven't lost any of my regard for you. Perhaps you'd be blunt enough to answer that you deserve respect, while I don't. Nevertheless, remember that I'm offering you money you could use to help the people in this wretched place."

"You know it isn't that simple."

"You make it complicated."

Gwynn caught sight of a pamphlet lying on Raule's desk. He picked it up. "Doctor Lone," he read aloud, "presents a revolution in medicine: the frontal lobe severance. Criminals and lunatics become obedient and docile with this quick and cheap procedure." He looked up. "What's this?"

"A gentleman who sticks a pickaxe in your eye socket and cuts your brain in half."

"And the recipient of this service lives?"

"As long as the pickaxe is clean, so that there is no infection. Perhaps you should tell your boss about it. Doctor Lone proposes his patients as a labour force to replace slaves."

"Intriguing." Gwynn returned the pamphlet to its place on the desk.

"I happen to think not." And then she gave a slight shrug and said suddenly, "Shall I show you what does intrigue me?"

"By all means."

Raule got up from her chair. "This way."

Gwynn followed her down the hall to the little laboratory. She opened the door. As he took in the collection of defective births, his eyebrows lifted.

"They're evidence," Raule said. "Do you like them?"

Gwynn moved up to one of the shelves and gave the jars on it a closer study. Finding the double-ended foetus, he picked up the jar and turned it around, examining it from all angles. "Evidence of what?" he finally said, putting the jar back.

"That all isn't well. That things are not right. Hardly a revolutionary idea, I know. But then this came along. Catch."

Gwynn fielded the jar Raule tossed to him. It contained the crocodile baby. He looked at the baby closely. "Quite a little charmer. Is it supposed to make me feel paternal?"

"It isn't supposed to do anything. Or rather, it did have a purpose, but it was incapable of fulfilling it. It couldn't even live."

Gwynn peered closely at the thing in the jar. "You're saying this is real, not a fake?"

"It's real, unfortunately. It came out of one of your Ikoi women. In answer to a prayer, I was told. This child was intended to be the saviour of her people, but its head and body ended up around the wrong way, and it died."

"You believe that?"

"I'm not sure. But I don't have a more credible explanation to offer. I do know what that thing is, though."

He looked at her expectantly.

"It's you, Gwynn. You, and Elm, and all of you who went wrong long ago and couldn't make yourselves right. I don't know what you lack. I wish I knew."

With a soft laugh, Gwynn threw the jar back to her.

"All right," he said, "I believe I understand your subtly made point. I won't take up more of your time." He turned his back and started to leave.

"Stop."

He halted in the doorway.

"Twenty thousand. For the sake of the people here in Limewood. And I want half paid up front, just for agreeing to this."

"Half witchdoctor, half leech." He laughed again. "It was simple after all, wasn't it? You can have twenty thousand."

Raule nearly kicked herself for not demanding more. She showed a bland face. "We are agreed. Now, kindly leave."

"Certainly, madam." Gwynn inclined his head, then departed down the corridor. Raule waited until she could no longer hear his footsteps. Then she picked up the jar and spoke to its occupant:

"It looks like we're in the money, little god. Maybe you've brought me good luck."

Most of the Horn Fan's cavaliers spent the morning before the battle exercising their horses at the Mimosa Tier Sporting Club. Afterwards,

Gwynn went with Marriott to the baths, to which the press of heat and humidity had driven a crowd.

"Your horse was jumping well today," Marriott remarked, when they had settled into the pool, with chiffon-clad girls attending them.

"I thought I'd better get him ready to vault over piles of corpses," Gwynn said, letting himself loll in the water, as one smiling sylph rubbed a violet-scented shampoo into his scalp, while another massaged his shoulders.

"Aye, that's the right talk. It's been too long since we've had a really good fight. I'm looking forward to it." Marriott sounded entirely earnest.

"Then you can look forward on my behalf, too, while I watch my back."

"Ah, now, don't say you don't miss it. It's in your blood as it's in mine. War, my friend. Elm was right. A man needs to step into the fire."

"You seem in good spirits," Gwynn ventured.

"I'm feeling alive, Gwynn. It's been a while. I'm fierce again. I only hope that will be enough."

With a sense of foreboding, Gwynn asked, "Enough for what?"

"To die a worthy death. My hands shake. I told you, didn't I? This is the best way out, Gwynn. The honourable way. I haven't had a bad run, all in all. But I'm not going to get any further. I don't mind it ending now."

Gwynn felt a certain weariness. "All right, Marriott. If you die, can I have your emerald cufflinks?"

"Sure. You can have all my cufflinks."

"That's too generous."

"Don't mention it."

Gwynn dunked his head under the water, and stayed submerged for as long as he could hold his breath. He imagined himself adrift on an ocean, floating like a castaway's bottled message.

Having a good time. The stars are warm, the night sands shine like silk. Wish you were here.

Gwynn poured a small brandy, topped the glass up with soda, and took it out onto the balcony. He looked down onto the Corozo's front terrace, thinking about making a midnight flit out of Ashamoil. If he stayed, he might as well go to Memorial Bridge and blow his own brains out, and save the bother of getting shot by someone else.

But if he went, he couldn't ask Beth to leave her work and come with him. It would be unreasonable, ridiculous; and she was certain to refuse.

And he couldn't go alone, and leave her in the city. It wasn't just a question of putting her in a dangerous position. Forcing honesty into his inner dialogue, he admitted that he *wouldn't* go alone. The truth was, he wasn't ready to part with her. And now, he wondered if he ever would be.

The sense of delight was still there inside him. Having likened it to a flower when he first felt it, his thoughts now inclined to the analogy of a seed: a nucleus, interred deeply, disclosing its first secrets into the private darkness around it, while the vast part of its potential was still a latent dream. When he contemplated its unfolding, he felt a luminous stir in his heart. And was it comic, he asked himself, that he was likely to die so soon after discovering it, before he'd had a chance to do any-thing more than simply admire its existence?

He answered his own question with an artificial smile.

He thought of going to her; but in the end, he decided not to. He was embarrassed about the idiocy he was going to take part in when the sun rose; and he feared that his emotions would run away from him, and he would lay himself entirely open to her. He felt no readier to do that than he did to relinquish her company.

Hart the strongman lay beside his sleeping wife in their bed in the single room they lived in. It was the middle of the night, but soon she would be rising to go to work at the cloth factory where she laboured sixteen hours a day, day in, day out. Her homely, exhausted face, dear to the strongman, looked softer and younger in the dim light. Lifting his head to look over the top of his feet he could see their child, sleeping soundly in her cradle at the foot of the bed.

"I heard something, pet," Hart said to his wife, quietly so as not to wake her. "At the Usurer's Head. I was answering nature, out the back. I'd nicked up a little drainway to have a crap. Some fellows don't think twice about moving their bowels in public view, but you know I've got sensibilities. I'd found a nice dark spot. While I was there, a pair of right jackasses came outside. I heard them pissing on a wall. While their water flowed, they talked. They weren't quiet; only a deaf cabbage wouldn't have heard. One said something quite interesting to the other—something that certain people in Customs and Excise might be interested to hear, it occurred to me. You know I'm a dutiful man, a good citizen. I made a report. And I found out what some people will pay for hearsay. Makes you wonder if they know what money's really worth at all."

Hart's wife shifted in her sleep. She began to snore gently. He nudged her. She grunted, then returned to breathing quietly.

"Our little girl," Hart went on, "what can we hope for her, if she grows up a pauper? I know you want more for her than what we can give her. It makes me sick to the bones to think of her working like a dog all day, like you do, poor woman. No. I want my daughter to have a fine life. So this is a start." Hart picked up his wallet from where it lay on the bedside table and took out some folded banknotes. "Five hundred florins," he said, rubbing them in his big fingers. "That goes in the bank first thing tomorrow. And there'll be more, if someone gains by what I passed along. There'll be much more. I'd tell you, pet, but I know you wouldn't like it. You've got too many worries. Let me carry this one. A man's strength has to be good for something, doesn't it?"

Hart folded the notes away and put the wallet back on the table. He lay down beside his wife, trying to forget that there was now this secret between them.

FOURTEEN

THE AIR OVER Memorial Bridge was charged with the smell of horse shit, ripening in the heavy heat of the morning. Invisible cicadas shrilled over the rumbling riverside factories. The two war parties faced each other at either end of the bridge. On the south bank, the Horn Fan had forty mounted men, and some two hundred on foot, Elm having called up every brawler and roughneck on his unofficial payroll. On the north bank, the larger force of customs police and their allies was assembled. Between them, the statues overlooked the battlefield. Designed to be viewed from a distance, each one stood some twenty feet tall, on top of a six-foot plinth, on the inside of the balustraded parapet wall.

The Horn Fan's cavaliers were all perspiring in their formal clothes. Grooms had been working on their horses since the small hours of the morning, and all the animals had braided manes and coats gleaming like satin. Elm, on a white thoroughbred, was out the front making a speech about sacrifice and glory. Up in the van of riders, sitting on his blinkered horse between Marriott and Elbows, Gwynn looked at the faces around him. While they puffed on last-minute smokes and imbibed liquid breakfasts from flasks and bottles, far too many were grinning like loons. Elbows looked stern and noble—Gwynn didn't know how Elbows pulled that off, but somehow he did—while Marriott looked too peaceful. Elei was somewhere in the ranks towards the back, as Elm had wanted him in the battle, saying, "Let him win his spurs." Of the senior circle, only Biscay was excused from the fighting. He had come in a sedan chair to watch. Tareda was watching too, from a carriage with smoked glass windows and thick curtains.

While the war parties waited like chessmen before a game, a stir of activity was going on around them. A throng of curious souls had gathered, lining up on the terraces beside and above the bridge, crowding at windows and on roofs. Kids from the slum gangs were prominent in their bright costumes, darting around like dragonflies; hawkers were doing brisk business selling breakfast sausages and pies; several journalists from the city papers had taken up positions close to the bridge, notebooks in hand. Below, in the centre of the river, a party boat had dropped anchor, and a troop of smartly turned out people stood on the deck, craning their necks, a number making use of opera glasses to observe the goings on.

This is going to be a shambles, Gwynn thought with certainty, dragging on his twentieth Auto-da-fé of the morning. Elm did not have a strategy. He had given no orders, save that they were to charge towards the foe and be valiant. Gwynn wondered about the horses. The Horn Fan's mounts were trained to stay calm in a fight and were used to gunfire, but they weren't accustomed to action on this scale, and Gwynn suspected that when they ran into the battle they would try to run right back out again.

Not expecting to survive in the case of defeat, he had bet most of his money on a victory. The bookmaker had given him eight to one against the Horn Fan, saying cheerfully, "They're going to wipe the bridge with you. But the punters like my odds. From my point of view, today is a great day for you to die."

While Elm was talking, Gwynn checked his guns. He had his usual two revolvers, plus two others inside his coat, extra spare cylinders for reloading, and the Speer—he had found no better rifle in Ashamoil— slung across his shoulders.

Elm concluded his speech. Wishing his men luck, he retired to the back of the field. His newfound boldness did not stretch to his personally leading the charge. That task would go to Marriott, who had been first to volunteer for it. Now Marriott turned to Gwynn.

"Ah, this is good! I feel I've a pack of wolves inside my blood!" he growled, and gave an ostentatiously savage laugh.

"I am," said Gwynn, "ecstatic for you." Marriott and he had always watched each other's backs. He didn't expect any such vigilance from his countryman today. Getting ready, he looped his reins over his saddle horn, and shortened the Speer's strap.

Marriott snorted, then laughed again, and clapped him on the shoulder. "We'll be drinking from the skulls of the tax collectors to-night, my friend—whether we're alive or feasting in the halls of the valiant dead!"

And then Marriott drew his weapon, a great war hammer he had taken from a dead man in the north years ago, and bellowed the order to charge.

Gwynn touched his spurs to his horse's flanks, and it leaped away at a gallop with the others. The air filled with the clangour of horseshoes falling on stone. The enemy cavalry was a surging mass of dark blue uniforms ahead.

To Gwynn's left, Sharp Jasper rose in his stirrups, howling, baring his jewelled fangs. To his right, Screw-'Em-Down Sam brandished an elephant gun. Steering the horse with his legs, Gwynn sighted down the rifle's length, chose an oncoming rider, and fired.

As he squeezed the trigger, deafening fire erupted all around him. A rider on the enemy side came off his horse and was trampled by his onrushing comrades. Gwynn couldn't see if anyone on his own side was hit. With a mental apology to the equine genus, he aimed for the horses, and was rewarded with the sight of two galloping beasts falling down and several others tumbling over them, throwing their riders.

Marriott forged ahead alone, insanely, into the vanguard of the enemy, swinging his hammer left and right. His horse went down, but as he fell he caught hold of a man, dragging him out of his saddle. As Marriott tried to mount the horse another man levelled a pistol at him, but was shot by Gwynn.

Gwynn had no intention of reaching the middle of the bridge. Jock-eying out to the right-hand verge, he picked up his reins and tried to pull his horse to a halt next to a statue; but herd instinct had taken over its mind, and it refused to slow down. Gwynn eyed the next statue, a monument to an amazon. The plinth was about level with his waist. Having no time to think about whether it was really such a good idea, he pushed his rifle around to his back, brought his feet up so that he crouched on the saddle for a moment, and jumped.

He landed on the plinth securely, if roughly, colliding into the statue's knee. When he had steadied and turned around, his horse had vanished into the melee. The situation on the bridge was now congested chaos. As Gwynn had guessed, many of the horses were trying to flee—though all the ones he noticed wore the blue and black caparisons of the Customs Office—and fallen animals were obstacles for all the riders. While some men remained in their saddles, most got down to fight on foot. Many had abandoned their firearms in favour of bayonets and swords.

Sheltering down behind the amazon's stalwart legs, Gwynn sought targets. Someone else—it looked like Elbows, though it was hard to see through the black gunsmoke that already clouded the air—had done as he had, and was sniping from behind a statue on the other side.

Opportunities for clear shots were few and far between. Gwynn settled for keeping the rifle in one spot, and firing when a foe crossed his sights. By the time the gun emptied, he had killed six men. He briefly considered switching to pistols, but decided he'd rather have the rifle's accuracy, and started to reload it.

In the middle of doing so, an impact slammed into his right arm. The force of it knocked him backwards off his perch.

He would have fallen off the bridge entirely, if the balustrade had not run behind the statues. He managed to grab it with his left arm—violently knocking his teeth against it at the same time—and hung on desperately.

His right arm had a hot spit running through it, but the limb obeyed him when he willed it to move. Bearing with the pain, he hauled himself up, and got a knee on top of the wall. Thinking to get down beside the statue and lie low, he edged along on his stomach, breathing in gasps, hampered by the Speer, which was wedged under him.

As soon as he was past the plinth, he rolled off the wall, and landed in a crouch on the ground. Immediately, something came around the statue and whistled down towards his head.

Gwynn jerked the Speer up. The barrel blocked a scimitar, and fire tore down his arm. Now he could see the blade's wielder: a man with a goatee, dyed saffron yellow, which put Gwynn in mind of a merkin.

Gwynn jumped to his feet, at the same time pushing the rifle sharply counterclockwise. The twisting motion turned the blade aside, putting an opening in Merkin-beard's guard, which Gwynn took advantage of, aiming a kick at the man's kneecap.

Gwynn heard and felt bone break. Merkin-beard screamed, staggered, and dropped the scimitar. Gwynn let go the rifle, drew his left-hand pistol, and fired three shots into the chest below the saffron tuft.

As his vanquished foe sank to the ground, so did Gwynn. He spared a look at his arm. There were two half-inch holes on the outside of his sleeve, one above and one below, going through the muscle on an angle. And, just for extra fun, all his front teeth ached and felt loose.

A man came charging at him with a bayonet. Gwynn missed his first left-handed shot, only barely hitting in time with the second. Gwynn dodged as the man fell towards him, and put a second bullet through his skull.

The fighting had spread out along the bridge; but the main fray was up at the north end, which meant the Horn Fan had to be winning. Gwynn hardly credited his eyes. And then he really had to blink, for out of the drifting, livid smoke, a solid black shape appeared. It was his horse, lightly trotting, as if it was out in a pleasant field somewhere.

"Where have you been—sightseeing?" Gwynn sighed. As the horse didn't answer, Gwynn crawled into the saddle with a large shrug of his mind, and rode up the bridge. He shot three more men, and realised he had shot the last two in the back. The forces from the Customs Office were retreating. From somewhere far ahead, he heard a voice roaring in Anvallic, "Victory!"

"You were lucky—again," said Raule, sewing the last stitch in Gwynn's wound. She tied the thread and snipped it. "It's a nice clean hole. It should mend right, though it's going to give you some well-deserved discomfort for a while."

"We were all lucky," Gwynn said. *More than lucky*, he added silently. *Something changed the rules.* None of the Horn Fan's cavaliers had died or been seriously injured. A few men had lost their horses, most of them to broken legs; and that was all. No wonder Raule seemed in a good mood—she'd had little work to do in return for the twenty thousand.

He wanted to go to Beth, but Elm had ordered an immediate celebration at the Diamantene. He was already gone, with Elei. Elm's son had killed a man, and had himself escaped unscathed. The bravest and luckiest hero of the day was Marriott, without a doubt. He had killed Nanid, crushing the man's skull with his war hammer.

After one of the novices had bandaged his arm, Gwynn sought Marriott out. He walked past Elbows, who wore the serene look of a man who had vindicated himself, and found Marriott having a cut on his jaw attended to by another young nun. Far from looking happy to be alive, his expression was pained.

His mouth twisted in a bitter smile. "Well, this I didn't expect, Gwynn."

Gwynn made an effort. "Come, being alive can't be all bad."

"But when a man had other plans, my friend; when a man had other plans . . . "

Gwynn walked away, and went to look for a washroom.

He keenly felt himself to be more of an observer of the party at the Diamantene than a participant in it. While his colleagues rutted on couches and the verminous floor—Elm had brought a bevy of choice whores to the club for the occasion—Gwynn sat with Marriott, and got drunk.

He should have been correct. The battle should have been a disaster. He had no idea how the idiotic confidence of the others had triumphed over reality, but it unarguably had. While not wishing to look a gift horse in the mouth, he could only wonder at the implications of the day's events.

Bookmakers' boys arrived with envelopes. Every man, it seemed, had bet heavily. Gwynn took his and pocketed it carefully. Marriott, however, had none.

"I was so sure," he said, "that I was going to die."

All Gwynn could do was buy him another drink.

Some time into the party, a messenger arrived with word for Elm. After listening, Elm came over to Gwynn.

"We've caught our voice in the dark," he said. "I want you to take care of it. There's a wife, one child. Standard fix. Are you sober enough to remember an address?"

Gwynn nodded.

"Room seventeen at the old Cheesemakers' Guild on Cato Street."

"So, who . . . ?"

"If you can believe it, the strongman from the fucking funfair."

Gwynn remembered that Hart had been at the Usurer's Head. He didn't know the strongman, but was surprised nevertheless. Going by appearances, he had always taken Hart for a quiet, straight character, not a man to gossip, or interfere with others' affairs.

"That's certain?"

"Certain as word ever is. What, he's a friend of yours?"

"No. Just doesn't strike me as the type."

"A man hears something not meant for him, he gets greedy, gets ideas," Elm shrugged. "Then he gets killed."

"When, then?"

"Do it by Hiverday. You'll be taking Elei along. Today was all well and good, but he needs to learn the nuts and bolts."

"Will do."

Elm went away. Gwynn looked around until his eyes found Elei. The boy was on a couch, hardly visible under two naked beauties. Elm hadn't openly designated an heir, but he was obviously fond of his youngest child. If Elei survived to an adequate age, his father's favour might hand him the Horn Fan's leadership over the heads of his older siblings, who currently assisted in running Elm's interests in other cities. If that happened, Gwynn mused, times could become very interesting indeed.

He didn't go any further in thinking about the future. When it was over with Beth—he still believed it couldn't last—he wasn't sure he'd want to stay in Ashamoil. Wavering a little, he stood up. "Time for me to be going, I think," he said to Marriott.

"Before you go," said Marriott, "look at my hands."

Gwynn looked. Marriott's fingers were trembling.

"On the bridge, they were steady again. But see them now—they're like virgins on a wedding night!"

Marriott began to weep. Gwynn sat back down again and embraced his friend with his good arm, unable to think of a single word to say. He stayed, nursing his last drink, while Marriott swallowed shots doggedly, until he finally passed out.

Gwynn dragged himself very wearily up the stairs. He paused at the top, blinking in the light. As he walked around to the lane to fetch his horse he kept his eyes down, aware that he was staggering a bit, and that he still had on his clothes from the battle, bloodstains and all. He didn't want to meet anyone's gaze. He gingerly mounted into his saddle, gathered the reins, and rode to see Beth at last.

He expected her to be angry or at least annoyed with him for not telling her about the battle, but she was not. She shrugged phlegmatically, and said she had read about it in the papers.

"You look seedy," she observed.

"You look beautiful," he said.

She led him to the bed, and left him there.

All afternoon, he fell in and out of dark sleep. The first time he woke, he found he was naked. In his other waking interludes, Beth was sometimes present, sometimes not. Once, he felt her hands moving up and down his body, whisper-light, describing slow gyres. Later, he noticed her attention dwelling on his bandaged arm and his various bruises, as though the damage interested her. If that was so, he could understand. He had no particular objections.

The next time he woke and saw her staring, he roused himself to give a sardonic smile. "Should I have broken my nose, or lost an eye?"

"No, that wouldn't do at all," she said.

"I almost knocked a few teeth out," he murmured.

"I wouldn't have been at home to you."

"You're crueller than me, madam."

"I'm afraid," she said, "your conceit defines you. With nothing to be conceited about, you would be a different man."

He came further awake. "You don't credit me with enough imagination, my dear. I would adapt myself to the circumstances. I would have false teeth made of red coral and gold, and a glass eye—no, many glass eyes; I would collect them. I'd have them in every kind of glass—ruby, silvered, frosted, etched, lustred . . . "

"Well," she said, "I suppose I wouldn't mind that. I admit, I had taken you for holding a more conventional idea of beauty."

"Perhaps I do," he allowed, "but I dare say I could alter my tastes."

She smiled. "Most people would try to conceal such injuries, but you would replace them with embellishments. Do you think of your flesh only as a type of garment—truly interchangeable with coral and carnival glass?"

"If we're only talking about appearances, I suppose I do, up to a point. It's all matter."

"The skeleton wears muscle, muscle wears skin, skin wears clothing?"

"Just so. A face is a mask made of skin; an eye is a marble connected to the brain."

He reached and traced a line from the corner of her eye to the roots of her hair. She kissed him on the forehead, then got up and left. She closed the door, and soon he heard her working in the studio.

His thoughts drifted. Not only him, but the very nature of the world seemed to have changed. The Horn Fan's miraculous victory, the crocodile baby, the lotus man, if he wasn't a fake; these things gave him cause to wonder. If Beth's theory of multiple worlds was true, he mused, and his world had mingled with another, that other world had laws he didn't understand. Such another world could be akin to a plant which, when transferred to foreign soil, grew out of control; or even like an infectious disease. What if there was a world that could alter everything it touched, and make it strange? Beth would cast herself as its owner, in all likelihood; but she could as easily be merely one of its odd creatures, its hybrids, its symptoms.

"Discretion is always essential." Gwynn spoke in an undertone to Elei, who rode abreast of him along a brick-paved lane between a terrace wall and the back of a cannery. The clip-clopping of their horseshoes covered their conversation. "If questions are asked—and sometimes they do get asked; not every official in this city is a friend of your father's—we shall need an alibi to say we were elsewhere tonight."

"Then, we are visiting our witness?"

"Just so." The shadow in the lane was too thick for Gwynn to see his charge's face; however, he sensed the boy's shy pleasure at having been correct.

This was the first time that Gwynn had had anything to do with

Elei, who had been at a boarding school in Phaience before his year in Musenda. So far that night Elm's son had shown himself to be attentive, calm and quietly amiable. His manner betrayed no indication of either greed or ruthlessness in his character. Gwynn wondered whether those qualities were present and precociously well concealed, or in fact genuinely absent.

The lane brought them to Chime Song Square. Gwynn reined his horse to a stop in front of an arch in a wall, which led to the yard of a house with a red window on the second floor, through which a light came. They tethered their horses in the yard, unstrapped packs from their saddles, and climbed up a short flight of steps to a tiled porch. Set back in a deep architrave was an old, carved sandalwood door with a brass knocker in the shape of two entwined figures. Gwynn lifted the knocker and rapped. Presently, slow footsteps could be heard approaching. The door was answered by a handsome woman in a gown of velvet the same deep red as the window, cut low to reveal shapely breasts. She smiled and held out her hand, and Gwynn crossed her palm with banknotes.

The woman gestured for Gwynn and Elei to come into the house. Inside, all was rose-tinged gloom, with furniture draped in satin dust-sheets, and thick perfumes hanging in the spaces of the air. She led the way to a bedroom and left Gwynn and Elei there. They changed into the clothes they had brought in the packs: rubber-soled boots, black jackets with hoods, and black scarves. When they emerged, the woman led them to a back door. It opened onto a wet and rancid drainage lane, hardly wider than Gwynn's shoulders. He walked ahead, with Elei following.

"She would say we were with her?" Elei asked, keeping his voice down.

"That's right. A holiday excursion for you."

"And she would be believed?"

"If no one contradicted her."

"Why do we trust her?"

"She's an honourable woman; at least, she honours the cash she's paid. And, yes, someone could offer her more, but then she'd have to weigh that against the cost of crossing your father."

Elei asked no more questions. They pulled the scarves up to cover their faces. Gwynn led them for half a mile or so, along back ways that eventually brought them to a dim street lined with buildings which at one time had been grand. Many of them bore the old engraved names of municipal offices, banks, guildhalls, and other places of similar importance. Like most of the buildings in the district, they had been converted into cheap housing at least a century ago and hadn't seen a workman's hammer or cleaner's brush since. The yellow sky and the light of distantly spaced lamps showed, above the porticoes, great crowded fantasies of baroque stonework and sagging racks of iron balconies.

Gwynn halted at a building with grey marble columns and two carved stone cows flanking its front entrance, and sank into the shadows of the doorway under the pediment. Elei pressed himself between two pilasters on the other side of the door. Fishing in a pocket, Gwynn brought out a set of steel picks, and went to work on the lock. It was a surprisingly good one for such a run-down place, and springing it took him longer than he would have liked. But at last he coerced it, and pushed the door open gently.

In the lobby there was the sound of old age snoring. Gwynn flicked his lighter on. A wrinkled doorkeeper or janitor lay on a cot, against a wall painted with a pastoral fresco, nearly erased by the depredations of time and vandals. Gwynn handed the lighter to Elei, and took a small bottle and a sponge from a pocket inside his jacket. He tipped the bottle onto the sponge, releasing the sugary fumes of chloroform into the air. He held the sponge over the old man's mouth, until his sleep deepened into unconsciousness. Then he set foot on the stairs and climbed, his rubber soles making no sound. To Elei, who was treading with an acceptable minimum of noise, he gave an approving nod.

Number seventeen was on the fifth landing, and this time the lock gave no trouble. The door opened onto a single poorly furnished room divided by a wooden screen. There was no curtain or blind on the window, and the night-glow coloured everything in the room with an amber wash.

Beckoning Elei to follow, Gwynn walked up to the screen and looked over it. On the other side there was an old brass bed, with a woman asleep in it, alone. A cradle at the foot of the bed contained a sleeping infant. Gwynn noted the woman's very plain face, the sour smell of her, the awkward shape of her body under the sheets, and the sheets themselves, which bore a dreary pattern of pale green flowers.

He took a slow breath. His injured arm hurt, and the chloroform had brought on a headache in the middle of his skull. Gathering himself together, he took out the bottle and sponge again and entered the sleeping area. As he leaned over the woman, she started to wake. He swiftly covered her face with the sponge, holding it there until she was overcome. From the other side of his jacket, he slipped out a narrow knife and a pair of pliers. He proffered these to Elei.

"I'm to do it?" Elei whispered.

"If you want to."

Elei took the implements slowly. He looked uncertainly at the pliers. "What am I to do?"

"Have you been told what this is about?"

Elei shook his head.

"Her husband's error was one of conversation. Therefore the reprisal will be delivered via the organ of conversation, the tongue. That is your father's preferred method of dealing with a situation of this kind. It makes a point."

Elei nodded.

Gwynn decided the boy could do the whole thing. He wasn't in the mood for being in this squalid place, doing this squalid work. He leaned against the wall, and lit an Auto-da-fé. "Take your coat off and roll up your sleeves. You don't want to walk outside covered in evidence," he advised. Elei complied.

"Now, lift her so she's sitting, and tilt her head back." When Elei had done that, Gwynn instructed, "Open her mouth, grip the tongue with the pliers and pull it upwards. Where it joins the floor of the mouth, cut down, as far towards the back of the mouth as you can."

Elei followed these steps as Gwynn described them. "I can't see what I'm doing. There's a lot of blood," he whispered after a few seconds.

"Work by feel."

Elei obediently poked and sawed with the knife. Eventually, he removed the tongue. Holding it in the pliers, he asked, "Where should I put it?"

"Anywhere. On that shelf will do. Clean yourself up and we'll go."

Elei deposited the tongue on the shelf Gwynn had indicated. There was a washstand to the right of the bed, with water in a pitcher. Elei rinsed the knife and pliers, wiped them dry on the sheets, and handed them back to Gwynn. He washed his hands, turning his head to look at the woman, a mild curiosity in his face.

Loud wet noises were coming from her throat. Presently blood bubbled out of her nose and mouth.

"She's dying now?" Elei whispered.

"Yes."

Elei finished washing. Gwynn checked the woman. She was dead. He started to lead the way out. Elei touched his sleeve, and he halted.

"What?"

"What about . . . ?" Elei tilted his head towards the cot.

"Nothing. Leave it."

"For mercy?"

"For insurance. A person who doesn't care if they die can easily kill you. If you make an enemy and leave him alive, make very sure he has something to live for. I prefer to kill my enemies, but your father is a more sophisticated man than I."

Elei nodded.

Gwynn took them out and back along the route they'd come by. They were going down a narrow stair when a noise behind his head alerted him to quickly move aside. He did so just in time. Elei's vomit splashed down the steps.

"I'm sorry," Elei rasped when he stopped. "I'm really sorry . . . " Even in the dim light, his mortification was plain to see.

"Elei, a point of etiquette. If you think that's going to happen, a warning to the person in front is considered good manners. Unless you thought you'd test my reflexes?"

It was supposed to be a joke, to make light of the incident, but Elei took it seriously, like a younger child, with a look of deeply wounded pride.

"Elei, I am teasing you."

"Oh."

"Are you all right?"

"I think so. Do you have to tell my father?"

"Not unless he asks."

"He wouldn't think to ask about something like this, would he?"

"Probably not."

"Good," Elei said. He straightened his shoulders. "I won't ever be sick again when I kill someone."

With Gwynn leading on, they returned to the house with the red window without further incident. They changed back into their ordinary clothes and took their leave of the house's mistress. When they were out in the yard, Elei asked whether they might go to the Diamantene for a drink. His mouth, he said, tasted rotten. Gwynn acquiesced, and so they rode to Lumen Street.

As it happened, several of the others were at the club. Tareda was on stage, and Marriott, Sharp Jasper, Elbows, and two juniors called Porlock and Spindrel, had a table up at the front. The red-eyed beetles were gone, but some of the pythons remained, fat and indolent, spoiled by the clientele, who now treated them like lap-dogs, and overfed them on leftovers and candies. Gwynn noted that Marriott was making an effort to keep his gaze away from Tareda, but the imprint of tragic love was on his face. Meanwhile, Jasper and Elbows greeted Elei with avuncular bonhomie. Naturally they wanted to know how he'd fared. Gwynn cupped one hand in the other, the sign for a job carried out, at which they gave Elei much congratulation. Elbows slapped his back and told him he would be the boss one day. Elei accepted their compliments with modesty.

Jasper bought Elei a strong cocktail. One of the juniors would have given him some joss, if Gwynn had not forbidden it. Elm wouldn't mind Elei getting drunk with his men, but he'd be less than pleased if the boy was allowed to get really vilely wasted.

All the men bought Elei drinks, and the night lurched on. The talk turned to fishing. Elbows wanted to make a trip up the river to catch trout. Gwynn kept a conscientious eye on his charge, and tried not to show the lack of gaiety he felt.

Tareda finished her set, and came over to the table. Encouraged by his surrogate uncles, a flush-cheeked Elei asked Tareda if she would do him the honour of sitting beside him. Smiling down at him like an older sister, she told him he was his father's son. She sat down in a chair that he somewhat clumsily pulled out for her, and started asking him questions about his family in Musenda and the day-school he'd been going to there. Marriott stared at empty space.

Gwynn finished his drink and went to the bar to get another. He was paying for it when he heard the single shot.

He sprinted back, thrusting people aside. Into the silence which had fallen in the club, he heard Sharp Jasper's voice rise, shouting the foulest profanities. He reached the table, and saw Elei on the floor, curled up on his side. Tareda, Sharp Jasper and Elbows were all bending over him. Marriott was missing.

"Tell me," Gwynn breathed.

Tareda looked up. "He got excited, and put his hand on my tit. I pushed him off me, and then Marriott shot him," she said flatly.

Elei's face was distorted in pain. On each exhale of breath, he let out a thin scream.

"It's in his gut," Jasper said. "It might be worth taking him to that doctor friend of yours. Unless you want to run, right now."

"We should all run," Elbows said, a muscle in his cheek twitching.

Gwynn felt distant, as though he was a different person, somewhere else, watching the scene through a telescope. He knelt down, and tried to see the damage. The entry wound was on the left side of the boy's trunk, a couple of inches below the ribs. Gwynn had expected to see a large caliber hole, but it didn't look bigger than a twenty-two. The blood oozing out of it was dark.

He looked up and down Elei's back. He couldn't see an exit wound.

Without any idea where the bullet had gone inside the boy, there was no way to say how serious it was.

"I'll get him to the hospital," he heard himself volunteer. "He was my responsibility. You two," he ordered Spindrel and Porlock, "carry him. Somebody get word to Elm."

Both juniors looked as though they expected Elm to jump out of the shadows at any moment. Moving gingerly, they lifted Elei, who uttered a long mewling whimper as he was raised.

"You sure?" Jasper gave Gwynn an odd look.

Gwynn nodded. He continued to feel far away. Then he said, "Marriott's gone?"

"Into the night."

"Take my carriage," Tareda offered.

"Thank you, I was going to," Gwynn said. "Someone will give you a ride." He gestured sharply at the two youths bearing Elei, and all of them moved past the other patrons, who all sat in perfect, frozen silence, looking anywhere but at the hapless party from the Horn Fan.

PART THREE

FIFTEEN

HALF-AWAKENED, RAULE turned over and sought sleep again. But the knocking on her door kept up, and she heard the sister calling her name.

She roused herself. "What is it?" She groped for clothes in the dark.

"Gunshot injury," came the sister's voice. "A boy. There's a man with him, one of those cavaliers. They're in the surgery now."

Raule hurried downstairs, after the sister, into the hospital's tiny surgery. The casualty was laid on the table, chest bared. He was conscious, and groaning in distress. Raule wasn't surprised to see who the other man was.

Gwynn wore the look of an angel of death suffering from bad nerves. He was pressing what looked like a dinner napkin against the wound. He stood back to give her room.

"Why aren't I rid of you?" Raule scowled. "Don't try to answer. Who is this?"

"Elei, Elm's son," Gwynn said quietly. "He was shot about ten minutes ago. Be assured, I'll—"

"Pay me for my trouble? Yes, you will." Raule soaped her hands. "Did you shoot him?"

"No."

Raule looked at the entry wound.

"It's still inside him," the sister told her, preparing an injection of morphine.

Elei raised his head. "Am I going to die?" he gasped.

"Maybe not," Raule said.

While the sister gave Elei the needle in his hip, the door opened, and more nuns filed into the surgery, carrying cloths, kettles and basins. Soon, Elei vanished behind a wall of gowns and wimples.

Gwynn backed out of the room. In the corridor, when the door had swung shut behind him, he leaned against the wall and passed a hand over his eyes.

He was alone, having sent Porlock and Spindrel back with the carriage. He looked at his watch. It was ten to three.

He went to Raule's office. Trying the door, he found it locked. He remembered the keys that hung in the entranceway, and went and got them. One opened the door, and he went in, found pen and stationery, and wrote to Beth, telling her that he had been involved in some trouble, and that it might be wise for her not to be at home for a few days. He signed the letter and sealed it in an envelope. Letting himself out, he jogged to the nearest main street, and looked up and down it for a likely messenger, for his horse was still back at the Diamantene. Few people were about. A couple embraced in a doorway, absorbed in each other. Someone lay on the pavement, wrapped up in a blanket.

Then Gwynn found what he was looking for. Down a side alley, a group of youths sat idly around a fire in an oil drum. A sequined red vest, twinkling in the firelight, caught Gwynn's eye.

He approached the group, whose heads went up at the sound of his steps. He spoke to the sequinned one.

"You, do you want a job?"

A delighted expression crossed the boy's face briefly, before he schooled his features into nonchalance. "Maybe. What job?"

Gwynn held out the letter. "Deliver this." He gave the address of the house on the Crane Stair, and proffered fifty florins.

"When?" said the boy.

"Right now," said Gwynn.

"Hey, I'll do it for twenty!" said a smaller boy. The one to whom Gwynn was talking turned around and boxed his ear.

"Sorry," he apologised to Gwynn.

"Just get going," Gwynn said.

The boy gave an amiable shrug, and loped off down the street.

"Move your carcass!" Gwynn shouted.

The boy picked up his pace.

Gwynn returned to the hospital, where he took a seat on a wooden bench outside the surgery, and lit a cigarette. His wound throbbed fiercely, and he had a bad headache again. There would be laudanum, somewhere; but he quelled the urge to go and find it. He didn't need a fuddled mind right now.

Whether Marriott had actually meant to kill Elei, or had meant to fire a warning shot and was betrayed by his shaking hands, didn't matter. Marriott was now a dead man, unless he'd left town and had already gone far, and Gwynn doubted that. Marriott might be hiding, but he wouldn't leave the city that had Tareda Forever in it.

Gwynn smiled bitterly to himself. He had not expected to ever understand Marriott's obsession so thoroughly.

Elei's death would be a warrant for his own. If Elei lived, Elm would still very likely want to punish him for failing to keep the boy safe. If he had only himself to think about, he could run, or fight. At worst he'd be shot dead, which would be better than a trip down the river in concrete shoes.

However, he had Beth to consider. He had no idea whether her strange power over men's hearts would save her from Elm's malicious whim, if things went badly. But if he stayed in the city, gave himself up—he could hope that any punishment that Elm wished to inflict would fall directly on him, and Beth would be safe. It seemed he was capable of sacrifice after all.

He went through the whole packet of Auto-da-fés. Surrounded by the squashed ends, he stared around. There was no light on in the corridors, but the surgery door had glass panels, and enough light came through that he was able to read the posters on a noticeboard hanging on the wall. They bore the seals of the church and various societies for public this and moral that, and were printed with lurid descriptions of venereal disease and tirades against 'unnatural vices'.

One denounced tobacco, "The Filthy and Dangerous Vice of Smoking, which Offends the Nose, Deadens the Palate, Causes Ageing of the Skin, and Enforces a Progressive Decrepitude of the Body Entire." Gwynn skimmed down to the last line: "Tobacco will Slowly and Surely Kill You."

And so will time, Gwynn thought. *But if you want the job done quickly, professionals recommend bullets.*

"Gwynn."

He started awake.

He was lying on the bench; he couldn't remember falling asleep. Raule was there.

She held out a little, squashed bit of lead on a tray. "You can thank providence for small bullets," she said. "It went into the stomach and stayed there. All that liquor in him might have slowed it down. If he doesn't get an infection, he'll be able to go home in a couple of weeks. Give it a month, and he'll be none the worse for wear."

"This isn't a dream, is it?" Gwynn said.

"How would I know?" said Raule.

Gwynn looked at the slug. He remembered thinking the wound was small. Marriott must have taken to using a light pistol, because of his hands.

"You are a queen of doctors," he said to Raule. He stood up. "How much do I owe you?"

Raule waved a dismissive hand. For a moment, she fixed him with a thornily complicated look. Then she turned and went back into the surgery, and closed the door.

Gwynn went outside, and started back to the Diamantene to get his horse. It was now six in the morning. He stopped at a kiosk to buy more cigarettes and a newspaper. The shooting was on the front page. Gwynn didn't read the article. He threw the paper in a bin, and composed himself to face Elm.

Tack and Snapper halted Gwynn in the garden outside the villa.

"You know the drill," Tack said.

Gwynn handed his weapons over to Tack, and spread his arms. Snapper patted him down thoroughly. He twitched when Snapper's hand closed over his wound.

"Sorry," Snapper said. After confiscating a knife from inside Gwynn's right boot he found no more weapons, and straightened, nodding.

"All right. He's in the pool."

Gwynn entered the villa escorted by the twins. Elm's private suite was at the top of the house, up three flights of stairs.

"If we have to kill you—" began Tack, as they climbed,—"we want to say it's been nice knowing you, Gwynn," finished Snapper.

"Likewise, gentlemen," Gwynn said cordially. If Elm decided to be vindictive, it would be Tack and Snapper who smashed his hands and set his feet in concrete and pushed him into the Skamander. Until then, they might as well all be civil.

On the top floor, they walked through a corridor lined with walnut panels and floored with a sculpted carpet. At the end, between two gold portrait busts of Elm, was the bathing chamber's frosted glass door. Snapper pulled a bell-rope on the adjacent wall to announce their presence, and then the brothers took Gwynn through.

The chamber was full of steam, softly lit by kerosene lamps in niches. Where the steam was thin, more gold statuary could be discerned: naked nymphs, sirens and angels, all bound to the marble walls with delicate gilt chains. A heating furnace was on next door, the hollow, windy sound of its burner faintly audible.

The first pool had water in it, but was unoccupied. A gold leaf screen concealed the second pool beyond. Gwynn stood still. Tack and Snapper pulled out pistols. Minutes passed, while water sloshed on the other side of the screen.

Finally, Elm's voice came out of the room's recesses.

"So, you show up. My son must still be alive."

More splashing followed the words. Gwynn tried to read Elm's intent from his tone and inflection, but his voice was a cipher.

"Yes," Gwynn said, simply.

"Tell me," said Elm's voice, "what his condition is."

"The doctor expects him to make a full recovery, if no complications develop."

Water moved.

"I was told," said Elm, "that Marriott shot him."

"Yes."

There was another long pause. Gwynn felt sweat trickling down his back.

At last, Elm ended the silence.

"Gwynn, I must decide what to do with you. Elei did a stupid thing, and the others should have been watching him when you weren't there; still, I have to choose someone to punish."

Gwynn fixed his eyes on the face of a statue.

"For now," Elm's voice said, "I'll assume the doctor's prognosis is correct. Therefore—for now—this is my judgement, on Marriott, and on you. This could be called an error of the heart, or an error of the prick; but I'm calling it an error of the hands. You will deliver Marriott's hands to me. You'll do it before midnight tomorrow. That's my justice, and my mercy, on you both. I trust you understand that my mercy is generous."

For an instant, Gwynn felt a wave of enormous, cowardly relief. In its wake came a wave of loathing: he imagined smashing Elm's skull into a wall, over and over, until it split like a pomegranate. After that, a stale, dry feeling entered him, and stayed.

Elm continued as though he'd said nothing of more than ordinary consequence. "Jasper had some people look for Marriott. They'll be at the Viol Arcade. Meet them now."

Thus dismissed, Gwynn turned around to go. Irrationally, he half expected to feel the bite of bullets in his back. None came. Tack and Snapper followed him out of the room, and returned his weapons. They were silent, and so was he. He buckled his ironmongery on and strode ahead down the corridor. The twins didn't follow him.

On the stairs, he picked up a roaring noise outside the villa. When he emerged into the garden he found rain bucketing from the sky, as if the bottom had fallen out of some celestial ocean. While he was in the house, the monsoon had arrived.

A sonorous voice of falling water, striking rooftops and pavements and plunging into the Skamander, echoed between the walls of the valley. Most of Ashamoil was gone from sight, hidden behind a solid grey-white curtain. Gwynn was drenched within seconds.

Going through the garden to the stables, he saw another person's figure coming towards him.

It was Tareda. She was as sodden as he, and had no shoes on. She walked up to him.

"I spoke with him," she said. "I did the best I could."

"Then you might have saved my life," he said.

She looked away from him. "What's going to happen?"

Gwynn told her.

"I'm terribly sorry," she whispered.

"Marriott adored you. You must have known that. He only wanted one smile from you."

"A lot of men adore me. I belong to Elm. I can't make exceptions."

Gwynn let out his breath slowly. "Forget I said that. I spoke out of turn."

"I have to go inside," she said.

Tareda walked past him. He felt insubstantial, like a ghost, as he kept on along his own way.

An hour later, he was waiting at the arcade. The shops were still closed up behind their iron grilles. He had not been waiting long before a pair of low types approached him. They introduced themselves as Nails and Pike.

"We found him," said the one called Nails. "He's at the Sangréal. Doesn't look in a hurry to go anywhere."

Gwynn knew the Sangréal. It was one of the waterfront's most wretched cellars.

"Is someone watching him now?" he asked.

Nails grunted an affirmative. "We'll leave word at the Diamantene if he moves," he said.

Gwynn shook his head and said, "No." He didn't want to be at Elm's club any more than he had to be. "Even the snakes there can listen and talk," he said by way of an excuse. He thought of an appropriate venue. "Use the Folly of Men. I'll check with you there tomorrow night."

"What time?"

"Eight."

"Will do," Nails said.

The two men left. Gwynn climbed into his saddle and rode through the rain, up the Crane Stair.

Beth came to the door in only a chemise. Her garret was stiflingly hot.

"I got your note," she said. "I'm not going anywhere. I have nothing to fear from your boss. You worry too much, Gwynn." She took his hand. "Come and see what I've been working on."

Gwynn opened his mouth, then shut it again. He had not told her any details in the letter, and, evidently, she wasn't interested in hearing them.

At that moment, he realised that he did not exist to her in the same way that he existed in his own perception. She held a copied version, an interpretation of him, filtered through the matrix of her priorities and desires.

Therefore, surely, he only held a copy of her.

He followed her into the studio.

"These are the first proofs," she said, gesturing towards a dozen etchings laid out on a drying rack. "What do you think?"

The etchings were similar in many ways to her scenes of oppressive architecture and elusive life which had so intrigued him. The new images retained the dark tone of ink and the monumental style of the buildings; they seemingly depicted the same imaginary location. However, the life of its inhabitants, where previously only alluded to, was now fully exposed. The doors and shutters were opened, to reveal the world beyond the walls.

Gwynn found it impossible to compose his opinion into words.

In depicting the hidden world, Beth's genius seemed to have deserted her.

The denizens of it resembled the carnival chimerae from her earlier work. However, they had crossed the line from the paradigm of protean whimsy to one of debased humanity: one man had a third, porcine leg; a woman had, instead of breasts, the single engorged udder of a cow; another woman's arms were two serpents, and the man kneeling between her spread legs had several pairs of secateur blades between his jaws in lieu of teeth and tongue; and so on. As before, they were engaged in sensual pursuits, but this time pleasure was absent. Their faces, which were all human, wore looks of contempt, idiocy and loathing.

Gwynn wondered if his eye was jaundiced; if, at the moment, with the concurrent events in his life, he was incapable of seeing beauty or feeling pleasure. But the more he looked at the images, the more he was sure of his judgement.

There was nothing among the sights before him that a madman could not have extracted from the cankerous recesses of his mind. He was further unsettled to see himself everywhere in them, or rather fragments of himself, as though he had been dismembered and strewn through the scenes. Among both those figures inflicting pain and indignity, and those suffering it, were many who in some way resembled him.

Hesitating to voice his uneasiness outright, he said, "I'm afraid I'm somewhat at a loss of understanding. What are these showing, exactly?"

"The acquisition of scars," Beth said. In reply to his perplexed frown, she instructed, "Stand still."

He complied, and she started unfastening his clothes. He felt like a shop mannequin. Presently, he stood naked to the waist. She stroked his skin, with the softest brush of her fingertips. Then she put her hand around his injured arm, and gave it a hard squeeze through the bandage.

In pain, he stared at her.

"That's real," she said. "The flesh is reality. It holds our memory far more faithfully than our minds do."

"Madam, what in the world—" he erupted; then his voice died, for her face came close to his, and he smelled her breath. Her mouth was a censer, from which a double odour flowed: the salubrious air of a rose garden, besmirched with the gore of a fresh kill.

He stood, shocked into passivity, while her hands traced his old scars and she said, "I have been jealous of you, because you wear a history of facing death. Anyone can wear beauty, but too often strength has no way to show itself and be admired. When I watch the acid bite into the metal, I imagine the metal is my skin. Do you understand?"

Gwynn shook his head. "Beth . . . " He looked into her eyes and found that at last the iron barrier was gone. In the bright blackness beyond, he saw something he knew of old.

Of all the things he had at times hoped to find there, something he might have created himself certainly wasn't one of them.

He frantically tried to think. The odour on her breath came from the vision he'd had at Vanbutchell's. Could the vision have been a true instance of prescience, a warning? If so, the smell might be a symptom of a disease, or a toxin; perhaps one of the chemicals she worked with was doing her harm.

"What is it, Gwynn?"

"I'm afraid you're unwell. You don't seem yourself."

"I've never felt better," she assured him. "I will find it tiresome, if you continue to worry about me. I'm an extremely healthy individual of my species."

She proved her physical potency. Her lovemaking was violent, and he responded in kind. Once, she slapped his face; and he found himself using all his strength to force her onto her front, thinking to pin her and take her in the way of an animal. He could not say whether he changed his mind and voluntarily loosened his hold, or whether she bested him; but he found her facing him again; and her hands flew up, and closed around his throat. It was no more than a playful grip; but he sensed an angry violence hovering beyond the game. While his body went on, almost by itself, having its pleasure, his spirits sank further, as the promise of unfamiliar territories receded past a horizon.

When they were finished with each other and had their breath back, he said, "You've gotten under my skin, it seems. I invited that, so I don't object. What I fear is that I've gotten under yours."

"You wished to change, did you? Well, perhaps so do I." Calmness had returned to her manner. She was lying on her side, smiling. But the smell was strong on her breath and in her sweat.

Her words surprised him.

"I imagined you as a catalyst, changing what you touch while re-maining unchanged yourself," he said.

"Romantic, but wrong. I sought you, remember. You've been the ingredient I needed."

"I'm not sure of that."

"Wait and see, then."

You've become dear to me, he wanted to say to her; but he found himself only able to say that he was tired, and couldn't stay, and that he would be busy with work the next day, and wouldn't be able to see her.

That afternoon, he lay on the couch in his sitting room, trying to rest, and to put himself in order. But he could find no peace of mind, as thoughts of Beth and of Marriott revolved around in his head like two carousel horses.

If he followed the letter of Elm's orders, he didn't have to kill Marriott. A man could survive without hands. He ought to offer Marriott the choice, perhaps. But in the end, he decided that since Marriott wanted to die, that would be better.

In the dead of night, Hart the strongman wrapped his wife's body in a clean sheet. Picking the burden up in his arms, he bore it to the house of a man he knew as a worker of magics.

The wizard answered Hart's knock, coming to the door in a black robe embroidered with arcane emblems in gold thread. Upon seeing what the strongman held, his old face creased into lines of deep sorrow.

"Master Vanbutchell." Hart spoke the name he knew the wizard by, and then was unable go on.

Vanbutchell the worker of magics said, "You understand, I can't bring her back. I can only give you a weapon. And there will be a price, and another price."

"I accept," Hart said. Tears fell from his eyes, so full of guilt's bitterness that they cut two bloody grooves down his face.

"Very well."

Vanbutchell led him through the house to a room which was empty, open to the sky through a round hole in the ceiling, and open to the earth through a matching hole in the floor.

"We stand in the athanor," Vanbutchell said. "This place is the axis and the matrix. Here, at certain times and with the appropriate material, one may perform unheard-of alchemies. Stop; come no nearer. I will tell you the price. To the universe, you shall make payment with your life."

"That doesn't matter to me."

"I also require a payment for myself. You have a daughter. Tomorrow, bring her to me. She will care for me in these years of my old age, and if she has the aptitude I will make a sorceress of her."

"Better you take her than the poor-house. You have my word; she'll be yours."

"Then leave what you carry," said Vanbutchell, "and go, and at this hour tomorrow return, and I will give you your weapon."

"Why must I leave her? She should be buried decently."

"The material. Her bodily remains will be transformed into the instrument of your revenge. Do you object?"

Hart bent his head. "That might be just," he said slowly. "Yes. It would be just."

He knelt, and lowered the sheet-wrapped bundle to the ground.

Vanbutchell put a hand on the strongman's massive shoulder. "I could give you something for your pain."

"No."

Vanbutchell nodded very sadly.

Hart left and walked home, where he held his daughter in his arms, and told her everything about her mother, not sparing the manner of her death or his part in it. Though she was too young to understand a word, he still felt a duty to tell her the truth. Then he lay awake, sometimes shedding more of the unnatural, corroding tears, sometimes losing himself for a brief time in a fantasy that his wife lay beside him, just a little distance apart.

The monsoon rains came the next day. He lay in bed and listened to the falling water, holding his daughter in his arms. When darkness came again, at last, he tried to play with her, but she was fretful. He changed and fed her, but still she frowned and cried. He started crying again, too, ordinary tears, this time, that ran down the raw gutters in his skin.

"The sky cries, you cry, I cry," he murmured. He walked up and down the room with her. The movement seemed to soothe her, so he did that until it was time go to Vanbutchell again.

The worker of magics took a long time to answer the door. He looked older. He said to Hart, "It wasn't easy; I've also paid a price." He went on, half-muttering, to himself it seemed, "But I have done well to enable this reckoning. There are too few reckonings; too much wrong is permitted. After this, perhaps we will find ourselves more discriminating and sober." Then he looked expectantly at the strongman.

"Her name is Ada," Hart said. He kissed his daughter softly on her forehead, then handed her into Vanbutchell's arms.

Looking intently at her small face, Vanbutchell gave a measured nod. "She may be a sorceress one day. She will have a new name."

"That's none of my concern," Hart shook his head.

"Remain there." Vanbutchell went away down the hall with the infant girl and disappeared into the back of the house. A short time later he returned, moving slowly, with something else in his hands.

It was a weapon, an axe. A four-foot shaft of black iron, with a two-foot, fan-shaped blade on the end. Vanbutchell held it out to Hart.

Hart took it, very carefully. It weighed heavy in his hands. The blade was bright, as sharp as a new razor, and it was engraved, with flowers that bloomed in elaborate patterns over the metal. He touched it gently, brushing his fingertips over the ornamented surface.

"Yes, it was made from the physical remains of your wife—may her soul soon rest," Vanbutchell answered Hart's unspoken question. "I did not choose the shape or create that pattern you see on the blade; it is simply what she became."

In the midst of his grief and horror, the strongman felt a surge of pride for the woman who had been his wife. A hard life had worn her out before her time. Now here, in his hands, was proof of the fine soul the world had never noticed. The thought could give him no comfort, but it galvanised his resolve.

He was no warrior; as a youth he had done a little soldiering, but it was twenty years since he had used his strength to do anything but entertain at the fair. However, he felt he knew the weapon in his hands as well as he had known his wife's body.

"Go well to your vengeance and your fate. I will tell your daughter that her father was a hero," said Vanbutchell, not without irony, but also not without sincerity. "I have done one other thing for you. Soon your enemies will believe you are dead. They will not be looking for you."

The sorcerer bowed, and then turned and shuffled away down the hall.

Outside, pummelled by the rain, Hart held the axe close against his chest. In his mind there was no doubt that the Society of the Horn Fan had been the agent of his wife's mutilation and death. There was no other candidate. He had a formidable enemy. But if he was to die exacting vengeance, that would only be a deserved punishment for his guilt.

SIXTEEN

WITH ALL THE depth and breadth of consideration that he could bring to the circumstances, Gwynn devoted the day to contemplating Marriott's murder.

He rose early and went out, cloaked in an oilcape. Almost no one was about in the heat and drenching rain. The Skamander churned; crocodiles drifted in the tempestuous water.

Not the river. Of that he was certain.

Three hours riding east along the river brought him to Ashamoil's verges and a new extension of the city, which in the short span of its existence had earned the name of Little Hell. Here were slaughter-yards, tanneries, knackers and glue factories, which had some eighteen months ago been forcibly relocated from their ancient premises to this new spot, in an effort by the city administrators to improve the central waterfront area. Gwynn had taken the launch past Little Hell many times, but had never visited it.

He found a wilderness of tin-clad sheds, and a stench so rancorous it stung his eyes. His horse tossed its head and snorted furiously.

From the saddle, he observed the activity in a slaughteryard. Pigs were being killed. A roof of tarpaulins sheltered the big dirt square from the rain, but animal blood and excrement made it a quagmire. Gwynn wasn't the only visitor at the yard: two haruspices squatted next to a gutted pig carcass with their robes tucked up around their knees, poking at the entrails with bamboo wands.

Gwynn considered swords, knives, daggers. He watched the men cutting the pigs' throats, observing the great effort with which they drove the knives into the animals' flesh.

It was true that lately Marriott had not been much of a friend. Gwynn didn't feel as close to him as he had in the old days.

But when all was said and done, blades were utilitarian. Even the finest sword was a kissing cousin to a butcher's knife. And he really didn't want to smell his old friend's blood, or feel the splitting of his flesh and the breaking of bone.

No. He would choose another way.

Taking leave of Little Hell, Gwynn rode back towards the middle of town, and took the road up Titan Hill to the war museum. There, he spent two hours in the cool, dry stone building's halls, in which he was the only visitor, looking at quiescent weapons. While some of them were interesting for technical, aesthetic or historical reasons, few suggested themselves as practical, apart from the guns. But if a blade was too intimate, a gun was too distant, and too casual, its ease of use constituting a kind of discourtesy that he didn't wish to commit.

Outside, a strong wind sculpted the rain into curtains of water and sent them flying into each other, one breaking upon the next. Gwynn rode downhill through the spray. It was now past midday, and he was hungry. He stopped at a cafeteria and had a plate of kippers and scrambled eggs, which he consumed without tasting.

Further along the street, by happenstance, he passed a square where a man was being hanged. The wretch jerked around, choking, the hangman having made the length of rope too short. Gwynn could only shake his head at the ineptitude. He watched until the body at last hung limp, though not still, for the wind pushed it back and forth like a lantern in a storm.

Outright strangulation would be grotesque, and difficult. He considered using chloroform, followed by some less violent method of suffocation, but discarded the idea as lacking style.

Which left poison.

It had merits. If the right substance was chosen, physical suffering could be avoided; it could be done at close quarters, but still with a degree of remove; and, in the matter of style, it was discreet, and a time-honoured element of tragic drama. For the doomed protagonist, poison was the sable dart that brought a strange, stylised death: a death with time for soliloquy, one in which the body did not collapse like a broken puppet, but could slowly turn into a statue on the stage, becoming a monument that preserved the meaning of the person.

In real life, it went without saying, such a flawless exeunt of the fated one was never a likely prospect. Nevertheless, the association was there, and Gwynn thought that if he was to be the author of Marriott's death, he wanted that death to be not completely nonsensical in relation to the life preceding it. The strongman's wife suddenly came to his mind, as an example of an absurd death. Mismatch produced comedy, but only up to a point, admittedly subjective, beyond which lay the territory of horror. That territory had an appeal of its own, of course; but only when the victim was a stranger.

The idea of taking Marriott's life by a horrific method entered his mind, if only as a hypothetical notion. He gave it thought, out of curiosity as to what the effects on his mind would be. Mentally rehearsing various scenarios, putting a homunculus of himself on the stage of his wildest imagination, seeing it perform grotesque atrocities with a silly, hypocritical smile, he was reassured of his limits. The homunculus was not him; even his unkindest side took no interest in causing Marriott to suffer.

It occurred to him that he had never actually betrayed a friend before. It was something he'd always managed to avoid.

No longer.

Gwynn decided on poison. But he had comparatively little expertise with it; therefore, in the spirit of increasing his knowledge, he rode across Fountains Bridge to the north bank, then through cobbled lanes in the university quarter, to the domed library, repository of a millennium of learning.

The library sat halfway up a hill, overlooking the river. That day, however, the view was only of the chaos of rain. Within an hour, Gwynn had found three locally available substances that were acceptable for his purposes. Feeling sure that Vanbutchell would have at least one of them, Gwynn remained in the reading room and pored through texts, looking for a clue to Beth's state. But in all the mazes of chemistry, biology and history, he found nothing.

He had spoken figuratively of getting under her skin; but could such an invasion be more than psychological? How ironic would it be if, for all his prior fears about the Horn Fan, the only thing inimical to her was he himself?

When he finally put the folios aside, the sun had gone down.

The air remained hot, and the rain still fell tempestuously. Everywhere, water gushed from spouts and streamed down the streets, rubbish swirling and eddying in its flow. Where there was no paving, the mud was deep. Overnight, Ashamoil had turned into a giant's uncouth water-grotto.

Gwynn rode down to the wharf fair for the sake of going somewhere.

Business was still going on, under red and blue tarpaulins. Most of the regulars were there, hustling a very small crowd. The strongman was understandably absent. Gwynn had arranged for another one of Elm's eyes and ears, a woman who went by the name of Sugar Mouse, to watch him. The dwarves wore grim looks while they somersaulted and cartwheeled.

Gwynn rode on, not paying a great deal of attention to things around him.

He almost rode into someone dashing around a corner. It turned out to be the Rev. He had no waterproof clothing on, and was sodden. He ran up to Gwynn.

"I know what you're up to!" the Rev shouted.

Gwynn eyed him in silence.

"I know," the Rev said again, "what you're up to. Don't do it. Please don't do it."

"Father, you are gibbering."

The Rev shook his head violently. "Rumour gets around. Your poor friend's well-known. There were many witnesses to the unfortunate incident at the club. Speculation is running high as to what will become of him. I hazarded a guess that circumstances would demand your involvement, my son, and therefore I followed your peregrinations today. This rain helped me to conceal myself. Your purpose wasn't hard to guess, for one who knows you. I know you don't want to do it!"

"You know very little; but you should know better than to listen to rumour."

"This will damn you!"

The Rev threw himself to the ground and lay prostrate in front of Gwynn. Gwynn nudged his horse forward. It stepped over the Rev, who scrambled to his feet, ran up alongside Gwynn and grabbed his ankle. Gwynn tried to twist out of the Rev's grasp, and found that he couldn't; the priest's grip was unexpectedly strong.

"What are you going to do now, shoot me?" the Rev challenged.

The few people in the vicinity had stopped looking at the sideshows, and were now watching the new attraction. Gwynn stared at the Rev as if he suddenly didn't know him.

"Shall I tell them what you're going to do?" the Rev hissed. "I can shout it out, and these people will hear. They'll tell other people. Will you shoot them all?"

"No one will care what you shout," Gwynn said, "least of all me."

"All right, then," said the Rev. "All right." He released Gwynn's leg and stepped back a couple of paces. He drew breath to yell; but his nerve failed him at the last instant. The bemused onlookers saw him standing foolishly with his jaw wide open, silently showing the inside of his mouth, as though to a dentist.

"Gentlemen, please excuse me," a voice came from somewhere near the ground behind the Rev. It was a placid, tired voice, and it came from the man who grew the lotus from his navel.

"I couldn't help but overhear." He tilted his head to look at the Rev and Gwynn. "It isn't my custom to interfere in the business of others, but in this case I feel compelled to. Priest, why don't you show him what holiness can achieve? What no other has been able to do, you could; release me from this stagnant existence. Without this lotus in me, I could find proper work, a wife; I could have children."

"I can't," said the Rev.

"That is a lie," said the lotus man.

The Rev looked uncomfortable, while Gwynn watched without evincing interest.

"Will he," the Rev spoke to the lotus man, "curb himself and not further betray his soul, if I can remove this thing which afflicts you?"

"You can only try."

"Sir, who are you?"

"I?" the man said. "A nobody, sir. Just a man of inaction."

Inside the hood of his oilcape, Gwynn's eyes narrowed. The lotus man noticed, and tilted his face towards Gwynn. "Bad day?" he smiled. "Well, perhaps tomorrow will be better." Then he beckoned to the Rev. "Come, do it; what have you got to lose?"

"You have no idea," said the Rev. But nevertheless, he did approach. He bent down, and stretched out his hand towards the tall pink blossom.

"One shilling," said its host. The Rev handed over the coin, and the man poked it away under his mattress.

While Gwynn looked on, the Rev knelt, grasped the lotus by the stalk with both hands, and pulled.

The lotus came out. It trailed a long root, to which threads of gore clung. The man let out a sharp cry, then a whimpering moan. Blood— bright, arterial—pumped out of the hole in his centre. The Rev dropped the lotus, and sat staring at the scarlet surge. The man was looking straight up with dark, liquid eyes that were full of disappointment. The Rev bowed his head, and buried his face in his hands.

"I have a request," the dying man whispered. "Plant that root in fertile ground. It's possible something good will come of it." The Rev either didn't hear the words or ignored them, so Gwynn dismounted and picked up the lotus.

It was then that someone said loudly, "Murderer!"

Gwynn looked to see who had spoken. But he wasn't being addressed. A scruffy bravo had a knife in hand and was about to throw it at the Rev's back. Gwynn could have knocked the Rev out of the way, but found himself instead with gun in hand, firing. The would-be assassin stiffened, staggered, and fell over.

Gwynn waved the smoke from the shot away from his face. "Anyone else?" he inquired.

The crowd rapidly dispersed.

Gwynn waited, but the Rev didn't look up or otherwise move. Meanwhile, the ex-freak bled to death. Gwynn left the Rev and rode down to the river. He thought of the mud under it: rotten, corpse-laden. To the limited extent that he knew anything about horticulture, he thought such ground would probably be fertile. He threw the lotus into the water.

That deed done, he took himself to the Folly of Men, where Nails waited for him.

Nails reported that Marriott still remained at the Sangréal. "He doesn't move none. Goes out to piss, is all."

"All right. Keep watching him anyway."

"As you wish."

Gwynn gave Nails some money, then went to Uncle Vanbutchell's. The alchemist was in. On this occasion he came to his door wearing a black robe and a black skullcap. There was no sign of the pyjamas, and his demeanour was neither angelic nor vague. He was able to sell Gwynn exactly what he wanted. He brought out a small china box, sealed with black wax. The price he named caused Gwynn to raise an eyebrow.

"That ointment is rare. You're lucky I had any in stock," Vanbutchell said. "Anyway," he shrugged his robed shoulders, "since you're going to pay for your evil, you might as well start now."

Gwynn didn't feel up to arguing. He counted out the cash and took the china box. Then he thought of something. He asked Vanbutchell whether he knew of any drug or poison which produced an aroma of raw meat and roses on the taker's breath.

"None whatever," said Vanbutchell. "Nothing that I sell, certainly."

"Could there be another reason, then; an illness, for instance?"

"Not that I am aware of."

Gwynn felt no sense that Vanbutchell was hiding anything. He left, trying to put his worries about Beth to the back of his mind.

The Sangréal stank like a latrine. Half-naked bodies writhed against each other in the ill heat and dark, on a floor of muddy tiles. A hand rose from the mass of flesh and clutched at Gwynn's coattails. Gwynn kicked out with his spurred heel. Someone yelped a ripe oath, and the hand recoiled.

Gwynn made his way towards the back of the room, looking for Pike. Seeing him, Gwynn made eye contact and jerked his head towards the exit. Pike looked at him with dull curiosity, then shrugged, and shuffled off.

The rear half of the room was taken up with small cots, on which decrepit junkies lay. Gwynn found Marriott against the back wall. The cot was too short for him, and his feet hung awkwardly over the end of it. A long brass opium pipe rested in his hands. His eyes were shut, in a face that had aged a decade. His skin was cinereous, his hair plastered to his forehead and cheeks in sweaty clumps. Next to his cot there was an unoccupied one. Gwynn sat down on it, and lit a cigarette.

"Marriott."

Marriott didn't stir.

It could be done right now, Gwynn thought. He let his own eyelids close, as he tried to work himself into the necessary frame of mind. In the face of Marriott's condition, the irony of his purpose wasn't lost on him.

"You . . . "

Hearing Marriott's husky voice, Gwynn opened his eyes again.

Marriott was looking at him. "You . . . it's funny . . . there were so many people, but you weren't there. I wondered where you'd got to." His mouth formed a lopsided smile. "I thought they must have put you in the river." He coughed, slowly turned his head, and spat on the sawdust. He rolled back. "How are you, Gwynn?"

"I'm well."

"How's Tareda?"

"She's well, too."

"Tell me about her, will you? Tell me everything. What kind of songs does she sing now?"

"The same songs."

"Then she's still unhappy," Marriott whispered. He drew on the pipe. "Do they all love her, still?"

"Yes."

"She's singing at the Diamantene tonight. Do you want to come?"

"Not tonight. Perhaps next time."

"Your rose-haired lady, eh? I can't pretend I'm not jealous. But I'm glad for you, too. Make her yours, my friend. Don't lose her." Marriott grunted, coughed, and raised himself onto his elbows and twisted to face Gwynn. "I'm glad you came to see me. I've been expecting you. I thought you'd have been here sooner. I was surprised when you didn't come with the with the others."

"Others?"

"Oh, I don't know. I've been dreaming a lot of people."

"This isn't a dream. You're awake now."

Marriott sucked on the pipe again. "It was my hands. I didn't mean to shoot the kid. I didn't even mean to draw the gun. My hands shook, Gwynn."

As if he were turning off a tap tightly, Gwynn quelled thought and emotion. "Mind if I have some of that?" he asked, motioning towards the pipe.

"Go on." Marriott passed it over to him. Gwynn put his cigarette down and took the heavy pipe in both hands. He allowed himself a breath of the sweet smoke, not too much. Before returning the pipe, he wiped the mouthpiece with his gloved fingers. Taking it back, Marriott gave a slow nod of his head, as if he knew what he was doing. He took a long drag. Gwynn watched him sink back down to a prone position and lie there, breathing quietly. Gwynn thought there might be nothing more. The poison was known to bring a sleep which eased into death as smoothly as steam vanished into air. However, Marriott began talking again.

"It's a good thing that a man can sleep so much, I think. A third of every day. Half if he tries. I'm remembering now, in Brumaya, when we got you out of the duke's prison, you were sound asleep. You wouldn't wake. Do you remember?"

Gwynn picked his cigarette up. "I remember."

"And do you remember that train we stole?"

"Of course. The ninety-seven."

"You made me shovel the coal."

"Because you didn't know how to drive the engine."

"Next time, I drive. You can shovel."

"All right, Marriott."

"I've been like a toad wishing for the moon." Marriott's voice was slurring. Gwynn had to listen hard to pick up what he said. "Thinking I could swallow it, like a pearl. I know what you've done. I spoke for you, for your honour. But this way you'll get to keep your lady. That's what I'd be thinking, if I were you."

Gwynn waited. The rise and fall of Marriott's chest slowed. Gwynn let a few more minutes pass, then checked Marriott's pulse. It was slackening. Marriott spoke no more words, and the next time Gwynn checked, he was dead.

Gwynn went out, and returned with Sharp Jasper, with whom he'd come in a carriage. Together they lifted the body and laboured up the back stairs with it. Nobody accosted them. Places like the Sangréal were accustomed to seeing bodies going out the door. Gwynn and Jasper lifted their load into the carriage, and shut the doors.

The downpour and wind had ceased, giving way to a night of hothouse calm. Jasper took the reins, and drove them to a quiet lane that ran up to the river's edge. They lifted the body out of the carriage.

"Do you want me to do it?" Jasper asked.

"I will," Gwynn answered.

Gwynn had brought lead weights, which he tied to Marriott's feet. Then he drew his sword and made two chopping cuts at the corpse's wrists. He nodded to Sharp Jasper, who came over, and together they rolled the body into the water. It sank quickly, Marriott's face an oatmeal blur, then gone. Gwynn straightened, breathing hard. His gloves still bore traces of clear, greasy ointment. He stripped them off, and threw them into the water too.

At the villa, Elm accepted the leather bag Gwynn handed him. He opened it, checking the contents. Sneering, he spat inside. Without a word, he looked up at Gwynn, and dropped the bag on the floor. Then he slowly cupped one hand in the other.

Gwynn went back to the Sangréal that night, took a cot and smoked himself into an abyssal stupor. As he went under, among the visions that passed through his mind was one of a small kernel, buried in earth, black, as though burned in a fire.

SEVENTEEN

WHEN ELM CAME to visit Elei at the hospital it was the second time Raule had seen the grandee at close range. The first time, after the fight on the bridge, she had received the impression of a man who liked to play the king. He had thanked her ostentatiously for her efforts, little though she'd done in the end, then extracted the hospital's payment from a jade chest full of newly minted notes. She'd hoped to never see him again.

He came with his huge twin thugs in tow, one holding an umbrella. He gave her a suave bow. The thugs bowed too, in unison, like a pair of comic mimes.

"Doctor, Gwynn says you believe Elei will recover completely," Elm said.

"With time and rest, yes."

"I would like to see him."

"Of course. The sister will show you."

"Thank you." Elm bowed again, before following the sister on duty, who walked with her face set straight ahead, as if she was accompanying the devil himself.

Raule leaned back in her chair, feeling sour inside. There was no doubt about her feelings regarding Elm. She hated having him set foot inside her little realm.

She sought inside herself for concomitant sentiments of pity for the victims of his business. No such sentiments were there. Her conscience was still a phantom. Disgust she could experience, but not compassion. Recalling Doctor Lone the lobotomist, Raule mused that it was as though her own brain had been operated upon, and some important

251

section of it excised.

She could recall the first occasion on which she had noticed her conscience to be missing. It had, in a way, been during a surgical operation.

It happened in the Copper Country, in a typical walled oasis town, a place with a hundred or so crude clay houses, and more goats and chickens than people. It was no paradise, but it sufficed as a base of operations for the soldiers-turned-bandits who had commandeered it.

Gwynn had by that time become their leader. After taking the town, he had made a speech to its people, instructing them in the advantages they would reap from providing his band with shelter. The bandits would pay for all that they consumed, he promised, and while within the town walls they would behave as grateful guests. When one of his men was caught attempting to rape a local girl, he underscored his words: he ordered the townsfolk and the outlaws gathered, and in front of everyone's eyes beheaded the offender.

The band, now numbering thirty-six, rode out a few nights later to ambush an approaching caravan. Raule waited in the surgery she had set up in one of the houses, with three town wives at hand to boil water and cut cloth for bandages. She recalled those three: unsmiling women whose eyes expressed a permanent shrug in the face of life's dealings.

Of the thirty-six, exactly half returned. Of those, few had escaped wounding. Two died before the morning. Disguised soldiers of the Army of Heroes had been riding with the merchants. The ambush was ambushed.

The surviving outlaws had managed to capture two of the soldiers who were with the caravan. From them, Gwynn—limping on a bandaged leg, having escaped crippling injury by an inch yet again, and as angry as Raule had ever seen him—and a couple of the others, extracted the information that there had been a tip-off from someone in the town. As the captives didn't know or wouldn't say who, Gwynn eventually ordered their throats cut.

The next morning, he ordered the whole population to assemble at the town's scaffold. His men and women, mounted on camels, flanked the townsfolk and commanded them to kneel in rows. Gwynn stood on the scaffold, leaning against the gallows, and asked for the guilty party to come forward. Up on the scaffold, also, was an iron bed, carried from a house and stripped of its mattress.

The people responded with silence. They, who collectively had accepted the presence of the intruders, had, as if by the whim of a wind, collectively become defiant.

"Consider this," he had spoken to their muteness. "If no one comes forth, we'll do the tedious old routine. One of you will die each minute until the one who had dealings with those soldiers names himself or is named by another."

A man called out, "You're not after truth! You only want to shed blood!"

Gwynn nodded slightly to Red Harni, who shot the man dead.

The blood spilling onto the sand didn't break the silence around the gallows. Gwynn allowed a minute to pass, then nodded to Red Harni again.

Suddenly a teenaged boy jumped up and cried out to stop, that he was the guilty one. And then a woman got up, screaming that she'd told some officers at a souk about the outlaws in the town. A riot of confession followed, with all of the people, young and old, raising their voices, each crying that he or she was the one.

Gwynn fired a shot. The noise brought an abrupt stop to the clamour, as the townsfolk looked around to see which one of them had been killed. As it happened, he had only fired into the air. However, the momentum of the protest was killed. The people's mad courage leaked away. Slowly, with the rifles of their erstwhile guests pointing at them, they all knelt down again.

Gwynn pointed to the boy who had confessed first, and snapped his fingers. The nearest bandit dismounted, took hold of the boy, and dragged him up to the scaffold. This time, no one else volunteered to be guilty.

The boy wore a martyr's otherworldly, very beautiful, near-idiotic smile while the bandits strung him up. They hung him first, not so as to break his neck, but only to cause him pain. Before he came too close to dying, two of them cut him down, then tied him to the bed with ropes.

Raule, ordered by Gwynn to stand by the bed in the capacity of surgical advisor, noted that once the boy had recovered his breath from the choking, the otherworldly smile returned to his face. It stayed there even when Gwynn drew a long, evil knife.

One cut opened the boy's shirt; a second drew blood. At the third cut, the boy screamed, never to smile again, and kept on screaming, for he hadn't been hindered with a gag. Raule found herself redundant, as Gwynn went about the work with dexterous precision. Soon there was garnet and coral and carnelian, the body's hidden riches, exposed to light, and its inner stink released into the morning air. Gwynn unhurriedly probed, sliced, severed. Now and then he paused to take a languorous swat at the flies that were gathering around the opened body. The village dogs, attracted by the smell of blood, gathered around the scaffold, Gwynn's own thick-furred, battle-scarred white hound with them, wagging its tail and barking excitedly at its master.

While watching the slow execution, Raule had recalled an old story of a prophet who at one point in his career was met by an angel who cut him open from throat to groin. The angel then washed the prophet's heart with holy water, and filled it with gems symbolising knowledge and faith. She had thought, abstractly, *Wouldn't we all like to imagine that we are so within, filled with valuable, beautiful and indestructible things, not this vulnerable and stinking offal?*

The boy's shrieks could have scraped the earth flat. Raule knew that the man shot by Red Harni had been right. Truth wasn't at issue. Whether there had been a betrayal or not, who was guilty and who was not, mattered not in the slightest. Gwynn had to give his remaining followers blood from somewhere, or they'd be wanting his; and he, Raule noted, was clearly taking pleasure in exorcising his frustrations.

He drifted around the bed, circling with limping steps, cutting and prodding. When Raule warned him that the boy was dying, he wound a loop of the entrails onto the knife, and slung it over the edge of the scaffold to the dogs. Jumping to grab the dangling morsel, the dogs dragged more down, each member of the pack securing a share, until, finally, all was unravelled.

The people kneeling below were silent throughout the entire execution. Their dignity was terrible, terrifying. That was when she had first realised something was wrong with her: when she stood there without horror or shame, without feeling anything save for that fear of the dignity of the meek.

Her reminiscence ended when Elm and his two solid shadows walked back into her office.

"You have my deepest thanks for saving my son's life," Elm said, and brought out a wad of cash in a gold money clip. He started counting off notes.

Raule raised a hand in refusal. "There's no need," she said coolly.

Elm gave a small shrug, and put the money away.

"I have a request," he said. "I'm confident that my son can be entrusted to your care, but I don't wish him to be near these sick people any longer. He must have a private room."

"Of course," Raule sneered. "I'll have the royal suite made up." She glared Elm in the eye. "There is not a cubic inch of private space in this building. It is as public, sir, as one of your slave pens. Your son is in a ward for non-infectious cases. If that isn't enough for you, I suggest you try another hospital."

Elm shook his head. "You may be a foreign witchdoctor with the manners of a goat, but you've proven yourself to be a skilled physician. I haven't seen any others in this city. My son will remain here."

Raule shrugged. "Then he stays in that bed. Bear in mind that he should not be anywhere under this roof. This hospital is for the residents of Limewood."

Elm raised an eyebrow. His mouth twitched. "You see yourself as something of a champion of the poor, don't you?"

"No. Just their doctor," Raule answered tersely.

"Don't you feel it getting under your skin?" he asked. She didn't answer. He pressed, "All the filth, all the misery, the wretchedness—don't you feel you'll never be able to scrub it off yourself?" He was smiling.

Raule pushed her chair out, and stood up. "Why don't you ask yourself if your trade gets under your skin? You can think about it on your way out." She motioned towards the door.

The smile stayed on Elm's face. "Have it your way, Doctor. But look after my son." He paused. "Perhaps you can think about the fact that your fate is now tied to his."

He turned his back and left the room, his duplicate goons following.

When they were gone, Raule let out a long, deep sigh.

That night, Jacope Vargey surprised her with a visit. With him was the girl Raule had seen before. Both of them were looking happy. They were going to leave Ashamoil together, with Emila, Jacope said.

"We'll find a better place," said the girl.

Raule wished them luck. Perhaps there was a better place. Who was she to tell them there wasn't?

The goodness in the world grew like moss in cracks, she thought. It grew, somehow, with hidden roots, nourished by something unseen.

Three nights after he killed Marriott, Gwynn rode to the Folly of Men, where he was due to see Sugar Mouse.

Sugar Mouse had news of the strongman Hart. "He's dead," the young woman said, tossing black ringlets back over bare brown shoulders. "Hung himself from the big fig tree in Chime Song Square."

Gwynn asked whether she had seen the body; she answered that she hadn't, but had heard the news from half a dozen reliable people. Gwynn paid her, and went to leave.

"Hey," Sugar Mouse said.

"What?"

"I haven't seen you with that red-haired goddess lately. You single again?"

She was about Tareda's age, a nice-looking girl. When Gwynn shook his head, she said, "That's a pity," and smiled from under her eyelashes. "But I bet you could be unfaithful."

Gwynn put a finger under her chin and tilted her head up. "Oh, yes. In ways I doubt have ever crossed your mind."

Her smile faded as she looked at his face. She moved his finger away.

"You know, you're a strange man."

"It's a strange world," he said softly.

She made a wry face, and seemed about to make a remark. However, at that moment a figure charged into the bar, and raced up to Gwynn. It was Spindrel. He looked upset.

"Shit, I've been looking for you for three fucking hours!"

Gwynn quelled the sigh that rose in his chest. Whatever the problem was, he didn't want to know anything about it.

"You're called for," Spindrel told him.

Gwynn pressed his lips together, while he silently ground his teeth.

Sugar Mouse smirked. "Enjoy your night, sirs," she said, and drifted away.

Gwynn stared past Spindrel's inquisitive look. Spindrel shrugged, and started to head out. Gwynn almost followed. But a thought made him grab the junior's arm and turn him round. Gwynn motioned towards the back door, and started shoving his way through the crowd. Spindrel swore, and went after him. Getting ahead quickly, Gwynn slipped through the back door, and let it swing shut.

Spindrel, stepping out a moment later, found himself looking down the black muzzle of a gun.

"If we go around the front," Gwynn hissed, "will I find a lynch mob waiting for me?"

"What?"

"If Elei dies, I'm for the river. You know that. Is he dead?"

"You mad bastard, it isn't the damn kid!" Spindrel gritted through clenched teeth. "It's Elbows. Elbows is dead."

Elm's gaze raked his assembled cavaliers in the manner of a rusty saw blade raking bare flesh.

"No ideas? Nothing?" he said. "Are *all* your brains pushing up the daisies?"

No one was meant to laugh at the joke, and no one did.

The assembly was not in the meeting room, but in the cool room in the villa's basement. A single lamp illumined forty men who knit their brows, adjusted clothes, took interest in their fingernails, scratched their scalps—did anything but turn a direct look towards Elm.

"What, in the name of all my whores," Elm said wearily, "do I pay you for?"

Not for expertise in the paranormal, Gwynn felt like answering. In the middle of the room, on blocks of ice on a steel table, lay Elbows' body. A blow with a sharp object had split his head open from his right temple to his upper lip. That wasn't the disconcerting thing, however. It was the flowers. Small, flat, five-petalled, pale green blossoms filled the wound, and were visible just under the surface of the surrounding skin.

Gwynn stood absolutely still, trying to make his face as blank as the room's white walls. He had seen flowers just like those ones before, and quite recently: in the strongman's bedroom, on the sheets.

However he looked at it, he kept returning to one thought: Elbows' post-mortem state indicated a meeting of the worlds of the living and the dead.

And such a meeting belonged, it went without saying, to the realm of the extraordinary—the realm into which he had been moving, or which had been moving into him, since the night he found Beth.

He heard Elm say, "The Customs Office is suspect, naturally. So is anyone else who had reason to top Elbows. Make inquiries. Further, two of you will guard my son at all times. Round the clock watch, standard shifts. And all of you, watch your arses."

Riding through drizzle back down into the city, Gwynn recalled his dispute with the Rev over the lunatic and the piano. He felt as though that lunatic was inside his mind now, and outside in the world, too, imposing the illogic of dreams onto thought and matter.

His mind, clinging to reason, approached the implications of Elbows' death logically. If, indeed, a spirit—whether the strongman or his wife—had acted from beyond the grave, why had it killed Elbows, when Elei and himself would have been the logical targets? The ghost wasn't fussy, perhaps; or it was working its way up to a finale. In either case, he had reason to be afraid.

Many of his colleagues had made signs to ward off the evil eye when they saw the body, but no one had ventured to mention the supernatural out loud. There had been clear signs of relief when Elm mentioned the Customs Office.

Gwynn rode to the Crane Stair.

It was obvious that things were worse with Beth.

By the volume of work she had produced, it was clear she had been labouring with scant rest. Her face was markedly thinned, and her eyes sat in shadows. The ambiguous scent from his dream clung around her, like an animal's musk. It seemed to Gwynn that she looked at him with the gaze of both a killer and a victim, a weapon and a wound: such was the thing he might have created, that he had seen at their last encounter.

She said very little. Drawings, hundreds of them, were stacked on the floor in her studio and her bedroom. She sat down on a chair, and closed her eyes.

Gwynn picked up a pile of sketches at random. Some were done in ink, others in charcoal and chalks. Every one of them depicted him, or a man very much like him. Going though them, Gwynn saw this man in situation after situation, none good: posed upon a bridge above a deary marsh, a solitary charcoal scarecrow; crouched in a dark doorway, grimacing at something unseen in a lane that vanished into blackness; on a wide, dark terrace, wailing silently at a brooding sky; with the dead, many times, standing over them holding a bloody sword or a smoking gun, lurking among the mourners around a grave, embracing a hanged woman, dancing a tarantella with skeletons; himself dead or dying, in empty streets, on the deck of a boat, on an altar; drowned in an undersea forest of kelp; rotting in chains in a dungeon; lying mysteriously beaten and abandoned in a drawing room; sprawled on a ghat, naked, phallic serpents surging around him, poised to strike.

He dutifully picked up another pile and looked through it. He came to an image that showed him standing next to a bed, on which lay an emaciated family of a man, woman and two children. His doppelganger faced out from the picture with a slyly inviting expression, one hand extended, indicating the family to the viewer, looking for all the world as though he was trying to hawk sessions of pleasure with the miserable supine bodies. The next drawing was almost identical, but it was his own body, in the same poor condition, that lay on the bed, and two sharp-faced boys who shared the salesman's role. As he went on through the distempered scenes his own figure became meaningless to him, like a word repeated too many times. Gwynn returned the drawings to their place on the floor, brushed chalk residue off his gloves, and faced Beth, who opened her eyes.

She studied his face, and nodded. "I didn't expect you to like them. I don't intend to show them to anyone."

"I confess I am relieved," he said. "Madam, I fear I haven't served you well as a muse."

"Oh no, on the contrary," she disagreed, with a shake of her head, "you're ideal. I couldn't have done better if I'd created you myself."

Gwynn sat down in the chair across from her.

"There's no wine," she said. "I haven't been out to buy any."

"Have you eaten?"

"I have eaten strange flesh," she said. She gestured at the stacked drawings. "And I have borne strange fruit."

Gwynn lit an Auto-da-fé, and dragged on it ferociously.

"You are unhappy," Beth observed.

"In accordance with your wishes, it seems."

Beth shook her head. "It is simply," she said, "that a basilisk cannot bear to look at himself in a mirror. I have reflected you, and the sight of your reflection has caused you pain."

"I came here to tell you," he said, "that since the night we met, my life has increasingly come to resemble a dream. On that night, I sought to change. I invited bewitchment. I couldn't have told you, then, what kind of change I sought. I only knew when I found it. But I lost it, all too quickly. Yet, the dream continues. Have you seen a split cranium, growing flowers like a window box? I saw that, a mere hour ago."

"My poor devil," she murmured. "You haven't understood your part in this. Do you know the purpose of art?"

"My instincts say that the purpose of art is to beautify life—but I am not an artist."

"You are more of one than you think. Art is the conscious making of numinous phenomena. Many objects are just objects—inert, merely utilitarian. Many events are inconsequential, too banal to add anything to our experience of life. This is unfortunate, as one cannot grow except by having one's spirit greatly stirred; and the spirit cannot be greatly stirred by spiritless things. Much of our very life is dead. For primitive man, this was not so. He made his own possessions, and shaped and decorated them with the aim of making them not merely useful, but powerful. He tried to infuse his weapons with the nature of the tiger, his cooking pots with the life of growing things; and, I believe, he succeeded. Appearance, material, history, context, rarity—perhaps rarity most of all—combine to create, magically, the quality of soul. That is why a rough sketch can have more power to move the viewer than the final, finished work does: the original is literally alive, and in making subsequent versions the artist runs the risk of merely reflecting that life. We modern demiurges are prolific copyists; we give few things souls of their own. Locomotives, with their close resemblance to beasts, may be the great exception; but in nearly all else with which today's poor humans are filling the world, I see a quelling of the numinous, an ashening of the fire of life. We are making an inert world; we are build- ing a cemetery. And on the tombs, to remind us of life, we lay wreaths of poetry and bouquets of painting. You expressed this very condition, when you said that art beautifies life. No longer integral, the numinous has become optional, a luxury—one of which you, my dear friend, are fond—however unconsciously. You adorn yourself with the same in- stincts as the primitive who puts a frightening mask of clay and feathers on his head, and you comport yourself in an uncommonly calculated way—as do I. We thus make numinous phenomena of ourselves. No mean trick—to make oneself a rarity, in this over-populated age."

She yawned, and rubbed her tired eyes. "I have come to believe that we steer our individual spheres of being through the spectra of pos- sible worlds via the choices we make, the acts we perform. Most people stick to known routes, and therefore they cannot travel far. They live too modestly, and perhaps too privately. Only by being strange can we move, for strange acts cause us to be rejected by whatever normality we have offended, and to be propelled towards a normality that can better accommodate us. There is always risk in eccentricity, but I have been lucky—no, I have been *careful*—I have moved slowly, in short steps, making the assumption that in order for there to be successful communication between states, there must be a state in between that partakes of both. And I have made use of the tools of symbolism and metaphor. The ancients took a wary attitude to art. The viewing of some pieces was restricted to small numbers of initiated scholars, for the mere sight of certain artefacts could cause unprepared people to be changed to stone, or trees, or beasts. Today, nobody cares; I can toil up here, making objects of power all day, every day, and not a soul will accuse me of sorcery." She gave a faint smile. "I have evoked an evil spirit. I summoned him—and now, all this work is my attempt to study him. He is not a good soldier, who fights only other soldiers; he is the criminal, who intrudes, and enforces his paradigm on others, casting them into the role of victim. But he cycles back; he returns to a position in the crowd, doing as they do. Scars he may have, but essentially he is marmoreal. He teases with the promise of a fuller change, a wounding unto death, and death's attendant drama, the release and reshaping of forms and humours . . . I have only imagined the stories he does not tell me." She sighed. "You are not him, yet you are him. I summoned you to me; that engraving was a very numinous object. No doubt many men could have played your role; but you are the one who sits here now."

"Then tell me what role I have played," Gwynn said, "because I fear I am playing the role of a madman; and I fear I have harmed you." He took a deep breath, and dug for words. "When I came to this city, I would have agreed with anyone who said there was little mystery left in the world. But in you, madam, first in your image, then in your living self, I saw the allure of something as far away and as secret as the stars. As I reached towards this unknown, I began to feel like a man who has ridden through a vast desert, never knowing anything but the sand around him and the dry road under him, then comes upon the mirage of a garden and a city, and finds that the mirage is real, and that it is bigger than the desert; that the desert was, after all his walking, only a small part of the mirage."

"Then you felt love, which is the state of feeling desire and the fulfilment of desire at the same time," she said.

"Perhaps you have the right answer. But to use your words, I returned to my position in the crowd. But that is not all. From my perspective, the laws of nature have changed. They began changing on the night I met you. I was dreaming, that night, and I followed a red thread to find you. I dreamed you had a scent of roses and blood; and the scent remains."

She smiled. "The salts of transformation. Reality, not dream. I think you have always been ready to see me as a creature of your dreams; to imagine that you were the traveller, and I the adventure, by means of which you might attain a happier state. You have seen magical things, and you have chosen to believe they belong to my sphere of being; and have you not identified yourself as a dangerous intruder—perhaps the only being who could harm me?"

All of a sudden, Gwynn felt exhausted. His wound throbbed with his heartbeat, as though a hammer was pounding a nail into his arm.

"I will tell you our stories," Beth said. Rising from the chair, she walked into the studio. He followed her out, but remained near the doorway, while she stalked across the room to the trapezoid window. "Once I told you I came to this world by changing places with a child who wanted to leave it—do you remember?"

"I remember you said you dreamed or imagined so."

"I dreamed," she said, "that I pulled a silk strand out of my mouth, and began to wind it around my head. It was the beginning of a cocoon."

The egg Gwynn had given her was still lying on the windowsill. She picked it up.

"Shall we find out what's in it?"

"If you wish; it's yours."

She crooked her arm, making as though to throw the egg against the wall. But then she gave a little laugh, and put it back on the sill. She stepped away from the window, folding her arms in front of her. "You're from far away, Gwynn. If ever you've felt lonely here, you don't have to look for a reason." She paused, perhaps expecting him to disagree, but he waited silently for her to continue.

"I have a memory of being very young, and crying for no reason that could have been apparent to anyone," she said. "One of my aunts asked me what the matter was; I told her that I wanted to go home. Of course, she told me that I was home already. I said nothing, but I was sure she was telling me a lie. I've always felt like a marooned traveller, even though I've lived in this city all my life. I came here to the river quarter, where everything's always coming and going, and life is nothing like the orderly society I grew up in, so that I could have an excuse for feeling like a foreigner. But now I want to go back home. Back to where I came from, before I changed places with that child. Once, I thought of all this in terms of a metaphor; now I believe in terms of a metamorphosis." She threw herself down on the bed, and flung her arms out. "I'm building my cocoon," she spoke towards the ceiling. "When I emerge from it, I shall be able to return home."

"What if I said I fear you are only building a labyrinth, a jail?"

"That's a thought I've had myself. But a labyrinth must have something living and rare buried in its wormy heart. A jail must hold a captive. Perhaps the rare creature, the captive, won't come into being until the prison is built for it. Perhaps it has to grow in there. You've taken a fancy to my larval form, but will you like my imago?"

Gwynn came right into the room. He shrugged. "For a long time, I have believed that it is human nature to invent the strangest explanations for the things that mystify us, and to believe in something beyond all we yet know of, because we cannot abide limits and endings; we are insatiable, and we desire the impossible. I prided myself on having no illusions—but, like any man, I must have desired them."

"The cocoon I have dreamed is spun from red filament," she said. "Would you say my mind simply made the dream from my body's familiar material, or would you believe that my body, my colour, exists in this form in order to make the dream possible?"

"That I cannot answer," he said. "It is your body, and your dream."

"Our dream," she said. "I have dreamed consciously, and my evil spirit has dreamed all but unconsciously, but our dreaming minds have the same power. To our dream, I brought the organising power of soul, while he brought the chaos of matter. He is more than strange, more than eccentric—he is calamitous. He tears the curtain between life and death. I, too, have observed a breaking of natural laws, and this is done by his power—and you, symbolically, numinously, by the laws of metaphor and image, are him. I told you that you were the ingredient I needed. You are the breaker of rules. *You are the unnatural which can alter nature.*"

"I am a man," Gwynn said. "I was born, I have aged, and one day I shall certainly die."

"Perhaps you could have it otherwise," she said.

He shrugged. "You once told me I wanted too little from the world. But the little I do want seems to be out of my reach."

"There speaks your bitter vein of winter," she said. "You'll have to decide how far you're willing to travel, my northern basilisk—if you do not wish to keep returning to the same place. Alchemy is happening, the process has begun, and you cannot remove yourself from it. But you may choose the state in which you finish, at the end. If you are looking for mysteries, I will always be one step ahead of you. You need only follow."

Gwynn shook his head slowly. "I fear the dead have a claim on me. I could believe all you say, madam; perhaps I do believe it. I could forget that I am myself, and imagine that I am an element of you. Perhaps I will die, and you will be left with your evil spirit, unpolluted by the human."

"Will you trust me?" she asked. "Will you wait, while the process takes its course?"

He let out a sigh, and looked at his watch. "I must go," he told her.

"You'll come back," she said.

He let himself out.

As Gwynn led his horse down the Crane Stair, through the half-tunnel of shadows under the cantilevered houses, he fell into a contemplative reverie. He thought:

I am always a different man; a reinterpretation of the man I was yesterday, and the day before, and all the days I have lived. The past is gone, was always gone; it does not exist, except in memory, and what is memory but thought, a copy of perception, no less but no more replete with truth than any passing whim, fancy or other agitation of the mind. And if it is actions, words, thoughts that define an individual, those definitions alter like the weather—if continuity and pattern are often discernible, so are chaos and sudden change.

He realised he was thinking more like Beth. This did not surprise him. And—he chased the thought in a circle—it did not surprise him because he was thinking like her.

When he finally went to bed, it was with heightened consciousness of the near parity of sleep and death. And as in the solitude of sleep, he was jailed by memory. In his dreams, he suffered a rendezvous with Marriott, in a labyrinth of stone passages that were ankle-deep in drifts of dirty snow and broken glass. It began with Marriott cutting his hands off so that he couldn't fight, and then his feet so he couldn't run, and then it got worse, and he spent hours immersed in pain from which he could not wake. He woke up to his alarm clock with his body drenched in sweat, his heart palpitating, his muscles cramped. He felt vile, and would have stayed in bed, but he had to go and take his turn minding Elei.

EIGHTEEN

RAULE WASN'T HAPPY about having Elm's henchmen continu-
ally hanging around in the hospital, and she made that fact known in
very plain, indeed crude, terms to Gwynn, when he arrived to take the
morning shift with Sharp Jasper. When he tried to word an apology, she
shut her eyes and waved him out of her office.

Elei had a light fever, and was drifting in and out of sleep. Gwynn
and Jasper whiled away the time with cards, using the bed as a table.
The Rev accepted Gwynn's invitation to join them.

Before the shift was over, Spindrel sprinted in with another junior.
They were wet and out of breath, and they looked afraid.

"Biscay's been snuffed," Spindrel gasped out. "Porlock too. It looks
like they were both killed last night. They're like Elbows—exactly the
same." Spindrel swallowed. "There's another meeting. We're here to
take over the watch."

Gwynn and Jasper abandoned their cards and exited with haste,
leaving the pool to the Rev. In no time, they were pressing their horses
through a boiling thunderstorm up the long, steep route from Limewood to Elm's villa.

"So, Gwynn, what were you doing last night?" Jasper asked.

"Sleeping," Gwynn answered.

"Same here." Jasper licked his sharp teeth, as he was wont to do
when he was agitated.

Other traffic had been making way for them, but at that moment
they were forced to the side of the street by a carriage-and-six coming
at furious speed the other way. The coachman, a bulky figure, hailed
them cursorily.

When it had gone past, the two cavaliers looked at each other. Jasper shook water out of his ears. Both had recognised the carriage: it was Elm's, the coachman either Snapper or Tack.

"Where do you reckon he's going?" Jasper said.

Gwynn shrugged, and shook his head. "To hell and buggery, perhaps?"

"This is getting too much," Jasper complained. "I think I want to retire and go somewhere peaceful."

"Careful what you wish for," Gwynn said. "There's nowhere more peaceful than a boneyard."

Jasper glared at him with ill will.

Biscay's corpulent body and Porlock's thin one lay in the cool room, the accountant sheared through the skull like Elbows, Porlock nearly cut in half through the waist, the wounds as clogged with blossoms as the gutters of late spring.

Screw-'Em-Down Sam was the only other person there when Gwynn arrived with Jasper.

"Sam, where's the boss?" Jasper asked. "We just saw his coach heading river-way, going like a freight train."

Sam pulled at his moustache with one finger and one half-length stub. "He collapsed," he said. "In here. It looked like a heart thing. Before he passed out, he told Tack and Snapper to take him to Gwynn's witchdoctor."

Gwynn wondered how Raule would react.

"I'm in charge," said Sam. After Biscay, he had been next in seniority. "Now, I don't know what shit's going on, but someone does. So first we're going to check up on our known enemies. There's a book from Elm's office up in the meeting room. Just take a page and go through the names. Work together—nobody goes alone."

"Then is that one page between two, or one page each, Sam?" Jasper asked.

"One fucking page each, Jasper. It's a long list."

The rain had fallen into one of its rare lulls. Going outside was like stepping into the hot, grey mouth of a beast that was holding its breath, building new and bigger storms in its belly. The trees in the garden stood with limp, dripping leaves, and the injured air of ill-used lovers, after their prolonged thrashing with water.

Gwynn loosened his cravat. He lit a cigarette and so did Jasper.

Jasper dragged deeply, and looked up at the sky. "What do you make of all this, Gwynn?"

Gwynn shrugged, and didn't answer.

"I thought you might leave, after . . . " Jasper trailed off. He coughed. "None of my business. You've obviously got reasons for staying. Still . . . "

"I know. We've seen three good reasons for leaving."

"Some men would take this chance to run."

"Some will."

"I'm staying, too. Funny, isn't it, how you discover your principles?"

"We'd better work out an itinerary," Gwynn said.

He felt as though he was living two lives simultaneously.

There was a lot of work to do, and Gwynn and Sharp Jasper had to go hard at it to keep to their schedule. News came that Elm was recovering, but Sam was still running things for the present. Elei's fever came and went. As Gwynn had predicted, the Horn Fan lost members; some twenty men jumped ship.

By the end of the second day, Gwynn and Jasper had interrogated thirty people. The dark man's teeth, gnashing a hairsbreadth away from a bound subject's nose, mouth or eye, elicited many names. Knowing it was a futile exercise, Gwynn put on a show of menace, and hoped Jasper didn't notice that his mind wasn't really on the job.

Late on the second night of their investigations they went to unwind in a quiet tea shop on the southern spur of the middle-less Burnt Bridge, to which their last stop of the day had brought them near. The charred arcs and struts of the wooden bridge had been shored up with steel scaffolding centuries ago; the scaffolding, quickly rusting in Ashamoil's humid climate, had been added to many times, but the old poles were never removed when the new ones were installed, and the bridge had consequently over time become reduced to a small element within a great lattice of rust. The rain was tearing the oldest rust away and throwing it against the tea shop's windows.

"We should visit the boss," Jasper said.

Gwynn was obliged to agree. "Tomorrow. We should get to the end of these house calls by lunchtime."

He rubbed his arm. The activity of the last two days wasn't helping the wound to heal.

The next day, the rain was dirty and the wind that blew was foul, as though the clouds had rotted from staying in the sky too long, the air gone bad in the monsoon beast's maw. Lightning hit the hilltops all day, felling a few tall trees in the gardens of the rich, and thunder boomed up and down the valley. Crocodiles still lorded it in the Skamander. Gwynn saw one up close as he rode along the Esplanade on his way to rendezvous with Sharp Jasper. It seemed the perfection of strength and sloth; hundreds of millions of years were in its eyes and its smiling, extravagant jaws. Gwynn thought it one of nature's better accidents that the stupid brutes with their tiny brains looked always to be contemplating abstruse baneful secrets or savouring extensive and intricate cruel plans.

He could have made time to see Beth, but he procrastinated. He went to the baths, instead, and lay in the water for an hour, alone except for the attentive young lovelies who soaped his hair and brought him drinks.

"I will live," said Elm, "and so will my son. Our house will not fall."

"You're doing great, boss," said Snapper.

"Jasper, is anyone else dead? Have you solved our mystery?"

That was the third time Elm had asked those questions.

"No one, and no," Jasper gave a repeat of his answer. "We're onto it. Everyone's working."

Elm closed his eyes. "Work harder. You're lazy dogs, all of you."

Elm lay in the bed next to Elei's. Tack and Snapper had moved into the ward with their boss. As all the other beds were occupied, Gwynn could only assume they were sleeping on the floor. Elm and his son were both heavily sedated. Gwynn wondered whether such a degree of medication was absolutely necessary. Raule wasn't around; she was out visiting the sick in their homes, according to the sister on duty. Was it that Elm just couldn't imagine the little efficient woman, with her worthy mission and acidic disapproval of immoral behaviour, as being capable of any kind of mischief? After considering the matter for a little while, Gwynn decided to keep his thoughts to himself.

"Gwynn."

Gwynn stepped forward.

"If my son doesn't live, I've decided what will happen to you. The river, Gwynn. You're useful, but if Elei dies, I won't want to see your face again." Elm let out a long, slow breath. "You can have that to fear. No doubt you fear it already. Yet you stay, like Marriott. I've been thinking that perhaps I shouldn't trust you. After I made you do that to Marriott, how can I really trust you?"

Gwynn showed an impassive face. "I believe I proved where my loyalty lies."

"Lies? Does it lie? That's what concerns me."

Then, abruptly, he fell asleep.

In the flooded cellar of an abandoned house in one of the quieter shabby streets by the river, Hart sat on the table that served as his bed. Between the table and far wall, where stairs went up to the street, five chairs with their seats above the water formed a line of stepping-stones. The chairs had been placed there by the old man who was the cellar's previous occupant. The old man had dropped dead of fright when he saw Hart, who had only come down the stairs in search of a hiding place out of the rain. Now the old man's corpse was in the water. Fish were in the water too, and they were feeding on the corpse. By daylight, which came through narrow windows at the top of the wall adjoining the street, Hart could dimly see them, small sharp shadows darting around the large one.

It was daytime now. Hart sat cross-legged, resting the axe across his knees.

"Pearl," Hart muttered. He'd started calling the weapon by his wife's name. "Pearl, love . . . " He trailed off, and pressed the blade against his unshaven cheek. "Love," he whispered, "are we really going to do this?"

Not knowing which member of the Society of the Horn Fan had

killed her, he had resolved to murder every one of them. But he had only killed three; and already his bloodlust was abating, and his plans for grandiose revenge had started to seem grotesque.

"I know you're a killer now, but maybe I'm not one." He stroked the blade. "I'm sorry, pet. I'm sorry."

The blade was cold and beautiful, and its bright edge spoke to him louder than words: was his love such a failing candle, ten years of wedlock so easily forgotten?

"Oh, love, pet . . . " Hart crooned over and over, feeling sadness wash through him as though it was he who lay half-eaten in the water. He wept, and his tears ran down the furrows in his cheeks. He sat and crooned and cried until he was hollow. But something rattled around in the void, something too gentle, too passive, too tightly bound in the service of notions of right and wrong.

That thing was surely his soul; what else could it be? He hated it for being a paltry soul, incapable of grandeur. Thinking of how small his soul was, he wondered if that was why he had always striven to make his body large and strong.

He laid the weapon down on the table, crawled across the chairs, and climbed up the steps to the street.

Into his face fell rain that stank and was yellow, rain like the piss of all the world's dogs. Blowing the rain around was a mucky wind, out of the jakes and the grave.

He went back down the stairs again. Disregarding the chairs, he sloshed through the water. He picked up the axe and held it next to his cheek. "Help me," he whispered. "Help me work it out, pet."

A door seemed to open behind his eyes. He saw a room, and in that room he saw Elm ordering Gwynn to kill his wife. Then he saw his old home. He saw the murder. He struggled to make the vision stop, and couldn't. He was made to see everything. When it was over at last, he bellowed in the cellar like a dumb beast.

NINETEEN

WHILE ELM STILL remained at the Limewood hospital, Screw-'Em-Down Sam tried to show that he was doing a competent job. No murderer had yet been found, but one could certainly be invented. A scapegoat was found in the person of a young man, a vocal opponent of the slave trade, who was known for making grandiose and vaguely artistic gestures—the previous year he had collected some fifty hands, arms and feet that slaves had lost to factory machines, and had hung them on wires, in front of a banner explaining their provenance, between the two central pylons of Fountains Bridge, facing all the river traffic—and he had fought in the battle on Memorial Bridge, and had lost several comrades. When interrogated, he was eager to claim responsibility for the deaths of Elbows, Biscay and Porlock.

Sam, striving for elegance, arranged an execution in which the idealist was taken out into the villa's gardens, to a grove of lilacs near the house, where, inside a small pavilion, a garotting post had been set up. The corpse was consigned to the river.

The next day was Croalday. Gwynn kept his usual appointment with the Rev.

"You really look like shit, my son," the Rev informed his adversary. "What have you been doing?"

"Getting into trouble, as usual." Gwynn lit an Auto-da-fé, and eyed the food on the table. It looked less thoughtfully prepared than usual; there were many strange minced and chopped messes, shiny with aspic and oil, served in upturned turtle shells. Feni, hovering near the table, explained that he had been forced into an economy drive.

"I recommend," he said, pointing to a pinkish concoction, "the olio of weasands, fatends and bungs. It's much nicer than it sounds."

"We're not fussy eaters, Feni," Gwynn said, and served himself.

"Are you still with Beth?" the Rev asked.

"I think I would have to say that I am," Gwynn said.

"That's good. Merely loving one other person won't save your soul, of course, but it's a beginning." The Rev filled his mouth with tripe and onions, then did his cigarette-and-matches trick.

"How do you do that?"

"Now, now; a magician shouldn't reveal his secrets. But I'll tell you. The cigarettes and matches are up my sleeves. I take them out and put them back again. It's a very simple trick, really."

"I think not. Even the most ordinary street magician has an unusual manner of moving his hands, a certain stealthy grace; and frankly, you're not graceful."

"Your point?"

"Allow me to digress first, and speak about certain phenomena I've recently witnessed. The first was an infant with the head of a human and the body of a crocodile—dead, happily."

"I know it," said the Rev. "That thing in the doctor's chamber of horrors."

Feni came with the silver teapot and lacquered bowl. Gwynn performed his usual ritual with the agate flask, and sipped. "The second phenomenon concerns three men, each killed by a heavy blade wielded with great force. In all three deaths, the wounds have been filled with inexplicable small green blossoms, which also sit under the surface of the skin around the wounds. Perhaps it wouldn't have been impossible to place them there, using chemicals to lift the skin; but the skin showed no sign of having been lifted or tampered with in any way."

He then explained about the strongman's bedsheets.

When he finished the tale, the Rev let out a dolorous sigh. "My son, my son. I am despairing."

"There's no time for that," Gwynn said, making an irritated gesture with his fork. "I believe my colleagues were murdered by a ghost. It struck randomly, and hasn't struck again, but I fear it will."

The Rev nodded, and released another sigh. "Ghosts are becoming more and more a common nuisance. It's all because we're getting sloppy in how we deal with the dead. But if you're going to ask me to perform an exorcism, I won't. Whatever happens to you as a result of your latest sins, you deserve it. I won't try to save you. I'll find someone else and begin again."

Gwynn shook his head impatiently. "I wasn't going to ask you for help. There's more, but I've told you all I intend to. It's enough to say that certain rules appear to have changed. I am trying to understand those changes. You have shown no surprise at the existence of the off-spring of a woman and a crocodile; and evidently phantoms are nothing remarkable to you. But to me, these things aren't ordinary."

"My son, of course they're not ordinary. But the explanation is perfectly simple. As I just said, ghosts are a result of human negligence; they're like rubbish in the streets. As for monsters and all things that transgress the laws of nature, they are God's doing. Through marvels, the holy presence manifests its power, for the benefit of particularly blind humans."

"Exactly the sort of gibberish I'd expect you to spout," Gwynn said with a weary sneer; but his disdain wasn't all that sincere. It was easy, comfortable to talk to the Rev, to cover the same sort of old ground.

"Who's talking gibberish, my son? I'm beginning to think you're uncheckably evil, and I fear I've wasted all my time with you."

"Really? Strange, when I was fearing that you hadn't."

The Rev attempted an insouciant shrug, but his eyes betrayed a surge of hope.

"I suspect," Gwynn said, "that what you do with those cigarettes is another transgression of the laws of nature. If I searched your coat, I'd find its sleeves empty, wouldn't I?"

It was Gwynn's intention to gather all the data he could. He thought to himself, with black humour, that in a world where anything could happen, a god could exist—and that could only add to his problems.

The Rev gave Gwynn a very long look. "I almost abandoned you," he said finally. "Perhaps I am not meant to. Very well. You've risked looking like a fool; that may be a sign of progress." He got up from his chair. "Come outside."

Gwynn followed the Rev out of Feni's, into the alley at the back.

The rain was in another lull. In its place there was solid damp heat. The alley was wet, the gutters full of stagnant water, while above, the monsoon clouds sweated and sagged in yellow masses, hanging over the upper floors of the buildings in the alley like folds of fatty skin. As Gwynn and the Rev stepped out, a bolt of purplish lightning shattered among the clouds. A breeze cooled the air for an instant, after which the heat absorbed it as effortlessly as a giant drinking a thimbleful of water.

Another trident of lightning flashed, followed by a mortar-burst of thunder. Looking up at the suppurating clouds, Gwynn was struck by a longing for black sky, stars, the planets, the moon.

"All right," the Rev said, "are you watching?" His saggy face looked like a bulldog's, hopeful of a bone.

"Like an eye at a keyhole, Father."

The Rev produced a cigarette out of the air. He produced a match. "Did you see where they came from?"

"No."

"Very well." The Rev removed his jacket. He showed Gwynn that there was nothing in the sleeves. He held out the jacket for Gwynn to inspect. Gwynn did so and, finding nothing, handed it back. The Rev rolled up his shirtsleeves and showed his bare arms. "Shall I strip?" he offered.

Gwynn shrugged. "It's a free city, Father."

The Rev lit the cigarette. He blew smoke rings. Ring by ring the smoke formed female faces that stayed for a few moments, until the vapours in the air softly absorbed them. The Rev exhaled again, three times, making a smoke sailing ship on a smoke sea, a smoke highwayman hanging from a smoke tree, a smoke boy catching a smoke fish.

There was a very long silence. Finally Gwynn said, "All right, I see."

"But you don't see the light, do you?"

Gwynn let out a deep sigh. "Is that something you've always been able to do, or is it a recently acquired talent?"

"Some things," said the Rev, "are private. They lie between a man and his God." He put his jacket on. "You haven't changed your viewpoint; that's obvious."

"I would prefer to believe you did it by your own agency," Gwynn said.

"Well, as nothing natural or unnatural has convinced you of God's existence, there was no reason to think my funny little show could. Will you mock me out here, or shall we go inside?"

Gwynn shook his head. "As I find the world becoming more and more ridiculous, I seem to be losing my capacity to look upon it with a ridiculing eye."

"Dinner will be getting cold," the Rev said.

Gwynn wondered what it was that the Rev had really lost.

He took a step back and looked away down the alley. "There is not an answer, is there?" he sighed. "Before now, perhaps you only did conjuring tricks; and now you have—what shall I call them?—occult powers. But even if you explained everything to me, I couldn't believe you, as I know you suffer from delusions." Again he shook his head, and said, "I am too tired. I will go home."

He walked away, his boots splashing through the puddles on the ground.

When Gwynn's figure had vanished out of sight, the Rev looked up. "I'm sorry, but you know it's the best I can do these days," he said aloud. "He lacks sensitivity; I won't venture to say whether those of us who ache lack gratitude. I suppose you know the answer."

The Rev, faced by the clouds, felt none of Gwynn's distaste for them. He could at least imagine something above them, obstructed by mere matter. It would be worse to have to look at a clear sky and still see nothing.

It wasn't until the next night that Gwynn found the resolve to go to the house on the Crane Stair.

There was a strong smell outside Beth's door; not the wild, living smell of roses and blood, but the common stench of a charnel house. The name-plate beside the door now read: **BETHIZE CONSTANZIN, THEURGE.**

Noises, and the muffled voices of several people, came from the other side of the door. Right hand on gun, Gwynn knocked.

The door was opened quickly; it was Beth who answered it.

The weariness was gone from her looks, and her former glamorous strength had returned. She was clad in the long, clinging green and gold gown that was her evening best. Her hair was styled elaborately, with jewelled combs and pins glimmering in the red coils.

"My dark gentleman," she said, with a slow smile, and embraced him. At close quarters, her scent overpowered the reek of carrion.

Gwynn held her tightly.

"Beth."

She stepped back.

"And would you," she said, "be death, or the devil?"

He said, "My answer has not changed."

She put an arm around his back, and guided him inside. "Come, my graveyard ghoul, and have a look," she whispered.

In the studio—the heat in the room was thick as wax, the fetor redolent of Little Hell—monsters stood, crouched, and reposed supine. They were the source of the pollution, for they were all composed from parts of carcasses, truffled with elements of vegetable and inorganic matter—orchids, pomegranates, machine parts, shards of glass.

They had many heads—of apes, hogs, horses, even a tiger—and many limbs. Rag-veiled figures worked around them, stitching and tying and gluing. Gwynn recognised these workers as scavengers of the same ilk as the ones that had, months ago, hurried to pick up the remains of the ill-fated pimp and his Blood Ghosts.

The room seemed to have grown in size to accommodate them all. And time, too, Gwynn thought, had done a trick; it seemed impossible that Beth could have gathered all the materials, let alone manufactured the sculptures, even with the help of the sinister assistants, since he had last seen her.

If they were the chimerae of Beth's imagination, taken off the paper and expanded into three dimensions, they emanated neither the rambunctious joy of the first generation nor the cruelty of the second; there was no sentiment in them at all. Yet, though unfinished, and crammed together in the studio like cattle in a pen, the figures had a presence Gwynn could not deny—a presence beyond the visual and olfactory onslaught. It was as though, he thought, the bodies of primordial titans had been excavated from the earth or dredged out of the ocean, complete with all the fragments from later ages that gravity and the shifting earth had pressed into them. Though so new, and though their material guaranteed them short lives, each alien brute was, by some trick, charged with the power of antiquity itself.

Gwynn felt diminished, outdone, an epigone, trumped.

"We can force something to exist by inventing its reflection," Beth said. "Now, here's a riddle for you: if a mirror reflects matter, what does matter reflect?"

"What," Gwynn tried to quip, "does it matter?"

Standing behind him, Beth grasped his shoulders. "All substance is ancient. You and I, our corporeal forms, these cadavers, began with the universe. The furthest past resides, albeit shuffled and reshaped, in the present. Living substance, flesh—this uncouth brawn, bone and hair— is our most accessible, potent medium of transformation. I learned that from you, my slaver's henchman, my assassin."

"These are not intelligent things," he murmured. "Their impurity appeals to me; their stupidity does not."

"They are the Lords of Misrule," she said, pressing against him, her voice buzzing against his neck like the wings of a wasp, and added, "These others are experts, connoisseurs, who said they were aware of my work, and offered their services. They have long traditions."

Gwynn heard her indistinctly. Having given his opinion, he felt all the dead eyes in all their bestial skulls staring madly at him. Sweat trickled down his face, while his mouth went dry. He tried to say that the sleep of reason brings forth monsters, but his voice uttered instead, "My bed is a nest of earwigs."

Everything in front of him shimmered in the heat. Forms melted, solidified, melted again.

The nearest monster, an amphisbaena with the heads of a baboon and an ass, stitched to the body of a buffalo cow, seemed to move its mouths:

"Do you not lust after the stink of the real?" said the baboon. "In the suspicious cellar?" said the ass.

Suddenly, Gwynn felt galvanised by the very fact of his modernity. He was the only one who didn't seem to be having fun; and that, he felt, wouldn't do at all. Pulling himself together, he shrugged Beth's hands off, and smiled cruelly. "I shall show you the stink of the real," he said, and drew Gol'achab from its scabbard. In one sweeping movement, he severed the baboon head.

The head of the ass began to weep.

One of the scavengers limped over and picked up the fallen head. Taking a bone needle from somewhere inside its rags, it put the head back in place and started stitching the skin.

Beth grabbed Gwynn's arm. "Why did you do that?" she demanded.

"It provoked me," he shrugged.

"They're only *children*," she said.

Gwynn threw back his head and laughed. Sheer mirth banished his peevish temper; he was charmed, all argument kissed away. He kept laughing, while the scavengers shuffled up to him, disarmed him, and then, with clumsy but gentle fingers, divested him of his clothes. He was happy to be naked, in that heat; but one of the scavengers picked up a sack from the floor and opened it, and brought out a butcher's apron of stiff black leather, and a wide band of black cloth. The creature tied the apron around Gwynn's neck and waist, while another secured the cloth over his eyes. A third came up, and draped his shoulders with a black chenille cloak that smelled of beer and garlic. He managed to quieten his laughter, and to get some of his breath back, as they guided him to the bedroom.

The musk of the sphinx flooded his nostrils, while his bare feet waded through paper; it felt like all his unflattering portraits.

Fighting irritably with the ties, Gwynn escaped his cumbersome costume. He blinked, for the room was bright: twenty or more lamps hung from the ceiling. Beth sat on the edge of the bed, naked save for the jewels in her hair, her legs drawn up coquettishly.

She turned her head to the side, showing the lovely, muscular surface of her neck.

He knelt on the bed, sank back, and pulled her body down on top of him. He wondered how her odour had ever disturbed him; he sucked her breath in, filling his lungs with the perfume of her.

The scavengers remained in the room, squeezed around the walls. In voices smooth as tallow, they began to chant.

Listening, he made out the words:

> *Skull is a distillery of crime*
> *Throat is a brass gutter*
> *Heart is a bird asleep on the wing*
> *Spine is a saboteur's stair*
> *Right hand is a shadow*
> *Left hand is a root*
> *Eye is an eclipse*
> *Delly is a comotarium*
> *Arse is a silk-lined coffin*
> *Skin is a rag for bones*

"What are they singing?" Gwynn giggled.

"A love song," Beth replied.

"Well, then, quim is a casino," Gwynn said indistinctly, while hungrily kissing her there, "yours truly a prodigal . . . "

"That's the spirit," Beth enthused, stretching her legs.

> *Comes a ship to the night sands,*
> *Comes the mating of chaos and time,*

chanted the scavengers. Gwynn didn't feel any objection about the onlooking chorus. On this occasion, he understood, the quest for carnal entertainment was only part of a larger, more complex pageant, one which could not sit within the compass of human passions. With his mouth he stung, then soothed her: hers was the most perfect, ambrosial flesh in the world; and in its possession—he understood, in a latecoming moment of enlightenment—his own flesh felt unspoilt, sound and scathless; he became a creature without any history at all. As he tongued Beth's embouchure, he sipped, like an animal drinking rain out of moss, willing to undergo whatever consequences the ingestion brought.

Four voices spoke, all at once:

All you noble mannequins, you men and women with severe features, remarkable eyes and teeth like knives, I embrace you. You love the misty autumn moon, the summer frangipani, the profile of an elegant lover, the evening flight of cranes, the rain falling in the sea, and even some of your fellow human beings. Good for you!

::

I have been told that I will be taken to the centrifuge and the press, for the doctors are relentless optimists and believe that by heroic measures they will find something of worth inside me. Once a week, pitiless agents will collect my tears.

::

I have never disdained the house of memory, wherein wait such surprises as a row of pointed windows reflecting the sea, a mossy stone fist serving as a corbel, a broad-backed old woman plunging a hand into a wicker basket full of yellow apples, the sound of a loud, deep bell. Renown was won in the gutters of mourning, and at noon, love turned into a tiger.

::

Somewhere there are gardens where peacocks sing like nightingales, somewhere there are caravans of separated lovers travelling to meet each other; there are ruby fires on distant mountains, and blue comets that come in spring like sapphires in the black sky. If this is not so, meet me in the shameful yard, and we will plant a gallows tree, and swing like sad pendulums, never once touching.

He saw a light in the darkness in front of him. It illumined secrets in the flesh going into Beth's interior: hieroglyphics marked on her skin like tattoos, and, embedded among the marks, the fossils of tiny creatures, shaped like glyphs themselves, sun-things, moon-things, hooked stars, chambered spirals.

By now she had taken him in her mouth, and the deep pleasure seethed, fermented, was as strange as everything else. He felt a drawing pressure everywhere, as though he lay in the mouth of a giant who was spiriting humours from his deepest interior, turning him smoothly inside out through the honeycomb of his pores.

Then phosphor inflamed his every nerve, and a juggernaut with wheels of fire rolled through his body. He ignited, became smoke; a cloud of cinders, he tried to clot the sun; the sun fought, and burned him again, rarefying him into a subtler substance.

Gwynn briefly returned to consciousness of himself, as he and Beth arrived at a mutual, shivering, vortical and tidal climax. When the waves subsided at last, he fell back on the pillows, scalding hot, all but insensible, numb as a leper.

The scavengers filed out, returning to the studio, murmuring among themselves.

As she had on the night of their first encounter, Beth said, "Stay here. Sleep."

Gwynn couldn't stop his eyes from closing.

The caique glided down the canal in the jungle.

Her dreaming mind hung a chain of moons in the black sky above the colonnades of trees, and surrounded the boat with an escorting armada of water snakes whose heads glowed like live coals.

A garment of red silk enclosed her, clinging glove-tight to her body, and on her face she wore a mask of ruby glass. Her companion, who sat at the oars, blended into the background darkness, with only the folds of a black domino and the brim of a wide black hat coming forward into visibility.

While he rowed, she was speaking. "This little girl, when she was young, had a yellow felt ball, for playing with in the nursery when the monsoon kept her indoors. When she was very young, she loved the ball because it was bright and yielding, warm and light. But a day came when she loved the ball because she could turn it into the sun. By bearing it around the room, ardently, she made the hours of day pass, and by putting it to hidden rest in a trunk she made night fall. The day and night she made in this way were more real than the day and night outside, where she was forbidden to go. On that day, when the ball became the sun, she began her journey. Tonight, she nears her destination. Rose Ragged shall go to the Mystery Gala; she shall finish passing through dream, and come to the unfettered place where all dreaming is real, the universe she constructed long ago."

Her oarsman said nothing, but kept pulling the boat through the water.

They came to a crossing, where another canal intersected theirs.

"Left," she said.

"Mine or yours, madam?" he asked.

"Yours," she clarified.

He rowed them around the corner. The junction was the beginning of a maze of criss-crossing water routes, through which she directed them, past the eyes of large beasts, past flickering torches, past crumbling walls of stone and brick that intruded into the water, past swarms of orchids and clouds of pollen.

And slowly, the sky lightened. The moons remained, but ceded their luminescence, while the jungle gave way to a less dense forest of ferns and slender palm trees.

As the world brightened, her companion became, if anything, darker.

At last, he took the boat over to the bank and rested the oars, for they were coming to the edge of a cliff. He rose and stood, while she climbed out. The cliff was high enough that she could only see the sky beyond its lip, but she heard the murmur of open waters, and so knew the ocean lay below.

"Will you come with me to the edge, and watch the dawn?" she said.

He stepped out, and walked beside her.

They walked past the last palm trees, and came to the edge of the cliff. Far and vast, the ocean unfurled. Inexhaustible, tearing and mending, emerging from night, relinquishing terror, the deep calling unto itself. Light gathered on the horizon.

"I can stay but a moment," he said.

She did not look at him, knowing she would not see anything.

She said, "We are very close now."

And the voice of the ocean whispered, "Now, and now, and now, and now . . . "

And she heard the one beside her say, in a softened and bare voice, "I loved all I found in you, and desired all that I could not find."

Then she heard the sound of a sigh, and the sun came up, and the shadow beside her fell to the ground, where it stretched out behind her, a black, long, lone marker.

Gwynn woke late in the night, with a parched throat. Beth was deeply asleep. All the lamps had burned out, the curtains were drawn, and he couldn't see her face. He slipped out of the bed, and walked into the studio.

The scavengers were all slumbering on the floor. Gwynn studied the chimerae by the yellow nocturnal light. He tried to see only stinking idols, farcical things created by madness, but his eyes refused to. As though his perceptions had been altered—whether enhanced or damaged he had no way to gauge—he saw unveiled theophanies, intelligences not constrained by death, and infinitely superior to man.

He tried to imagine the ecstasy of creation that had brought them into being, but could not. He waited for the ass-baboon thing—now mended—or any of them, to speak. But they did not. Nor could they, it occurred to him, while their creatrix slept.

He recalled Beth's story of the imp in the box, and wondered, if he were to accept her invitation in full—if he stayed longer, slept longer—what manner of world he would wake to, and what place he would have in it. And would there come, he wondered, a day when his own consciousness depended on hers?

He walked to the trapezoid window, and stood there a long time, thinking of the dead, and wondering where they were.

In the end, having no compass for his desires, he yielded to his nature.

TWENTY

THE CLOUDS BURST, letting fall the heaviest rains the season had yet seen. Riverside buildings that weren't elevated were flooded, and a number of the flimsier ones fell into the river and were swept away.

But nothing could stop the forward motion of business. Gwynn was due to go and meet Sharp Jasper to take some guns up to the Colonel. He rose late, and deliberately lingered over breakfast in an eatery on Tourbillion Parade. He indulged in fried eggs, eel pie, and waffles with mangoes and whipped cream, for he was ravenously hungry. While he ate, he read the *Dawn Chorus* from front to back. There was no mention, anywhere, of Elm or the Horn Fan, which was unusual. The leading story was about a crocodile that had found its way to the ablutions chamber of a society family's hilltop villa. The fashion pages announced an invention, a chemical silk, with the melodious name of cuprammonium xephron. Borrowing a pencil from the waitress, Gwynn attempted the cryptic crossword on the puzzle pages, and solved half of it. Not a bad effort for a foreigner, he thought.

After his protracted meal, he rode down to the wharf where the Horn Fan's launches were berthed. Jasper and Spindrel were waiting. Gwynn got them away under a sun that was a pale vortex in the rain clouds, which filled the whole realm of the air, covering the city and the river with thick white fog. Other boats were visible only by their lanterns and the black puffs from their smokestacks, and navigation would have been impossible had the volume of traffic not been greatly reduced by the weather.

In the launch, the heat was so punishing that the three men stripped to the waist, and Tarfid, in the inferno of the engine room, worked in his undershorts. Gwynn lit a cigarette, out of habit, but it was too hot to smoke, and he let it burn down by itself.

He felt a dim absence of mind, and the sense of being a guest at an emptying party. Lost in thoughts that doubled back and criss-crossed each other like the tracks of blind explorers, he almost missed the Majestic's landing. The fog lamps at either end of it weren't lit. Gwynn cursed, cut the steam, and sounded a long, irate blast on the horn. The river was swollen almost to the level of the decking. Spindrel moored them, while Gwynn and Jasper re-donned their discarded layers of clothing. Leaving Spindrel with instructions to sound the horn if there was any sign of trouble, they stepped onto the landing and took the path across the lawn.

As they were nearing the hotel, Jasper ran his tongue over his baroque teeth. "This air . . . " he muttered.

Gwynn sniffed, and picked it up: the not unfamiliar whiff of something dead was afloat in the fog.

Gwynn wondered what it was going to be this time.

At the hotel, there was a peculiar quietude. Though lights showed downstairs and in some of the upper windows, there were no porters or guards under the verandah, no strains of music from inside.

Gwynn and Jasper stepped onto the verandah and went up to the door. Gwynn put an eye to one of the glass panels on the side, and drew his right pistol. He could make out the dark shape of the front desk in the lobby, but there was none of the usual movement of staff and guests. He shook his head at Jasper, who had also armed himself. Together, they went around to the back of the hotel. All there was as quiet as at the front.

Gwynn was standing slightly in front. "After you," Jasper said, motioning towards the door.

"Thank you, darling," Gwynn muttered. He pushed the door open, and slid back against the wall, ready to fire or run. Nothing happened. When it seemed no attack was going to come, he moved slowly around the door and looked into the rear hall.

The reason for the silence, the odour, and the absence of staff stared up from the floor with motionless eyes. The chandeliers dropped light on the corpses of a dozen guards, domestics and men in the uniforms of Colonel Bright's organisation. Most had been shot, a couple hacked and bludgeoned to death.

Gwynn and Jasper exchanged looks. In silence, they went around and investigated the rooms on the ground floor. In the lounge and the dining hall there were more corpses, stripped of valuables and weapons. Some lacked part or all of their clothing. Some civilian guests lay among the Colonel's dead men, but not a great many. Few people travelled during the monsoon, pleasure boats didn't run at all, and Gwynn recognised most of the civilians as permanent residents of the hotel.

An inspection of the kitchens yielded twenty or so murdered domestics, and an odd corpse: a man, near naked, dead like the rest, a meat-cleaver buried in his face. His arms bore the geometric ritual scars of an Ikoi soldier.

Gwynn prodded the dead Ikoi with his boot. "So the worm turns . . . "

"One worm, but where are the others?" Jasper muttered. "If he's the only one who got unlucky, it's hard to believe the others would have left the corpse here."

Gwynn shrugged. "A careless oversight?"

"Or he could be a plant. The Siba could have done this." Jasper sucked on his teeth.

They went down and checked the cellar next. The door to the stairs was open, and there were more bodies below, but no more of them were Lusan.

Jasper wiped his brow. "There's still the bar," he said. "Do you fancy a drink or several?"

"By all means," Gwynn said, "let's adjourn."

Back they climbed up the stairs, and made for the ground floor saloon bar. The bar had double doors of dark wood with green frosted glass panels, promising a masculine haven away from the whiteness and crystal of the rest of the hotel.

Sharp Jasper flung the doors open.

He took a step back. "Holy . . . " he breathed.

Gwynn stood still in the doorway. "To someone, it would appear."

Whoever had carried out the massacre, Gwynn gave them full credit for effort. The forty or fifty dead, mostly the Colonel's men, along with a couple of waiters, a few guards and some musicians, were laid out on the floor in an asymmetrical, but quite obviously deliberate, linear design of the same style as the tattoos on the dead Ikoi. The tables in the bar had all been moved out of the way, and neatly stacked against the walls to make room for the assemblage.

In the middle of the design three tall lamps stood ceremoniously, marking the points of a triangle. Their shades had been removed, and in place of them were wedged the heads of Colonel Bright, Corporal Join, and a third man, who Gwynn had seen a couple of times before, and recognised as the merchant who had worked the other half of the Horn Fan's racket. Whatever state Lusa's war had now come to, gatecrashers were clearly no longer welcome.

Jasper walked up to the Colonel's head and wrenched it off the spike. He gave it a disgusted look, then threw it across the room. It bounced off a wall, and rolled to rest near the bar.

Jasper stood in the middle of the room, and faced Gwynn. "Looks like it's over," he said.

Gwynn had to agree with Jasper. If and when Elm recovered, he might build up the Horn Fan's business again, but it would take time, and he wouldn't be able to pay the wages of men like them.

Jasper went to the bar and fixed himself a drink. Gwynn did likewise.

"To absent friends," he said.

"Absent friends," Jasper repeated, touching his glass to Gwynn's.

Half a bottle of brandy later, they ventured up to the first floor. On the stairs and in the rooms they found more dead, but no more artistic arrangements, and still no more Lusans. Gwynn's view was still that they had taken their dead with them, but he granted that anything was possible—and, in any case, he didn't greatly care.

They found Colonel Bright's suite thoroughly ransacked, with almost nothing in it left intact. The painting of the knight and the woman lay on the floor, slashed to ribbons. There was a square cavity in the wall behind it, where a safe had evidently been. The Colonel's desk held a few papers. They didn't look like anything particularly interesting, but Jasper gathered them up anyway. A check of the other rooms on that floor and the one above turned up nothing but more slaughtered soldiers and guests.

They left the Majestic through the front door, and returned to the launch. Jasper told Spindrel the news, while Gwynn headed them back to Ashamoil. Halfway back, the rain stopped, but Gwynn didn't increase their speed. The other two didn't complain. There was no reason to get back quickly, now.

Sunset was rusting the Skamander, the evening crocodiles gathering at the quays, when they finally returned. Screw-'Em-Down Sam didn't take the news philosophically. When he'd finished yelling, he sank down in a chair and fretted over how he was going to tell Elm.

Gwynn offered to. The other three looked at him askance.

"I should go down there anyway," he said, "and make sure the good doctor hasn't turned our boss out onto the street."

Sharp Jasper looked as if he was about to say something, but he didn't.

"All right by me," Sam shrugged.

As Gwynn was going, he heard Spindrel's hysterical voice—"*What are we going to do?*"

He caught Jasper's answering, "Get out of here."

Raule thoughtfully turned the small instrument around in the fingers of her right hand, observing its miniature, ludicrously dainty shape. Then she focused her eyes on the unconscious man lying on the surgery table.

"I'm really very sorry about your son," Raule said, softly, leaning down close to his face. "There was nothing I could do. His illness had nothing to do with the wound. It was a parasite, Margoyl's Worm; the autopsy confirmed it. The eggs usually reside in saliva, where they lie safely dormant; but if they enter the blood, they will hatch, breed like rats, and attack the vital organs. It is almost always fatal. One symptom is that the urine becomes blackish, and the stool yellow. When these signs were brought to my attention in your son's case, I let him know what had befallen him. When he realised he was unlikely to live, he described to me a certain act he carried out, on your orders. He cut his finger during this act, he said, but the cut was shallow, and he hardly noticed it. But even a small cut would have been a wide gate for the worm.

"In advance, I should also express my regret about your thugs. I know they were only doing their job, but I'm also doing mine. Surgery, it's called; the business of removing diseased, malignant and necrotic tissue from an organism. You are the tissue, in this case."

When she'd realised Elei was dying, it had been a simple matter to prepare a couple of syringes and, with the help of the nun on duty, swiftly administer them to the two bodyguards. The dose of morphine in each had been strong enough to fell a horse. It had done the job on Tack and Snapper very nicely.

Elm hadn't noticed when the twins fell asleep over their cards. He was too busy watching coloured dreams go by.

As far as she had been able to ascertain, Elm's love for his son had been real. But that in itself could hardly have moved her. "Animals try to rear their young, don't they? That's all," she uttered aloud. "How much can a parent's love for a child really weigh in the scales of virtue? It's only love for those not our own that counts for a great deal, surely."

There was no surely, of course. She was aware that her phantom conscience was no substitute for the real thing. But on the other hand, perhaps there was something to be said for the capacity to make moral judgements without interference from a conscience founded on the unreliable ground of emotion.

"Evil flourishes because the good aren't good enough," she murmured. "And sometimes the good just have bad days."

"I thought he was rather naive to trust you."

Raule looked up, and saw Gwynn, who had come silently into the room. She said nothing to him.

"I came here to make sure you were all right," he said, meeting her eyes. He folded his arms across his chest, bringing his hands away from proximity to his weapons. "But evidently you're still able to take care of yourself." He glanced at Tack and Snapper, whose bodies lay on the floor. "Are they still alive?"

"For now," she said. "Him, on the other hand . . . " She gestured towards Elm. "He's a crass and ignorant man, Gwynn. He isn't a worthy master."

"I know his character," Gwynn said. "We can all be crass and ignorant at times. The Horn Fan's finished in any case, you might like to know. But no doubt your contempt is righteous. Do what you wish with him."

"Thank you," she said sarcastically, "for the permission."

He shrugged. "You might also like to know," he said, "that you won't see me again. There's been little affection lost between us, in this city. Nevertheless, I'm hopeful of parting sans insults."

Raule considered, and surprised herself by nodding. "If we are no longer opposed," she said, cautiously. She put out her hand, the one that wasn't holding the slim little instrument.

They gripped briefly. She didn't smile, only said, "Try to stay out of trouble, gunslinger."

"And you, Doctor; after tonight, at least."

And so they parted.

When Raule was alone again, she began her work. It didn't take long. Finished, she washed her hands, then went to her office, where she sat down and wrote a carefully worded letter of resignation. She sealed the letter in an envelope and left it on her desk. Then she went to her laboratory, and took a final look at her collection of monsters. She looked particularly hard at the crocodile baby. She very nearly took it with her. But she decided that it belonged to Ashamoil, and left it where it was.

For three days, Gwynn was seen in unfamiliar places around the city, confusing people in suburban ballrooms and gin attics. He was observed to look over his shoulder frequently, as though he suspected he was being followed. He spent a lot of time cleaning his guns, and he didn't sleep.

But at last, Gwynn left this self-imposed limbo, and rode to Beth's garret. He feared he had acted perversely in stealing out; he imagined he could not find the will to leave because she remained, and therefore he hoped to find her there, and changed: back, he dared to dream, to the woman with whom he had spent so many happy, aimless nights and days. The rain still hung in abeyance, and the air was a cindery, nearly unbreathable soup, through which Gwynn's black horse trod heavily, neck bent and flanks foaming, like a beast pulling a monumental load.

The attic windows were dark. In the yard, Gwynn looked up and saw that the door at the top of the stairs hung slightly ajar. He threw his reins over a branch of the crabapple tree, and took the stairs two at a time. No sound came from beyond the door. He pushed it open.

The studio was bare.

Gone were the scavengers, gone all the art from the walls, gone the presses and metal tubs and the other ordinary paraphernalia. Gone, too, were the chimerae. The air smelled only of dampness and dust.

The bedroom was equally empty, except for the fireplace, which overflowed with burnt paper. Gwynn picked up a piece that wasn't completely blackened, on which a little of a picture remained: four fingertips, an espaliered tree branch, a coastline. Debris.

His lips formed her name, without sound.

There was a letter on the bed. He read it, and re-read it:

> *Your stillness was the stillness of a moment of uncer-*
> *tainty stretched out across years. You were the mourn-*
> *ing felt for lost and absent things, and the fear of loss*
> *to come; you embodied, at times, fascinating cruelty*
> *and exhaustion. Your gaze had the power to turn me*
> *to stone; but mine had the power of a mirror. We sepa-*
> *rate, I to the sky, you to the surface.*

Below was a sketch, in thickly wrought ink, of the sphinx stretched out on a divan of stone and creepers. The monster's face was turned three-quarters, her gaze directed at something outside the picture. Her expression was rapt, as though she sighted something more intriguing than herself. More writing followed:

> *It only remains to dry these wings in the new air, and*
> *to wish my friend the snake farewell, before I forget*
> *the forms of speech he understands. A sunlit wind is*
> *whistling up the river. I am excited like a girl, I who*
> *was never young, and in a moment I shall mount my*
> *trapeze and fly to the sky and the ocean and the great*

world beyond the walls. One riddle I shall leave, for
him to answer, if he can: where was my cocoon?

Gwynn ran back into the studio. The glass had been removed from the trapezoid window. The paint on the sill was scratched, almost gouged, in a way that could conceivably have been done by claws.

Gwynn bent down and put his nose close to the sill, and sniffed, trying to find a trace of her scent, which he failed to. He silently cursed his humanity, wishing for the senses of a beast. He leaned into the open air, and bent his head.

Something was caught in the net of creeper on the wall. It was the egg, the one he had given her long ago. Sunlight had faded its paint. He stretched his hand out and picked it up. It was wet, cold, and somewhat softened.

He thought of breaking it open to see what manner of creature was inside. The possibilities were boundless, but only if he did not break the shell and learn the truth.

He placed the egg on the windowsill. "Madam, was I not drowned half to death in you?" he murmured. "Have you taken another muse, some more versatile, volatile apparition? Am I but a residue?"

For his mind entertained a vertiginous fancy: she had taken some part of him, perhaps the best thing in himself, leaving this less dignified self behind, to vacillate between the irritations of ennui and of desire, and inevitably disintegrate.

He slumped over the windowsill, his eyes screwing out a couple of tears.

And into his blurred sight, something intruded. Below, floating, waving in a sudden zephyr:

One long red hair.

The very end of it was clasped in a tendril of creeper, some way below, the wind threatening to pull it free and carry it off.

Gwynn leaned out of the window and bent down, perilously far, stretching his arms. Still he couldn't reach the hair; and the wind claimed it.

But the wind lifted it up, and Gwynn's fingers, in their jewelled gloves, flew out and snatched it.

The hair dangled, swaying in his breath, a vanishing spiral, a fiery aspiration, a meteor's silent harmonic, a cipher without a solution, a wanton dancer.

What was he to do with it? Have it encased in a locket, and look at it now and then, as he had looked at the etching?

Then—he could not help it—he imagined the hair was imbued with potency; that in the flexible thread lay the very quiddity of Beth. And so he brought it to his mouth, rolled it between his tongue and teeth, and swallowed it.

He took that much of her with him, and the letter, for evidence, should he ever come to doubt that he had known its author.

Uncle Vanbutchell was in, and answered his door with unwonted alacrity. He had on his costume of pyjamas and smoking jacket. To Gwynn's inquiry as to whether he still had any Seas of the Moon, he replied that he had kept some aside, and he went away and returned with a phial, which he handed over with the instruction that three drops would be a very adequate dose.

"It has been a pleasure doing business with you," he said mildly. When Gwynn was out of earshot the alchemist added, "Well, it has been lucrative, at least."

TWENTY ONE

THE REV LEFT the Yellow House. Guiltily savouring the memory of a girl called Onycha, who had a waist cinched with a smooth brass corset and a neck lengthened with brass rings, he made his way to Feni's. The Rev walked slowly, with his coat and waistcoat unbuttoned, but still he puffed and panted, and felt his heart labouring to move his blood. He reached Feni's with great relief, and almost dived through the orange glass curtain.

Within, the Rev cast very surprised eyes upon his adversary. Gwynn occupied a table in a corner. He was bowed in front of a pot of tea, his hair fallen over his face. He didn't appear to notice the Rev's arrival. To the best of the Rev's recollection, he had never seen Gwynn in Feni's at any time other than their appointed one on Croaldays.

The Rev asked Feni for his usual Black Sack. "Make it a full one," said the Rev, eyeing Gwynn.

Feni shrugged, and complied. After opening the bottle and handing it to the Rev, he nodded in Gwynn's direction. "Your friend's been here a while. He's quite wasted."

"Well, he's a drug fiend."

"You might want to persuade him to go home, Reverend," Feni suggested. "Then again, you might rather stay here and drink, and see which of you dies first. Personally, my money's on him, but you never know."

"Pardon—dies?"

"You know, passes away. Snuffs the lamp. Checks out," Feni elaborated.

"Why should either of us die?" the Rev asked, with interest.

Feni nodded towards his sister and her friends at their noisy table. "My sister's cards, which never lie, indicate that someone will breathe their last here in my place tonight. I thought it was going to be your friend, but since you've shown up, it might be you. Maybe heaven will call you tonight, eh?"

"Heaven's forgotten my name, Feni. Perhaps it'll be you who dies, have you thought of that?" The Rev left money on the bar, and heard Feni's loud snort behind him, as he turned away and took his bottle over to the table where Gwynn slouched. Gwynn slowly raised his head, disclosing an unwonted state of dishevelment. His jaw was unshaven, his hair uncombed, his eyes alarming: the whites vexed to fuchsia, the pupils minutely constricted, leaving the pale irises to float almost empty, like two sea jellies, in their raw enclosures.

He smiled, horribly.

"Sit down, Father," he invited the Rev, motioning flaccidly at the chair opposite. "Sit."

"My son, what's up?" the Rev asked, taking a seat.

"The sky. The moon. The cost of living." Gwynn coughed. "Excuse my being insalubrious like this. It's a special occasion."

"What occasion?"

Gwynn picked up a phial that was on the table, and shook it liberally over his tea. He gulped from the bowl. "My resumption of bachelor life. Beth is gone. I am set at naught."

The Rev lifted his bottle to the level of his chin, then found himself setting it down again. For once, he fancied staying sober. He felt a certain amount of sympathy for Gwynn; but what he felt chiefly was glee at having his adversary before him in such a vulnerable state. The Rev judged that he now had by far his best chance—the best he might ever have—to seduce Gwynn into the way of faith. Immediately, with urgent excitement, he began to pray:

O Supreme God, crumble what is left of this man's reason.

Thou whose sweetness is ecstasy, whose breath is perfume and thunder, enter where there is loss, show thyself as the only proper telos of all yearning. Come to this soul, which lies in its tent of barren bounds, innocent of all knowledge of thee. Then be thou ardent and hesitate not to strike with thy blazing mouth; strike swiftly to inflict thy glorious and tender wound of benediction; and let not the struck one recover his senses, which have constrained him to a path of errors!

While addressing his absent deity thus, the Rev fixed his eyes intently on Gwynn, trying to discern whether his efforts were having any effect.

Gwynn set the tea bowl down, and straightened a little. Then, very slowly, his head tilted back until his eyes were raised heavenwards. At this sign, the Rev's heart hammered violently. Unable to contain himself, he cried, "What do you see?"

Gwynn frowned, as if straining to view something more clearly. The Rev waited without breathing.

At last, Gwynn fixed his red gaze back on the Rev.

"Nothing," he declared. His face creased in an expression of thorough disgust, and he tapped the phial with a fingertip. "I've known this stuff," he said, "to induce a better than average delirium. But tonight I see only the world's public walls, no matter how much I ingest. I'm beginning to wonder if the damned old bastard didn't sell me the wrong liquid. For all I know, this is ape piss."

Abysmally disappointed, the Rev sank back down. However, he wasn't about to give up. He concentrated hard on a new assault, while Gwynn sat listless. When he was ready he said, "All right, look up again."

"To what end?"

"If you don't try, you'll never know why."

With an air of tolerance sorely pressed, Gwynn raised his eyes again.

This time, afloat in mid-air for him to behold, was a countenance of breathtaking loveliness and inhuman intelligence. This face was both female and male, mature and youthful, serious and amused, dark with mystery and alight with passionate interest, from which, it could somehow be sensed, nothing was excluded. The wise, proud lips smiled, and a fragrance of frankincense and cloves drifted down. In the air beside the face appeared a hand, with a skin of hundreds of flashing jewels, grasping a sceptre of gold. The hand lifted the sceptre high, then began to swing it down in a graceful arc.

Gwynn reflexively ducked, and whipped out a pistol.

"Hey!" Feni yelled from the bar. "What the hell are you doing?" He couldn't see what Gwynn was aiming at, as the Rev had made it visible to Gwynn's eyes only.

Face, hand and sceptre all quivered in the air, and faded away. "Sorry," Gwynn muttered, returning his weapon to its holster.

"Yes, well, any damage you do, you'll be paying for," Feni cautioned him.

Gwynn resettled himself, and for some moments regarded the Rev with foggy circumspection. The Rev was slightly out of breath.

"It wouldn't have hurt you, my son!"

"That," Gwynn said, "was your god, I take it?"

The Rev was modest: "An utterly inadequate imitation of the Only Beauty, the Impregnable."

"I wish I had your hallucinations. However, if I wanted to watch a puppet show, I'd go to the fair. Kindly, don't do that again."

"My son . . ."

"Leave it, Father," Gwynn said wearily. "Just for tonight, desist in your efforts to destroy me. You're supposed to be the compassionate one."

"Which is why I won't abandon you. I was wrong to think of doing so before. I've invested too much."

"Well, you're going to lose your investment, I'm afraid. I shall be leaving this city, before the hour that passes for dawn." Gwynn picked up the phial and turned it around in his fingers. "I thought this might show me where she went to. But dreams, it appears, make fools and weaklings of us, and bring us low before swindlers. She is beyond all horizons, and I am forced to watch your sideshow. Without her there is never true bewitchment, but only a tedious flow of phantoms. I suspect her body and her soul were one; the one partook of the other's immortality. She and I were different species; I am far more like you, unfortunately. I admit I'll miss our argument, Father. Most people with whom a man like myself has occasion to sojourn on the road are poor conversationalists."

"Then I'll come with you," said the Rev staunchly.

"No."

"I'll follow you. You can't stop me."

"If you follow me, I'll kill you at the first opportunity."

"I don't believe you."

As Gwynn surveyed him with forbiddingly unkind regard, the Rev sighed. "Since you're out of your tree, I'll forgive your incivility."

The Rev was sweating. It would be too unfair if Gwynn upped and left, just when he was in a state of being potentially receptive to grace. In the privacy of his mind, he composed more vigorous prayers. Meanwhile, out loud, he kept hedging his bets. "I'm coming with you. I'm not afraid of you. I'll be your sidekick."

"A nauseating thought."

"I'll be your friend."

"Oh, for crying out loud . . . "

The Rev shrugged. He gave the impression of being in a sulk, with his arms folded across his chest, while inwardly he went on with his orisons.

After a long silence had passed, Gwynn spoke quietly. "You know, the wisdom which is now conventional claims that light creates shadows. But the facts are otherwise. Darkness came first and is infinitely older and more enduring than light. Light borrows a little space; then it dies or it moves on, and the dark exists again as if it had never been disturbed. If you go down the Skamander, away from this city, you can see all of the stars; and on moonless nights you can see almost nothing else, so void the world becomes. The stars seem gallant to go on burning amid such a great indifference; but they're tricksters, too. They draw your eyes away from what lies between them—the cavities, which are absolute. Absence is more truthful than presence, if truth is that which endures and never changes its nature. The stars must hate this city. How long before we devise a means of telling horoscopes with gas lamps?"

Gwynn finished his speech in a vehement tone. Then his eyes crossed, and he slid sideways off his chair.

The Rev saw Feni's sister and her friends exchange knowing looks. He spared a glare for them, then leaned down towards the floor.

"My son?"

Gwynn was getting up shakily. He found his feet, and moved at a stagger towards the back door, but missed it by several feet, and tried

to open a section of the wall. Hurrying over, the Rev guided him to
the doorway, and turned the handle. Gwynn swayed through, lost balance, and fell over on his face. He uttered a vulgar oath, tried to rise,
got halfway, then collapsed again. He lay panting in the gutter, a not
inconvenient place to be, for in a moment he was torrentially sick. He
vomited the remains of fire: wet ash and coal dust, then heaved up salt,
black oil, blacker pitch, and, finally, spat out a mouthful of quicksil-
ver. Only then, at last, did the spasms of his stomach subside; and he
crawled away from the mess and lay down, his head against the wall
and his legs sticking out into the alley, in which position he remained,
giving every appearance of physical and psychical incapacity.

The Rev watched this performance with consternation. "Hang on,
I'll fetch you a drink of water," he said, and hurried back into Feni's.

Patches of night sky glowed through a jumble of back stairs, awnings,
chicken coops and washing lines. It all swayed like the rigging of a ship
pitching up and down on rough waves. Gwynn squeamishly shut his
eyes. There were guns firing inside his skull, and they seemed to have
an endless supply of bullets.

"Determine the value of the sublime in a world whose everyday
is beyond redemption—boy, are you listening?" It was one of his old
schoolmasters speaking, out of a chicken coop, in which he was folded
up like a contortionist, his face pressed against the wire netting.

"I feel a bit seedy, sir," Gwynn heard his own voice protesting.
"Why don't you ask the priest?"

"I'm asking you, boy."

"I don't know. You tell me, sir. Or I'll burn you, fuck your whole
world sideways, destroy all you cherish . . . "

The hallucination couldn't answer, and it went away.

Gwynn made himself get up as far as he could, which was to his
knees. He wondered, irritably, when the Rev was going to come back
with the water.

Then he did hear someone coming. Not out of Feni's, but from further down the alley. He peered in the direction of the sound.

The approaching person was about a hundred yards away. It was a
pedestrian, tall and broad, and draped in a long oilcape. As the figure

drew closer it shed the cape, revealing a giant man, naked but for a bit of tiger skin around his hips. In his hands he carried something bright, that caught the light of the sky. Gwynn's eyes made out the shape of the axe.

Fear granted Gwynn a measure of sobriety and strength. Staying on one knee, he steadied his back against the wall, and pulled his right gun out. He held it in both hands and cocked the hammer back.

"Ah, you, at last!" he called out. "Let's see what manner of nemesis you are—a phantom within the mind, or without? Metaphysically, this is a very important question."

Hart's apparition was silent.

Gwynn waited, until Hart's figure was within fifty yards of him, and fired twice. If a ghost could kill living men, perhaps a living man could kill a ghost.

The strongman made a blurred motion, and kept walking.

Gwynn fired a third time, with an identical result.

By now Hart was close enough that Gwynn could see the furrows on his face, but he had no time to ponder their cause. He aimed at the middle of the broad chest, and released the three rounds remaining in the chamber.

Blur—blur—blur.

The axe blade deflected the bullets.

Adrenaline carried Gwynn to his feet. He staggered back several steps, pushing himself along the wall.

"Good, isn't she?" The apparition spoke in a voice that surprised Gwynn with its ordinariness.

"Who?" Gwynn said, stalling, while he took a reload from his belt. He dropped his pistol's loading lever, slid out the cylinder pin, inserted the new cylinder, slid the pin back and snapped the lever shut, a procedure that would normally have taken him about three seconds, but his fingers seemed to have lost their memory, and they moved at the mystified pace of somnambulists in a mangrove swamp.

"My wife. Her name was Pearl." Hart continued approaching, and Gwynn stepped back again.

"She told me who killed her. I'm going to kill the boy, and his father, but first I'm going to kill you."

Gwynn shook his head. "The boy is dead. So will the father be, soon. Your wife is dead, and so are you. Go back to your grave."

"My wife is not dead, little man. I hold her in my hands," Hart laughed. "Nor am I dead. You were deceived. You're the only dead man here."

"If you say you live, I say you die," Gwynn growled, with more bravado than he felt. Hoping the axe couldn't deflect two bullets at once, he drew his other gun and fired both together, as fast as he was able, until they were empty.

The strongman appeared to stand still, but the bright blade moved like a hummingbird's wing. Not one shot got through.

The strongman stepped forward, stood side on, and moved the axe down to the level of his hips, parallel with the ground, the blade behind him.

Gwynn threw down his useless guns, and ran backwards, feeling as though his legs were moving through a rough sea: one wave pushed him, and he almost fell; then another wave caught him, and pushed him upright again.

Gwynn's mind did giddy cartwheels. The weapon's speed was impossible: therefore, did the realm of the marvellous persist? If, having sought mystery and alteration, he was going to get those things in the form of ordinary death, it would be too ironic. One alternative, at least, was available: it was not really that the axe was impossibly fast, but that he was impossibly slow, missing all his shots, and hallucinating an explanation for his embarrassing lack of success.

He drew Gol'achab and a deep breath. "That's quite a party trick," he panted. "How does she do it?"

"Love is strong," Hart said. "And death is also strong." And he swung the axe.

Gwynn didn't fancy his chances of parrying it, but there wasn't a lot else to try. Fully expecting to be cut in two, he held Gol'achab two-handed and brought it down like a whip.

It connected, after all.

In the instant the steel sang, Gwynn pulled back sharply, and gave the hilt a sharp twist, using the curved blade to hook the axe down. The manoeuvre worked, granting him an interval for attack.

Gwynn lunged forward, lifting Gol'achab's point up; a feint, which seemed to work, as the shaft end of the axe swung up to block it, leaving the strongman's lower chest and belly unguarded. But when, at the last moment, Gwynn lowered his aim and thrust straight, the axe was there, and blocked the strike, with such force that Gol'achab was nearly knocked out of Gwynn's hand, and Gwynn himself was thrown far off balance. As he lurched back, instinct made him duck, and the axe whistled past above his head.

"He's sick," the Rev said to Feni. "I need water for him."

"I'll have to boil some," Feni said. He took an iron kettle off a hook and put it under a tap on the wall. He turned the tap, and a khaki stream guttered forth.

The Rev made a face. "After all these years I've been eating your cooking, don't tell me you get your water from the river, Feni."

Feni shook his head. "Rain tank. But where do you think the rain comes from?" He lit a burner and put the kettle on it.

While waiting for the water to heat up, the Rev and Feni heard the gunshots out the back.

"It seems your friend is meeting his fate," Feni commented.

"Absurd." The Rev glanced towards the back door. "He's shooting at bogeymen conjured by his addled brain."

Feni shrugged, "Maybe. But I hear two voices out there."

"Your head is full of your sister's superstitions," the Rev scoffed. All the same, he got up and went to the door. In a moment, he heard the clanging of metal on metal, and grunts of exertion. It certainly sounded like a fight. He remembered Gwynn's words about the murders. But was Gwynn battling for his life, or was he just madly banging his sword on a drainpipe? The Rev put his hand on the doorknob, then wavered.

The axe moved so swiftly, or Gwynn so slowly, that he was almost constantly on the defensive. He could dodge, retreat, catch the heavy blade as it swept down or across, and turn it aside; but no more. Whenever he tried to get inside the strongman's guard, the axe met and bettered him. His tactics worked no more effectively than they would have against a tidal wave or an avalanche. Many times, he failed to completely avoid the edge of the axe, and he began to accrue cuts. He staggered and panted, while the strongman was tireless and expressionless. In the gloom, his eyes were blank mask holes. A sheen of moisture on the broad face supported his own assertion that he lived; but he might have been the inert weapon, and the axe the wielder.

Gwynn feared the yataghan's slender blade might snap under the heavy blows—if his wrists didn't snap first.

He blocked a downsweeping blow that would have severed his right foot. Using all his might, he levered the axe up. In the same movement, he flicked Gol'achab around for an overhead strike, which he had to turn into a parry, as Hart took a stride backwards and whirled the axe one-handed, mirroring Gwynn's move, but getting to the crucial point faster. Gwynn deflected the axe again and backstepped rapidly, trying to get some space in which to catch a breath. The axe chased him. He stepped to the left, swung Gol'achab in another arc over his head, changed to a left-handed grip midway, lunged forward and aimed a blow at the strongman's temple on his undefended right side.

At the same time, the axe swept around, chopping along the horizontal. Gwynn would have been inside its circle, but Hart had shortened his grip on it, and the blade struck, passing through the sinew of Gwynn's flank like a hot knife through butter.

Gwynn pitched to the ground, a short, harsh scream escaping him. He tried to rise at once, shutting out the clamour of pain, but his long spurs tangled under his feet, and he scrambled and staggered without a shred of grace. He expected to die right then. But the killing blow never came, and when he looked up, he saw Hart standing, waiting, in no hurry.

Gwynn managed at last to make his legs raise him up. It wasn't such a bad wound, he realised. Not deep enough to be fatal. But that was an academic nicety. The next cut would kill him, or the cut after. With perfect certainty, he understood that he simply would not survive this fight, no matter what he did. He could only choose how he would lose it.

He took one breath.

And looking into the strongman's face, he saw a single strict path.

As he exhaled, he let Gol'achab fall out of his grip, and stood with his hands empty, spread in surrender.

The axe called Pearl didn't hesitate.

The Rev, who had been listening to the clanging go on, heard it cease. He listened for other sounds—for screams, or running footsteps. But he only heard chickens clucking.

The Rev got a grip on himself. Recalling that he had intended to go out, he compelled his hand to open the door, and his feet to take him outside.

Everything was very quiet. The agitated fowl aside, nothing moved or made a noise. Some distance off, two figures lay on the ground. The Rev called Gwynn's name. Neither figure stirred.

The Rev ran down the alley. He came to a huge slick of blood, and, heedless, ran through it. Reaching the nearest prone body, he stopped.

It was Gwynn, and he was dead. Something had sliced through his left shoulder down to the end of his breastbone. His eyes stared up, frozen wide open.

The other, lying close by, was alive. The Rev recognised the strongman from the wharf fair. By the great, strange, gore-coated weapon in his big hands, there was no reason to doubt how Gwynn had met his end.

The strongman looked up at the Rev. "She's waiting for me," he whispered. "She won't let me stay here alone. She forgives me, my Pearl, and now I can go to her." He smiled faintly, then he seemed to fall asleep. The Rev couldn't see any wounds on him. He sensed the soul moving, exiting the flesh like a tooth being pulled, leaving nothing behind.

The Rev turned back to Gwynn, and squatted down beside him. He closed his adversary's eyes with an unsteady hand, then passed his fingers through the air, causing a light to appear. It gleamed on blood, on shattered bone, and on numerous small flowers, lying within the wound.

The Rev started to weep. "I'm grieved, my son," he blurted through his sobbing, "and not merely because I've lost my chance to save our souls." Then he dragged Gwynn half upright by his coat lapels, and shook him hard. "It isn't fair! You'd begun to change—yes, you had!

I was making progress. I would have won! Do you hear me? I would have won!"

The Rev stopped shaking Gwynn's body when he realised it was literally falling apart in his hands.

"Oh, shit, shit!" the Rev repeated, the eloquence of his prayers deserting him. "Shit on you! Shit on me!"

The arctic wind rushed unimpeded over a waveless white ocean of snow, which broke, all around its perfect perimeter, against a dome of black sky. In the sky there was the white galaxy and, high in the north, the pockmarked pearl of a full moon.

It was the edge of the living world, a day's dogsled journey beyond the terminus of the northernmost railway. One of the younger sibyls had brought him there. He was eight or nine years old. He listened to the woman's voice, muffled by seal furs:

"We go no further than this. Yonder abide the dead in their domain. And when the living sun burns out and the living moon falls dark and all things that have life have come and gone, that world shall be the only world, and so it will be forever. All of time is but a shell floating alone on a still ocean; and the shell holds the universe; and the shell has a day of birth and a day of death, when it will sink into the ocean, and all it held will be lost, save for what is remembered in the memories of the dead."

He followed her gaze across the tundra to its distant end, where the whitened earth met the snowflake stars. The wind stabbed through his furs, clawing into his vitals. His hands and feet, his eyes, the bones of his face, all ached. Every breath he took was like swallowing ice. He couldn't stop his teeth from chattering, so he grinned, to show the sibyl that it was only the cold, and not her sternly sad prediction, that made him shiver. The sibyl smiled as if to mock him; yet, her mittened hand came out and drew him close to her, inside the folds of her fur cloak. Then her voice rose again softly, telling him stories he had stopped believing in but was not yet tired of hearing: tales of his famed ancestors, their deeds honourable and infamous, their contests, crimes and passions. He heard something in her voice that, years later, he would identify as nostalgia for things she never had known and never would.

The engine they returned in seemed a descendent of the beasts in the sibyl's tales. Riding in the sooty heat of its cab, he listened with avid interest to the engineer's explanation of how the machinery worked, and committed to memory everything the man told him about pipes, pressure, valves, fuel and the rest, thinking all of it marvellous. When at last he was in his bed, back inside the walls of the citadel, and on the cusp of sleep, his thoughts were all of the splendid engine and how he might scheme to persuade those in charge of his education to allow him to learn to drive one. When a dream came, however, it had nothing to do with that boyish hope. Instead of engines, or even of monsters and heroes, he dreamed of steel-built towers that were vertiginous and hollow, having no rooms, and intersecting the towers empty galleries through which mournful winds blew. Inside these shafts and passages white ravens frantically wheeled, hurling themselves into the blank walls in a vain search for an exit.

In that dream, he had wandered through the structure like a ghost, drifting as he willed through the walls that trapped the ravens. Now he returned to the towers again, as a man, and as a prisoner.

He lay at the bottom of a shaft whose walls were silvery, nearly like mirrors. White ravens and their reflections wheeled in its far heights. He lay on his back, held immobile by an invisible force. He felt something sharp in his mouth and realised that his tongue bore thorns. The only other physical sensation was of extreme cold, a depth of cold that would kill a living man, but which was merely uncomfortable for a dead one.

He wasn't alone. People were gathered around him. Marriott was up the front, as were Hart and his wife. Nearby was General Anforth, and next to him Colonel Bright, holding his head under his arm. Elbows and Biscay were there, and a background crowd of many other. All were observing him with derision writ large.

Colonel Bright turned to General Anforth and spoke: "I think we got him, sir."

"Better blow his brains out," said General Anforth, "just to be sure. Who's got a gun?"

"There's no need for that, gentlemen," Marriott said. "The one that'll do the job with real finesse is on its way."

Anforth looked at his watch. "If it doesn't arrive soon, we must organise a lynch mob," he said with authority.

The Rev picked up Gwynn's right hand. Unlike the strongman, Gwynn wasn't going quickly: the Rev sensed the lingering dregs of life, the spirit cleaving to the flesh.

"Well, what a dog's dinner," he muttered. "And I . . . would you believe, I've just thought of a salient point? I dare say you won't mind if I expound. Consider: despite your execrable attitude towards your fellow human beings, your appalling lack of interest in them, you were curious about beasts and the natural world. And I could believe—yes, I'll believe it, to ease my heart—that your interest in things so unlike yourself, at least in physical ways, was evidence that you, too, yearned for the divine to recognise the divine in all things. In time, if you'd survived, you'd have come home. I shall believe this, my friend."

The Rev wiped his eyes. "If I clutch at straws, it will hardly be the first time. Isn't that what all the faithful must do? You, too, thirsted for the infinite. I must believe that, if nothing else. You, too, wished for the unnamed thing that was lost and is mourned in human hearts. It occurs to me now that my thinking has been faulty: we do not feel God's absence. We feel the absence of all that is lost to God, that which has set itself apart and refuses to return, believing itself to be in exile."

Realising that he was babbling, the Rev stopped, and held Gwynn's hand in silence for a while. He felt the soul clinging tenaciously to the world—afraid to leave and face the terrible fate awaiting it, no doubt.

"I know you're still here," the Rev spoke again, eventually. "You know that if you don't leave, I'll have to banish you? Anything of you left in this world would undoubtedly cause trouble. But there's no need for us to hurry. Not just yet."

He had to wipe his eyes again. He conjured a lighted cigarette into his mouth and drew hard on it. "What a mess, eh? I wonder if you can hear me. Because there's a story you should hear. I should have told it long ago, perhaps. I thought you would have been cynical then, and I still think you would be now, if you were alive. But it could be that you can see things from a different perspective now. My son, I must try to the last to convince you to repent, believe and submit; there's a chance for you, even now, to avoid falling into the welter of the unclaimed."

The Rev paused to tap ash onto the ground. "You've seen my gimcrack little conjurations, and perhaps justifiably doubted their importance as evidence of the divine majesty. But when I was a young man I had less frivolous talents. When God gets close to us he makes us do strange things; and God was very close to me. Nowadays the church finds the topic rather embarrassing. The paper pushers and pew polishers don't really like God to get too close, you see. Supreme power can only be dangerous to public morals. Perhaps I should have used that angle with you—you might have been sympathetic. But I digress, and there isn't time for that, is there? God told me to live among lepers. He instructed me to touch them, and to make their affliction my own. And can you imagine what started happening next? Miracles, my son. Miracles!"

The Rev found his throat suddenly dry. He decided time wasn't so short that he couldn't make a quick trip back to Feni's for his drink. "Don't go anywhere, my son," he adjured. "I'm just running back to get a little hair of the dog."

Gwynn looked up at the people looking down at him. They were talking among themselves in a language he couldn't understand. Now and then one of them would point at him, and an angry or a jeering murmur would go up in the crowd.

The Rev wasn't there, but Gwynn could hear his voice.

Afraid of what was going to happen to him, more intensely afraid than he'd ever been of anything, Gwynn faltered. Pride abruptly deserted him.

"Don't go. Don't leave me here," he begged awkwardly with his thorned tongue.

TWENTY TWO

COMING BACK OUT with bottle in hand, the Rev squatted down beside Gwynn's body again. "I was just thinking," he told his late adversary, "that in all the times we talked, we never once got drunk together. That seems a pity."

He took a swig, and sniffed tears back. "But what was I saying? I took on the pains of others, yes. The sick, the crippled, the mad. God worked through me to heal them. I must admit, my poor friend, that it's refreshing to not have to argue that point exhaustively with you. As for me, I healed up in a matter of days, always. I never questioned why I should have to suffer each debility in order to banish it. In fact, I admit I welcomed the suffering, believing that it refined and rarefied me. I was sure it made me more worthy of God's favour. If you weren't in such an unfortunate predicament, I dare say you'd be laughing quite gleefully at that, eh? And you know, I didn't question why God had chosen me, either. It seemed most natural to me that I should be graced with the divine presence and called to a divine task. You can't imagine what it's like to be besotted with the power of the infinite. My arrogance was ten times yours!

"Back in those days, the days of my pride, I used to roam from village to village. In one village there was a girl. Her body was crippled, her face disfigured, her mind slowed and deranged. Her folk had found her guilty of fornication. It was a serious crime back then, and so they had stoned her, not quite to death. They brought her out and showed her to me, thinking I'd applaud their righteousness. In my anger, I called down fire from the sky. Well, that certainly surprised them! I rather surprised myself, too, because I'd never even thought of trying to do such a thing; but it proved quite easy. The fire burned every person in the village. You've never felt such heat! Men, women and children, perhaps two hundred, all blazing like torches. Everyone but the girl and I were consumed.

"When the fire finally burned out, we two were covered in the ashes of her folk. She said nothing to me; she didn't show any reaction at all. I readied myself to heal her. I took on her injuries, and for three days I was stricken as she'd been, while she was restored to health and beauty and intelligence. During those three days she tended to me, all the while never speaking a word. On the fourth day, when my faculties were recovering, she asked me why I'd done what I did. Why hadn't I simply healed her and left it at that? She asked me what devil I served. I told her I served no devil, but the Transfinite, the Unanswerable Deity. She told me I was mistaken. Then she got on a mule and rode out of the village.

"I watched her go. It was when I lost sight of her that I felt the blissful presence leave me. How can I describe it? It was like losing all my limbs, all my senses, all joy and all hope, all at once. I went mad, and stayed mad for a very long time. I tore off my clothes and rolled in the villagers' ashes.

"In my madness, I learned the new extent of my miraculous powers. I called up firestorms and burned the rocks and sand. I found out how to hatch insects from my hands and scorpions from my feet. I learned the minor buffoonery you've already seen. I could do everything except feel God. It goes without saying that I railed at the heavens. I screamed for forgiveness and for answers. Did my sudden talents for arson and jack-pudding tricks come from God? If not, then from whom? Had the girl been an ordinary girl? Or an angel sent to test me, and if so, what was the test? Why I had been raised so high, only to fall, and did God know I would fall?"

The Rev's voice had risen to a shout. He checked himself. Lowering his volume to a soft but urgent pitch, he went on. "My madness was a firestorm in itself. Eventually it burned out. I lay alone, naked, one night, and realised I was sane again. God was still absent, but my reason had returned. I chose to believe that the test I'd failed was one of whether I could love my fellow man as I loved God. Your people are not unwise, after all: love of the perfect Deity may prevent us from loving imperfect man! But God's will is to restore the lost; and that can't be done without loving them. Therefore I resolved—and you must imagine my abject humility—to return to the healer's path, do God's will, and await forgiveness and a restoration of the light.

"I didn't guess what was coming, but perhaps you do: my healing powers were gone. I couldn't so much as cure a headache or a blister! Ever after, I have only been able to perform utterly useless miracles. I can't even make booze!" The Rev sneered acridly at himself; then tears started afresh down his face. "What went wrong? You at least seem naturally damned, my son. You didn't have to suffer the agony of a fall from grace. You can't know!"

The Rev's weeping and wailing reached Gwynn at the bottom of the shaft. Sheer annoyance with the Rev's maudlin speech caused Gwynn to grasp the shreds of his pride and dignity around him. His tongue had grown as stiff as an acacia branch, and the thorns transfixed the roof of his mouth, so that he could no longer speak at all, and could only direct a thought at the Rev:

Father, life—my mistake, death—isn't a bed of happy whores and a fountain of wine over here, either. I shudder to think of the tableau you and my mortal remains must present. Would it be entirely beyond you to speak a few dignified, if bootless, words of comfort and hope, or else make some sort of jest to lighten the occasion; or, if either effort is bound to overtax you, would you at least embrace the virtue of silence?

But while Gwynn could hear the Rev, the Rev was insensible to Gwynn's attempts to communicate. At length he stopped crying. He wiped his nose on his sleeve, cleared his throat, and addressed Gwynn again.

"What am I going to do? Who will I argue with now, eh? You mad bastard. A woman! You could have lived without her. That other poor fellow, the strongman, was probably a good man. I should be sitting with him, praying for the peace of his soul. But I don't know him. I know you, by which I mean that I know you're the most iniquitous, the most wretched, the least worthy man I've ever met. But on Croaldays, with you, I was a man conversing with a friend over a meal. Without you I'll just be a bum in a bar. I should pray for your soul; but if you were alive I think you'd disapprove; and it doesn't really matter, because God doesn't listen to me anyway."

Good call, priest. I'd rather not have insult added to injury, Gwynn thought. He tried to close his eyes to the mob surrounding him, but his eyelids were as immobile as his tongue.

"Just let me speak to you," the Rev said. "Who else will I ever be able to talk to? Listen: God seeks lovers. God is not tame. God is the dancing stork in the water-meadow and the tiger in the night. The loneliness, the ache for the lost, that causes dogs to bark at nothing and the whole species of the crocodile to do nothing but kill and sleep for a hundred million years: you must have known it when you lost your woman. You had courage of a sort, and you loved beauty. You loved God's world. You were, you—"

The Rev couldn't keep it up. "Bugger it all, you were the very antithesis of grace. You wallowed in deliberate ignorance, as happy as a pig in shit. Multitudes would say it's right and just and a damn good thing that you died young, and a sign of God's great mercy that you died quickly. The good and the wise would claim that this world will be a better place without you in it. That I would selfishly disagree makes not a fig of difference. I tried to play the panderer, to seduce you on God's behalf; instead, it was I who came to feel love for you. So, if you've failed tonight, so have I: I have still failed to love all mankind.

"At least you've suffered; that's something. There might be some expiation. And if for you, then perhaps for me too. I just want that old divine love back."

After that, the Rev couldn't speak for some time. He had no idea, anyway, what further things he could say.

He looked at Gwynn's face, which was masked with blood and bituminous muck. The Rev took out his pocket handkerchief, doused it in the Black Sack, and went to work. The Black Sack proved an effective solvent, and the Rev was able to do a good job with Gwynn's appearance, even sloshing the liqueur into his mouth and wiping his teeth clean.

"There," he muttered huskily, screwing up the handkerchief and tossing it away when he was done. "Not exactly a good-looking corpse, my son, but better than before."

And then, in his misery, an idea visited him on wings.

It was a terrifying idea, but beautiful also. There was something very right about it. Only—

"I'd want to be properly wasted," he muttered. "Far, far gone . . . "

After voicing this thought, the Rev rose abruptly. Acting in a hurry, in order to have no time to change his mind, he once more dashed back into Feni's. When he emerged again, he had in hand Gwynn's bowl of tea and the phial.

The Rev returned to Gwynn's side. With bravado he emptied the remainder of the phial's contents into the bowl. Then he placed one hand on Gwynn's forehead, as if in a blessing, and with the other hand raised the bowl in a toast.

"Here's to you, you poor devil! I always knew you'd be the key to my salvation." The Rev spoke with bonhomie to encourage himself. He couldn't afford to slow down and think, or, he feared, he would not dare to try the plan which had presented itself to him. "If a man gave up his life for yours—if he died as you died—would you turn from your sinful ways? Would your body remember its own pain and recoil from inflicting pain on others? It could be hoped; though, more likely, you'd remain a degenerate scoundrel to the end of your days. But whether you turn to righteousness or not, whether I succeed or whether I fail in bringing your soul to God, doesn't matter now. It doesn't make a beggar's penny of difference, because an offering of equal worth will be made."

Concluding thus, the Rev raised the bowl and poured all the tea down his throat.

The tea was strongly tarry, with a brackish aftertaste that might have been the flavour of the drug. Within seconds, the Rev felt drowsy. In another few seconds he slipped down into the pool of blood. One arm fell across Gwynn's body; then he lost the power to move his limbs.

"So I'll sacrifice myself to save myself," he mumbled blearily. "See, you faithless world, this is my big comeback! For one night only!"

Even in his heyday, when he'd been the famous miracle man of the wilderness, the Rev had never tried to resurrect the dead. It had always seemed a blasphemous thing to attempt. Whether or not he could have accomplished it even then, he knew he certainly shouldn't be able to now, in his present state of disfavour. Nevertheless, as he felt chemical forces suck him into a silent, unlit slough, he wasn't afraid of failure.

He seemed to lie in this dense vacuity for a long interval, but at last it evaporated, and visions came to him. He saw paradise and captivating houris at first, and then things he had no words to describe, things which were terrifying and at the same time desirable beyond measure.

There was music, or something like music.

Something breathed. The breath blew the music across the face of the world, across all worlds. Something was flying forever, alone and endlessly through profound night.

The Rev felt abysmal sorrow, resounding fear. He wanted to die; he wanted someone to kill him.

He tried to pour himself into the abyss. Instead, the abyss poured itself into him.

It materialised high above Gwynn, up in the shaft where the white ravens still wheeled. It stooped, and began a floating descent: a serpent of nebulous white vapour, its wreathing form as elegant as an equation, a crown of ghostly diamonds on its long head. Orderly rows of steel teeth lined its thin maw, and under two ridges on its skull were eyes like frigid stars. Gwynn identified it as the Coldrake. The clustered onlookers drew back as it came down, and all of them bowed low as if to visiting royalty. The Coldrake made a bow in return. That was the last moment of comedy.

It undulated before him. As it moved, it produced sounds like the pumping and hissing of steam machines, and it uttered a single cry, the shriek of a saw gnawing through metal. It circled around him, and then fell over his face like a caul.

It enfolded his body in its coils and tightened, drawing itself inside him until he could no longer see it, though he could feel its presence by his own diminishment where it passed. It spiralled, questing for sustenance, penetrating everything it encountered, with the effortlessness of mist flowing among the leafless branches of trees in winter.

It knew the way. It was going home.

The Rev mumbled in his sleep, "He push etern'ty in your heart too. No 'cepshions. Etern'ty. Insash'able thirsh for the inf'nite. Like the doggiesh an' the pariah tigersh in the night. Think I'm high 'nough now, my son. I'm trailing clods of glory. Don't go 'nywhere, jush 'tay there. All right, thish it, watch the priesh jump. Where thou hash gone, lemme go in thy plash . . . "

If a person had been watching from a window or stair in the alley, they would have seen, when the Rev finished speaking, an inexplicable force begin to act upon the body of the saturnine man lying under the priest's awkwardly draped arm. From the terrible wound, bits of shattered bone spat like melon seeds from a boy's mouth. Also ejected were the flowers, in a burst of clotted confetti. The left arm, which had been hanging at a grotesque angle, moved into a normal position, and the split ribcage could be observed to rejoin, and the muscle and then the skin to knit over it. The other wounds closed up with less drama; and then, when all was set to right, the repaired chest began to gently rise and fall.

After this had taken place, the imaginary observer's ears would have been assaulted by a horrible cry from the throat of the priest, as his own body tore open from shoulder to breastbone, and his heart split in two.

TWENTY THREE

GWYNN SMELLED BLOOD.

I'm alive, was his first thought.

Impossible, the second.

Better find out, the third.

He opened his eyes. Saw yellow sky, chicken coops and the rest. For minutes he lay still, just breathing, too stunned to do more than that.

Volition returned slowly.

He had been aware of an arm across his chest, and had assumed it was his own. He now determined that it wasn't his. The grey flannel sleeve identified its correct owner.

Gwynn turned his head, relieved to find out that he could move again. Half a breath later he found out how fast, as he instinctively leapt to his feet to get away from his gory bedfellow.

He looked down at the Rev's corpse, and kept looking, at the Rev's staring eyes, and at the Rev's wound. Finally, Gwynn felt his own shoulder, where that wound should have been. He felt his side. His clothes were drenched in blood, and slashed to rags; but that was all. He took his gloves off and felt his skin with his fingertips, but couldn't find so much as a paper cut in any place where the axe had struck him. Only the half-healed wound in his arm was still there, throbbing not a little. He did have numerous vague aches, and overall felt exhausted and unwell. But his body was, basically, intact.

It was harder to appraise the condition of his mind.

He tried to make sense of the little scene around him. He saw the strongman, lying still, and Gol'achab on the ground. He saw the tea bowl and the empty phial, and he remembered how much of the Seas of the Moon he'd taken. He also remembered words the Rev had said, or seemed to say, while . . .

While I was dead?

Gwynn picked Gol'achab up. The blade had some new notches. With sword in hand, he checked Hart for signs of life. There were none. There were no signs of how the man had died, either. One thing about the corpse was certain, however: it was flesh and blood.

He sheathed Gol'achab, and turned his attention to the axe. Gingerly, half expecting it to rise of its own accord and attack him, he prised it out of the dead strongman's hands. Turning it in the dim light, he studied the blade with its engraved flowers, the pattern now marred by numerous scores and dents.

He laid it down beside the giant man's body.

Memories came, floating through his head, in disarray, long ago tangling with last week. Irritated, he called his faculty of recall to order.

There had been a childhood in a fortress in a frozen country with stints at a boarding school abroad; years spent in a mercenary army, then years as a desperado in a desert, then new employment as a henchman to a grandee called Elm, whom he had abandoned to a sticky end. He recalled a liaison with a red-haired artist called Beth Constanzin; he had found her, followed her—to the threshold of a world where matter was as malleable as thought.

He searched his pockets until he found her letter, and drew it out. The paper was dripping red, the writing and the picture obliterated. He could only recall the gist of it, and fragments of the words: *your stillness . . . excited like a girl . . . great world beyond the walls . . .* and the last riddle. While he sat in Feni's he had thought of many possible answers.

The letter was slippery. Gwynn let it slide out of his fingers.

He remembered dropping his sword in the same way: that, and the stroke that followed, he certainly could not forget. His death had not been a counterfeit trick of delirium. His bones remembered breaking, his nerves remembered the shocking flood of agony, with too much exactitude.

In that mad moment, he had remembered Beth's words: *Only by being strange can we move . . . He is more than strange, more than eccentric—he is calamitous. He tears the curtain between life and death.*

And, so, he had done the strangest thing.

Consenting to stop his mortal machine, he had wildly hoped to transcend his mortal existence and follow her. Not that he'd had much choice; but the clarity of purpose had been there, nevertheless. Under the circumstances, he'd done the most he could. He had not hoped to survive in the flesh. Yet, he was here, animate matter, a man.

But to what, truly, could he ascribe his survival? To that abject act of surrender, to the hair he had devoured, even to the Rev's god? To some other factor, singular to himself? Had he reached the threshold of immortality, only to be dragged back from it by the Rev? Or had he been rescued from annihilation?

Where, when, how, and who, was he?

There were no immediate answers to those questions.

He went to look for his guns. While he was retrieving them, fat raindrops started to spit from the clouds. Within seconds the rain was heavy. In another few seconds it was crashing down. He stood still in the downpour, letting the water wash over him until it ran clear. He took gulps of it and gargled, for there was an atrocious taste in his mouth.

That was when he remembered being sick, and he looked around for the ashes and all—and for little green flowers, too. But he was belated. All kinds of filth, dislodged from the gutters by the hurrying water, swirled and eddied down the alley, undifferentiated.

Uncertainty reigned supreme, and Gwynn, like one seeking sanctuary, re-embraced it.

He pushed his hair back, and scratched his jaw, grimacing at the rough stubble on his skin. Realising he was stooping, he straightened his bearing. And then, slowly, he walked back to the bodies.

"You said you could heal yourself, didn't you?" he addressed the Rev. The Rev stared up into the rain.

Gwynn stood and waited for a while, but the Rev's condition was looking rather permanent.

Turning away, Gwynn eyed the strongman, and felt an old urge. He saw no reason not to give in to it. He put his hand on Gol'achab's hilt; but then his eye fell on the axe. To use it would be, he felt with certainty, tasteless, inappropriate, a gross transgression of propriety; and for that reason, he picked it up. Ignoring the protests his bad arm made at the weight, he swung it. The blade plunged through the massive neck easily. Gwynn laid the axe down again, feeling lighter in mind.

With a further painful exertion of effort, he hoisted the Rev's body onto his shoulder, and carried it back up the alley to Feni's. He brought the Rev in, and deposited him on a chair.

Feni stared. Feni's wife and her friends stared. The soused journalists swivelled around on their bar stools, and stared. Ignoring them, Gwynn addressed his dead opponent for the last time.

"If you saved me, I'm not sure I ought to thank you, Father. You yourself said that without sacrifice there can be no glory. I came to believe something similar—but how am I to know now? The moment when I could have found out is over, and perhaps there'll never be another. Tonight, I don't know who won, and who lost. I can't say that I hope you won. Still, I hope you found what you were looking for."

Leaving the Rev in the chair, Gwynn walked up to the bar and opened his wallet. The leather had protected the banknotes inside. He counted out a small sum, and then a much larger one.

"That's for the tea," said Gwynn to a slowly blinking Feni. "This here is for the good father's funeral."

He went out through the bead curtain.

Feni gazed at the Rev, then at the money. He expected it to disappear, or turn into dry leaves or pieces of dead men's skin as money from the realm of ghosts ought to. It didn't.

Feni rummaged among his bottles and found something that was pretty much pure alcohol, wiped a glass, and poured himself a generous drink.

As Gwynn climbed the Corozo's stairs, the night-noises of the building's inhabitants reached his ears. The smell of furniture polish and burnt toast was there, unchanged.

On getting inside his rooms, he made a beeline for the washstand, and made himself clean with three quarts of sage and orris water, shaved, and soaped his hair until there was no trace of blood left. He selected attire suitable for travelling: black doeskin trousers, an ivory lawn shirt, a double-breasted waistcoat in bice and pigeon damask, a serviceable black broadcloth riding jacket, a cream linen cravat which he tied loosely, and comfortable, solid boots. He combed his hair and tied it with a black ribbon. His person thus attended to, he gathered all his weapons together on his desk, and cleaned and oiled the lot.

He packed belongings into two saddlebags. All the uncanny fashions he'd worn in Ashamoil he left on their hangers, including the peacock coat. After a moment's hesitation, he also left behind the mandragora flask, and restrained himself to taking Auto-da-fés and some brandy for nights on the road. Once he was done, he went back into the bedroom, and stepped up close to the mirror.

There was nothing in his face that had not been there for years.

As a test, he took out a knife and made a small cut on the palm of his hand. It bled in the normal way, and didn't miraculously heal.

He tried believing in the Rev's god. He couldn't, to his relief.

"In truth," he said to himself, "if a god really was responsible for giving me my life back, I'm curious about such a god's motivation for letting a fellow like me back on the streets of the world. It hardly seems an unambiguous act of grace."

Gwynn turned away from his disdainful reflection, and extinguished the lamps in the room. He returned to his desk, and opened the drawer in which *The Sphinx and Basilisk Converse* lay flat, inside its wrapping paper. He hesitated, caught by a wild fancy that the picture might have changed. He indulged in imagining himself courted by a new mystery, a new trail to follow, that would bring him to Beth again, wherever she had gone.

Just as he had left the egg unbroken, he almost left the etching wrapped; but at last, he felt a rare need for certainty.

He removed the paper.

He looked over the picture, until his eye was sure: it had not changed in the smallest detail. He re-wrapped it, and closed the drawer.

The monsoon still drummed on the roof. Gwynn fastened his oil-cape around his shoulders, and set his wide-brimmed hat on his head.

It was nearly time to make his exit.

He had to stand knocking on the Limewood hospital's door for several minutes before a young sister finally opened it. She had obviously been crying.

"The doctor isn't here," she said sharply, and went to shut the door in Gwynn's face.

Gwynn caught the door and shouldered his way in, with a terse apology, and informed the sister that he wouldn't be long. Leaving her protesting behind him, he went up the hall and entered the ward where Elm had been. Another man occupied the bed. Gwynn looked around the other wards. No Elm.

He passed the same sister in a corridor. "The laboratory," she said, quietly, not meeting his eyes.

Gwynn went there. The room was dark. He could hear breathing, slow and heavy. He went out and fetched a candle from the hallway, and brought it in.

Elm was in a chair, sitting in an awkward, limp fashion.

Gwynn went closer. The grandee's mouth hung slack, and saliva glistened on his chin. His left eye was covered by a cotton patch. His right eye blinked slowly.

"Elm?" Gwynn stepped nearer again.

The eye swivelled and looked at Gwynn. It was the eye of an animal in pain. Or, perhaps, not quite an animal. There was possibly some human intelligence there, trapped. In the dim light, Gwynn couldn't really tell.

The chair in which Elm sat was in front of the dissecting table. On the table were three objects: the jar with the crocodile child in it, a small pick-like tool, and a book. The book was marked with a sheet of paper. Gwynn put the candle down, and opened the book at the marked page.

The piece of paper proved to be Doctor Lone's pamphlet, with a sentence circled: *Criminals and lunatics become obedient and docile with this quick and cheap procedure.*

The book was Raule's journal. At the top of the page she had written that Elei was dead, and that she had resigned her post. There followed a note regarding Tack and Snapper: *The two large gentlemen were, I have been told, victims of an unfortunate misunderstanding, involving agents of the Knackers and Renderers Guild. Consideration for the reader's sensitivities forbids me to pen the details of this accident;*

323

inquiries should be directed to the soapworks next door. The rest of the writing was a rather disjointed discourse on the workings of conscience. The final sentence read: *Evil flourishes because the good are not good enough.*

Gwynn looked back at Elm, and considered.

While contemplating, he tore the page out of the journal, and, with the candle, burned page and pamphlet in the laboratory sink. He put the little pick away in a drawer. Feeling better now that the evidence was erased—not that he really thought the remnants of the Horn Fan likely to pose much danger to Raule—he went to look for the sister again.

He found her in a ward. She left the side of the patient over whom she was praying, and spoke to him in the doorway. "I'm the only witness. No one else has seen it," she said. She was calm. "Do you wish to kill me?"

He shook his head. "I am going to relieve you of this . . . encumbrance," he told her. "Regarding all that has occurred, I hope no one troubles you, though unfortunately I can't guarantee they won't."

A pause. "Thank you," she said finally.

"Don't mention it."

Gwynn walked back to the laboratory, and sat down on a bench facing Elm. "Well," he said, "it seems we're all going our separate ways."

Elm's eye blinked.

"I'm sorry about Elei," Gwynn said. "He wasn't a bad kid. And then there's Tareda to think of, isn't there? But I dare say she'll look after herself." Gwynn paused, trying to judge whether Elm was taking any of his speech in. It was impossible to tell.

"I'm surprised at the doctor, but perhaps I shouldn't be. And I can't deny that I'm rather pleased." A faint smile crossed Gwynn's features. He cocked his head, still studying the eye in front of him. "Are you capable of wanting vengeance, I wonder? It doesn't seem so, but perhaps you'd like to die. That's a wish I can always grant. We could go and watch the lights on the river first, and then I could finish you off. What do you say?"

It seemed to Gwynn that Elm stirred slightly.

"Think about it for a moment," Gwynn said.

He cast his gaze over the shelves of monsters. He got down off the bench, and went to stand in front of the jars.

In the dim light the pitiful things took on a menacing aspect. Gwynn found the crocodile baby. He brought it into the candlelight and examined it closely. It still looked flawlessly real, no fake but a genuine anomaly.

"Are you another residue?" Gwynn murmured to it. Then he took it over to Elm, and held it in front of Elm's eye.

"In a sense," he said, "this is your last son."

Elm's head listed; he drooled. Gwynn unscrewed the lid of the jar, lifted its occupant out, and stuffed the thing into one of Elm's pockets.

"Come," Gwynn said, "we should be gone."

He gripped the seated man under the arms and hoisted him up. Once standing, Elm proved able to walk with a stumbling gait. He was completely disinterested and placid as Gwynn led him out of the hospital. Gwynn took them around the back to fetch his horse, then, leading the horse with one hand and Elm with the other, he walked the short distance to the river.

Once there, Gwynn stopped in the black shadow of a warehouse close to the water. He took a couple of paces back from Elm, who, now that he was no longer being led, stood still, in the rain, his eye opening and shutting with the regularity of clockwork.

Gwynn drew Gol'achab, and ran it through Elm's belly.

Elm collapsed, jerking around and gagging. Gwynn kicked him a couple of times, then cut his throat. He wiped the sword on Elm's sleeve, and then bent down and shoved the body into the water.

Very quietly Gwynn said, "I have no excuses, Marriott."

Then he swung into the saddle, and set off through the streets.

On the way out of Limewood, he passed the Orchard. Red and green lanterns guttered under tarpaulin awnings at the edges of the square, and in the centre, in a space open to the falling sky, two blurred boys strutted in a circle.

Disciplining himself, Gwynn quelled the urge to ride to the Crane Stair. Taking a different route uphill, he headed for the railway station.

EPILOGUE

THE SIGN READ: DEAD BULLOCK SOak. Whoever wrote it had run out of space for capital letters on the board.

It was a sign with no town. Beyond it there was only a wide area strewn with rubble. A sandstorm of terrific force looked to have had gone through and levelled the place.

Raule led her camel up what was left of the main street. Human and animal bodies lay all around. She checked every person. They were all about a day and a night dead.

It had taken her six months of travel before she'd at last decided to go home. She'd found that General Anforth was dead and her own name and face were long forgotten, but otherwise nothing about the Copper Country had particularly changed. She had travelled to Dead Bullock Soak to take up a position as town doctor. Had she arrived a day earlier, she would have shared in its inhabitants' fate.

Towards the end of the street the brick rear half of a single house was still standing upright. Raule stopped in front of it. An old man sat a-doze in a chair within. When Raule's shadow crossed his face he opened his eyes.

He spoke at once, and with sarcasm. "Ye'd be the doctor. Good of ye to finally get here."

"Are there any other survivors?"

"Flies. Mayhap a few lizards, Doctor."

Not willing to give up hope, Raule went out into the ruin again and made a thorough search. It was a waste of effort. She returned to the half-house, where the oldtimer was now cooking a meal on a griddle.

"Was it a storm?" she asked him.

"D'ye think I saw?" he replied, not looking at her. "I was in here, a' cowerin', as is the privilege of age." But he then went on in a quieter voice, "No, it weren't no act o' nature. And I won't be no liar. I saw. Ye'll call me an old childish fool, but I still know front end from nether, thank ye. It were stone, but it were up and a' runnin'. Come from yonder out back o' the southwest butte. 'Twas an enigma that were abroad last night. Now ye can call me mad, and go tend to the needs o' the lizards, or what else ye will."

Raule saw no point in staying. She rode on, towards the butte, which poked up from the flats about two miles out of the town. After coming to the butte and passing it, she found herself approaching a march of sandhills. Out in front of the sandhills stretched an avenue of huge, strange, fossil formations: they had skulls, spines and limbs, like the skeletons of beasts, but equally involved in their shapes were traceries of petrified vegetation and ancient, pitted metal. It could be imagined that the dunes, in their millennial shifting, had reorganised all the trash that had fallen into them over the ages into this almost orderly scheme. The formations were well preserved, as though the sands had kept them hidden for a long time, and had only moved away recently, like a retreating sea, to expose them to sight. Perhaps the force that had flattened Dead Bullock Soak had also moved the sand.

Raule rode her camel along the avenue, marvelling at this kingdomless court. At the point where the hills took over, Raule rode up the first slope, and kept riding in a straight line. She rode that way for three days. Her water ran low, but staying faithful to the impulse that had caused her to choose that path, she kept riding. If fate had not guided her home to be a healer, she wanted to know why she was back in the dry old country, alone and adrift again. If she was being led to die, she would accept it. But she would not accept the shame and disappointment of being unplaced in the world.

Bloody-mindedly, she allowed her water to run out.

When near to dying of thirst, she heard camel bells, and human voices. A band of Harutaim were riding up from the west. She managed to reach them, and they didn't object to her riding with them that day, or the next; or the next year, or the year after that. From their witchdoctors she learned much, and gradually she became respected as a witch-doctor among them. And in those years she rebuilt a core to replace the one she had lost—grain by grain, and in much different form.

In the nomads' land, which was a land of lines, many lines, with space as such being incidental filler, a negative concept, Raule occasionally wondered whether she had escaped from a doomed world—escaped from nowhere to somewhere. An equal number of times, she wondered whether she was part of something left by a world which had birthed itself into a new, more gracious state—a state beyond apprehension by that which remained, dry, linear as bone, as the veins in a dead leaf.

Both thoughts came to her less often as the years went by.

The wind coming in off the Edge tugged at his long hair. The escarpment that plunged down to the Salt Desert was a bare hundred feet away across the no-man's land of coarse scrub and withered grass.

In the other direction lay low hills, on which the necropolis was built. On the other side of the city of the dead was a city of the living, in which crimes were tried not in courts but in theatres. The new playhouse out on the barrens beyond the necropolis was the latest venue for fashionable people to be seen while seeing justice done.

A new-fangled marvel lit the open-air stage: windmill turbines on the wasteland turned the power of air in motion into the power of light. Under incandescent globes far brighter than gas lamps, Gwynn rested his left hand on the hilt of his sword, while his right hand adjusted the silk half-mask he wore. The mask was black, the defence's traditional colour; his opponent's mask was white.

The noisy crowd hushed as the master of ceremonies stepped forth to read out the charges. A light that no one could see came into Gwynn's eyes as he breathed in the people's excitement, their bloodlust. They loved to watch him kill, and if he died they'd love to watch that, too. He felt their ambiguous yearning as an all-over caress that reached to him through the air.

As a successful blade-at-law, he enjoyed popularity with all levels of society. He had rooms at one of the city's best addresses, furnished with marble floors, gilt mirrors and a grand piano; his collar was pinned with a jewel presented to him by the Justice Minister's daughter; he employed a valet, a secretary and a cook. His image proliferated on souvenirs: china and celluloid figurines, playing cards, lucky charms, knife handles, note paper; his face was even printed on mock-votive candles.

The MC finished the brief reading and folded the document away. To the crowd's applause, he spread his arms wide, the rhinestones on his robes dazzling in the new lights. "Ladies and Gentlemen, the trial will now commence!" he cried. "I give you the Champions of Dispute!"

Gwynn and his opposite stepped forth onto centre stage. The modish audience clapped and cheered wildly, shouted, "Hail! Hail!" and waved kerchiefs and whirligigs above their heads.

Gwynn's white-masked opponent was a tall, muscular woman. He recognised her as Madame L____ C____, one of the better swords in the city, and one who nearly always prosecuted. His client was Moldo Ramses, the well-known hatchetman from the Hrid family. The charge was murder, therefore the fight would be to the death, theoretically, though such a dramatic ending was unlikely in practice, when typically someone would yield first.

A couple of Gwynn's colleagues from the Vamamarch Matador Temple, who were watching from a private box, waved discreetly. Though the Vamamarch was one of those societies of duellists which expected its members to accept the most lucrative cases offered to them (and contribute a percentage to the common purse, which paid pensions and medical expenses, and provided for bereaved relatives), some leeway was allowed for personal tastes. Gwynn's tastes occasionally led him to take on certain cases for less than his usual fee, or for no fee at all. Hence, he had acquired a reputation for possessing a noble character, and even for being something of a hero—or, at least, in the assessment of one contemporary commentator, one of those parties who are able to fulfil the public need in the event of genuine heroes being absent or, for any reason, unpalatable. It was people like the Hrid, however, who kept him in funds well enough that he could afford to indulge in those sporadic noble acts.

He managed to keep his personal life out of the papers through an equal application of discretion and bribery. There were rumours of a past, tragic love affair; however, no one could deny that he gave the impression of a man without burdens. And, in truth, his heart was at most times light. He appreciated the consensual aspect of the duel; he had a great deal of leisure time; he patronised artists and scientists; his appointment book never lacked for soirées and parties. He was known to be an atheist, and to hold views opposing slavery, and as such was particularly welcomed in liberal and progressive circles. He would energetically debate philosophy, aesthetics and metaphysics, but could not be drawn into arguments about theology, a subject of which he claimed to be utterly weary.

He never encountered Raule again, nor heard any word of her. Nor had he witnessed any more impossible phenomena since leaving Ashamoil. His memory for dreams never improved; a thorough, swift oblivion consumed the vast majority of his sleeping hours. But a handful of times, over the years, he woke with the memory of a dream in which Beth appeared, sometimes as a woman, sometimes as the sphinx. Occasionally he contemplated her riddle, turning his answers around like the blades of a windmill. The cocoon hung within a dream, within her heart, or even his, within the eaten hours of his sleep, or in the midden of the past, or the abyss of the future, the ever-unknown beyond the edge of each moment, or it was woven everywhere throughout the world, and through him too. Or it was elsewhere, in some place, some circumstance of being, at which he could not point his eyes, any more than he could point them at the dark side of the moon.

Madame L____ C____ drew her blade with a flourish. With equal showmanship, Gwynn drew his comically named sword, and smiled for the audience.

It was a hard fight, but he won. He would win many more, fighting duels in that city until his long black hair turned to the grey of polished iron. Beyond that point, however, the account of Gwynn's life becomes a monkey with many tails (a situation with which its subject would surely not have been displeased). Its endings can be broadly classified into three groups: the humdrum—his health fails, years of hard living exacting their natural and long-overdue price; the frightful—where, for instance, the Rev's miracle comes undone, and during a reception or some similar public festivity he splits apart where the strongman's axe struck him; and the fabulous.

From the latter category—which is the largest—one of the most enduringly popular versions relates how, in those latter years when, although still famous, he was no longer the object of many dreams, Gwynn at last came to lose a fight badly. While he lay, swiftly dying, on the stage in the respectfully hushed theatre, a presence was felt by many of the spectators. "Atrociously old and primitive, and exceedingly cold," were the words of one who sensed it.

While this presence was disturbing the audience, something else broke through the roof of the theatre. The witnesses concurred that it appeared to be some sort of large beast, but falling plaster obscured it so that no one saw it clearly. It remained on the stage only a few moments, then lifted itself with great speed and exited through the opening it had made. Several people in the front rows were injured by falling pieces of the roof.

There was concurrence as to its smell, which witnesses described as redolent of a murder in a rose bed. Finally, the people who had felt the first presence agreed that it departed upon the intruder's entrance. The general opinion was that while the latter did not project such an appalling character as the former, it posed more danger to bystanders. The incident became the talk of the town for a fortnight. The respective natures of the two entities generated much speculation, as did the question of Gwynn's fate, for when the commotion was over it became clear that Gwynn was gone. All that remained on the stage was a quantity of his blood—absorbed by the floorboards and also by some plaster dust, which souvenir hunters quickly collected—and his clothing, within which was found a thin, perfect cast of skin, sloughed like a moulting serpent's. The clothes and the skin, and the famous sword Gol'achab, vanished into private collections; the public had to make do with the blood. (It is a fact that in the eastern region of the Teleute Shelf red dust is still sold as a talisman against the evil eye, but the theories about the origin of this superstition are easily as numerous as those concerning Gwynn's departure from life.)

It remains to note that in Ashamoil, during the regime of the Floating Generals, at the time of the dry season when the maculate horn vines blossom in that city, something unprecedented swam in the Skamander. It flopped up onto a quay: the body of a huge crocodile with the head of a man. It reared on its stumpy back legs and showed the lotus growing out of its scaly belly, and proclaimed itself to be a god. It said nothing more, for a single shot through its forehead killed it instantly. The marksman was never located, and when the bullet was retrieved it was found to be of a type that had not been made in the last three hundred years.

The monster was embalmed and put in the Natural History Museum. Shortly after its installation, a vandal cut off its head.

ABOUT THE AUTHOR

K.J. Bishop lives in Melbourne, Australia. Her stories have appeared in Aurealis, Fables and Reflections, and The Year's Best Australian Science Fiction and Fantasy Vol. II. The Etched City is her first novel. She can be contacted at her website, www.kjbishop.net.

Printed in the United States
1116000004B/40-42

7/04